CONSPIRACY OF BLOOD AND SMOKE

Anne Blankman was born in upstate New York and studied at Union College, during which time she did an exchange in York, England – a place she's always dreamed of returning to. She has since worked as a youth services librarian. The idea for her debut novel, *Prisoner of Night and Fog*, came to her after she learned about Hitler's beloved half niece who shared his luxurious Munich flat. Anne began wondering what it would have been like to be a young girl growing up within the Nazi elite's inner circle – and if it would have been possible to break free from it. This is the follow-up to that book. You can visit her online at www.anneblankman.com

By Anne Blankman and available from Headline

Prisoner of Night and Fog
Conspiracy of Blood and Smoke

CONSPIRACY OF BLOOD AND SMOKE

Anne Blankman

headline

First published in Great Britain in 2015 by
HEADLINE PUBLISHING GROUP

1

Cataloguing in Publication Data is available from the British Library

ISBN 978 1 4722 0785 2

Typeset in Sabon LT Std by Palimpsest Book Production Limited,
Falkirk, Stirlingshire

Printed and bound in Great Britain by
Clays Ltd, St Ives plc

Headline's policy is to use papers that are natural, renewable and
recyclable products and made from wood grown in well-managed forests
and other controlled sources. The logging and manufacturing processes are
expected to conform to the environmental regulations of the country of origin.

HEADLINE PUBLISHING GROUP
An Hachette UK Company
338 Euston Road
London NW1 3BH

www.headline.co.uk
www.hachette.co.uk

To my daughter, Kirsten – I cannot give you forever,
but I promise to love you for that long.

PART ONE
THE ATTACK

Strength lies not in defense
but in attack.
—*Adolf Hitler*

1

THE GIRL KNOWN AS GRETCHEN WHITESTONE BICYCLED down the country lane. Desolate fields, their grasses winter-brown and glistening from the afternoon's rainfall, stretched out on either side of the road. The first strains of twilight darkened the distant hills to black, and nearby a few muddy sheep grazed, pausing to gaze blank-eyed at Gretchen as she pedaled past.

Beyond the long line of poplar trees rose the Oxford Psychoanalytical Clinic, a stone lion of a building turning gray in the dusk. Gretchen coasted down the drive and stopped under the portico, leaving her bicycle leaning against a pillar. The front door handle was cold in her hand as she twisted it open and stepped inside.

Walking into the mental clinic's reception hall felt like walking into a luxurious hotel lobby. The wood-paneled walls were dotted with watercolor paintings, the parquet floor covered with red Turkish carpets. The first time Gretchen had seen it, she'd been shocked, for she had expected stark white walls, men and women writhing in straitjackets, and the throbbing hum of an electric current machine. Her guardian had smiled at her confusion, saying the clinic was designed to treat its patients, not imprison them.

A nurse sat behind the front desk, going through a sheaf of papers. 'Good afternoon, Miss Whitestone,' she said in the clipped accent that Gretchen had found so difficult to understand when she'd first arrived in England. 'Your father should be finished seeing patients for the day, so you may go right up.'

'Thank you.' Gretchen didn't bother correcting the nurse – Dr Alfred Whitestone wasn't her father; her real papa had been dead more than nine years – but it was best not to discuss the matter, and thus encourage questions that were too dangerous for her to answer. As far as the staff knew, she was an ordinary German immigrant who had been taken in by a kindly English family. If only the truth were that simple.

Gretchen hurried up the twisting stairwell to Alfred's office. The third-floor corridor stretched out, its yellow-and-white tiled walls broken by a succession of closed doors. The patients were downstairs for their painting and flower-arranging therapeutic classes, so the place was quiet. A house of lunatics, Gretchen's school friends had whispered, but she knew better. She'd spent too many years at her honorary uncle Dolf's side not to recognize true darkness – and this was not it.

Just thinking of Adolf Hitler threw her heart against her ribs. *Don't*, she ordered herself, walking faster. She hated the way he still crept into her head. Worrying about him was foolish: hundreds of miles and the gray waters of the English Channel separated them. Even if he was looking for her, he'd never find her. She'd hidden herself too carefully for him to pick up her trail.

But she still had to pause outside the office door, waiting for her pulse to slow, before she knocked.

4

'Come in!' Her guardian sounded distracted; he was probably lost in a case study or a patient file, struggling to untie the dark knots in the minds of those he had pledged to help. Gretchen hoped that someday she could be half as accomplished a psychoanalyst as him.

'Hello, Dr Whitestone,' Gretchen said, stepping into his office and squinting in the sudden muted light. A single green-shaded lamp burned, leaving most of the room in shadow. The doctor sat at his desk, tidying a stack of manila folders. 'I've just gotten back from town. The study session went well,' she added, knowing he would ask, although it still seemed strange to have a parent who inquired about her schooling.

These conversations between the two of them had become a daily habit; she would stop by his office after school and they would chat for a few minutes before walking home together, leaving her bicycle at the clinic for her to pick up on her way to school the next morning. They rarely talked about anything but school or the clinic, but, even so, it was nice to have someone's full attention and to know that if she did want to discuss something else, he was willing to listen.

'Now, Gretchen,' he said gently, 'we've been over this before. Please call me Alfred.'

Gretchen flushed. Even though she'd been a member of the Whitestone household for seventeen months, she still sometimes forgot to call her guardian by his first name. Addressing an adult so informally – especially one she hadn't known since girlhood – went against everything she'd been taught by her parents.

Most of her parents' rules were wrong, she reminded herself, and forced a smile. 'Yes, Alfred.'

His gaze held hers for a moment longer, his expression serious. 'I don't make the request lightly. You're my daughter in every sense of the word that matters.'

Gretchen swallowed against the sudden tightness in her throat, thinking of her father. He had never said such things to her, but she had known he had loved her by the way he danced with her around the kitchen or sat with her when she woke up from a nightmare. Loving Alfred wasn't being disloyal to Papa, she reminded herself for the thousandth time. It was finding a way to keep living, no matter what happened. 'I know,' she managed to say.

Whitestone blinked several times and turned away, busying himself with the folders in a filing cabinet. 'You said the study session went well?'

'Yes. Though the French exam will probably still be dreadful. Anyway, it's half past six, and Julia must be frantic that the rolls have gone cold by now.'

'Poor Julia.' Whitestone locked the cabinet and turned to Gretchen, smiling. Cold rolls were a long-running family joke – Alfred was frequently late to supper, and once had been so wrapped up in work that he'd forgotten about a lavish dinner party his wife was throwing, resulting in the infamous cold-as-rock rolls. 'We'd best get home, then,' he added, ushering her out of the office.

Together, they started down the hall. Although Gretchen tried not to see them, she couldn't help noticing the missing wall tiles, the scuff marks on the floor, the flickering bulbs in the electric light fixtures. Up here on the third floor, far from the probing gazes of potential patients and their families, the clinic's meager finances showed themselves.

As their footsteps echoed up and down the hall, Gretchen glanced at Alfred. As always, he was his comfortable, dapper self: a thatch of black hair above a square of a face, dark eyes behind gold-rimmed spectacles, and a blue suit that somehow managed to appear freshly pressed although it had been worn all day. He looked just the same as he had when they'd met

6

months ago at her mother's boardinghouse in Munich. Then he'd been a stranger on sabbatical, wishing to observe the psychological oddity of rising politician Adolf Hitler. He'd planned to write a profile on Hitler for a medical journal, one that would garner him enough professional acclaim that he'd be invited to serve on the staff of a prominent London hospital.

But he'd never written it. In order for her to be safe, she had to remain anonymous, which meant the Whitestones had to, as well. So Alfred had continued trudging along at his job at this mediocre clinic, and kept his article on Hitler locked in a desk drawer. Because he cared for her, she knew.

'Do you ever regret it?' she asked as they entered the stairwell. 'Staying here, I mean, when you could have gotten a job somewhere else.'

'Of course not.' Whitestone spoke briskly. 'If I'd written about Hitler, we could have attracted a lot of attention. We mustn't give anyone a reason to look at us too closely. Your safety is more important than anything.'

What had she done to warrant such unwavering love and self-sacrifice from this family? There were no ties of blood or years of shared memories between them. But there was something deeper, something she hadn't experienced until she'd met Daniel.

The thought of her beau relaxed the clenched muscles of her stomach. She pictured his eyes, brown mixed with gold, watching hers while he grinned, the left side of his mouth lifting higher than the right. *It's all right*, she heard him saying in his sharp Berliner accent. *Nobody but my family knows where we are, and they'll never tell anyone.* He would cup her chin in his hand, propelling her closer until their lips were almost touching, and say the words she desperately wanted to believe. *We made it. You'll never have to see Adolf Hitler again.*

She needed him to be right. Because she knew if she and Uncle Dolf met again, he would have her killed immediately. If not for her 'blood sin' of loving a Jew, then for the secret she'd uncovered about him. The one that had broken them apart. The thing that ripped her from sleep, night after night, leaving her gasping in the dark, pressing a hand over her mouth so nobody would hear her.

'We should hurry,' she said through numb lips. 'The boys must be hungry.'

They collected spare mackintoshes, umbrellas, and galoshes from the front hall and set off across the damp fields. Light from the clinic's windows tossed gold onto the ground, turning the drying raindrops to flecks of glitter. About two hundred yards away stood the Whitestones' home, a large brick house perched alongside a rutted lane that gradually widened as it stretched into the city. On the back porch, Gretchen and Dr Whitestone kicked off their galoshes, then stepped into the warm kitchen where Cook bustled over the Aga stove.

'Get on with you,' Cook grumbled. 'Keeping poor Mrs Whitestone waiting these twenty minutes.'

Gretchen tried not to smile. She found Cook's complaints soothing, for she heard them at least a couple of times every week, but here no one ever sighed with disapproval or said one thing while meaning another. Unlike Mama.

Her stomach twisted. She joined Dr Whitestone at the sink, gazing at the water sluicing across her hands until her worries about her mother slipped away.

Dr Whitestone took Gretchen's arm. 'Come along.' There was a slight catch in his voice that made her peer at him, but his face was calm.

From the dining room, Gretchen caught a giggle and someone whispering, 'Hush!' She frowned. Ordinarily, suppers

8

at the Whitestones' were noisy affairs, between her three foster brothers chattering about their day, Julia chiding them about their table manners, and the boys' governess sighing into her soup about yet another stupid comment her beau from the greengrocer's had made. The quiet felt unnatural.

Was something wrong? Gretchen hurried across the kitchen, hearing Papa's old warning in her head: *Silence means someone's waiting to hurt you.* Had something happened to Julia and the boys? She pushed the dining room door open, ready to run inside, and stopped short.

Paper streamers dangled from the chandelier. Candles flickered from Julia's best silver candlesticks, which were set on the lace-trimmed tablecloth that normally came out only on Sundays and Christmas. A hand-printed sign reading HAPPY BIRTHDAY GRETCHEN – the boys' work, no doubt; she recognized the shaky *T* as Jack's – had been hung over the green-and-gold-striped wallpaper. Beaming under their party hats were Julia and her three sons, Colin, Andrew, and Jack, aged twelve, ten, and eight like stepping-stones, all flame-haired and freckled like their mother. Sitting next to Julia was Gretchen's friend Mary. The governess must have been given the night off.

'Happy birthday!' they shouted.

'But . . .' Today wasn't her birthday. She had turned eighteen back in July.

Then she saw Julia's small frown. Of course. Her old self, Gretchen Müller, had been born on 18 July 1914. Gisela Schröder – the name on the false identity papers she'd bought in Switzerland two autumns ago, when she and Daniel had fled Germany – had been born seven months later, so today, 21 February 1933, was indeed her eighteenth 'birthday'. She'd kept her real first name, reasoning that no one would look for her here, but she'd assumed parts of the fictitious Gisela's identity, including her birth date, to fill in the holes in her own.

Confusion wrinkled Mary's forehead, and the boys looked bewildered. They didn't know who she truly was, or that it wasn't her birthday. She had to react, and fast, before they started to wonder at her silence.

'Thank you,' she said. 'This is lovely. I've never had a birthday supper before.' Last year, Julia had tried to give her one, but she'd declined, feeling uncomfortable at the thought of the Whitestones going to that much expense for her. Apparently, Julia hadn't wanted to give her the chance to refuse again.

'Never?' The boys goggled and everybody laughed.

'It isn't just supper,' Julia said. 'There will be presents and cake afterward.'

Tonight she wore a patterned silk dress and had forced her hair into a sleek chignon, a marked change from her usual tweed skirts, lace-up shoes, and unruly curls. The boys wore their typical short trousers, kneesocks, and sweaters, but everything was clean, without a single stain or rip, practically a miracle in the rambunctious Whitestone household.

Something brilliant and warm unfolded in Gretchen's chest. They had dressed up for her sake.

'We have one surprise that won't wait.' Julia beamed. 'You can come in now,' she called.

Gretchen's heart leapt. She turned toward the doorway. In the hall beyond the dining room, she glimpsed a tall young man. He moved so fast toward her, he was little more than a blur of a black suit jacket and trousers. But she recognized the muscular line of his shoulders, the confident tilt of his head. *Daniel*. Everything within her blazed to life.

10

2

GRETCHEN DASHED TO HIM. HOW HAD HE MANAGED
to come tonight? He was supposed to be at work, covering
a society dance at a local country club for his newspaper.
Before she could say a word, he had wrapped an arm around
her, pulling her so close that she felt his heartbeat thudding
through his jacket. Then he kissed her, a quick peck on the
mouth. He pulled back, grinning.

'Surprised?' he asked. 'I traded assignments with another
reporter. He's at the country club tonight, poor soul.' Daniel
dipped his head low, brushing her ear with his lips so only
she could hear him. 'Seeing you has made all the groveling
worth it.'

'Having you here is the best birthday gift I can imagine.'
She stood in the circle of his arm, drinking him in even
though she had long ago memorized the sharp planes of his
face, the olive tint of his skin, the fall of his dark hair. There
was nothing gentle or quiet about him – the first time she
had caught sight of him, she had thought she had never
seen such fierceness – but in his embrace, she felt protected.

As though she could withstand anything, as long as they were together.

Alfred cleared his throat. 'I take it Daniel's appearance is a success, then.'

His words pulled Gretchen back to herself. Blushing, she slipped from Daniel's embrace and introduced him to Mary. They shook hands, her friend's smile faltering when she glanced at his left arm hanging rigidly by his side.

Gretchen caught her breath. *Please don't say anything*, she silently begged. Daniel was still so self-conscious about his injury.

But Mary sat down without another word, and Gretchen exhaled in relief. There was no flush in Daniel's cheeks as he seated himself across the table. He hadn't noticed.

Mary nudged Gretchen and wiggled her eyebrows, mouthing, *He's so handsome!* Gretchen managed a weak smile. At school tomorrow all of her friends would probably demand to know more about Daniel and why the devil she hadn't introduced them. She'd have to come up with excuses to fob them off; she could hardly admit that she'd kept them apart on purpose, fearing she and Daniel would slip and say something about their old lives in Germany. Nobody could know who they really were or what they were hiding from.

As Cook came in with the soup, Julia turned to Daniel. 'Daniel, dear, how's work?'

'About what you'd expect.' The tips of his ears turned red. 'I'm a reporter at the *Oxford Mail*,' he explained to Mary. 'I write the society column.'

In her lap, Gretchen's hands tightened into fists, the fingernails cutting into her palms. Although Daniel's tone was light, she knew how much the words cost him. Working as a society reporter at a daily tabloid was a steep fall from his old job back in Germany at the *Munich Post*. That paper was one

12

of the last publications left that was unsympathetic to the burgeoning National Socialist Party, and its reporters had been writing investigative articles about Hitler for over a decade.

Every time Daniel had gone to the *Post* office, he had risked a beating, for Party storm troopers sometimes loitered outside, waiting for a chance to attack him and the other reporters. Despite the danger, Daniel had loved the work: He had believed that he was doing something important.

Now he wrote about high society folks' clothes and balls and romances. It was a decent job, for it paid enough that he could afford a room in a lodging house in town, and he never went hungry.

He hated it.

'The job is an excellent starting point,' Alfred said quickly. Gretchen's hands uncurled in her lap. Thank goodness for Alfred; he always knew what to say. 'Just you wait, Daniel – it won't be long before you prove yourself and all the best editors in England are clamoring to hire you.'

Daniel's laugh was forced. 'Thanks, Dr Whitestone. You're very kind.'

Then Jack started begging Daniel to tell him pirate stories, as he always did, and soon everyone was laughing at Daniel's tale about Captain Jack sailing the seas, searching for buried treasure. Before Gretchen knew it, they'd eaten the roast beef, creamed potatoes, and peas and were sitting in the parlor, having cake while she opened presents.

She smiled over the hair ribbons and hand-drawn pictures from the boys and the bottle of perfume from Mary. She got a string of pearls, her first grown-up jewelry, from Alfred and Julia, and a German edition of her favorite book, Hermann Hesse's *Siddhartha*, from Daniel. He must have scoured the cramped bookshops on High Street to find it. She ran her hands over its leather cover, marveling at its softness, while the metal grille in the fireplace glowed red-hot. Faintly, she heard the telephone ring from the front hall.

'Do you like it?' Daniel nodded at the book. 'I remembered how sad you were that you had to leave your copy behind in Munich.'

How had he remembered something so trivial? 'I love it,' she said, smiling at him. 'It's perfect.'

He leaned closer. 'Did you see what Winston Churchill said in today's paper about the debate at Oxford University?'

She didn't follow British politics as keenly as Daniel did, and it took her a moment to remember who Churchill was. He'd been a prominent politician during the Great War, but these days, he was a writer and a benchwarmer in the House of Commons, a position so inconsequential that he no longer had any say in policy decisions. The only reason she knew that much was because Daniel had to write about him for the society pages whenever he visited his cousin, the Duke of Marlborough, at nearby Blenheim Palace.

'The debate?' she asked, dredging through her memories. On the other side of the room, the boys had clustered around the coffee table, begging Julia for another slice of cake, and Alfred was asking Mary about school. 'Do you mean that talk at the university a couple of weeks ago?'

'Yes, when the students debated whether or not Englishmen have a responsibility to fight if there's ever another world war.' Daniel fished a newspaper clipping out of his pocket and handed it to her. 'Look what Churchill said about it.'

She read the smudged newsprint:

Mr Churchill recently spoke at a meeting of the Anti-Socialist and Anti-Communist Union, saying, 'My thoughts fasten on Germany, where the rumors about

14

Jewish persecution and possible pogroms have grown louder since Mr Hitler slunk into office last month. I understand the Nazis better than most in England, for I was recently in Munich, where the Nazis tried to bring about a meeting between me and their leader. Hitler wants war. And we ignore him at our peril.'

It had happened at last, what Daniel had wanted for so long and despaired of ever hearing: an English politician had spoken scathingly about Germany's new chancellor. When she and Daniel had first arrived in England, they'd been certain someone influential would listen to their warnings about Hitler. On his days off, Daniel had taken the train to London and loitered outside the Houses of Parliament. As soon as the politicians ambled out, he dashed after them, saying he had important information that would gravely affect their foreign relation policies.

A few of the men had stopped, listening with polite smiles, then thanked Daniel and advised him to write to his local MP instead. Most of them hadn't broken stride. It had taken Daniel months to accept the truth: nobody wanted to listen. They were too desperate to hold onto this fragile peace. Too worn down by the years of want and economic depression and hungry bellies. They would placate Hitler for the promise of quiet lives, full stomachs, steady jobs.

She looked up to find Daniel watching her. 'Finally,' he said, 'someone in England understands how dangerous Hitler is.'

'At last,' Gretchen said with relief, then paused, biting her lip. 'But everyone says he's a has-been. What difference can he possibly make?'

'I don't know. We could go to his house in Kent – that's not so far away – and tell him what we know about Hitler.' Daniel's face lit up at the thought.

Gretchen's heart sank. She had hoped that Daniel had finally accepted that English politicians weren't interested in listening to them. Even if Mr Churchill was willing to meet with them, he couldn't have Hitler removed from his chancellorship post. The best thing she and Daniel could do for themselves was move on.

'Can't we forget about Hitler just for tonight?' Gretchen said.

Daniel's face fell. 'Of course.' He took the clipping back, pasting on a smile. 'You deserve to be happy, especially on your birthday.'

Cook appeared at the door. 'I beg your pardon, Mrs Whitestone.' The words squeezed out between each rapid breath. 'Mr Cohen's landlady just rang.' Her gaze skittered to Daniel. 'She said she would have gotten word to you sooner, sir, but you were out of the office all afternoon on an assignment.'

Daniel had been crumpling up the discarded wrapping paper. His left hand convulsed around the ball of red gift wrap, a sure sign that the damaged nerves beneath his skin were turning to fire. 'Why does she need to talk to me? What's happened?'

Gretchen went still.

'You received a telegram, sir,' Cook said. Her hands fluttered around her sides. 'Your landlady wouldn't have thought anything of it except . . . Well, sir, it's a foreign telegram.' She hesitated. 'It's from Germany.'

A hush fell over the parlor. Daniel jumped up. His face had gone sheet-white. 'What did it say?'

His voice was so hoarse, Gretchen scarcely recognized it. She understood his concern: telegrams were expensive, and his family would only have paid for one if they had needed to get in touch with Daniel immediately. There was no one

16

else in Germany who knew where he lived. Something important must have happened.

Nerves twisted in Gretchen's stomach as she rose. Cook said, 'Mr Cohen, your landlady didn't want to read your mail. I'm afraid I've told you all I know.'

Gretchen took Daniel's good hand in hers, but he didn't seem to notice, turning instead to Alfred and saying shakily, 'Please, can you take me back now? I need to see the telegram straightaway.' He didn't wait for Alfred's response, glancing around the room, his eyes unfocused. 'I apologize for breaking up the party.'

'You must go at once,' Gretchen said. 'Shall I come with you?'

'No. Stay, enjoy the party.' When he leaned forward to press his mouth to her cheek, his touch felt so light she might have imagined it. 'I'm sure it's nothing,' he murmured in her ear. 'Maybe it's good news. Perhaps one of my sisters is getting married.'

Somehow she managed to pull her lips into a smile. 'Maybe,' she agreed. 'Tell me as soon as you can.'

He nodded and squeezed her hand. The flurry of leave-taking began: Cook fetching Daniel's and Mary's coats, everyone shaking hands and saying farewell, the little boys bouncing around like tops from too much cake and excitement. Then Daniel, Mary, and Alfred were gone, the front door creaking shut behind them. Gretchen stood in the parlor, listening to her guardian's car rumble to life in the lane alongside the house, its tires crunching over the gravel drive as it took Daniel away.

That night, alone in her bedroom, she rested her head on the door. The smooth coolness of the wood was soothing. From down the hall, she heard the boys going to bed: the splash of

17

water in a basin, the rustle of sheets being turned back, the low murmur of Julia's voice as she read them a story.

Downstairs, Cook hummed as she scrubbed the supper dishes, and a sudden burst of static, followed by classical music, sounded from the parlor. Alfred must be listening to the wireless. When he'd returned from dropping off Daniel and Mary half an hour ago, she'd been waiting for him, desperate for news. But he'd shaken his head, saying Daniel had preferred to go to his room and read the telegram by himself. Surely he'd get in touch with her tomorrow.

Gretchen had nodded, her throat tightening. What could have happened? Was his family all right? She knew he missed them terribly. Sometimes he said that he felt as though he had no family anywhere, with his parents and sisters hundreds of miles away in Berlin. She understood how he felt: she had no real family left, either, except for her mother, since her father and brother, Reinhard, had been killed. With seventeen months of silence between her and Mama, she supposed they might as well be dead to each other, too.

She looked around her bedroom. It seemed the same, untouched by her nerves. Safe. She loved the feather bed covered by a flowered duvet, the simple maple wardrobe, the walls papered with pink roses, the cheap reproduction prints of all the artists Hitler despised: Klee, Kandinsky, and Picasso, the colors bright, the shapes surreal. They reminded her of a drawing she'd made in her primary school's art class. When she'd shown it to Hitler, he'd sighed, saying, *Whoever paints the sky green and the grass blue is feebleminded*. She'd burst into tears and thrown it into the kitchen stove.

Well, he didn't make her decisions anymore. She slipped her revolver out of her schoolbag and put it in the cardboard box on top of the wardrobe, where it was too high for the maid to dust.

18

It was a pity she couldn't practice shooting, but she couldn't risk her guardians finding out that she'd secretly bought the gun last summer with the pin money she'd made watching a neighbor's children. They would never understand why she needed it. To her, owning a revolver was as necessary as air. When she'd been growing up in Hitler's inner circle, she'd never met a Party man who didn't carry a knife or a pistol. Uncle Dolf himself was one of the best marksmen in Munich and he had taught her how to shoot when she was small.

Her heart started to pound. But instead of sliding to the floor and covering her face with her hands, as she used to do, she stared at herself in the mirror and said the words that she forced herself to say every night. 'Adolf Hitler killed Papa.'

Saying them didn't change anything; Hitler had still gotten away with murdering her father nine years ago. All because Papa had known that Uncle Dolf had been diagnosed as a psychopath – a diagnosis that Gretchen doubted her father had believed – when they'd recovered at the same military hospital during the Great War. Hitler had been terrified that the information would destroy his burgeoning political career.

And so he'd shot Papa during a street fight between the National Socialists and the state police, gambling that no one would notice in the confusion. As usual, he'd been lucky. It wasn't until two summers ago, when Gretchen had met Daniel and they had investigated her father's death, that she'd real-ized the man she'd adored for years was a criminal.

Now she bit her lip to keep the tears at bay. Saying the truth didn't change what had happened. But every time she said the words to herself, she felt stronger.

Since the last time she had seen Hitler, he had lost the presidential election, but the National Socialists had continued to surge in the polls, and last month President Hindenburg had appointed Hitler to the chancellorship, the second highest position in the country and his due as head of the largest political party in Germany. He was powerful now, more powerful than in the years she'd known him, except in one crucial way: he didn't own her anymore.

She changed into her nightdress and snapped off the lamp, plunging the room into a blackness broken only by the slivers of moonlight showing through the curtain. Whatever news had been in Daniel's telegram, she prayed it had nothing to do with the nightmares of their past.

3

DANIEL STILL HADN'T TELEPHONED BY THE TIME Gretchen left for school the next morning, and some of the tension melted from her shoulders. If the news had been dire, he would have told her. Everything must be all right.

When the dismissal bell rang, she slowly put her books in her schoolbag, wishing she didn't have to leave. Here she always felt normal, surrounded by the simple majesty of science, the smooth logic of mathematics, the precision of Latin. Every question had an answer. Unlike the questions that tormented her about her old life.

As she wove between the girls in the corridor, she caught snatches of their conversations – tonight's assignment on *The Merchant of Venice*, the French teacher's too-tight blouse, the sixth-form girl who'd been caught in a pub with a university undergraduate – but the words brushed against her like butterflies' wings, soft and barely felt. If only she could giggle and chatter as easily as the other girls. Sometimes forcing a laugh or a light-hearted comment required more energy than she could manage. She wasn't like her classmates, and she never would be.

It didn't matter, she told herself as she reached the front hall. In a few months, she would graduate and enroll at a university, so she could become a psychoanalyst. More than anything else, she wanted to heal diseased minds. She hadn't been able to help or change her brother – the whole family had been trapped in the twisting tunnels of Reinhard's brain, afraid to risk angering him – but she could save others. After seeing the patients at Alfred's clinic, she now understood that many mentally ill people weren't violent, unlike her brother. But surely there were more like him, cold and sadistic, who liked torturing family members for sport. She wanted to help them all.

Outside the weak strains of February sunlight touched the bicycle she'd left leaning on the brick building. As she hopped astride, Mary appeared beside her, out of breath, her coat unbuttoned over her blue school uniform.

'Where are you off to?' she asked.

'I'm going to see if Daniel's home,' Gretchen said. 'If he has an evening assignment, he takes an hour or two off in the afternoon to spend with me.'

A grin creased Mary's round face. 'Then I shan't keep you. But I'll want all the details tomorrow. Especially how you managed to keep such a gorgeous fellow under wraps for so long. We all knew you had a beau, but I'd no idea he was so splendid! Does he have any friends?'

Gretchen smiled, thinking of the graduate students who lived in Daniel's lodging house: hard-bitten, coffee- and gin-swilling young men who were far more interested in garnering top marks and landing high-paying jobs someday in the City than in the proper students at a girls' school.

'Yes, but they're not what you'd call your cup of tea.'

'Lucky you, then, for catching such a delicious drink.' Mary paused. 'Is he ill? Because of his arm, I mean.' She flushed as

22

Gretchen looked at her. 'It's none of my business, but I couldn't help noticing.'

'He's fine,' Gretchen said quickly. There was no way she could tell Mary the truth – that some National Socialists had beaten Daniel right before they'd fled from Munich. Going to a hospital would have been only a temporary reprieve before Hitler's men found them. By the time they'd reached Switzerland, Daniel had insisted he was much better and they should reserve their dwindling money for false identification papers, not doctors' fees. The whole time his bruised muscles had swelled, pressing against the skin until the cells died, leaving his arm hanging uselessly by his side. Then the muscles had slowly atrophied, contracting until his arm was little more than blood and bone.

'Oh, so he'll be getting better, then.' Mary brightened. 'That's a relief!'

'The nerve damage is permanent, I'm afraid,' Gretchen said. Now that she was finally talking about the matter with someone else, the story rushed out. 'Alfred took him to a specialist in London last summer. The doctor said Daniel's lucky to have any use of his arm at all. Some days, his arm feels numb. Other times, it feels as though it's been set on fire. The pain will come and go for the rest of his life.'

'How dreadful!' Mary put a hand to her mouth. 'He must be very brave, to cope with such an awful injury.'

'He's the bravest person I know.' Gretchen leaned across the bicycle handlebars to squeeze Mary's hand. She wished they could whisper and giggle about Daniel like ordinary school chums, lying on the rug in Mary's room, flipping through magazines, half listening to the wireless, talking about boys and whatever came into their heads. Just as she and her old best friend, Eva, used to do.

A lump rose in her throat. She and Eva were lost to each

other now, as they must be, and no amount of crying or praying would change that. Swallowing hard, she released Mary's hand.

'You're a good friend,' she said. 'I'll see you tomorrow.'

Mary smiled uncertainly. 'Are you all right? You look sad.'

Forcing a smile, Gretchen nodded. She was as all right as she ever could be. After bidding Mary good-bye, she pedaled down the narrow street lined with a jumble of stone and stucco buildings, past a couple of housewives pushing prams and some university undergraduates wearing their required long black robes. Overhead, clouds choked the sky, gilding the shop windows and the black automobiles crawling down the avenue with silver.

Daniel lived in a narrow, three-story house on Iffley Road. Gretchen left her bicycle leaning against the front steps and rang the bell. After a moment, the door opened and Daniel's landlady, a middle-aged woman in a tweed skirt and green sweater set, peered out at her. She didn't smile, as she usually did.

'Oh, Miss Whitestone, please come in.' She ushered Gretchen into a parlor crowded with old-fashioned furniture and around a wooden table so wide that Gretchen had to walk sideways to reach the sofa. Daniel often joked that he was afraid to breathe in there or risk breaking one of Mrs Mitchell's precious things.

Gretchen folded her hands in her lap, waiting for Mrs Mitchell to go to the foot of the stairs and call to Daniel to come down, as she usually did. Instead, she went to the desk in the corner, unlocked a drawer, and took out an envelope.

'Mr Cohen asked me to give you this,' she said, crossing the room and pressing the envelope into Gretchen's hand. 'I'll give you a moment to read it.'

24

She strode from the room, leaving Gretchen staring after her in confusion. Daniel had never left a note for her before. She tore open the envelope.

> *My Gretchen,*
> *Aaron was attacked. He's in the hospital and the doctors aren't sure if he'll survive.*

She gasped. She remembered Aaron Pearlman, Daniel's cousin, so well. He'd let her stay with him and his sister, Ruth, for a night, when she'd had nowhere else to go. She turned back to the letter.

> *The National Socialists were having a parade through Munich. Apparently, nowadays everyone is supposed to salute as they go past. But Aaron didn't. Several of the National Socialists left the parade and beat him in the street, while others watched and did nothing. Ruth screamed at them to stop, and they only laughed at her. The doctors say he has massive internal injuries.*
> *I must go back. By the time you read this, I'll have already left. The men who beat Aaron need to be brought to justice. Don't worry – I'll be careful. I'll use my false papers, and I'll contact my old colleagues at the Munich Post. They have a far-flung network of informants, and if anyone knows who's responsible, they will. Once I have the men's names, I'll give them to Ruth, so she can tell the police. I don't know if they'll arrest the guilty men, as there are plenty of National Socialists on the police force. But I'll have done something, at least. I can't live with myself if I don't try.*
> *I will come back to you as soon as I can.*
> *Your Daniel*

The paper shook in her hands. Returning to Munich was suicide. Daniel couldn't hope to sneak back into the city undetected; surely his face was too well known. As the despised Jew who'd dared to fall in love with Hitler's 'sunshine', he would be hunted down and killed.

She read the letter a second time, as if by seeing the words again she could somehow change their meaning. Daniel had written in German, even though they'd been careful to talk only in English since they'd disembarked from the ship at Dover months ago, tired and hungry and with only nine pounds between them. No possessions, no spare clothes, nothing but each other and the false identification papers they'd paid so much to get. Gretchen's dry eyes burned. And now Daniel had plunged back into the nightmare.

She got up and stumbled out of the parlor and down the front steps. Her legs were trembling so badly she could barely clamber onto the bicycle. She pedaled down the road, heading northeast, toward home, all of her movements automatic. Dimly, she heard automobiles gliding past and the rattle of a pram's wheels on the pavement. Daniel's letter rustled in her coat pocket.

Somehow she got back to the Whitestones' house, although she couldn't remember bicycling there. Moving like an automaton, she went through the parlor, where Julia, the governess, and the boys stopped talking to stare at her. The effort to lift each foot onto the next step seemed like too much, but she managed to get up them and into her room. Then she curled into a ball on her bed and let the tears come.

What if Daniel made a mistake – trusted the wrong person, walked down a street where somebody recognized him, or forgot to respond to his false name, Leopold? There were so many things that could go wrong.

She had to concentrate on the flow of air in and out of

her lungs, just so she could breathe. In her mind, she saw Daniel flashing his confident, lopsided grin, and her heart ached. Daniel wasn't who she had thought she wanted, when they had met. But he was who she needed. Now and always, he was who she needed.

The door opened, but Gretchen just pressed her wet cheek to the bedspread, rounding her shoulders, as if she could pull herself into her own private grief. The mattress dipped as someone sat down next to her.

'What's happened?' It was Julia's voice. She smoothed Gretchen's hair from her face, just as Gretchen used to wish her own mother would do. Gretchen closed her eyes, clinging to the sensation of Julia's fingers, light and cool on her scalp, and the whole story streamed out.

When she had finished, there was silence for a moment. Then Julia sighed. 'He'll return as quickly as he can. Daniel loves you with his whole heart. Alfred and I knew that from the moment you two showed up on our doorstep.' She laughed a little. 'I'll never forget the sight of you – so pale and skinny and exhausted. It was obvious Daniel was in terrible pain, but he wouldn't let Alfred inspect his arm until he saw that I'd gotten you something to eat.'

She hesitated. 'You're lucky, Gretchen, to have a young man who places his duty to his family above his own safety and happiness. There aren't many who would be so brave. He'll be back before you've had time to miss him.'

Shaking her head, Gretchen said nothing. Julia didn't understand. How could she, when she had never attended a Party rally in the Circus Krone where the hundreds of people in the audience roared, '*Sieg Heil, Sieg Heil!*' or lingered over coffee at Café Heck, listening to Hitler go on and on about his future plans? *I shall do the thing the rest of the world would like to do*, he'd muttered to one of his comrades while

27

she'd traced the wet circle left by her glass on the table, sixteen and bored. *They don't know how to get rid of the Jews. I will teach them.*

If Hitler found Daniel, he would show him no mercy.

'Rest,' Julia said. 'Everything will seem better in the morning.'

But nothing would be different tomorrow; Daniel would still be gone. Gretchen opened her eyes and stared at the ceiling. Beside her, Julia murmured reassuringly and smoothed her hair. They stayed that way for a long time.

Six days dragged past. At breakfast, Gretchen half listened to the wireless and scoured the morning newspapers, reading every article about Germany, searching the tiny print for Daniel's name without finding it. During the day, she lost herself in her lessons and could almost forget Daniel had left. But then the memory of Daniel's leaving would crash over her like a wave, pinning her to the ocean floor.

After school, she slumped on the parlor sofa, staring at the same geometry problem, willing her frozen brain to work. Alfred and Julia were listening to the wireless. From the kitchen, Gretchen heard Cook humming as she prepared supper, and thumps and shrieks of laughter drifted downstairs from the nursery. It should have felt like an ordinary afternoon, but everything seemed unfamiliar, the mundane routine transformed by Daniel's absence.

The tinny voice from the wireless sliced into her thoughts. 'Germans are in a state of shock today,' he was saying.

Gretchen bolted upright. 'What did he say?'

Julia set down her knitting, concern etched on her face. 'Gretchen, are you all right—'

'Shh!' Alfred leaned forward. 'We need to hear this.'

The announcer continued in a smooth voice, 'At

nine o'clock last night, February the twenty-seventh, Berlin was the target of a terrorist attack heard around the world. Person or persons unknown set fire to the Reichstag, the building where the German legislative assembly convene. According to some sources, the fire may be the work of either the Nazis or the Communists, Germany's two most powerful political parties. For our listeners who don't follow German politics, the parties are bitter rivals and have battled each other for supremacy in the Reichstag for the past few years.'

Gretchen barely breathed, afraid to miss a single word.

'Today, President Hindenburg and Chancellor Hitler declared a state of emergency and issued the Decree of the Reich President for the Protection of the People and the State,' the announcer went on. 'The decree suspends all major civil liberties, including freedom of expression, freedom of the press, and freedom to assemble. Letters, telephone calls, and telegrams may be intercepted by the police at any time. We have been told that there is widespread panic in the streets of Berlin, and its residents fear more imminent terrorist attacks.'

The announcer paused for breath and then launched into another story. Gretchen's mouth had gone as dry as sand. Was Hitler responsible for the fire? Throughout her childhood, the Communists had been the National Socialists' fiercest opponents, and Hitler despised them. He had taught her that Communism was like an infectious disease spreading down from the vast Russian steppes. *A political system designed by Jews meant to enslave non-Jewish nations*, he used to say, tapping her nose playfully.

'My God,' Alfred said in a hushed voice. 'Gretchen, do you think Hitler is behind this?'

'Maybe.' She knew too well that he would stop at nothing, even murder, to advance his political career. Now, in one night, he had been granted two of his most fervent wishes: a means to destroy the Communists and to monitor the German population. Thanks to this presidential decree, nobody was assured of any privacy in Germany.

And that meant no letters from Daniel. He wouldn't contact her for he wouldn't want anyone to read his mail and learn her location. Thank God he was in Munich, hundreds of miles from the chaos in Berlin. But that was no guarantee he was safe.

Julia crossed the room to sit next to her. 'Hitler can't hope to get away with it,' she said firmly. 'Sooner or later, people will realize how wicked he is and have him removed from office.'

Gretchen couldn't find her voice. Maybe Julia was right, but what if Daniel was in trouble right now? He could be dead or imprisoned, and she had no way of finding out.

Somehow, Gretchen managed to slog through her lessons, bicycle home, sit in her bedroom staring at blank pieces of paper that should have been covered with her homework assignments. She read every newspaper she could get her hands on, but none of the articles about Germany mentioned Daniel's name. They focused on the Reichstag blaze instead. A twenty-four-year-old named Marinus van der Lubbe had been arrested on the scene. As he was half blind, it seemed impossible that he could have set the fire by himself, and no one else had been accused yet.

The information gave Gretchen pause. If Hitler had ordered the fire set in an effort to frame the Communists and create a national emergency suspending civil liberties, then wouldn't he have chosen a better scapegoat? It didn't make sense. The sensation of déjà vu swept over her. Something about this fire seemed familiar, but she couldn't pinpoint what it was. As far as she could recall, Hitler hadn't been mixed up in arson before. She was too worried about Daniel, though, to puzzle over it further.

At school, nobody asked what she thought of the mysterious fire in her homeland, although several of her friends wanted to know how Daniel was faring and when he would be back. She shrugged, too heartsick to answer.

'Now, Gretchen,' Mary said five days later, linking their arms and guiding Gretchen away from the cluster of girls on the school's front steps, 'you needn't put up a brave front with me and the other girls. It's obvious what's happened to Daniel.'

Gretchen started in surprise. 'It is?'

'Of course.' Mary gave her a sad smile. 'He's gone back to Germany to live, hasn't he? I daresay he's awfully handsome, but there are plenty of other fellows out there, and any of them would be lucky to have you. Just wait. It won't be long before you've forgotten all about him and moved on to somebody else.'

A hysterical laugh bubbled in Gretchen's chest. *This* was what her friends thought she was worried about? That Daniel had broken things off with her? How little the English understood what was happening in her country. In a way, she supposed she couldn't blame them – the terrorist attack in Berlin must seem like a dream to them, here in their snug homes, where they had enough coal to warm them and food to fill their bellies.

Many people in Oxford were poor, too, for the Depression had struck here, as well. But they didn't know how it felt to see the streets of their city swarming with men in different political party uniforms, truncheons in their hands. They didn't know how it felt to watch one shoddily constructed government after another collapse, and to go to bed hungry most nights while your parents wept because they didn't have the money to feed you.

Gretchen's eyes met Mary's, which were shining and sympathetic. She pushed her laugh down deep inside. It wasn't Mary's fault that she didn't understand.

'Thanks,' she said. Mary beamed and they returned to their cluster of friends to talk about the upcoming geometry exam.

When she got home, Gretchen slipped into the front hall and leaned against the wall. It was a relief to be alone, where she didn't have to paste on fake smiles for anyone's benefit, answer Julia and Alfred's concerned questions about Daniel – *No, I've heard nothing yet* – or smile at her friends' misguided concern. She could clutch her throbbing head in her hands, praying that she would get something from Daniel, a letter, a telegram, *anything* to let her know that he was all right. Even though part of her knew he wouldn't dare getting in touch with her.

From upstairs, she heard the boys shrieking with laughter. Sighing, she automatically reached for the pile of afternoon post on a side table. Nothing from Daniel. But her hand paused over the final envelope, where 'Miss Whitestone' had been written in unfamiliar script.

She ripped it open. It was from Daniel's editor at the *Oxford Mail*, saying that he had received a strange telegram this morning from Munich and was enclosing it in hopes that she would be able to decipher it.

Her heart surged into her throat. She pulled the telegram from the envelope.

They know the Lion has returned.

The Lion – it must be a code word for Daniel. He'd been named for the Old Testament Daniel, who'd been thrown into a den of lions. Only a friend would have known that.

Lion wanted for murder in Berlin. Not seen in days. Possibly dead.

32

4

A CRY BURST FROM GRETCHEN'S THROAT. HER MIND seemed to have frozen; all she could think over and over was *no*. She stared at her fingers, tightened to white on the telegram; somehow they looked unreal.

From the kitchen, she heard Julia asking if she was all right, but her mouth wouldn't work. *Dead*. She wouldn't believe it.

She flipped the telegram over and shook the envelope upside down, as if there might be another piece of paper, something that said this had all been a terrible mistake, and Daniel was fine and on his way back to England even now. But there was nothing else except for the name of the man who had sent the telegram, typed neatly under the message: Fritz Gerlich.

Then there was no mistake. Herr Gerlich was the anti-National Socialist journalist whom Daniel liked and respected more than any other. Although they hadn't worked together, they admired each other greatly. She still remembered his quiet gaze and soft voice. He wouldn't have written this telegram unless he was certain it was true.

33

Something about the message swam to the front of her consciousness. She stared at the telegram again. Why would Daniel be wanted for murder in Berlin? He was incapable of killing, of course, and he was in Munich, hundreds of miles from the capital.

She took a deep breath but the pressure in her chest didn't ease. This must be how the National Socialists planned to get rid of him. They'd found out that he was back in Germany, but they mustn't have been able to find him or they'd simply kill him. Instead, they'd set the police on his trail. Thoughts blew about her head like leaves in a windstorm. *Focus*, she ordered herself. Falling apart wouldn't help Daniel.

She began to pace. Daniel had been spotted by his enemies, but they hadn't captured him. Somehow, he'd managed to get away. Perhaps he'd used his old sources to help him – when he'd worked as a reporter in Munich, he'd had a network of contacts throughout the city, including in the police force. Maybe someone had tipped him off about the upcoming arrest. He was too clever not to understand his precarious position. He was brave, but he wasn't reckless.

He would have gone underground. He might still be alive.

Gretchen stopped pacing. There was no decision to make; no options to consider. She knew what she had to do.

Julia's heels clicked on the floor as she hurried into the room, with Alfred close behind. 'What is it?' Alfred asked. 'We were just having tea when we heard you cry out. Are you hurt?'

Her hands shook as she handed him the telegram. 'It's Daniel. I have to go to him.'

Alfred and Julia scanned the telegram, then looked up as one, their faces pale. 'I'll get in touch with the police in Munich,' Alfred said, 'and see what we can find out.'

'They won't tell you anything!' Gretchen shouted. 'Many

of them are National Socialists!' She took a deep breath, struggling to lower her voice. '*I* have to do it. There's nobody else.'

Alfred's face seemed to crumple. 'Absolutely not! It's far too dangerous.'

'Darling.' Julia laid her hand on his arm. 'She loves him,' she said quietly. 'And I think Gretchen will go, whether we give her permission or not. Don't make this harder than it already is.'

He started to argue, but Gretchen barely heard him. She made for the stairs, calling back, 'Daniel's in trouble. And I'm going after him.'

Gretchen raced to the wardrobe in her bedroom and flung its doors open. What did she need? Her old false papers, and a few changes of clothing, nothing too English looking, pleated skirts and silk blouses and woolen stockings. She grabbed clothes off hangers and tossed them onto the bed. Money. She had thirty pounds saved, not nearly enough, and it was at the bank. Here at home, she had only a couple of half crowns in her purse.

No matter. She'd figure something out. She was leaving tonight.

She stood on a chair to reach the cardboard box she'd hidden on top of the wardrobe. Inside the box, the revolver gleamed dully. She tested its weight in her hand. About two pounds and eleven inches long. She would have preferred a smaller pistol, like the Walther that Hitler had used to teach her. But the Webley Mk IV wasn't bad – she could inflict tremendous damage with this weapon.

She pulled a suitcase out from under her bed and tossed the unloaded revolver and a box of .455 caliber bullets inside. It'd been months since she'd fired a gun, but she wasn't worried about her aim. Hitler had taught her too well for her to be rusty.

Just as he had taught her to fight before her opponent had a chance. *Strength lies not in defense but in attack*, he used to say as they pushed her brother's toy soldiers across the carpet. This time, she would take his advice, she decided as she folded clothes. She would remember everything he'd told her and use it to keep herself alive.

Two hours later, Alfred drove her through the deepening blue-black of twilight to the train station. Gretchen watched the familiar streets, with their long rows of brick and stone houses, rise up and fall away. Alfred had argued with her for a long time. He'd shouted it was foolhardy; an invitation to death. Nothing he'd said had changed her mind. She'd made her decision.

In the end, when Alfred had realized that she wouldn't stay and she'd promised again and again to be careful, he'd relented. Julia had said that Gretchen should change her appearance as much as possible, and colored her honey-blond hair brown with Cook's hair dye. While the strands were still wet, she had cut them into a bob hairstyle that barely reached Gretchen's ears. Gretchen had watched her transformation in the mirror without a word. Between the pink powder on her cheeks and the sleek cap of brown hair, she looked like a flapper: modern and daring, so unlike the proper National Socialist girl she had once been.

There were some things, though, that couldn't be changed: the shape of her face, the color of her eyes, the curve of her mouth. Hitler would still recognize her. Of that, she had no doubt. Over the years, he'd watched her grow and change, and he had a photographic memory. No amount of time or cosmetics would confuse him. Just as she would recognize

36

him, regardless of how much he might alter his appearance. He could change the cut of his hair, shave off his smudge of a mustache, gain one hundred pounds. It didn't matter. She would always know the brilliant blue of his eyes.

At last, she'd stood in the front hall, clutching a suitcase, while the boys trooped in to say good-bye. As she had hugged them, Gretchen felt their small bodies shaking from sobs. She hadn't been able to keep hers back anymore. This family, with their questions about her day over supper, their smiles when she earned good marks, their laughter when she and the boys chased one another in the garden – this family was exactly what she had once thought she couldn't have. Saying good-bye to them felt as though she were ripping away a piece of herself.

In the seat beside hers, Alfred cleared his throat. 'Julia and I want you to have this.' He nodded at the leather wallet lying between them. 'It's five hundred pounds. We've been saving it for you, to go toward your university schooling and setting up your own psychoanalytical practice someday. It should cover your expenses.'

Five hundred pounds – it was more money than she'd ever seen in her life. And these people, who had no obligations toward her, no ties beyond simple affection, wanted to give it to her. Tears burned her eyes, and although she opened her mouth, she couldn't say a word. Alfred seemed to understand, for he smiled a little. 'All we ask is that you come back to us. We couldn't bear it if something happened to you.'

The lump in her throat hardened into a rock and she whispered, 'Thank you.'

At the train station, the platform was crowded with university students heading to London for an evening out, and tired-looking mothers with small children, eager to get to their country homes after a long day shopping in the city.

37

As a train whistle screamed in the distance, Alfred clasped Gretchen's hand. 'You'll need to be strong,' he said. 'Going back won't be easy on you, and I don't mean only the physical danger.'

She raised her chin, pretending a confidence she didn't feel. 'I'm fine,' she lied.

Alfred raised his eyebrows. 'I'm afraid,' he said quietly, 'that if you return to Munich, you'll have to cope with memories that you aren't yet ready to relive. You've undergone significant emotional trauma. Having to confront it again may be more than you can bear. I wish you would stay. But I know you won't.'

As the crowd swelled around them, jostling them closer together, Alfred gripped her hand tighter. 'Remember everything I've taught you about psychology. Use it to anticipate how others might act. It could be your best protection.'

'I promise.' She wished she knew how to thank him for everything he had done.

There was so much pain in his face. He wouldn't kiss her, she knew – he was too reserved for that – and so she pecked him on the cheek. The air filled with the squeal of brakes as the train pulled into the station. 'I know I've never called you "Father,"' she said, 'but you have been one to me.'

His eyes looked damp. 'You'd better hurry. Get yourself a decent seat.'

She joined the crush of passengers boarding the train. Once she'd found a third-class seat, she watched Alfred through the window. He walked back and forth on the platform, shoulders hunched beneath his overcoat, head downcast. Miserable. Gretchen had to hug her purse to her chest, so she had something to hold onto. The train lurched forward, picking up speed until Alfred was only a dot in the distance and then he was nothing at all.

5

BY FIRST LIGHT, SHE WAS ON A SHIP BOUND FOR CALAIS, standing on the deck and squinting in the sunshine that bounced off the steel-gray waters of the English Channel. France was a brown line on the horizon. From behind her, she heard the low murmurs of the other passengers braving the cold in their heaviest overcoats as she was, eager to taste the salt-scented air and hear the waves slapping against the belly of the boat.

She leaned on the ship's railing, staring at the growing shape in the distance until her eyes ached. After so long, she was about to step back onto the same piece of land that contained Germany. Where Daniel might still be alive, and her brother and father softened to dust beneath the ground, and, as far as she knew, her mother lived among the marshlands of Dachau. She shaded her eyes from the glare with her hand, so none of the other passengers could see her tears before she blinked them away.

For the hundredth time since she'd left Oxford the previous night, she wondered what had happened to Daniel. Was he safe and in hiding somewhere? Who was this mysterious victim he was supposed to have killed, and what secrets had been concealed by the real murderer?

For she had no doubt that there had been a real crime, a real victim; the National Socialists weren't stupid and their power was limited. They needed a body lying in the morgue – a body they had put there, so there wasn't a possibility of the true killer being caught and destroying their case against Daniel – and evidence they had manufactured, to convince Berlin's police force to issue a warrant for Daniel's arrest. If the National Socialists wanted a legal-looking means of getting rid of Daniel, they'd hit upon a clever one: murder was a crime punishable by execution.

Gretchen shuddered, watching the vast docks of Calais rise above the sea. She'd have to be smarter and faster than the National Socialists and the police combined, if she wanted to get to Daniel first.

Before midafternoon, she had boarded a train, where she sat in a crowded third-class compartment with a harried-looking mother and three small children. At one of the station stops, she wired a telegram to the Whitestones, saying she had reached France. After that, there could be no more communication between them, she knew, not until she was out of Germany again and on her way back to them.

The trains were slow and some didn't run at night, so after switching her pounds for marks at a public exchange, she slept in a grubby hotel down the street from the station. In the morning, she left on a train headed for the border. As the hours passed, she watched sunlight glimmer on the fields flickering past, trying not to think, for thought would only bring fear.

That night, she curled in a corner of her seat, clutching

her purse. When she woke in the gray dawn, the people sharing her compartment were still asleep, sprawled in their seats. Out of habit, she touched the gold hooked charm on her necklace; the *Hakenkreuz* had been her sixteenth birthday present from Hitler, and the metal felt warm against her fingers. She'd been wearing it when she'd fled from Germany. For reasons she couldn't understand, she hadn't been able to bring herself to throw it away – perhaps because it was the only thing she still possessed from her old life. Last night in the train lavatory, she'd put it on again, hoping the swastika charm would help her blend in when she reached Munich.

She drew up the window shade. Pine forests flashed past the window. Sometime during the night they had reached Bavaria. In the deepening pink of early morning, it looked the same, the land of her childhood: woodlands dark with trees, mountains cutting a jagged line along the horizon. A thin layer of snow glittered with frost. She had to look away to catch her breath. She was close to Daniel now. If he was still in Munich, they were only hours apart.

I will find him.

By three o'clock, the train had arrived in Munich, and she walked the streets of her city again. After so many months of having to translate English into German in her head, hearing her native tongue everywhere was overwhelming. The words seemed to crash against her ears like ocean waves.

She imagined that everyone she passed turned to look at her. When she looked in shop windows, though, she saw nobody was paying her any attention. For the moment, she was anonymous, a brown-haired girl in a gray loden coat, moving quickly as though she were late for an appointment. Not as though she were afraid someone might recognize her face.

41

Swastika banners, flecked white from the snow spitting wearily from the sky, dripped bloodred down the fronts of narrow stone and brick buildings. Burghers in camel-hair coats and office girls in brass-buttoned jackets hurried up the cobblestone street. A clump of working men in tattered trousers and stained shirts trudged past, probably looking for work since they weren't at the factories.

Housewives carrying string bags scurried to the Viktualienmarkt to haggle over meat and bread. Young children skipped beside their mothers – here the school day ended at one o'clock, so classes had already been let out. A couple of skeletal cats slunk down the pavement. Somewhere, streetcars clanged.

Only the children looked happy. Everyone else walked with their heads down, shoulders hunched against the cold, sneaking nervous glances at a group of men in khaki plus fours and red swastika armbands. Gretchen shrank against a building. She knew those uniforms. The men were members of the Sturmabteilung, the same unit to which her brother had belonged.

Gretchen turned away from the street, pretending to study the cigars on display in the shop window. What if the men recognized her? Both she and Reinhard had been well known among the National Socialists as the martyr's children, and she'd met many of her brother's SA comrades over the years.

She watched the men's reflections in the window. They looked to be in their late twenties or early thirties. Too old to have been Reinhard's friends. She might be safe.

A harsh shout cut into her thoughts. More SA men jogged down the avenue, their hands on the knife sheaths clipped to their belts. One of them called, 'Faster! Before the rat gets away!'

They charged into an office building, the door banging

shut behind them. None of the Müncheners seemed to notice, their faces turned away, their footsteps fast.

Gretchen's legs shook as she forced them forward. She flipped up her coat collar and pulled her broad-brimmed hat lower, hoping it obscured her face. Why were the SA storming someone's office? And why was no one reacting? Her legs ached to run, but a girl racing along the street would only attract attention. She walked faster, her suitcase bumping her knees as she counted building numbers. Fritz Gerlich's newspaper office was on the left. She'd never been there before – when she'd known Gerlich, he had been working as a historian, but last year he'd taken over the anti-National Socialist newspaper *Der Gerade Weg*. Praying he was at his office today, she hurried up the snow-dusted steps.

Inside, the lobby was dim and empty. The sound of shuffling papers pulled her to an open door.

The room had been ransacked. Gretchen stopped short in shock. Desk drawers yawned open drunkenly, their contents strewn across the floor: books, pens, paper clips, loose sheets torn from spiral notebooks, the sort Daniel used when jotting notes for a story. Chairs lay on their sides. Pots of paste had been flung onto the ground, leaving a mess of cracked glass and congealed white glue.

Fritz Gerlich crouched in the middle of the room, gathering papers into a tidy stack. He looked as she had remembered: a slight figure with dark hair combed back from an oval face and thoughtful eyes behind wire-rimmed spectacles. In his plain navy suit he reminded her of a schoolmaster.

Sighing, he tried to fit together ripped pieces of paper, then shook his head. When she stepped forward, her shoes clicking on the wooden floor, he looked up. 'May I help you, Fräulein?'

Her new hair color was a better disguise than she'd

43

anticipated. She tipped her hat back, so he could see her face. 'Herr Gerlich, it's me – Gretchen Müller.'

'My God,' he murmured, crossing himself. Hastily, he got to his feet and hurried to close the door. 'What on earth are you doing here? You shouldn't be in Munich,' he said before she could reply. 'It's far too dangerous for you.'

'I had to come after I saw the telegram you sent to the *Oxford Mail*.' Nerves had tightened her voice into something she scarcely recognized. Through the window, she heard more shouts from the street and the tinkle of glass shattering. Perhaps someone else's office was getting destroyed. 'Do you know what's happened to Daniel?'

Gerlich leaned against the door, his expression solemn. 'No. I haven't seen him in over a week.' He sighed. 'Herr Cohen's cousin had died before he'd arrived, and the boy's sister had already returned to their parents' house. Herr Cohen was most distraught.'

Aaron. Gretchen could still see him, standing in the shabby parlor he'd shared with Daniel and Ruth. Watching her cautiously, for as a Jew he must have been afraid to say much in front of her. But he hadn't turned her away. He'd let her stay with them. And now he must already be underground, buried by sunset as Jewish tradition demanded, slowly turning to earth himself. She couldn't fathom how devastated Daniel must be.

Behind his glasses, Gerlich's eyes met hers. 'I saw Herr Cohen a few days after he arrived here, when he stopped by my home. He had been beaten. Some Nazis had spotted him on the street and attacked him. They knew who he was. They'd taken his money and papers. I gave him enough money for a room for the night, but it was all I could spare. A couple of days afterward, there was an announcement in several of the Party-sponsored newspapers that he was wanted by the Berlin

44

police for murder. They claim he killed a young woman named Monika Junge. I've asked around, but there's been no word of him since.'

Gretchen clasped her hands tightly together so she wouldn't fly apart. Her suspicions were true, then: the National Socialists had seen Daniel and were after him. In her mind, she saw him crouching on the ground, arms over his head as SA men surrounded him, kicking and lashing with truncheons. Through the tangle of jackboots, she saw his dark eyes closing in pain as they pummeled him, a line of blood trickling from his hairline to his chin. A sick feeling twisted her stomach.

'You have no idea where he might be now?'

Gerlich shook his head. 'I wish there was more I could tell you, Fräulein. I sent the telegram to Herr Cohen's editor because I wanted his friends in England to know what had happened. I never intended for you to come back . . . especially on such a day as this.' He knelt on the floor, his knees popping from the effort, and started gathering torn papers again.

'What do you mean? What's happening?' She glanced around the wrecked room; she'd forgotten about it in her desperation to learn about Daniel. It was easy to guess who had ordered the vandalism: there was no one in Munich whom Hitler hated more than Gerlich. They had openly despised each other for years.

'The city is under attack.' Gerlich rubbed his forehead, as if in pain. 'SA groups have been pillaging businesses all day. Several men came this morning. They were quite effective, as you can see.' He waved a hand at the garbage-littered floor.

'How can they hope to get away with it?' She was bewildered. After the disastrous street shoot-out in which Papa had died, Hitler had pledged that the Party must appear as a respectable organization. They beat or killed their opponents, but only if there wasn't a chance of getting caught.

45

Gerlich picked up an overturned wastebasket. 'The National Socialists took over the city's police force today.' He sounded weary. 'Did you know Heinrich Himmler?'

She remembered him well: pudding-faced, spectacled, soft-spoken, with a smile always twitching his lips. He was the head of the Schutzstaffel, the Party's racially selective unit. Once she'd worked in the office adjacent to his at the Braunes Haus, the National Socialists' Munich headquarters. She nodded, filled with dread.

Gerlich set a handful of pens on his desk. 'Today he was appointed Munich's acting police chief.'

Then what Hitler had always promised would happen: the Party and all branches of the government were becoming one. His plans, uttered casually over drinks at Café Heck or spaghetti suppers at his apartment, rushed back to her. He'd said he would start with the police, for whoever controlled the prisons and punishments controlled the people. The *Gleichschaltung*, he called it. Coordination, the period of time when the National Socialists would bring everyone in the Fatherland into line. It was meant to be a complete revolution redefining the whole of society until it matched Hitler's vision.

Her breath was coming too fast. With the police force under the National Socialists' control, she couldn't depend on them for help. She thought of Daniel's old colleagues at the *Munich Post*. They'd cared about him. Surely they would help her find him, if they could. She had to get to their office straightaway.

'I must go,' she said to Gerlich. She clasped his hand in gratitude. 'Thank you for sending the telegram. I owe you a debt I can never repay.'

Concern was etched in every line in his face. 'I'm afraid you have little to thank me for. I've only brought you into

46

danger and—' He broke off as somewhere a door groaned open and shut. 'What was that?'

He rushed across the room and leaned his head on the wall, listening. His face had become a mask of terror. 'They're coming back!' he whispered.

Boots tramped outside in the lobby. Motionless, Gretchen listened to the sound divide into separate footsteps. Easily a half dozen. And coming closer.

'Is there another way out of here?' she demanded, but Gerlich shook his head.

She ran to the door and opened it a crack. A group of SA men, their expressions grim with purpose, strode across the lobby. Walking in the lead was an extremely short man missing an arm.

Instantly, she knew who he must be – Max Amann, the head of the Eher Verlag, the National Socialist publishing business. There was no one else in the Party who looked like that. Perhaps he wouldn't know who she was. They might have seen each other at minor Party events – parties and speeches and dinners, she couldn't remember now – but that would have been a few years ago, when she looked much younger. Maybe he would believe she was Gisela Schröder, the girl on her false papers, and let her go. Gently, she eased the door shut.

'It's Amann,' she said.

Beside her, Gerlich paled. 'He's come to arrest me. For years, he's sworn to put me in jail himself, if he got the chance. Nothing else would bring him here.'

There had to be a way out of this place. Gretchen scanned the small office: the rubbish-covered floor, the overturned desks, the window overlooking the busy street. She raced to the window and tried to force it open, but it had been painted shut. She and Gerlich were trapped.

47

The doorknob started to turn. She watched it, mesmerized, unable to move.

The door was flung open so hard that it banged into the wall. Amann stood in the entryway, his blue eyes fixed on Gerlich. Behind him, several SA fellows loomed like a brown wall.

Amann glanced at her. 'Who's this?'

She fumbled for her false papers in her purse. Please, *please* let him not look at her too closely. 'My name is Gisela Schröder—'

He snatched the papers from her and scanned them. 'They seem to be in order. Perhaps we ought to take her along, too, though. Only our enemies would come here.'

God, no. She knew what would happen if they forced her to accompany them. Sooner or later, one of Reinhard's old comrades would recognize her. She wouldn't last long after that – a bullet to the back of the head, if they were feeling lenient; hours of torture, if they weren't. Blood drained from her face.

She raised her gaze to meet Amann's, praying her expression looked calm. With one hand, she smoothed the collar of her coat, reaching inside with her index finger and snagging it on her necklace. Quickly, she pulled it out, so the swastika charm lay, gold and gleaming, against the gray wool of her coat.

'This isn't where I meant to come.' She sounded breathless even to her own ears. 'I had the wrong address.'

Amann glanced at her necklace. 'A foolish mistake to make today, Fräulein.' He waved a hand dismissively. 'She's one of us,' he said to his SA subordinates. 'Let her go.'

Gretchen snatched up her suitcase with shaking hands. 'Thank you.' She looked at Gerlich. What about him? She hated the thought of leaving him behind. *I'm sorry*, she tried to say with her eyes, but he merely shook his head, mouthing, *Go.*

The SA men separated a little, leaving a hole between their bodies for her to sneak through. As she darted between them, she smelled the sweaty linen of their uniforms, mixed with the staleness of cigarette smoke. Under her blouse, a thin line of perspiration slid down her spine. Hitler's old birthday present had saved her life. But Amann might still remember her. She ran across the lobby – another second and he might yell at his men to go after her—

From the office, she heard screams of pain and the sickening smack of fists meeting flesh. *Gerlich*. Her heart lurched, but she couldn't go back.

She dashed toward the front door, hitting it with the flat of her hand so it heaved open. She plowed down the steps into the crowded street, startling a flock of pigeons fighting over crumbs on the sidewalk.

The birds' harsh cries echoed as they flew into the snow-white sky, but Gretchen barely heard them, concentrating on the street ahead. More businessmen in suits and housewives in woolen coats; no familiar tall, lean figure in a fedora. Daniel might be somewhere in the city, though, perhaps only feet away. Maybe his former colleagues knew where to find him. Or maybe – her heart clenched – maybe their offices were being attacked, too.

A streetcar trundled to a stop at the corner and she ran to get onboard before it continued on its route. She sank into a seat at the back, keeping her head down, praying nobody would look at her. The *Post* office was a quick ride away. Perhaps the SA were already on their way to the newspaper's building; they seemed to be going after their old enemies today.

She had to get there before they did.

6

THE STREETCAR LET HER OFF TWO BLOCKS AWAY FROM the newspaper office. The muscles in her legs screamed to *run*, but she managed to walk, eyes scanning the avenue, searching for a potential threat. Snow was falling softly now, the flakes hitting the back of her neck and sliding beneath her coat collar, so cold that she couldn't stop shivering.

She turned onto the small, crescent-shaped street called Altheimer Eck. The road was empty, and the air carried only the hiss of snow hitting the ground and the rustle of a few swastika pennants hanging from windows.

She made for number 19, where the *Munich Post* kept their offices. She was halfway up the front steps when something hit her shoulder, smarting like a bee's sting. Surprised, she looked up to see tiny, dark objects raining down on her. They landed on the stairs with metallic clicks. For an instant, she thought they were coins, until she picked one up. It was the letter *A*. Someone was throwing trays of type into the street.

Her head snapped up. In one of the windows above, a

man's face peered through the glass, grinning down at her. He wore the khaki cap of the SA.

She was too late.

Behind the grinning face, she caught the whirl of movement – the flailing arms of men fighting – and through the open window, she heard the crash of chairs or tables hitting the office floor. Someone was laughing.

More letters fell, striking her cheeks and shoulders. Dazed, she turned and stumbled down the steps. Behind her, wood smashed into stone. She spun around. Broken chairs littered the front steps. As she watched, another sailed out the window, landing at her feet and splitting apart. She jumped back, biting her lip so she wouldn't scream.

Was Daniel trapped up there? Had he stopped by the office to ask his former colleagues for help? Or perhaps he had been sleeping there, desperate for a place to stay where the landlord wouldn't ask him to register with the papers he no longer had?

She stared at the windows. If Daniel was in there, she wished she could see him, so at least she could estimate how badly hurt he was. But all she glimpsed were brown-clad shoulders, jerking as though struggling with someone.

Panic sealed off her throat. Suddenly she could feel her brother's fist plowing into her stomach, so hard she couldn't breathe; could feel her knees smacking into the floorboards as Reinhard flung her down. Her vision faded to black. She thought she could smell the faint tinge of his cologne, and she let out a strangled whimper.

Stop, she ordered herself, sucking in air until her eyesight widened from a pinprick to a circle. She couldn't let herself relive her brother's beating every time she saw people fighting. Daniel deserved the best from her, and that's what she would give him.

She had her revolver in the suitcase, but she couldn't use

it – the SA would have sent a group to arrest the reporters, so there would be too many to shoot; she couldn't incapacitate them all and help the reporters get away. If she went inside the office to look for Daniel, her false papers might not withstand scrutiny a second time.

The clattering of shoes on cobblestones interrupted her thoughts. Two men were walking toward her, talking in low voices. They looked at her with open curiosity, and she realized how strange she must appear – frozen on the pavement, surrounded by broken chairs and typesetter's letters. She had to start moving before more people entered the street or the SA and their captives left the building. As long as she gave no one a reason to look at her twice, she was safe, and as long as she was safe, she could look for Daniel.

Her legs felt wooden as she walked back in the direction from which she had come, checking over her shoulder to make sure no one followed. She had failed. Now there was no way she could talk to Daniel's old colleagues. And who knew what awaited those men once they were hauled to the city jail? For so many years, she'd seen Hitler throw aside issues of the *Munich Post* and drop his head into his hands, moaning that the reporters' smear campaigns would ruin him. Even from his new home in Berlin, he wouldn't forget them. He would enjoy taking his revenge.

The streets filled again with burghers and housewives and shopgirls. The air smelled of snow and soot. Vehicles choked the roads: private automobiles, the low-slung Horchs and Opels she hadn't seen in so long; a streetcar, blue sparks shooting off its cables as it rounded the corner ahead; horse-drawn carts carrying empty burlap sacks. Police wagons rumbled over the cobblestones, and a couple of policemen, their faces obscured by driving goggles, whizzed past on motor scooters. Arrests must be occurring all over the city.

If only she knew someone powerful enough to help her and loyal enough to be trusted. Just *one* person.

But she was alone.

More police whistles shrilled, so nearby that she jumped. The man walking alongside her shot her a startled look. She had to get off the streets. Her good luck couldn't last forever. Sooner or later, someone would recognize Hitler's former pet.

A narrow alley yawned between two stone buildings. She darted into its darkness. Rubbish bins had been shoved against the wall, and the stink of decaying food and coffee grounds and cat piss assailed her nose. She didn't care. She leaned on the wall, letting the iciness of the stones seep through her coat, the almost painful sensation steadying her.

There was someone she could go to for help.

Eva.

She wrapped her arms around herself, shivering in the cold wind that whipped down the alley. Contacting her former best friend would be mad.

But for the first time in months, she didn't shove thoughts of Eva out of her head. Her once dearest friend: sweet, laughing, sport-mad Eva, who loved photography and Karl May cowboy stories and skiing. Their thirteen years of friendship gone in an instant when Gretchen had found out that Eva had secretly been dating Hitler. For two years, two of the people she had loved most in the world had concealed their romance from her. The betrayal still tasted bitter in her mouth.

How could she possibly go to Eva? How could she trust her again?

Footsteps pounded in the street beyond the alley. Gretchen shrank against the wall. The opening between the buildings was so narrow she caught only a flash of a brown suit and the frightened whiteness of a man's face as he ran past. Two

SA fellows were close on his heels, shouting, 'Halt! Social Democrat swine!'

Surprise washed over Gretchen. So they weren't only arresting reporters, but the liberal Social Democrats, too. Were any members of the opposing political parties safe? Or were they all being rounded up – everyone whom Hitler perceived as an enemy? If Daniel was still free somewhere, he couldn't stay that way for long, not with the police force and SA groups flooding the city.

She had no choice. If she wanted to find Daniel, there was only one person who might be willing to track down his location and keep Gretchen's reappearance a secret. It was a risk she must take.

Surely Hitler had thrown Eva over by now; a Bavarian shopgirl wasn't marriage material for the new chancellor in Berlin. In the time she and Eva had been apart, she wouldn't have become a dedicated National Socialist, Gretchen knew. Eva had never cared a pin about politics. By now, she probably had a new beau, and without the old string tying her to Hitler, she might listen to Gretchen. She might still care about her. Gretchen felt something swell in her throat. Just as she still cared for Eva.

She crouched on the ground, trying to curl into herself, so if anyone happened to glance into the alley she would look like a shadow between the bins of rubbish. She was going to have to wait here awhile. At least one hour. By then the SA men should have brought the *Munich Post* reporters to jail and filled out their intake papers. Enough time for Daniel to be processed, if he had been among those captured.

A newspaper, wet and wrinkled from the falling snow, lay on the cobblestones. She brushed it clean. It held today's date – Thursday, 9 March 1933 – but as she skimmed the front page, she saw no mention of Himmler's police appointment.

Apparently today's events had been a surprise for Munich's residents. How like Hitler to strike quickly before anyone anticipated his plan, and then strike again, before anyone could react. Clever. But she could be clever, too. And she had an advantage that few people did: she'd spent years at Hitler's side, drinking in his advice as though it were water. She knew how his mind worked. That knowledge might be the only thing that kept her alive.

So many people saw him shouting during his speeches and thought he was emotional. Spontaneous and authentic. But she'd sat in a corner of the parlor, playing paper dolls or sketching, while he'd agonized over the proper words to use at his next appearance. She'd watched as he practiced hand gestures in front of a mirror – a closed fist smashing into an open palm for emphasis, a hand soaring at the end of a sentence – while Papa nodded in approval. Behind that passionate facade lurked a calculating brain. He knew what reaction he wanted from his followers and how to provoke it. There was very little he did that was unrehearsed. She suspected that was why he seemed to disappear so completely into each role: one moment he was the red-faced, shouting speaker; the next, he was the gentle savior, accepting a bouquet of wildflowers from a child with a soft smile. He knew how to vanish into whichever person a particular crowd wanted him to be.

She crumpled the sodden newspaper in her hand. Very well. She would become like him. She'd transform into whatever role she needed to. She'd put feeling aside and reason things through, like he would. Beginning with: could she trust Eva?

There was no way of knowing for certain. Once, though, they had shared so much. Several months after Eva's parents had temporarily separated – Gretchen had never found out why – Eva had journeyed to Dachau for the summer with Gretchen and Reinhard to stay at their grandparents' house.

It had been a magical time. They had slept in a narrow bed beneath an open window, and every day they woke to the cackle of chickens and the rich scent of manure. They'd played hide-and-seek with the local children in the abandoned munitions factory, and the days had been long and shaded green. Years later, when Eva had been stuck at a convent school in far-off Simbach, they'd written each other faithfully every week, and Eva had once mentioned how much she'd treasured Gretchen's kindness during the strangest time of her life.

Maybe Eva still remembered.

In the distance, church bells pealed, slow, solemn notes that hovered in the air before fading. Half past four. At least another thirty minutes before she could telephone Eva – it would probably take that long for the *Munich Post* reporters to be hauled to the city jail and processed. She prayed Eva still worked at Herr Hoffmann's photography shop; so much could have changed in the year and a half she had been gone. Shivering, she crouched in the shadows and waited.

The bells were ringing five o'clock when Gretchen emerged from the alley. The streetlamps hadn't been switched on yet, and only the illumination from lit windows broke apart the descending gloom.

She darted into the first beer hall she came across to find a public telephone. Inside it was smoky and warm. As her eyes adjusted to the dimness, she saw that banners of different political parties were draped across each of the long trestle tables. She had forgotten the custom – each party or workers' union had their own table at beer halls, strictly reserved for its members. When she was younger, Reinhard and his SA comrades had sometimes taken her with them to the National Socialist table at the Hofbräuhaus, where they could eat cold cuts on rye bread and pretzels for almost nothing, while a brass band played.

Now the political tables were empty, except for a few men in SS uniforms, hunched over their beer steins. Nobody sat at the workers' union tables, either; presumably it was too early for the men to have left work for the day. A brass band played on the stage, but even beneath the wailing tubas, Gretchen could hear how unnaturally silent the beer hall was.

Before any of the waitresses could approach her, she hurried away from the main room, making for the long corridor where the lavatories were located. A public telephone hung on the wall by the men's room. She snatched up the receiver and dialed the exchange for Herr Hoffmann's photography shop. Somehow her fingers still remembered the numbers. The telephone buzzed twice in her ear before someone picked up on the other end.

'Photo Hoffmann,' chirped a cheerful voice. *Eva*. She sounded the same – sparkling and bright, like quickly moving water in a creek bed.

Tears clogged Gretchen's throat and she had to force the words out. 'Eva? It's me.'

There was a pause. Finally, Eva whispered, '*Gretchen?*'

Gretchen bit her lip, wondering whether she could trust Eva. But what choice did she have? There was no one else to go to. 'Yes.'

'You're alive!' Eva cried. 'I knew it! Everybody said you must be dead, but I wouldn't believe it. Where are you? The connection is wonderfully clear.'

'I'm here. And I need your help. Please, Eva, I'm begging you.'

Silence hovered over the line. Gretchen gripped the receiver so tightly her fingers started going numb.

'All right.' Eva sounded cautious. 'What do you need?'

Gretchen sagged against the wall in relief. 'Thank you.' She glanced down the corridor, but nobody was coming. 'The SA arrested the reporters from the *Munich Post* this afternoon. I need to know if Daniel Cohen was among them, or if he's already in jail. He would probably be an important enough prisoner to be housed at the central precinct.'

'Who's Daniel Cohen?' Eva snapped. 'The Jewish boyfriend you never told me about? I had to hear about him from my boss after you disappeared. But I guess we girls must have our secrets,' she added in a changed tone, and Gretchen understood what she wasn't saying: neither of them had been honest with each other about who they had loved. 'How the devil am I supposed to find out if he's been arrested?' Eva demanded. 'Do you really think the police would give me that sort of information?'

This was the difficult part. 'Not you. But your boss is an important man in the Party. They would tell him.'

'How do I trick Herr Hoffmann into ringing up the police station and asking – never mind,' Eva interrupted herself. 'This is something you truly need to know?'

'More than anything.'

Eva blew out a breath; it sounded like a thunderclap over the telephone line. 'Very well. I'll come up with some reason when I ask Herr Hoffmann. Be at the Englischer Garten at half past six at our favorite spot. If I can find out anything, I'll know it by then.'

She banged down the receiver, leaving Gretchen standing in the corridor, listening to the whistle of the disconnected telephone line. Hoping her friend wouldn't betray her.

7

THE SUN WAS SETTING IN A POOL OF ORANGE AND RED when Gretchen reached the Englischer Garten. At the massive park's entrance, she looked back at the Königinstrasse. The long street stretched out in both directions, the ends falling into shadow. She could barely make out the skinny stone boardinghouse where she used to live. On the front steps, a woman was brushing off the snow with a broom.

Even from a few hundred yards away, Gretchen could tell the woman was short and plump. Not her mother, then. Someone else must run the place now.

The patch of pavement where Gretchen had skipped rope and Reinhard had thrown jacks was empty, and the bedroom window where she had hung red curtains she had sewn herself was now lined with lace draperies. It was as though the Müller family had never lived there, all traces of their lives gone. For a long moment, Gretchen stared at the house. Inside was Mama's bedroom, where Mama had showed her how to hem skirts, the two of them laughing together at Gretchen's uneven first attempt. Her own bedroom on the third floor, where she'd found her cat lying on her pillow, its neck broken. And Reinhard's room on the floor below, where she'd accused him of killing Striped Peterl to get back at her. Where Reinhard had punched her in the face and thrown her to the floor, and when she'd begged him to stop, she had barely been able to speak around the blood pooling in her mouth.

Trapped air burned in her chest. She hated herself for thinking of her brother again, for letting the memories overwhelm her, just as Alfred had warned. *Reinhard is dead*, she reminded herself. She'd seen his SA commander kill him on Hitler's orders because, thanks to her investigation into Papa's death, the Müller family had become an inconvenience. Nothing could bring Reinhard back. He couldn't hurt her anymore.

That was a lie. He could still hurt her, and she knew it. Every time she thought of him, the familiar, old panic clawed its way up her throat until she was gasping. With a massive effort, she turned away from the boardinghouse, her eyes stinging. *Keep going*, she ordered herself. *Do this for Daniel.* His name forced her legs to move, slowly at first, then faster.

Inside the massive park, the snow-whitened fields were turning blue in the deepening dusk. Gretchen hurried along the curving paths, the back of her neck prickling. At the supper hour, the walkways were crowded with men on their way to their rented rooms or to a beer hall for a cheap meal. She didn't hear the tweet of police whistles or the rumble of wagons from the street; perhaps the arrests were over, at least for the day.

Ahead stood a thicket of chestnut trees. Between their trunks, Gretchen saw the sun tipping over the horizon, a blazing ball sinking into black. In the final seconds of daylight, she made out a figure standing within the ring of trees: slender, dressed in a three-quarter-length coat, a cloud of dark blond

60

hair peeking out from under a fashionable porkpie hat. Eva. She had come, just as she had promised. Love for her old friend surged through Gretchen. After everything that had shoved them apart, she had still been able to count on Eva.

There was no one else near the trees; no brown blur of SA uniforms under the leafless branches. Still Gretchen hesitated. *For Daniel*, she told herself and moved off the path, ducking under the low-hanging branches to reach the center of the clearing. Snow crunched under her feet, and Eva whirled at the sound, her eyes wide. Then she smiled and ran forward, flinging her arms around Gretchen. Through the heavy layers of their coats, Gretchen could feel the bones in Eva's back.

'I didn't think I'd ever see you again!' Eva pulled away, tears glittering in her eyes. Sobs rose in Gretchen's chest, and she gripped her friend's hands. She couldn't stop staring at her. In the chiseled angles of her face, there was nothing left of the plump girl she had been. 'Nobody seemed to know what had happened to you – some people said you must be dead, and Adolf said we weren't allowed to mention your name again.'

Gretchen froze. 'Adolf? You call him Adolf?'

'Of course.' Eva smiled. Tears had cut tracks through the powder on her cheeks, showing the pale skin beneath. 'What else would I call my beau?'

Gretchen's fingers slid from Eva's. Hitler hadn't thrown Eva over. They were still dating. She backed away, reaching across her body with her free hand to touch the side of her suitcase, feeling for the bulge of the revolver. Her gaze swept the bare trees. In the dusk, they looked like black skeletons, and on the pathway behind them, a couple of dark shapes ambled along. She recognized the shape of the men's heads; they wore knitted woolen hats, not peaked SA caps. She was still safe, for the moment. But Hitler's men might be waiting beyond the swell of the hills.

She dropped her bag on the ground and started undoing the buckles, her movements quick and jerky. The revolver was unloaded, but she could fill its chambers with bullets in a matter of seconds.

'What are you doing?' Eva sank to her knees beside Gretchen. 'You look ill.'

'Tell me what you've learned about Daniel.' She glanced back again. Nothing except trees and a field intersected with empty walking paths. She unfastened the second buckle.

'He wasn't arrested.' Eva's voice was matter-of-fact, her gaze steady. Gretchen remembered how Eva twisted her hair around a finger if she was fibbing, like the time she'd sworn to her mother that she and Gretchen hadn't snitched the cooking brandy from the kitchen.

Eva was telling the truth.

Daniel might still be alive and safe, somewhere. Perhaps it wasn't too late. 'Thank you,' Gretchen said, and she couldn't stop the hot tears from filling her eyes.

She half rose, scanning her surroundings. No one. Maybe Eva really had come alone. The sky had already turned black, but no stars had appeared yet. Another few minutes and the darkness would be so complete that she'd be at the mercy of night and whatever it concealed. She had to get away as quickly as she could.

'Did you learn anything else?' she asked Eva, who shook her head.

'Herr Hoffmann telephoned the central station – I made up a ridiculous story about wanting to know about Herr Cohen out of respect for my long friendship with you, and happily I think the boss had been hitting the bottle again because he didn't seem to find it strange at all. Anyway, loads of reporters from the Socialist and Communist newspapers were rounded up today, but your man wasn't among them.

The policeman said they didn't have anyone with that name registered as an inmate.'

It was better than she'd let herself hope. Gretchen embraced Eva, quick and hard. 'I'll forever be grateful to you.'

'You'll always be my friend. Always.' Eva's breath was warm on Gretchen's cheek. 'But you can't stay in Munich.' She hesitated. 'He still talks about you,' she added softly, looking away from Gretchen, fiddling with her gloves as though she were embarrassed. 'I don't know what happened between you, but he hates you now. I won't tell anyone you're back, I promise. But I can't protect you.'

Chills raced up Gretchen's spine. Hitler hadn't forgotten her. Deep down, she'd known he wouldn't – in his eyes, she had betrayed him too thoroughly to be ignored or cast aside. He might have his men looking for her even now. She knew the strength of his willpower all too well – once he settled upon a goal, nothing would swerve him from it. As long as he lived, he would want her found and punished. Back in England, she was beyond his control. Here, if the National Socialists found her, she was dead.

In the shadows, Eva's face was white, her eyes dark as coals. Impulsively, Gretchen snatched her hands. 'Come with me. We can leave Munich together.' She almost blurted out that Hitler was dangerous and had killed her father, but stopped herself in time. She must go slowly. Instead, she added, 'You have to see what kind of a man Hitler is, if you know how badly he wants to hurt me.'

Eva pulled her hands free. 'I can't.' There was a plaintive note in her voice. 'I love him. And nobody understands. Not you, not my parents. They think I ought to be married and having babies. And Adolf keeps me a secret. He's always saying that he'll never marry me.

'Never.' Her face twisted. 'And I've spoiled myself for other

63

men. Nobody will want me now, but it hardly matters because I only want him.'

Revulsion coursed up Gretchen's throat. *Spoiled.* Eva must have made love with Hitler. Her former second father and her old best friend, lying together, their limbs tangled. Gretchen stared at the black lines of the trees, willing her mind to go blank.

Eva was sobbing. 'I know it's a sin. And I've had no one to talk to, not since you've been gone.' She pulled a handkerchief from her pocket but didn't use it, twisting the fabric into a rope instead. 'Sometimes I wish I could die rather than go on like this. I tried back in November.'

Her words pulled Gretchen back into the conversation. She gasped. 'Eva, you mustn't—'

Eva raised agonized eyes to Gretchen's. 'My family had gone out for the evening. I stayed in, hoping Adolf would call, but when he didn't, I – I just lost my head. I took Papa's Great War pistol from the bedside table and shot myself in the neck.'

Unconsciously, she stroked her throat, as though she could feel the bullet plunging into her skin. 'My sister came home early and got me to a doctor. Adolf was so worried when he found out. He was in the midst of a campaigning trip but he rushed back right away. He brought me flowers.'

She gave Gretchen a small smile. 'You understand, don't you? You must, for you've known him practically your whole life. He's different from other men. He believes so completely in himself and his vision for a new Germany, and who am I to stand in his way? I must be grateful for whatever he's able to give me.'

Gretchen couldn't help thinking of Geli, Hitler's half niece. They'd been good friends, too, until the day she'd seen Geli dead on her bedroom floor. Suicide had been the official verdict, but she'd never been able to accept it. Geli had been too alive, too merry to kill herself. And yet here was Eva, fun-loving and vivacious, playing with death, too. What had Hitler done to her friends to change them so drastically?

'You deserve a man who's proud to be with you,' Gretchen said, 'not a man who hides you away—'

'It's my choice,' Eva interrupted. She raised her chin, as if daring Gretchen to say anything else, but Gretchen was silent. She knew too well how people believed what they wanted to – she had done the same for the first seventeen years of her life.

So she kissed Eva on both of her cheeks, saying, 'Thanks. I'll never forget you.' Then she buckled her suitcase again and squeezed between the tightly clustered trees toward the pathway leading out of the park and into the darkness covering the city.

In a pocket of copper beeches, she stopped to gather her thoughts. The blackness was heavy between the trees, and she felt hidden from the world. Was Daniel still in Munich? Probably not, as no one seemed to have seen him in days. Which meant there was only one possible place he could be – Berlin. He would be determined to uncover what had really happened to the woman he was supposed to have killed – not only because he wanted to clear his name, but also to prove the National Socialists were murderous thugs.

Somehow, she would have to find him in the capital. She looked at the sky. It was an unrelieved black. Soon the stars would appear, and with them, the night express to Berlin.

And she would be on it.

She took a streetcar to the central train station. Leaning her head against the window, she watched the familiar streets trundle past. A memory tugged at the corners of her mind, begging to be let in. Finally, exhausted, she surrendered to it.

She had recognized those copper beeches in the park. Hitler had taken her and Papa there when she was six, back in the days when the Party was new and its leader was still an obscure politician. They had veered off the path, tramping through the woods where the trees crowded so close she could barely see the pewter sky above.

'Adi, aren't you afraid to travel without bodyguards?' Papa had asked. 'There are some in the city who would like to kill you.'

Uncle Dolf had laughed. 'I take every precaution with my life, Müller. Besides, I have a skill few know about.' He had nodded at Gretchen. 'Walk ahead of us a bit, my sunshine. I'll tell you when to stop.'

She had hurried into the clearing, her thin-soled shoes sinking in the snow. When she reached the center of the tree-ringed circle, Uncle Dolf had shouted for her to halt, and she turned to watch them, waiting obediently. The men stood a few dozen yards behind. Papa wore a woolen cap, but Uncle Dolf was bareheaded. He never seemed to feel the cold.

'Throw a snowball high into the air,' Uncle Dolf called as he pulled something small and dark from his waistband. 'Pack it tightly!'

Gretchen rolled the snow into a ball and flung it upward as hard as she could. She heard a popping sound. The snowball exploded in a shower of soft powder, raining fine white crystals down on her.

She whirled around.

'Adi!' her father shouted. 'What do you think you're doing?'

Uncle Dolf was smiling and tucking his pistol into his waistband. 'I knew exactly what I was doing, Müller. As you can see, I'm an excellent shot. Even better than in our days together during the war.'

Gretchen's legs had locked her in place. Uncle Dolf had shot at her. And he was *smiling*.

He strode toward her. With a gloved hand, he grabbed her chin, tilting her face back so she had to look at him. 'Why so grave, my child?' His lips twitched as though he were trying to suppress a grin. 'You weren't frightened, were you? You know better than to be scared of your uncle Dolf!'

Politeness forced her to nod. 'Of course not, Uncle,' she said, and he laughed, pulling her close in the quick embrace he always had for her.

'Stop acting like a nervous old woman, Müller!' he shouted to Papa, releasing Gretchen and tramping on ahead. 'Your daughter has stronger blood than you!'

Papa rushed to her side. 'I'm sorry, Gretl.' His face was paper-white. He took her hand, and they followed Hitler farther into the woods. 'I'm certain you weren't in any real danger.'

She had nodded because she wanted to believe him. Fathers protected their daughters, and besides, Uncle Dolf liked to tell her stories about the Great War and listened to her singing and praised her looks. He loved her, and he wouldn't do anything to harm her. She was sure of it.

Now, twelve years later, she touched the suitcase on her lap, feeling the curve of the revolver through the leather. After the snowball incident, Hitler had insisted on teaching her and Reinhard to shoot. Everyone ought to learn how to handle a weapon, he had said, wrapping her little fingers around the Walther's handle while her father watched, objecting until Hitler had spun on him and told him to *keep your mouth shut, can't you!* and Papa had finally slid into sullen silence.

She was glad of those lessons now.

Even though it hurt to owe Hitler anything.

*   *   *

The streetcar let her off down the street from the Munich Hauptbahnhof. In the early evening, the station was packed: exhausted-looking commuters leaned against pillars, briefcases dangling from their hands; burghers in fine suits clogged the platforms, skimming newspapers while waiting for trains to nearby towns.

Gretchen walked along the platform reserved for the night express to Berlin. It was crowded, mostly with men and women, dressed in their traveling best, clutching their suitcases. Most of them had their backs to her, their eyes trained on the long line of track. A short fellow, hands in his pockets, dressed in a camel-hair coat; a beanpole of a man in a pinstripe suit, striking a match to light a cigarette; a middle-aged man who'd taken off his cap to smooth down his curly gray hair; and a tall man, turned away from her, the lines of his broad shoulders tight beneath his dove-gray woolen overcoat. There was something slightly off about his shoulders – the right one was raised a little higher than the left. She knew those shoulders and the injury they concealed. Her heart shot into her throat; she could barely breathe around it.

Daniel. Everything within her screamed his name. She bit down hard on her bottom lip so she wouldn't make a sound.

She lifted one foot, pushed it forward, then lifted the other. Slowly, slowly. Another step. Another.

Through the tangle of the travelers' bodies, she caught snatches of Daniel as he shifted position and stood in profile: the curve of his cheek and an unblinking dark eye; a fedora tipped low, shadowing his face, so what she could see best was the strong line of his jaw; and his feet, the heels lifted slightly off the ground, as though he had rocked forward onto his toes, ready to run at a second's notice.

She wove through the crowd, unable to look away from

him. He turned, his gaze flashing over the people gathered on the platform. She knew the instant he saw her: everything in his face changed, the narrow eyes widening, the clenched jaw loosening, lips parting as he mouthed her name.

He lunged forward but she shook her head, and he stopped, nodding in silent comprehension. They must give no one a reason to look at them.

All around them, other travelers chatted and shifted from one foot to the other, bored and tired and ready to leave. Gretchen moved between them, keeping her eyes trained on Daniel's. He didn't move. He just stared at her. As she got closer, she saw a spiderweb of brown lines surrounding his left eye. It looked as though he had been punched and the bruised blood vessels were almost healed.

He moved toward her, pulling her close, wrapping his good arm around her shoulders. Through their clothes, she felt his heartbeat, a thundering rhythm. She breathed him in, those familiar scents of oranges and boy and warm skin, but he pulled back, cupping her chin in his good hand.

'What are you doing here?' he asked.

'I had to come. Herr Gerlich telegrammed that you were in trouble.'

His eyes burned into hers. 'You came all this way for me?'

She hadn't finished saying 'Of course' before he bent down and kissed her. His lips were warm and insistent. She closed her eyes so there was only the welcome blackness and the heat of his mouth on hers.

Finally they separated and gazed at each other. He almost smiled and pushed a strand of hair back from her face. 'Your hair,' he murmured. 'It's a good disguise.' He seemed to catch himself and looked at the other passengers, but nobody paid them any attention. She and Daniel probably looked like an ordinary girl and her beau, reuniting after time apart. He turned back to her, his expression grave. Then he led her toward the rear of the platform, which was empty.

'You must have sacrificed so much to find me,' he said. 'I'm sorry to have brought you into danger. Do you know what's been happening today around the city?'

'Yes.' She squeezed his hand. 'It's terrible about your colleagues going to jail.'

He looked grim. 'I can't imagine that Hitler will ever let them out.'

A shrill blast pierced the quiet. A train shot along the track, its headlamp sharpening from a fuzzy white orb to a small circle. She had to press her lips against Daniel's ear to be heard as its brakes screamed, filling the cigarette- and soot-stained air.

'Why are you still here? I thought you would have left Munich by now.'

'I've been hiding out in a flophouse, working with the *Post* reporters to find out more about this murder I've been accused of.' He grimaced. 'We haven't gotten anywhere. And now they've been arrested . . .' He trailed off, blinking hard.

She gripped his hand tighter, wanting to distract him from his depressing thoughts. 'Are you going to Berlin? To investigate this murder?'

He touched her face, the faintest grazing of his fingertips along her jaw. 'Yes. I don't have a choice. My false papers were stolen. I still have my real ones, though. But if I try to leave under my own name, as a wanted murderer . . .' He shook his head, unable to finish.

Gretchen nodded. They'd had to flee Munich so quickly that they hadn't had a chance to retrieve their own papers and had had fake ones forged so they could enter other countries. She'd never gotten hers back. After they'd settled in Oxford, though, Daniel's cousins had sent him his papers,

70

because he'd wanted to use his true identity when he looked for work. 'We'll find a forger to make you new ones.'

'I can't, Gretchen.' He kept his gaze steady on hers, grim and unblinking. 'I have to prove my innocence.'

She made an impatient noise in her throat. 'Even if you prove you're innocent, Hitler won't let you leave the country.'

Daniel's eyes were clear and determined. 'Hitler's power is limited, at least for now. President Hindenburg can remove him whenever he wants, without the Reichstag's approval. So Hitler must tread carefully. If I can get proof that the National Socialists are behind the murder, I'll give it to a foreign corre-spondent friend I have in Berlin. He'll have the story printed in his paper in England. It'll be an enormous scandal for the National Socialists. All eyes will be on Berlin, and they'll have to let me leave the country.' He gave her a grave smile. 'And the best part is, the world will know the National Socialists are criminals. I might be able to destroy them once and for all.'

The boldness of his plan stole her breath. Could he truly convince everyone what sort of people Hitler and his men were – and push them from power forever?

A couple of men sauntered by, munching on rolls. Gretchen was silent until they had gone, thinking. 'I don't understand why they're blaming you for a murder that occurred in Berlin. Why not accuse you of a crime here in Munich?'

Daniel shook his head. 'I don't know. But I aim to find out.'

The train squealed to a stop beside the platform. Porters flooded the crowd, grabbing trunks and bags.

'Is it safe for you to go to Berlin?' she asked. 'I mean, you grew up there – surely you'll be recognized.'

'I'll be fine.' He looked exhausted, but calm. 'Berlin's like a dozen little cities. Most people live and work and go to

71

school in their own district. The area where I grew up is on the northern outskirts. If I keep to central Berlin, no one will know me.' He took a deep breath. 'I really want to go home, just for a short visit, if it's not too risky. I miss my family so much.' His voice sounded gruff.

Just looking at him made Gretchen's heart ache. 'We'll find a way to see them,' she said quickly. 'And prove your innocence. I swear it.'

Her fear must have shown in her face, though, for he said, 'I have to go to Berlin. If I don't clear my name, I'll either be caught and executed or I'll have to find another forger to make me false papers and hope they're good enough to fool the border agents. Even then, I'll have to live under an assumed name for the rest of my life. Everyone will think I'm a murderer. I couldn't bear that, Gretchen. The shame my parents would feel . . .' He glanced away.

The train doors opened with a metallic groan. People surged forward, eager to board the train and get settled for the night's journey.

Daniel kissed her cheek. His touch sent a line of fire down to her feet. 'You mustn't come with me. It's too dangerous, Gretchen. Please, go back to England straightaway.'

She thought of the police wagons rumbling through the streets, carrying who knew how many journalists to jail, just because they wrote for Socialist or Communist newspapers. Herr Gerlich, telling her to go, helping her when he must have known that he was about to be beaten and arrested. Aaron attacked in the street because he hadn't saluted. Eva's deadened blue eyes, and Papa and Reinhard lying beneath the ground, and Mama banished to her parents' farm in Dachau while Hitler remained untouched. For the last year, he had crisscrossed Germany in his airplane, campaigning, giving speeches, making promises, shaking supporters' hands, watching his men parade in the streets. Biding his time.

She couldn't leave. For Daniel's sake, for the sake of everyone who had fallen under Hitler's hand, she had to stay and help prove that the National Socialists were behind this unknown woman's murder. She remembered sitting in Hitler's parlor, listening as he thundered on about the Jews. *The parasites are poisoning us from within*, he'd said, one hand punching the air. *Germany will never regain her health until she rids herself of her most noxious pest*. Gretchen's stomach twisted at the memory. She couldn't pretend that she didn't know how deeply Hitler hated Jews – and that he wanted them dead. He had to be stopped. As the leader of a Party publicly tied to a murder, he would be.

She looked at Daniel. 'I'm going with you.'

His face tightened. 'No. If you come, I won't be able to protect you. Gretchen, you need to go back, so you can be safe—'

'Final boarding!' the conductor shouted.

Gretchen gripped her bag tightly and rushed across the platform before Daniel could stop her. As she climbed the train's steps into the dimly lit corridor, she heard him breathing behind her, quick and hard, as though he were angry. Or frightened.

Together, they walked down the corridor flanked with first-class compartments, finally stopping when they found an empty one. He didn't speak as he loaded their bags onto the overhead luggage racks, but a muscle clenched in his jaw.

Silently, they sat on the velour seats, Gretchen taking his hand, needing to maintain a physical connection with him. The train lurched forward. She leaned against him as the train picked up speed, watching the twinkling lights of Munich fall away as they raced into the darkness.

73

PART TWO
THE FATHER OF ALL THINGS

Struggle is the father of all things . . . It is
not by the principles of humanity that man lives or is
able to preserve himself above the animal world,
but solely by means of the most brutal struggle.
—*Adolf Hitler*

8

DANIEL PULLED DOWN THE WINDOW SHADES, CLOSING
out the night. As he slipped off his coat, Gretchen studied
him: although only two weeks had passed since they'd seen
each other, he looked thinner, the hollows beneath his cheekbones more pronounced. He must have had to go hungry
many nights.

'We ought to move to a third-class car,' he said. 'This
carriage is far too expensive.'

The thought of sitting in a compartment where the seats
were crammed closely together, unable to speak freely for fear
of others overhearing, and sleeping among strangers made
Gretchen's flesh crawl.

'We need the privacy—' she began as their compartment
door opened and the conductor poked his head inside.

'Tickets?' he asked.

Daniel reached for his wallet, but Gretchen shook her
head and paid with some of the Whitestones' money. Daniel
opened his mouth to protest, then looked away. She could
imagine how it wounded his pride, to have her pay for him,

but he probably didn't have more than a handful of coins at this point.

Once the conductor had left and Daniel had closed the compartment door, they sat beside each other again. He wrapped his good arm around her shoulders, drawing her close, and she rested her head on his chest, listening to the reassuring beat of his heart against her ear.

'Tell me everything,' she said.

'Aaron's dead.' Daniel's voice was thick. When she twisted in his arms to look at him, she could see his eyes shining with unshed tears. 'He died before I reached Munich. Ruth and his parents had him buried in the Jewish cemetery. Then they emptied out their apartment and moved back to Frankfurt. I hadn't told them I was coming – I was concerned someone might intercept a telegram. So when I showed up in Munich and found everyone gone, I had to talk to Aaron and Ruth's neighbors to find out what had happened. They said Ruth had told them she couldn't ever return to the city where her brother had been killed.'

His arm fell from her shoulders and he dropped his head into his hands. 'I went to the *Munich Post* offices,' he said quietly. 'I wanted to ask my old colleagues to dig up information about Aaron's assailants. They said these kinds of attacks have been happening all over the country, and it would be practically impossible to find out who was responsible.'

His hands hid his face, but she heard the agony in his voice. 'I didn't realize the nightmare their lives have become. They've been living on the run for months.' He took a shaky breath. 'For a long time, they haven't dared to print their bylines in the paper.'

He lowered his hand. His eyes were wide and unfocused, as though he were trapped in the past. 'When I left the office, I saw a couple of SA men hanging about in the street. I remembered them from my reporter days, when I used to cover Hitler's speeches. They recognized me, too, and dragged me into an alley. I tried my best to hold them off but . . .'

He sighed. 'They took my money and my false papers – my real ones were at my rooming house. Later I was able to go back and get them, but of course I can't use them as a wanted criminal. Anyway, those men probably would have killed me if a group of elderly ladies hadn't happened to walk by right then and said they were going to get the police.' He managed a small smile. 'Those old ladies saved my life. Ever since then, I've been moving from one flophouse to the next. The reporters lent me some money, enough to get by, but I didn't have enough for new false papers. I thought about asking my parents for help, but I was afraid the police might go through their correspondence. I don't want to get them in trouble. And then the Party papers announced that I was wanted for murder in Berlin.

'The SA fellows who beat me must have told other people that I was back in Munich. All I can think is that some National Socialists in Berlin got word of it. This is how they plan to get rid of me, in a way that appears perfectly legal.' He closed his eyes. Fatigue had tinted his face gray. 'And the people who would have protested have been arrested. I don't know if any of my colleagues escaped the roundup. Maybe Herr Gerlich did.'

Gretchen placed her hand on Daniel's knee. Beneath his slacks, the muscles around his knee felt rigid. The rhythmic rocking of the train swayed their bodies slightly. 'I'm sorry,' she said. 'He was arrested, too. I was with him when the SA came.'

Daniel's eyes opened and he stared at her. 'You were with Gerlich? How on earth did you get away?'

The whole story tumbled out. By the time she had finished,

79

Daniel had moved closer to her and gripped her hands tightly, his gaze never leaving her face. 'Thank God you escaped. If anything had happened to you . . .' He looked down for an instant, then back at her, the muscles in his throat working as he tried to swallow.

The sight of him struggling not to cry was contagious; tears slid down her own face. 'We'll clear your name so we can get out of here. We can do it, Daniel.'

'Once we're back in England, we'll tell people what's really happening in Germany. We'll have proof this time, proof nobody can ignore. My story will be enough to get me a newspaper job anywhere.' With the tips of his fingers, he wiped away the tears on her cheeks. 'Then we'll live. Really live, Gretchen, without any more fear. I swear it.'

She smiled and kissed him. The familiar feel of his lips on hers made a sob rise in her chest. Her Daniel, who made all her jagged edges smooth. Only an hour ago she hadn't been certain if she would ever see him again. She pulled back and wiped her eyes.

'Oh, Gretchen.' Daniel's face twisted. 'I'm so sorry I've put you through this. I'd give anything to keep you safe.'

She couldn't stop staring at him, as if turning away for an instant might make him vanish. 'Just don't leave me again—'

She broke off as the train jerked to a halt, its wheels emitting a loud metallic shriek. In the sudden silence, she could hear her heart racing in her chest. Why had the train stopped? A scant thirty minutes had passed since they had left Munich; they had hours to go before reaching Berlin.

Daniel yanked up the window shade. In the darkness, the lighted windows of a small town appeared like squares of gold. Gretchen frowned. She recognized the buildings' steeply pitched red tile roofs and the whitewash of their stone walls.

They were at Dachau. But the train should have gone straight through without stopping.

'Something's happening.' Daniel looked grim. With his good hand, he grabbed her suitcase off the overhead luggage rack, then his. 'Let's go.'

'Daniel, there could be a perfectly good explanation—'

'One thing I've learned over the last couple of weeks is to trust my instincts. And they're telling me there's no good reason for this train to have stopped. Come on.' He practically threw her coat at her and she slipped into it, her nervous fingers fumbling at the buttons until she gave up and peeked into the corridor.

A couple of men in SA brown stood at the opposite end with their backs to her, talking to people in another compartment. Even from a distance, Gretchen could hear a woman's shrill voice saying, 'You've no right to barge in here! I'd finally gotten my baby to sleep and now you've woken her up!'

'Our apologies, Frau,' one of the men said. 'We're looking for a middle-aged fellow. Brown beard, spectacles, a bit plump. Have you seen him?'

'It's all right.' Gretchen sagged with relief. 'They're looking for somebody else.'

Then the SA man turned and she saw his profile. A shiver shot down her spine. She knew him. It was Werner Bayer, one of Reinhard's old friends. There was no way he wouldn't recognize her; they'd been acquaintances for years.

She shrank back into the compartment. 'We have to get out of here! One of the SA fellows – I know him!'

Daniel's jaw tightened. 'Come on. *Now*,' he added when she stood, frozen.

Clutching their suitcases, they crept into the corridor. Gretchen didn't dare look back at the SA men, but she heard the rumble of their voices. Her heart pounded as she followed Daniel down the corridor toward the end of the carriage.

'Hey, you! Where do you think you're going?' called someone from behind them. It was Werner; she recognized his slight lisp.

She couldn't move. But Daniel turned, looking annoyed. 'What is it?'

Footsteps sounded on the carpeted corridor, coming closer. 'Why are you getting off? This isn't a scheduled stop.'

Daniel's face broke into a rueful grin. 'Try convincing my girl here of that. I've finally gotten her to agree to go to Berlin with me for the weekend and now she's got cold feet and is whining that her reputation's going to be ruined! I'll have to ring a friend of mine to drive us home so her father doesn't find out.'

The SA fellows laughed. 'Hard luck!' one of them sympathized. 'All right, get going.'

'Thanks.' Daniel tipped his hat. How had he managed to think so quickly? At another time, Gretchen would have been impressed; now she was too anxious to feel anything else. Whistling, Daniel hurried along the corridor, Gretchen at his heels. He wrenched open the carriage doors and clattered down the metal steps, Gretchen following closely. They walked toward the small train station, Daniel muttering, 'Act natural. Somebody might be watching.'

They stepped into the brightly lit station and pretended to study a display of maps until the train roared forward. Through the window, Gretchen watched the locomotive lumber past, gaining speed every second until it was nothing more than a black line reflecting starlight in the north. Releasing a pent-up breath, she glanced at Daniel.

'Let's go,' he muttered. 'The stationmaster's looking at us.'

Together, they went outside and stood on the platform. The harsh wind blew right through Gretchen's coat, and she shivered.

'That was good thinking on the train,' she said. 'However did you think up that story so fast?'

He shrugged. 'Habit, I suppose. When I was a reporter in Munich, I had to make up stories all the time to get potential sources to talk to me.'

It was a side of him she hadn't seen since they'd moved to England: quick-witted, daring, confident. Despite the circumstances, she couldn't help being glad she'd seen it again. She knew Daniel never felt more alive than when he was digging for the truth.

'I'm afraid we're stuck here for the night,' Daniel said. 'There won't be any more trains until morning. Are there any cheap lodging houses in town?'

Gretchen knew why he asked; as a child, she'd often spent summers in Dachau at her grandparents' farm. 'Not really. This is a small town, Daniel, and it's mostly houses. If we do find a boardinghouse with a vacancy, the proprietor's sure to ask for our papers.'

'Which I can't show him.' Daniel heaved a sigh. 'The temperature must be near freezing. We can't possibly camp out in the marshlands and we can't stay here or the station-master will get suspicious.'

They looked at each other. Gretchen knew what he was thinking by the uneasiness in his expression: of her grandparents' farmhouse on the northern outskirts of town, where her mother might be living.

'They won't like having you there,' she said quickly. 'But they won't turn you in, I'm sure of it.'

'I can't imagine the place will be under surveillance,' he said, almost to himself. 'Nobody knows you're back in Munich, right?'

'Only Herr Gerlich and Eva.' Neither added what she hadn't said – that presumably the only people Gerlich could tell about her return were his jailers. As for Eva, they could only hope she would keep her promise to Gretchen and maintain her silence.

Daniel nodded. 'There's nothing for it, then: we'll have to stay at your grandparents' house, at least for the night.'

'It's a long walk,' she warned. Her stomach cramped with anxiety at the thought of seeing Mama again. It had been so long since they'd been together, and she knew too well that Mama wouldn't understand the choices she'd made. Did she still love Gretchen? Or were the bonds of blood and years not enough? She pushed the questions away and tried to keep her tone light.

'We'd best get started,' she said.

Hefting their bags, they began walking. Gretchen watched their breaths make white clouds in the air. A dusting of snow lay on the ground.

Dachau's white houses looked ghostly in the night. Gretchen and Daniel headed east, to skirt the town, and walked alongside the Würm River. Overhead, more and more stars winked into life, painting the marshlands and the rushing river waters silver.

Gretchen pictured the town's layout in her mind. On Dachau's outermost northern limits stood her grandparents' farm and the old powder factory, separated from each other by a forest and a river. The powder factory was a thirty-minute walk from the station, her grandparents' home at least another twenty. They had almost an hour's worth of walking ahead of them.

Fog curled on the ground, and they had to step carefully between the gaping holes in the marshland, from where the big breweries in Munich had cut swaths of peat moss to make beer. As the starlight sprinkled down on the fields, Gretchen saw that the ruined farmland looked dead.

She was too exhausted and cold to talk. Daniel seemed to need silence, too, for he said little as they plunged into the forest, where the pine branches tangled so thickly overhead that they could barely see the light of the stars. Through the filigree of tree trunks, Gretchen spied the massive white concrete wall encircling the former munitions factory. It had been abandoned for years, since the end of the Great War, and she remembered playing hide-and-seek there as a child, darting between the whitewashed civil servants' villas, laughing. Now she heard nothing but the whine of wind between the trees.

They turned left, making for the western edge of the woods. Gretchen's legs shook from hunger, and her vision wavered. She couldn't remember the last time she'd eaten. Maybe on the train into Munich, but that had been luncheon, about nine hours ago. She stumbled over a tree root and Daniel's hand was instantly on her arm, holding her upright. His touch felt so familiar, so right.

Tears trickled from her eyes, trailing an icy line down her cheeks. He wiped them away, his fingers twitching, a sure signal that his old injury was troubling him again.

'Are you in pain?' she asked.

'I'm fine.' He was white to the lips.

'You don't need to do that,' she said. 'Try to pretend you're all right when you're not. I wish you'd let me help you sometimes.'

He gave her a tired smile. 'Gretchen, you don't know how much you already do.'

She smiled back at him. They continued walking in the darkness between the trees, but Gretchen carried the heat and the light of his words with her, keeping her warm, helping her believe, if only for a moment, that they were safe.

9

THE FARMHOUSE SAT IN THE MIDDLE OF A FIELD. FROM far off, it looked as Gretchen remembered: a large, old house made of dark wood silvered with age. As she grew closer, breathing hard from a stitch in her side, she saw that some of the blue shutters with heart cutouts were missing or hung cockeyed. Several roof tiles were gone. The farmland her grandfather had plowed for his potato fields had surrendered to mud and weeds. Clay pots on the front steps lay on their sides, cracked, spilling dirt across the porch.

At the far end of the mud-choked fields, Gretchen stopped in confusion. What had happened here? Her grandparents never would have let the farmhouse fall into such disrepair. She shot a wary look at her surroundings, but she saw no one. Had the National Socialists sacked the place?

'What's wrong?' Daniel asked.

'It's a mess.' She looked over her shoulder at the outbuildings: a barn, a couple of sheds, a henhouse, but they were quiet, the doors shut, no lights showing between the wooden slatted walls. The place was quiet as a tomb. 'Let's go in,' she added, shaking off her unease.

They knocked repeatedly and had to wait for several minutes before shuffling footsteps sounded on the other side of the door. It opened and a woman, bent with age, peered out at them. She carried a kerosene lantern, its yellowish flicker washing over her face. She wore a knitted woolen shawl over a white nightgown. A blue kerchief was wound around her head, but Gretchen didn't need to see her hair to know who she was. *Mama*. She let out a half-gasping sob.

Mama stared at her with red-rimmed eyes. Her cheeks, once so fair and soft, stretched tightly over her cheekbones. She opened her mouth to speak and a strange whistling sound streamed out. Dark holes dotted her gums. She was missing half of her teeth.

Gretchen froze. 'What happened to you?'

'Gretl, is that truly you? Your hair . . .' Mama stretched out a trembling hand, then let it fall, as though she were afraid to touch Gretchen.

'I dyed it.'

'Why would you do such a thing? Your beautiful hair – oh.' Mama's expression hardened. The words seemed to whoosh between her missing teeth, making it difficult to understand her. 'You did it to look like *him*, I suppose.' She looked past Gretchen, her eyes narrowing as they swept up and down Daniel.

Daniel removed his hat and nodded at her, his face carefully blank. 'Good evening, Frau Müller.'

Mama glared at him. 'Why are *you* here? Isn't it enough that you took my daughter from me? Do you have to come back and rub my nose in it?'

'Mama, please.' Gretchen laid a hand on her mother's arm. 'It wasn't Daniel's fault that I had to leave Munich.' The words she longed to say felt heavy in her mouth: *it was Uncle Dolf's fault; he's the real monster!* But she didn't dare say them. She and Daniel needed to remain on Mama's good side, if they wanted to be allowed to stay.

'We just need a place to spend the night,' Gretchen said. 'Please, Mama. We won't be any trouble, I promise.'

Tears clogged her throat. She couldn't believe that she had to beg her own mother for shelter. *This was what Hitler did to us*, she thought bitterly. His insidious lies had torn them apart. For the thousandth time, she wished her father had been assigned to any regiment besides the 16th, in which he had met Hitler during the Great War. There was no telling what their lives might have been like, if not for that one turn of fate.

Sighing, Mama held the door open for them. They slipped past her into a filthy parlor lit by the glow of Mama's lantern. The fireplace looked cold and black, and the box where Gretchen's grandfather used to keep the woodpile was empty. Ice crystals glittered on the wood-paneled walls. Months of rain and wood smoke had darkened the windowpanes. The watercolor painting above the mantel had been ripped; someone had stitched it together with red thread.

'What happened to the farm?' Gretchen asked. 'Where are Oma and Opa?'

'Your grandparents are dead,' Mama said dully.

'*What?*' Gretchen gasped. 'What happened to them?'

'They fell ill last winter.' Mama curled a hand over her mouth, hiding her missing teeth. Each word was accompanied by a soft whistling sound. 'Pneumonia.' She walked into the kitchen.

The backs of Gretchen's eyes stung. Not Opa, who liked to smoke pipes in the evening and tell stories about his childhood, back when artists had flocked to Dachau to paint the ever-shifting landscape with its play of sunlight and shadow.

And Oma, who smelled of cherries and could roll a piecrust perfectly on her first try and used to guide Gretchen's young fingers on knitting needles.

Daniel wrapped his good arm around her. 'I'm so sorry.'

She buried her face into his shoulder, counting her breaths. One. Her grandparents had been old. Two. She and Daniel were still alive, and they had to do whatever it took to stay that way. Three – she stopped, remembering that Hitler had taught her this calming method years ago, when she had been anxious about a school exam. She'd rather drown in grief than use any of his tricks. Even if they worked.

She pulled back from Daniel. He smiled a little, running his knuckles down the side of her cheek. 'Go and talk to her,' he said quietly. 'You haven't seen each other in ages. I don't want to get in the way. I'll stay out here.'

How did he know what she needed, without being told? She nodded her thanks at him and followed Mama into the kitchen. This room was worse than the parlor: The cast-iron stove was cold and coated with a layer of grease, and the brown linoleum-topped table was gritty with spilled food. The tin bathtub her grandparents used to fill with water from the well sat in the middle of the floor, its bottom wavering under a film of soap-scudded water.

How could Mama live in such filth? At the boardinghouse, she'd been a stickler for cleanliness, washing the linens, scrubbing the lavatories, scouring the windows with vinegar, and beating carpets on the back steps. What had happened in the past eighteen months to change her so completely?

'You must be hungry,' her mother mumbled, but Gretchen laid a gentle hand on her shoulder and guided her down into a chair.

'Please,' she said. 'What's happened here?'

Mama sighed and undid her kerchief. Her hair fell forward

like a curtain, shielding her face. Silver threads glinted among the blond strands. 'After they died, I couldn't keep up with the farm. There's so much work to be done, and I can't afford to pay anyone to help me . . .' She trailed off.

'And you?' Gretchen forced herself to ask, praying the answer wasn't what she suspected. 'What about your teeth?'

Mama cradled her head in her hands. 'It was the night you and your Jew left.'

Slowly, Gretchen lowered herself into a chair. Even through the haze of the months, she remembered each detail of the final hours she and Daniel had spent in Munich. They had caught a train to Dachau, intending to beg her grandfather for his car so they could drive over the border. They'd been walking near the old powder factory when Mama had appeared. She had assumed they would avoid the town center and keep to the outskirts, to decrease the risk of running into their pursuers. When she had warned them that SA men had already arrived at the farmhouse, Gretchen had seen their chances of escape evaporate like mist. Until Mama had given them her life's savings and they had hiked to Ingolstadt, where they'd boarded a train bound for Switzerland.

'When I got back to the farmhouse,' Mama said, her voice hissing between her missing teeth, 'the SA men were beating Opa. They wouldn't believe him when he said he didn't know where you'd gone.' She raised her head, tears shining in her eyes. 'They tore the painting over the mantel. You know how Oma loved that picture. Then they hit me.' She touched her lips.

They must have hit her many times, to knock out so many teeth. Gretchen felt sick. This was her fault. While the SA had attacked her mother and grandfather, she'd been hiking through the countryside with Daniel, safe and unhurt and starting a new life.

She took her mother's hand. Mama's fingers felt cold, and the backs of her hands were knotted with blue veins. They'd never been pretty hands. Red from preparing meals for other people to eat and washing clothes for the boarders to wear. Nails broken and skin mottled from endless labor to keep Gretchen and Reinhard fed and clothed.

But Gretchen had loved those hands. They had protected her.

'I'm sorry, Mama,' she said. Tears streamed down her cheeks. For once, she didn't try to stop them.

'I know, Gretl,' her mother said. She didn't squeeze Gretchen's hand back, but she didn't let go either. 'Just as Herr Hitler would be, if he knew what had happened. The Party has grown too big. When it was small and within Herr Hitler's control, it was a good organization. Now it's expanded beyond his grasp and there are rogue members doing wicked deeds in his name.'

Gretchen snapped her head up to look at her mother. Thin and pale in her old nightgown, her face painted yellow by the light of the lantern on the table. This was what Mama told herself, so she could keep going. Alone on a dying farm, abandoned by the people she'd thought were her friends. Oblivious that the man she admired so greatly had killed her husband and ordered her son's death.

'Uncle Dolf isn't who you think—' Gretchen stopped. Her mother's eyes were steady on hers. And bright with tears.

Gretchen glanced at the dirty kitchen and thought of the fields that probably wouldn't yield many potatoes in the fall. What harm was there in letting Mama believe what she needed to? She had no power, no influence, nobody to listen to whatever she might say. The truth seemed crueler than a lie.

Gretchen clutched her mother's hand. 'Yes, Mama,' she said. 'I'm sure Uncle Dolf would be very sorry, if he knew.'

10

HER MOTHER TOASTED BREAD FOR GRETCHEN AND
Daniel. As they ate in silence, Gretchen watched Daniel
sneaking glances around the kitchen, his expression pensive.
She realized a city boy like him had probably never seen a
home without running water or electricity before. This must
seem like another world to him.

She thought of the Whitestones' kitchen: bright with electric light, an icebox full of fine cuts of meat. And the cupboards
in her family's old kitchen, so often empty, when they had
lived in an apartment and Papa had been alive. She could still
hear Papa's hoarse mutter that he wasn't hungry. But she'd
seen the way he'd looked at the pieces of turnip on her plate.
He'd been starving, and had pretended he wasn't so she and
Reinhard would have something to eat. His hatred for the
Jews made a horrifying kind of sense: he'd needed someone
to blame, and Hitler had suggested an easy scapegoat.

When they were done eating and had thanked Gretchen's
mother for the meal, Mama took their plates, careful not to
touch Daniel's fingers. 'Gretchen, you may stay as long as you

want,' she said without looking at him, her voice shaking. 'You're welcome to live here.'

Gretchen's heart ached as she watched her mother carry the dishes across the room. 'Mama, I can't. Daniel needs me.'

'Fine,' her mother snapped. Her back was ramrod straight as she stacked the plates beside the dirty ones on the counter. 'Go to bed. Your Jew can have the spare room at the end of the hall.'

Her Jew. Mama couldn't see him as anything other than that. Swallowing a sigh, Gretchen led Daniel upstairs to a long, dark hallway lined with three bedrooms. She pointed at his door, but couldn't bring herself to look at him. What must he think of her, with a mother who despised him so deeply that she couldn't call him by name?

'There are extra blankets in the armoire,' she mumbled. 'I'm sorry, Daniel.'

He placed his index finger under chin, propelling it upward until their gazes met. 'It's fine. I already knew what she thinks of me.'

She clung to him for a moment, listening to the reassuring thump of his heart. 'We can do this, can't we?' she asked, needing to hear him agree. 'Prove your innocence?'

'Of course.' He sounded so much like the Daniel she'd known in Munich, brash and confident, that she couldn't help smiling. When she was with him, anything seemed possible. Somehow they would clear his name and show the world that the National Socialists were responsible for this Fräulein Junge's murder. With foreign eyes watching Berlin, Daniel would be permitted to leave the country, and they could go back to England and the life they'd been building together. The future rolled out before her like a length of twine, long and curving but wonderfully tough and strong.

'Good night,' she said, kissing him before slipping into

another spare room. Curled up under the heavy blankets, she let herself think of the Whitestones and tears rose to her eyes. They could have no inkling how desperate things had gotten in Germany, and must be so worried about her. In the darkness, she clasped her hands together and prayed she got the chance to see them again.

The express to Berlin didn't leave until nightfall. A day stretched out in front of Gretchen and Daniel, waiting to be filled. After a meager breakfast of scrambled eggs, they sat in the parlor, talking about this mysterious murder Daniel was supposed to have committed. Who had this woman been and why had she been killed? Without knowing more information, though, it was useless to speculate, and finally they gave up in frustration. The investigation would have to wait until they got to Berlin; in the meantime, they had to find ways to make the hours pass.

Daniel chopped wood for the cast-iron stoves that her mother used to heat the farmhouse; Gretchen filled the kitchen tub with fresh water and scrubbed all the dishes clean. As she went into the yard to toss out the water, she glimpsed her mother slipping into the henhouse. She followed Mama inside.

In the dark coolness, she saw her mother reaching into the straw for eggs while hens pecked at the feed on the ground. Gretchen helped gather the eggs into a basket.

'You said you came here from Munich,' Mama said. 'Did you visit Reinhard's grave there?'

Embarrassment flushed Gretchen's face. She hadn't even thought of her brother's resting place. She shook her head.

'I haven't been back myself.' Mama gently placed more eggs into the basket. 'Reinhard's friends in the SA paid for the tombstone. They said it was beautifully carved.' Her voice broke on the last word. Alarmed, Gretchen tried to touch her, but her mother shied away.

'No, Gretl,' she said hesitantly, 'there's something I need to tell you – something I've been thinking about since Reinhard died. It wasn't his fault that he became . . . well, what he was.'

Gretchen glanced at her mother in confusion. 'What do you mean?'

For a long moment, the only sound was the hens clucking and the rustle of straw. Then Mama let out a low moan and sank to the ground, dropping the basket. 'It was your father's fault,' she said.

Something icy grabbed Gretchen's insides. What was Mama talking about? Slowly, she lowered to a crouch beside her mother. 'I don't understand.'

'He wanted Reinhard to grow up to be like Herr Hitler.' Mama dropped her hands from her face. Tears trapped in her wrinkled cheeks shone like silver threads. 'He was determined to treat Reinhard just as Herr Hitler's father had treated him. It was all because of that story Herr Hitler confided to us once.'

The words tumbled out as though Mama had been holding them inside for a long time. 'His father often whipped him. One night, when Herr Hitler was a small boy, he heard his father coming down the hall to beat him. He was determined to get away and tried wriggling through the window. But he couldn't quite fit. So he took off his clothes and was almost through when his father opened the door. Herr Hitler snatched up a bedsheet to cover his nakedness. His father laughed and laughed at him. He even told Herr Hitler's mother to come and look. From then on, he called Herr Hitler "the toga boy". Papa said it sounded as though Herr Hitler had been toughened up from a very early age.'

Suddenly pieces locked together: Papa striding toward Reinhard, drawing his belt free from his trousers. Whipping him over and over, saying someday Reinhard would be thankful. Kissing Gretchen's cheeks or dancing with her around the kitchen while Reinhard sat in the corner, sulking. Why had they been treated so differently? Even as Gretchen asked herself the question, she knew the answer: Papa had coddled and loved her because she was a girl. Her gender had kept her safe. But Reinhard, the boy, the one who was expected to have a job someday and make a success of himself, had been treated in the same manner Hitler had. Whipped and humiliated and mocked.

Gretchen surged to her feet. Papa, the man everyone had told her was so kindhearted. Misguided, his mind wracked by warfare, but good deep down – that was what she had promised herself the whole time she'd been living in England. Air seemed to vanish from her lungs. Perhaps the man she'd loved and missed so much hadn't existed at all.

'How could you do that to Reinhard?' she choked out.

Mama's eyes gleamed with tears. 'Papa thought he was turning Reinhard into a leader. We didn't dream he'd turn out so differently from Herr Hitler – so cold and unfeeling. And he *did* die protecting you,' she added, sounding defensive.

Gretchen remembered the lie she had told her mother, a tiny piece of comfort she had hoped would help Mama get through the years. The truth swelled inside her mouth until she was bursting to let it out, but she didn't speak. The pleading on her mother's face was unmistakable – perhaps a part of Mama suspected that Reinhard had died in another manner, but she needed to believe what Gretchen had told her. Gretchen turned away from her mother and braced her hands on the wall, feeling the wooden splinters digging into her palms. The pain was welcome – it was something to feel besides this widening hole within her rib cage.

'I don't understand,' she said at last. 'Papa knew that

Uncle Dolf was diagnosed as a psychopath when they were recovering at the military hospital together. How could he want Reinhard to be like him? How could he remain friends with Uncle Dolf and bring him into our home?' The last words felt as though they had been wrenched from her.

'Herr Hitler a psychopath!' Mama snorted. She picked up the basket and began gathering eggs again. 'As if your father ever believed in that sort of nonsense. Those mind doctors are quacks, Gretl. Papa knew they must have been mistaken about Herr Hitler.'

The last pieces fell together in a rush. Gretchen had read the letters her father had sent to her mother during the Great War. He'd written that he'd heard the doctors talking about Hitler, but he couldn't believe that their whispered words truly applied to him. He'd known the truth, but hadn't accepted it. That was why he'd tried to turn his only son into a reflection of his dearest friend.

But Reinhard had grown up so emotionless, while Uncle Dolf was all fire. Papa must have feared he'd made mistakes in Reinhard's upbringing, to make him so different from Hitler. Eventually their parents had taken Reinhard to a doctor – and received the same diagnosis that Hitler had gotten. It had been her father's death warrant. Maybe then her father had finally believed the truth about Hitler. Or maybe he had continued to think that psychologists were charlatans. Either way, his knowledge had gotten him killed. When the National Socialists had attempted to overthrow the Munich government, he'd warned Hitler not to let his overwrought nerves get the best of him again – and Hitler had realized that Papa had known about the diagnosis from five years earlier and had to be eliminated to prevent the embarrassing secret from ruining his future political chances.

Gretchen wondered if Papa had figured out what was

97

happening, in that brief second between Hitler's pressing his pistol into his back and firing. Had he realized that the man he'd loved as a brother, the friend he'd tried to turn his son into, had been a monster?

The air inside the henhouse was so stifling that she couldn't breathe.

She shoved the door open and ran across the fields. She needed a place to hide from the world. Beside the barn, she sank to her knees and let herself cry. Poor Reinhard. He hadn't had the chance to grow into his own person. Maybe the early lack of their mother's touch had coiled something inside him, and their father's beatings and jeers had only twisted it tighter.

Maybe, if things had been different, she and her brother could have been friends.

Or perhaps he still would have grown up broken and emotionless; she couldn't pretend to understand all the mysteries of the human mind. But her beloved papa had helped to shatter what should have been whole in Reinhard. The man she'd adored and whom she'd needed to believe in so badly.

She wiped her eyes with the backs of her hands. Surely the answers weren't this easy, though, were they? Her parents' mistreatment of Reinhard must have affected him, but that couldn't be the sole reason he had turned out sadistic and distant. There had to have been something else within him, something that had been in him from the start.

Maybe Hitler had been involved in shaping her brother's personality, too; he'd certainly spent a lot of time with them while they were growing up. He'd taught them that they were special, separated from the so-called mongrel races because of their Aryan blood. Had Hitler's teachings given Reinhard permission to hurt others – because he thought they were subhumans and didn't matter?

And what about Hitler? Had his upbringing, which she

knew almost nothing about, warped him into a hate-spewing politician? She thought of his brother and sisters and shook her head. She'd once met his older half sister, Angela, a kindly, middle-aged lady, and she'd heard stories about his other siblings. They had sounded ordinary enough. Certainly Hitler's childhood must have helped to form him, but it wasn't the only factor.

Gretchen rested her burning forehead in her cold hands. How desperately she wished Alfred were with her right now. But she could imagine what he would say: *Reinhard may have been ill-treated but he was responsible for his actions. He chose to harm people, just as Hitler chooses to hate. We are each our own person, separate from our family, not wholly formed by our experiences. We decide who we want to be.*

Resolutely, she got to her feet and brushed dirt from her stockings. Maybe the Papa she'd loved and mourned had been her own creation. Her real father had been either deluded or wicked; at this point, it hardly mattered which. He was gone, and now she'd never know him. But she was alive and whole. And she chose to see with her own eyes, however painful and ugly the view.

11

GRETCHEN KNEW SHE WOULD PROBABLY NEVER SEE HER mother again. They embraced, stiff as strangers, but she saw the pleading in Mama's eyes before she and Daniel started on their long trek back to the station to catch the night express to Berlin. *Pleading for what*? Gretchen wondered as they walked across the snow-dusted marshlands. Forgiveness for hurting Reinhard? Or had Mama been silently asking her to stay? Gretchen was incapable of doing either.

It was a long night on the train, fractured by a dream of Papa beating Reinhard. She had woken up, the smack of Papa's belt on her brother's flesh echoing in her ears until Daniel had heard her crying, and had wrapped his good arm around her, asking, 'What's wrong?'

Out of habit, she glanced around their first-class compartment, even though she knew they were alone. Then she told Daniel about the way her father had 'trained' Reinhard, the words hesitant at first, then spilling out so fast she barely stopped for breath. Daniel didn't speak until she was finished, but his arm tightened around her a few times. When she was done, he had said, sounding furious, 'Don't you dare start feeling sorry for Reinhard. When I think about what he did to you . . .' He trailed off.

In the moonlight streaming through the curtain, she saw the muscles in his throat constricting as he tried to talk. 'Whether or not your father mistreated him, your brother still chose to beat you. Nobody made him do it.'

'Maybe my father did, by raising him like that—'

'No.' Daniel's tone was sharp. He held her close, his breath a warm flutter on her cheek. 'Maybe your brother was predisposed to act a certain way because of the things your father did to him and the people he grew up around. I don't know much about psychoanalysis, but I don't believe that we can blame our actions on our upbringings. If we could, then nobody would be responsible for anything they do.'

For a moment, she was silent, thinking. There were no simple answers, and she doubted that she would ever fully understand the inner workings of Reinhard's and Hitler's minds. But she had to admit that she agreed with Daniel: people were accountable for their actions.

The tension melted from her body, leaving her muscles as smooth and pliant as liquid. She turned into Daniel's embrace and slept undisturbed until dawn.

Early in the morning, they got off at the Anhalter Bahnhof. The station was crowded with passengers: thin-faced, shabby, clutching umbrellas and wax-wrapped sandwiches, the two things that Daniel said Berliners never left home without.

As they joined the throngs of people streaming out of the station, Gretchen caught the black flash of four men's uniforms. They stood at the entrance, their heads swiveling as they surveyed the people walking past. SS men; she recognized the death's head emblem on their caps.

Her legs shook so badly she wasn't certain if she could

keep walking. Who were they looking for? Had they guessed that Daniel had come to Berlin, or learned that she was back in Germany? If she stopped and reversed direction, people might wonder why. Somehow she forced herself forward. She glanced at Daniel. He stared straight ahead, his lips compressed into thin lines.

They walked on the edge of the crowd, so close to the SS men that she brushed against one of them as she passed. His eyes flickered over her without interest, and then went on to the people behind her. She let out the breath she'd kept inside. The men hadn't been looking for her or Daniel. Hitler didn't know she was in Berlin. They were still safe.

She followed the mass of passengers outside into air so bright and cold that her teeth turned to ice. The city exploded all around her: double-decker omnibuses trundling along the avenue, an S-Bahn train roaring overhead, a streetcar rumbling closer while its cables shot off blue sparks, and gleaming automobiles gliding past.

The sidewalks were jammed with pedestrians. By the station entrance, a couple of men were singing a folk song, their caps on the ground to catch spare pfennigs. Strips of traffic-blackened snow lined the curbs.

A wall of smells hit her: roasted chestnuts, perfume, cigarettes, car exhaust. Berliners' crisp accents wrapped around her like a cloak; they sounded so different from the slower, blurred sounds of the Bavarian dialect that she was accustomed to. She had been to the capital once before, but the trip had lasted a matter of hours, and time had turned the memory into a distant haze. She had forgotten what an *alive* city Berlin was. The panic from the Reichstag fire almost two weeks ago seemed forgotten now, or at least skillfully hidden. Here, Hitler seemed far away, as though his influence hadn't yet touched the capital.

102

'It's beautiful,' she said. Daniel gave her the first genuine smile she'd seen since they'd found each other at the train station.

'You'll find it very different from Munich.' Hefting his bag with his good hand, Daniel started walking, Gretchen falling in step beside him. 'Liberal, diverse, full of art and culture and painting and music.' He frowned at a group of SA men across the street. They stood outside a café, laughing, patting their pockets, probably looking for cigarettes or loose change for a cup of coffee. 'At least, it was when I was growing up.'

They walked faster. When they'd woken at dawn, they'd decided to go to his parents' house first, to beg them to flee the city. Daniel was certain it wouldn't be long before Hitler initiated a sweep of mass arrests in Berlin, as he had just done in Munich. The Cohens' religion – and who their son was – meant they were in danger.

Daniel hadn't been in touch with them since he'd returned to Germany because of the new decree that had suspended privacy for letters and telephone calls. Now he didn't dare call them or send a telegram. If they went to his parents' street, though, he thought they should be able to tell by watching the house if it was under surveillance. It seemed the safest option.

They took an S-Bahn train to the Waidmannslust district on the northern outskirts of the city. As they walked from the station, Gretchen heard church bells pealing eight o'clock. The houses were small and tidy, set back from the streets by narrow strips of lawn. There was no clang of streetcars, no rumble of omnibuses, only the high-pitched giggles of children playing hopscotch. This part of Berlin was another world.

Clutching their suitcases, they walked down the quiet road. Although Gretchen hadn't seen the Cohens' home before, she recognized it, for Daniel had described it so many times:

103

a tiny white house, surrounded by trees. Stripped of their leaves, the cherry and apple trees were black lines against the snow-scattered grass.

There were no men in brown or black uniforms walking the street; no faces peering through windows down at them. Her heartbeat slowed. The house wasn't being watched; Daniel had been right.

Together they went up the front steps. Daniel's mouth had relaxed into a smile. He rang the bell. They listened to it chime inside the house, then to the clicking of footsteps coming nearer. The door opened and a slender, dark-haired woman in a green woolen dress stared at them. Then she let out a low sob and flung herself into Daniel's arms.

Quickly, Gretchen dropped Daniel's hand and stepped back so she wouldn't be in the way. She smiled as Daniel hugged the woman.

'My boy!' she cried. She pulled back, framing Daniel's face with her hands. 'You've grown too thin! And your arm!' She ran her fingers from his shoulder to his wrist, the color draining from her face. 'Your arm feels so skinny. I had no idea the injury was so bad.' Tears glistened in her eyes.

'I'm all right.' A dull red crept up Daniel's neck. 'We'd better get inside, Mama, just in case.'

'Of course.' Frau Cohen held the door open for them. As Gretchen passed, Frau Cohen's smile froze for an instant, then slipped away. Unease raced up Gretchen's spine. She had imagined they would be glad to meet her at last – after all, Daniel was always saying how open and welcoming his parents were.

They walked into a parlor cozy with jammed bookcases, red velvet sofas, dark wooden tables, and brass lamps. They set their suitcases on the floor. Frau Cohen hung up their coats on hooks by the door, then led them into the kitchen, where a middle-aged man in a navy suit was setting his dirty dishes next to the sink. His long, muscular build and dark hair proclaimed he was Daniel's father as clearly as any introduction. He glanced at them as they came in, then stilled, his bowl falling from his hand to land with a clink on the counter.

'Daniel,' he choked out, and grabbed his son in a tight embrace. Gretchen heard a strange gasping sound and saw that Daniel's shoulders were shaking. It was the first time she'd seen him break down and cry. She looked away, her eyes stinging.

'I didn't do it,' Daniel was saying. 'I didn't kill that woman—'

'We know that!' His father drew back. Tears glittered in his eyes, but he was smiling. 'What are you doing here? You always said it was too dangerous for you to come back.'

'I had to warn you.' Daniel looked his father straight in the face. 'You and Mama and the girls need to get out of Berlin. I'm in Hitler's sights, and that means the rest of you are, too. Go somewhere else, start over where he can't find you.'

'Son, you're being melodramatic.' His father smiled, probably to take the sting out of the words. 'We're safe enough, provided we follow the law and don't get mixed up in things that don't concern us—'

'This discussion can wait,' Frau Cohen interrupted. 'He looks ready to drop, dear. Sit down and I'll fix you something to eat.' She hesitated, her gaze sliding to Gretchen. 'You too.'

Gretchen's heart sank. She hadn't expected this coldness, but she understood it: to Daniel's parents, she must be the Nazi princess who had taken him away from them. Quickly, she sat down at the wooden table, folding her hands in her lap, as though she could draw into herself and disappear. Daniel sat beside her, beaming. For his sake, she must pretend she hadn't noticed his parents' snubs. She managed to smile at him.

Herr Cohen sank into a chair across from them while Frau Cohen bustled around the kitchen. His eyes didn't leave Daniel's face. 'I can't believe it. Daniel, you look so grown. The last time we saw you, you were still just a boy.'

'He turned nineteen without us.' Frau Cohen set their plates on the table. She had fixed them enormous sandwiches, with pickles and potato salad on the side. The bitter aroma of coffee percolating drifted from the stove. Gretchen's stomach contracted with hunger. She murmured, 'Thank you,' and ate with her head down, so she didn't have to look at the disapproval on Daniel's parents' faces.

'I hated missing everyone's birthdays,' Daniel said. His voice was warm; thank goodness he hadn't noticed his parents' reaction to her yet. She knew that would hurt him. 'Are any of the girls here?'

'Inge and Edda are at the library, studying for an exam, and Mathilde's already left for a friend's house.' Frau Cohen poured everyone a cup of coffee. Gretchen wrapped her cold hands around her mug, grateful for its warmth. She studied the kitchen while Daniel and his parents talked about his sisters. It was so strange to see Daniel's childhood home for the first time, as though she were glimpsing a part of him that he had kept hidden until now.

The kitchen was small and plain, with a black cast-iron stove and a white metal icebox. Mint-green curtains framed the window overlooking the backyard. There were framed photographs on the wall, and Gretchen smiled at the black-and-white images of Daniel as a child, all legs and arms and ears. Then she thought of Mama's dilapidated farmhouse, and her cheeks warmed. Part of her couldn't help wondering if Daniel sometimes looked down on her – after all, his father was an electrician, his mother a seamstress, and they had a lovely, middle-class home, so unlike the shabby two-room apartment she'd lived in when her father was alive and a struggling, uneducated cobbler.

Then she looked at Daniel's easy grin and her fears slid away. She knew him inside and out, and he didn't care a pin about class differences.

'Gretchen, excuse my poor manners,' he said. 'I'm so excited to see my parents again, I completely forgot to introduce you. Mama, Papa, this is—'

'We know who she is,' Frau Cohen interrupted in a voice like ice. 'And she's not welcome under this roof. A meal is fine, but she can't stay.'

'No, you don't understand,' Daniel said hastily, his grin fading. 'Gretchen isn't a National Socialist anymore—'

'You don't even say Nazi now.' His father shook his head. 'Perhaps it's you who has changed, Daniel.'

'I won't use derogatory terms anymore. Not for anything,' Daniel said quietly. Gretchen's hands tightened on her cup until she thought the coffee-warmed porcelain would burn them. She'd taught Daniel that Nazi was Bavarian slang for country bumpkin, and he hadn't used the word since, out of respect for her. Just as she no longer uttered the vicious terms she'd once used for Jews. They'd agreed there must be no more cruel words between them.

'Now you're defending Nazis!' His father threw up his hands and paced the room. 'Hasn't this girl caused us enough grief, without you adding to it? She took you from us! If it hadn't been for her, you would have returned to Berlin long ago and found a respectable newspaper job or gone to a university. We wouldn't have to live in such agony. Every night we wonder if you're still alive or if you've been arrested.' He shot Gretchen an accusing look. 'Or hurt again.'

'Stop.' Daniel looked shaken. 'None of this is Gretchen's fault.'

'Of course it is!' Frau Cohen burst out. 'She brought you to Chancellor Hitler's attention! We cannot condone your relationship when it may cost you your life.'

Guilt was a vise around Gretchen's chest. They were right. She was to blame for Daniel's precarious position. If they hadn't fallen in love, Hitler would have considered Daniel merely one opposition reporter among many. Unknowingly, she had signed his death warrant.

'I understand,' she said. 'And I'm sorry.' She wiped at her brimming eyes with the back of her hand. There was nothing else she could think of to say. Quickly, before she could change her mind, she got to her feet and walked out of the room. She would sit on the porch and give the Cohens some privacy.

'Gretchen, wait!' Daniel called. She heard his chair scraping on the floor as he rose.

'You're better off without her,' his mother said. Gretchen stepped into the parlor and grabbed her coat. Frau Cohen's voice drifted after her. 'Haven't you written us that you hate England and your job and feel alone? That you long to return to Germany and a real life, even under a false name, but you daren't leave her because she needs you too much? Haven't you said all of those things?' Her voice had gotten higher and higher until she was practically screaming.

Gretchen recoiled as though she had been punched. Was that how he truly felt?

She had to get out of there. Blindly, she grabbed her coat and suitcase and rushed out the front door, into a lightly falling snow. Her movements felt jerky, as though she were a puppet on a string. She was a burden to Daniel. He had stayed with her in Oxford out of a sense of obligation, not love. Some part of her mind registered the snowflakes hitting the back of her neck and sliding under her blouse, trailing long lines of dampness down her spine, but she didn't feel cold, only numb.

She shrugged into her coat and hurried down the front walk. A memory raced through her head: stumbling with Daniel through the darkened Munich streets, his injured arm crumpled against his chest, his eyes meeting hers as he said that he would give up everything to be with her.

He had. But he had regretted it.

She reached the street and began to run.

12

SHE HAD GONE HALFWAY DOWN THE BLOCK BEFORE Daniel caught up to her. His hand fastened around her wrist, forcing her to stop. 'Gretchen, please,' he said. He must have been running hard; he was out of breath.

'Please,' he said again. 'You don't understand.'

She stared at the pavement, which was slowly turning white under a carpet of snowflakes. 'Did you really write those things to your parents?'

He sighed. 'Not exactly. Give me a few minutes to say goodbye to them, and then I'll explain everything.'

'You're not going to stay with them?'

'No.' His breath made miniature clouds in the air. 'If the only problem was their disapproval, we could room with them, at least for a few days. I stayed at your mother's house, after all, and that turned out fine. But I don't want to put them in danger and . . .' His voice caught. 'I choose you, Gretchen. Every time, I'll choose you.'

Her dry eyes burned. She nodded, but the motion felt disconnected, as though someone else had stepped inside her body. As Daniel rushed back to his parents' house, she watched him go, a navy blur in his suit. He must have been so eager to reach her that he'd forgotten his overcoat. For some reason, the thought made her throat thicken with tears.

The street was empty except for a black automobile driving past, its tires crunching in the snow. Across the road, a woman emerged from her home with two tiny children, bundled up so tightly in their coats, hats, and scarves that Gretchen couldn't guess at their gender. This was where Daniel had grown up, this ordinary suburb where fathers went to work in the morning and mothers stayed home with little ones and children attended school. Sweet and simple and so unlike her own childhood that they might as well have been from different planets.

As she watched, Daniel left his house and walked toward her, carrying his suitcase. Beneath his fedora, his face was pinched and pale.

'Let's go,' he said shortly, and started walking.

'I hate the thought of you leaving your family,' she replied, falling into step beside him. She didn't want to ask the next question, but she had to know. 'Why stay with me? When you hate living in England so much?'

The line of his slumped shoulders looked dejected. 'It's true I've been miserable in Oxford,' he said quietly. A sudden wind kicked up, sending little swirls of snow dancing across the street. 'My job is a joke. Without real news to report, I feel empty, as though I'm merely marking time. I have no friends to light the Sabbath candles with. No relatives to celebrate holidays with, no one I dare talk to about my past.' He hesitated. 'I'm lonely.'

'I can do those things with you,' she protested. 'You already celebrate holidays with the Whitestones, but I'll have Sabbath dinner with you every Friday night. You can teach me the Jewish customs. I'm sure it won't be long before you can find a proper newspaper job, and you can talk to me about your memories whenever you want.'

His smile looked sad. 'We can't fill all the holes in each other's lives. That's too much to expect from one person. Love isn't enough. There needs to be more – friends, a satisfying job, school, family. In England, all I have is you.'

For the first time, she realized how alone he must have felt. He had always seemed cheerful, so she had assumed he had been happy, too. He had been protecting her, even then. Suddenly she could feel the cold from the snowflakes landing on her cheeks.

They kept walking, their footsteps muffled by the snow. She couldn't say anything. Was he breaking things off with her?

'I'm expressing myself badly,' Daniel said. 'I love you, Gretchen, please don't doubt that. But we need more in our lives than each other.'

They had reached the S-Bahn station. She stood on the corner, the wind whipping her coat. She knew she loved him with every piece of her heart, with every breath she took, just as he loved her. What if it wasn't enough to tie them together?

'I don't know what to do,' she said at last. 'I want you to be happy more than I want you to be with me.'

His hands brushed hers. His were freezing, and she realized they had both forgotten to put on their gloves.

'We'll figure things out,' he said. 'I promise. But we'd better get out of here before one of the neighbors recognizes me.'

Together they hurried into the station. Neither of them said a word as the train roared along the track, carrying them back into Berlin's dark heart and whatever step they would take next. But every time she looked at him, his injured hand was twitching, a definite indication that he was in pain, and she wished she magically knew how to make everything in their lives right again, wounded bodies and hearts alike.

When they reached downtown, Daniel used a public telephone exchange in a café to ring a journalist friend, to find out where the murder victim had lived so they could rent a room close to her old home. Gretchen stood with her back to the street, pretending to study the loaves of bread in the next-door bakery's display window.

In the glass, she glimpsed a bloodred flicker. An enormous swastika banner fluttered from a building's facade. She couldn't look away from the reflection of the black hooked cross. She was so close to Hitler again. For all she knew, in another minute she might see his automobile drive past: a black Mercedes now instead of the red one they'd ridden in together in Munich. These days, he probably sat in the back, a more dignified position, which befitted Germany's newest chancellor, not up front with the chauffeur as he'd liked to do when he was still a rising politician.

Or they might see each other in the street, Hitler striding out of the Hotel Kaiserhof, where he had tea every afternoon, as she'd read in the English papers. He'd be distracted, arguing with one of his men when he noticed her, his electric blue eyes widening, his mouth opening in a startled shout. No disguise would fool him. If they saw each other, she wouldn't be able to escape from him a second time.

Daniel appeared at her elbow. 'My friend can't meet with us until luncheon, so we have two more hours.' His tone was clipped and impersonal. She knew they needed to speak as strangers in the street, in case someone was listening, but she couldn't help thinking that he sounded just as he had when they had first met – as though they meant nothing to each other. 'If anyone can ferret out the address, it's Tom Delmer. He's a correspondent for Britain's *Daily Express* and accompanied Hitler on his campaign trips last year.'

'Is he trustworthy?'

'Absolutely. My editor at the *Post*—' Daniel faltered, and she knew he must be thinking of his imprisoned colleagues. 'My editor liked him. That's an infallible endorsement, in my opinion. For now, it's best if we keep on the move until we see him.'

Together, they walked the long, curving streets, passing time until they could meet Herr Delmer. When they reached a crowd on a corner, Daniel didn't put his hand on the small of her back, as he usually did when they were in a cramped place, and he didn't talk. Gretchen was accustomed to his stream of conversation, the words tumbling out as though his thoughts ran so fast that his mouth had to struggle to keep pace.

His silence made her so uncomfortable that she studied the surroundings, desperate for a distraction. Everywhere she looked, she saw a fractured city: art galleries with modern paintings hanging in the windows alongside butcher shops and bakeries plastered with posters of Hitler; fancy French restaurants across the street from soup kitchens; a group of people chatting on a street corner, the ladies sporting the short hair and pale face powder of flappers, the men in artists' berets, while a few feet away, a handful of young fellows in SS black glared at them. On nearly every lamppost, white placards with Hitler's face painted in red had been pasted. Someone had scribbled in black ink across one of the pictures, giving Hitler buck teeth and crossed eyes.

Beside her, Daniel muttered, 'It looks so different. I . . .' He trailed off, and Gretchen followed his gaze. Across the avenue, a police officer in a blue greatcoat and a helmet with a metal insignia walked with a man in SA brown. They were talking companionably, and the storm trooper held a muzzled dog's leash. Each wore a shiny silver whistle hung from a cord around his neck. They looked as though they were on foot patrol.

'Are they working together?' Gretchen asked, but Daniel only shook his head, looking bewildered. Down the street, church bells chimed twelve. It was time to meet Delmer.

They crossed the street to the Romanisches Café. The large building was an ugly stone block, and its revolving door moved ceaselessly, swallowing and disgorging customers. Gretchen and Daniel stepped inside.

For an instant, they were enclosed in a triangle of glass and darkness. Warmth emanated from Daniel's body, and she half wished she could rest her head on his shoulder, breathing in his scents of soap and oranges. But she couldn't. Not with this new awkwardness between them.

The café's harshly lit interior was divided into sections: a glassed-in terrace, a small room on the left, and a larger room on the right. A circular staircase wound up to a gallery where men leaned over chessboards, arguing good-naturedly with one another.

Daniel led her toward the right. The room was crowded with round tables and wrought-iron chairs. Men sipped coffee and scribbled or sketched in notebooks. Women with faces powdered white and lips colored scarlet wrote and drew, too.

Lady artists and writers, Gretchen realized, unable to stop herself from staring. She'd never seen such people before in her own country. When she was little and lived in the Schwabing district, she'd wanted to walk home from school past the sidewalk cafés, so she could see the city's painters and sculptors sipping coffee and talking about art. But Papa had forbidden it, saying those people were degenerates.

115

A dark-haired, broad-faced man of about thirty stood when they approached his table. He wore a plain three-piece suit. Beneath his beetle brows, his eyes were sharp. 'I didn't think I would see you again, Herr Cohen.' He shook Daniel's hand, his expression cautious. 'I heard about the opposition papers being shut down in Munich. It's the devil of a business.' He glanced at Gretchen.

'This is Gisela Schröder,' Daniel said, giving the name on her false papers.

'Tom Delmer.' He bowed slightly to Gretchen and gestured at the chairs.

They ordered lunch: schnitzel with potato salad, beet salad, and two slices of rye bread for Daniel, a couple of open-faced sandwiches spread with minced pork, onions, and peppers for her and Delmer, and coffee for all of them.

Delmer leaned across the table toward them, speaking impeccable German. 'You asked on the telephone about Monika Junge. I can't tell you much. She was killed the day after the Reichstag fire, so naturally her death was eclipsed by that.'

'You were on the scene of the fire yourself, weren't you?' Daniel went silent as the waitress clunked down their plates and bustled off.

Gretchen ate quickly, scanning the other customers. They all seemed absorbed in their own conversations or notebooks.

'Yes,' Delmer replied, 'I was at the fire. I was milling about outside with the other reporters when I spotted Hitler's motorcar arrive.' His dark eyes watched them over his cup's rim. 'I joined his retinue and got into the Reichstag that way. It was quite a chaotic scene, as I'm sure you can imagine, and the story's only grown stranger – the police arrested three Bulgarian Communists here in Berlin yesterday. They'd already

116

arrested a Reichstag deputy, too, a Communist, and a half-blind Dutchman. They're saying all of them are involved in a Communist conspiracy, which a lot of people think is a pack of lies.'

His words gave Gretchen pause. Something about the fire sounded familiar – as though she had lived through this before. But that was impossible, wasn't it? She had felt the same way when she'd first heard about the fire on the radio, when she was sitting with Alfred and Julia. It didn't make any sense. Shaking off the sensation of déjà vu, she concentrated on what Delmer was saying.

'Hitler's clamoring for the supposed arsonists to be hanged,' he continued. 'A foolish thing to do, since it only reminds everyone he's an Austrian outsider.'

Gretchen understood: in Germany the sole method of execution was decapitation. Unbidden, a picture rose in her mind: Daniel, his arms fastened behind his back, being led to the guillotine, where a straw basket waited to catch his severed head. Panic tightened her throat. They had to find a way to prove his innocence, no matter what happened between them.

'I didn't kill that woman,' Daniel whispered urgently to Delmer. 'If I can get the evidence to you, will you publish it in your paper in England?'

Delmer looked Daniel straight in the face. 'Yes. It'll go on the front page, I promise you that. But I can't write the article without definitive proof – you're a reporter, you know the rules. No theories, no suppositions. Just facts.'

A muscle tightened in Daniel's jaw. 'I may have been a hack for the past year, but I still know how to report the news. I'll get you the story.'

'Good.' Delmer opened a small spiral-bound notebook. 'Speaking of facts, here's what I've found out. Fräulein Monika Junge died on the night of February twenty-eighth. She was a prostitute and quite young, only twenty. She was walking along the Tauentzienstrasse, just beyond the Kaiser Wilhelm Church, at about half past nine when a car pulled up beside her. According to witnesses, a man jumped out of the backseat and called her name. When she turned, he shot her in the head. He got back in and the car raced off. She was dead before she hit the ground.'

'Any theories about why she was killed?' Daniel asked. For once, he wasn't taking notes. Her heart plummeted as she realized why – in case they were captured, they wouldn't have papers with them that could drag other people into trouble.

'I've no idea.' Delmer closed his notebook. 'Maybe a jealous boyfriend did it. Or a lunatic or someone she looked at the wrong way, who knows. She lived at the Fleischer Rooming House off the Alexanderplatz, but that's all I was able to ferret out.'

Daniel rose and clasped the man's hand. 'Thanks, Herr Delmer. I'm much obliged.' He hesitated. 'We saw something strange on our way here – a policeman and an SA man walking together, as though they were on the same foot beat. Do you know anything about that?'

Delmer sighed. 'Germany's a new world. About two weeks ago, one of Hitler's ministers began recruiting men from the SA and the SS to work alongside the Berlin police force.' He glanced around the room, but no one was looking at their table. 'Be on your guard. The city's transforming even as we speak.'

So they couldn't even trust the police. Gretchen thought of the Sturmabteilung and the Schutzstaffel units. Since the Party's early days, the SA had served as a private army of sorts, providing muscle and protection for Hitler. The racially selective SS was a newer department. She had imagined both divisions remained entrenched within the Party. But now . . .

It was starting. What Hitler had always promised – the Party and Germany were becoming one. The union that she had once thought sounded so perfect. Now it terrified her.

She followed Daniel and Herr Delmer outside. The dry alpine wind pushed through her wool stockings into her skin. She tried not to shiver. 'Which of Hitler's ministers ordered the Party to infiltrate the police?' she asked.

Delmer turned up his collar against the cold. 'Hermann Göring.'

He continued talking, but Gretchen pulled back into her thoughts. She remembered Göring, although she hadn't seen him in years. He'd been shot in the same gunfight that had killed Papa. Afterward, he and his wife, Karin, had fled to Austria, and later they had moved to her native Sweden. When they'd returned to Germany several years ago, Gretchen hadn't seen them because they had settled in Berlin. Karin had died, Gretchen recalled, a month or two after she and Daniel had left Munich.

Göring was a vain man, constantly preening in his peacock blue suits, a dazzling sight in a sea of SA brown. And volatile – she still felt the ice of his eyes boring into hers when she'd accidentally knocked a glass knickknack off a side table in his parlor years ago. *Clumsy child*, he'd raged, and Papa had squeezed her shoulder, a silent order to apologize. *I'm sorry*, she had mumbled, and Göring had laughed, ruffling her hair, saying it was only a cheap trinket. Even back then, she'd sensed there was something unsafe about a man whose moods changed with lightning speed. And now he was in a powerful position in Hitler's cabinet. She couldn't imagine what he might be planning.

As she turned back to the conversation, she heard Delmer saying, 'And remember – you'll have to move quickly because of the Enabling Act.'

Gretchen glanced at Daniel, but he looked confused, too. 'What's the Enabling Act?' he asked.

'It's a piece of legislation that Chancellor Hitler has just proposed.' Delmer's expression was grim. He stepped closer to them, lowering his voice. 'Germany's been operating under a state of emergency since the fire. Hitler says he needs to be able to combat possible future terrorist attacks without any restrictions. If the Enabling Act passes, it shifts legislative powers from the Reichstag to him.'

Gretchen gasped. She understood what that meant: Hitler could act alone. He could pass his own laws without the restraining powers of the Reichstag, which was peopled by members of different political parties.

He could become a dictator.

Her heart clutched. If the Enabling Act was passed and she and Daniel were caught, Hitler could have anything done to them that he wished. He wouldn't have to bother with the legalities of trials and prison terms. Instead, he could have them tortured for as long as he wanted, perhaps while he watched, before he finally had them killed. They would be entirely at his mercy.

She shot Daniel a panicked look. His face had gone dark. 'When's the next Reichstag session scheduled to start?'

'On the twenty-third. You've got twelve days.' Delmer shook his head. 'The act will get passed; it's gained tremendous support within the Reichstag and in the papers. Everybody knows how elderly and ill President Hindenburg is – Chancellor Hitler will take complete control of Germany. You'll never be able to escape. Even if we publish proof of your innocence in my paper, the Party will merely cook up new charges against you.' He shook Daniel's hand. 'You don't have much time, Herr Cohen. Good luck to you.'

120

13

HERR DELMER NODDED FAREWELL TO THEM AND MELTED into the crowds streaming up and down the sidewalks. Blindly, Gretchen reached for Daniel's hand, squeezing hard when she found it.

'My God,' she breathed. 'We have to get out of Germany, while we still can.'

'You should.' Daniel started walking, and she fell in step alongside him. 'I have to see this through, Gretchen.' He dipped his head, bringing his lips to her ear. 'If I can prove that the National Socialists killed Fräulein Junge, the news could destroy Hitler's reputation. Maybe President Hindenburg will have him removed from office. His career will be over.'

'But you'll have to accomplish this in less than two weeks!' Gretchen hissed. 'If you don't find the proof before the Enabling Act passes, then . . .' She couldn't bring herself to finish.

'Then I'm as good as dead,' Daniel finished for her. His face was white, but calm. 'I understand the risk. It's worth it to me.'

They reached a street corner and stopped, waiting for a

break in traffic so they could walk across. From the corner of her eye, Gretchen studied him. There was something inside him, a length of iron that she had not recognized until this moment. It was selflessness, she realized. The absolute certainty that there were things that mattered more than his personal safety and he was willing to die for them.

She didn't know what to do about this new distance between them – but she knew she would never leave him.

'Then I'm staying, too,' she said. 'I'm seeing this through with you to the end.'

He shot her a sharp look. 'You could die, too.'

'I know.' Her hands were shaking so badly that the suitcase thudded against her leg over and over. She had to swallow twice before she could speak. 'It's worth it to me, too.'

He must have seen something in her expression that convinced him that she meant what she said because he nodded, interlacing his fingers with hers. 'Very well. There's no turning back now.' He took a deep breath, like a swimmer bracing himself before diving into icy water. 'Let's visit Monika Junge's old rooming house. It's possible the other residents know something.'

They crossed the street. In her head, Gretchen heard Hitler's voice: *a moving target doesn't get shot*. Grim determination lengthened her strides. Yes, she would remember his advice and use it against him to anticipate his every action. Before, in Munich, she hadn't known who she was dealing with. Now she understood him, as well as anyone could claim to. He wouldn't deceive her again. Whatever he did next, she would be ready.

But she couldn't stop feeling his eyes burning into her back, although every time she looked behind her, he wasn't there.

* * *

122

On the eastern end of Berlin, Gretchen and Daniel stepped into a narrow street where the harsh wind cut through their coats. Weak sunlight filtered between the tightly crammed buildings, so the houses stretched long shadows across the snow- and soot-grimed cobblestones.

Here no uniformed National Socialists walked or swastika banners hung from windowsills, and the adults moved slowly, their steps weary as though the years of hunger and spiraling unemployment had left them hollow. Daniel had been right; Berlin *was* like a dozen different cities. But would one, Gretchen wondered, eventually swallow the others?

Children streamed into the streets, laughing and calling to one another. Gretchen almost smiled at two girls wearing identical hair bows; once she and Eva had begged to be dressed alike, too, but their mothers couldn't afford the extra fabric for new dresses so they'd made do with matching red satin ribbons.

As she walked, she scanned the structures for Monika Junge's old rooming house. Up ahead, a hand-printed sign had been pasted in a window: FLEISCHER ROOMS TO LET. LADIES ONLY. The building looked like the others – a dingy gray facade stretching up four stories, and a heavy wooden door topped by a plaster archway embossed with scrollwork.

Gretchen glanced at Daniel. 'Ladies only,' she said, trying to keep her voice light so he wouldn't hear the nerves in it. 'That leaves you out. I'll inquire about a room, and see what I can learn about Fräulein Junge.'

His face twisted. 'Gretchen, I don't want you going in there alone.'

'I can manage,' she said quickly. If she waited longer, she might lose her nerve. 'Watch from across the street.' Sweat had pooled at the base of her spine, making her silk blouse stick to her skin. 'I'll be fine.'

Before she could think herself out of the decision, she hurried to the door. A middle-aged woman in a severe black dress answered the bell. 'Yes? How may I help you?' She stubbed out her cigarette in the dirt-filled flowerpot on the front step.

'I'd like to rent a room.'

The woman looked Gretchen up and down, her thin lips curling as though she had tasted something bitter. 'Nothing available.'

'But there's a sign in the window—'

'There's nothing available for you,' the woman snapped.

Over the lady's shoulder, Gretchen saw a front hall with plaster walls, stained brown in places, probably from water damage. There was no furniture, not a table or an umbrella stand, just a black telephone sitting on a chair.

What sort of rooming house was this? Her mother's old boardinghouse in Munich had been shabby, but it had at least attempted to be comfortable, with flowered sofas, wallpaper, framed watercolors.

'We only take girls with references,' the lady said.

Gretchen felt Daniel's gaze drilling into her back. It would be so easy to run to him. But she had to keep going, if she wanted to help him. She forced a smile. 'I must have misunderstood. When I saw Fräulein Junge a few weeks ago, I thought she had said there was a vacancy here.'

'Monika Junge?' The woman raised her eyebrows. 'You don't look like any of Monika's friends.'

'We weren't close.' Gretchen's face felt hot. 'I was sorry to hear about her death.'

The woman opened the door wide. 'Come in. We can't be too careful,' she added, leading Gretchen into the front hall. 'I'll show you the room.'

The door banged closed behind them. Walking up the

steps felt like climbing a hill in the dark; shadows and frigid air encased the stairwell. As Gretchen followed the landlady, she tried not to think of Daniel standing outside, probably with his fingers drumming on his thigh, a habit he slipped into when he was anxious.

The landlady rattled off the rules as they went up. 'You can rent at monthly or weekly rates. Breakfast and supper are provided, but no luncheon. There's a shared lavatory down the hall, and baths are permitted once a week. Each girl gets her own water basin, a lockbox she can store under her bed, and a supply of candles – we haven't electricity, you see. When you come and go, you have to sign in and out every time, no exceptions. My name is Frau Fleischer, by the way.'

So far, the regulations sounded ordinary enough. Gretchen relaxed a little.

As they reached the second-floor landing, sunlight straggled through a window, sparkling on a diamond ring on Frau Fleischer's finger. Gretchen nearly stumbled over the top step. A diamond ring, when Frau Fleischer couldn't afford electricity. Unease shivered up Gretchen's spine. There was something strange about this place.

'Here's your room,' Frau Fleischer said, pushing open a door. Peering in, Gretchen realized for the first time how hard her mother must have worked to hold onto her position as a boardinghouse manager; in Munich, the rooms might have been small boxes, but each resident had had her own.

Eight cots had been jammed into the long, narrow room, with two bureaus shoved against a wall. A single window poured pale winter sunlight across the women lounging on the beds or standing by the gramophone in the corner. They looked about her age, some a bit older. Three of them wore Chinese dressing robes; another lay asleep in bed, her bare shoulders peeking above the blankets, and two more were fully dressed in pleated skirts, woolen cardigans, and knee-high green leather boots. They hovered by the gramophone, arguing over which record to listen to next.

'Play nice, girls. Monika recommended a new guest, so be polite.' Frau Fleischer's voice cut through the chatter. Her long fingers grasped Gretchen's arm and pulled her forward. 'Supper's at six. If you're late, you miss it.'

'What are we having?' the girl who Gretchen had thought was sleeping asked, her eyes still closed.

'Lung soup. And no complaints!' the landlady warned as the girls groaned. 'It's food and it's hot, and none of you would be eating anything if it wasn't for me.' She glanced at Gretchen. 'You'll stay in tonight, naturally, and we can settle accounts. If you haven't had your medical checkup, I can arrange for it first thing tomorrow.'

The door slapped shut behind her. Alone, Gretchen turned to face the girls, who were watching her warily. Maybe this place was a kind of women's hostel; she knew that big cities like Berlin had such establishments, a single rung up from shelters for the indigent. But why weren't any of these girls at work? And why did she need to visit a doctor? Unease clenched her stomach.

Nobody spoke. The record spun around, its handle lifted so no music spilled from the horn-shaped speaker. A pile of blankets on a bed moved, and a black-haired head popped up, its owner yawning. 'Who's this?'

'I'm Gisela,' Gretchen said. She sat down on the only bare bed in the room. It was next to the window, and cold air pushed through the glass, right into her skin. It was obvious why no one else wanted to sleep here. 'May I have this bed?'

Silence stretched out. One of the girls went back to the gramophone, snatching the record out so clumsily that the needle scratched across the black grooved surface. At last, a

126

girl in a Chinese dressing gown said, 'That was Monika's. It doesn't seem right, someone else taking her place.'

'I was friends with her,' Gretchen said. Maybe if she could get them talking about Monika, she'd learn something useful. 'I don't know what happened to her – all I heard is that she died last week.'

For a moment, nobody answered. Some of the girls looked away. One of them sat up in bed, wiping at her eyes with the backs of her hands. 'She was shot.' Her voice was bleak. 'You'd best start unpacking. There's a lockbox under the bed for your valuables. Frau Fleischer already took Monika's things down to the office, so it should be empty. You'll have to ask her for a key. You can store your clothes in the bureaus.' She reached under her pillow, pulling out a pack of cigarettes, her robe gaping open to expose collarbones jutting beneath her pale flesh.

Gretchen knelt on the floor to pull the lockbox out from under the bed. It was a gray metal box with a hinged top. She set it on the bed and hesitated. She hated the thought of unpacking her things, for if she needed to get out quickly she'd have to leave them behind. And she couldn't let any of the girls see the revolver she had rolled up in a blouse – they'd be sure to ask questions.

They were watching her. Probably wondering why she waited. Slowly, she unfastened her suitcase, looking out the window's smudged glass. Daniel stood on the other side of the street, his bag at his feet, his fingers beating a rapid tattoo on his thigh, as she'd expected. If only she could wave to him, so he'd know she was all right.

She carried the blouses to the nearest bureau. The other girls had gone back to what they'd been doing when she'd come in: sleeping or staring at the ceiling or squabbling about music. She reached for a drawer, but the girl in the Chinese dressing gown appeared beside her and yanked it open.

'Not this one,' she said, and scooped out a handful of something white. As Gretchen watched, the girl placed the paper packets on the nearest bed, the little white squares stark against the navy chenille spread.

All of the girls spun around to watch the redhead open the packets. Nobody spoke or moved; they seemed to be holding their breaths.

The packets were filled with a fine white powder. Gretchen frowned. Headache medicine?

A petite brunette slid off her bed. Instead of dissolving the powder in a water glass, as Gretchen had expected, she leaned over the packets and inhaled sharply. A ring of white dusted each nostril. She rubbed at her nose and sighed.

Then she opened her eyes. The pupils had grown so large they nearly swallowed the irises. She smiled faintly at Gretchen. 'Want some? It's cocaine,' she added. 'It makes you forget everything.'

Gretchen took a step back. 'No, thank you.'

The girls shrugged and swarmed onto the bed, snorting the powder and sighing. In the corner, the record skipped in place, the needle caught on one discordant note.

Gretchen eased back to the bed with her armful of blouses and dumped them into her suitcase. She would leave before anyone noticed she was gone. There was no way she could stay here.

As much as she wanted to disagree with everything Hitler said, she couldn't help remembering his warnings about the dangers of nicotine and alcohol. *Impure substances weaken our blood*, he'd said to her once when she had asked why he didn't like to drink beer. *Your Aryan blood is the best part of you*, he'd added, cupping her chin in his hands, and she'd nodded, understanding. She was a girl made of blood and muscle and bone. But of the three, only her pure blood separated her from the mongrel races. She had believed she must never taint it; Uncle Dolf had made her promise. A Jew's touch would infect her with their virus, turning her into a Jew from the inside out.

But he had been wrong, she thought as she slipped across the room, clutching her suitcase tightly. Behind her, she heard mattresses sighing as the girls lay down, surrendering to the cocaine.

Her hand hovered over the doorknob. In her mind, she saw Hitler's face as he had looked the last time they had seen each other, right after he'd learned about her and Daniel. White with shock, his eyes bloodshot and disbelieving. *You're too trusting, Gretchen,* he'd said. *Everywhere, the Jew disguises himself . . .*

Daniel, true and straightforward, so unlike the men of lies she'd known before him. Even though he'd hated his life in England, he'd stayed for her sake.

She couldn't give up. For Daniel's sake, she must be willing to do anything.

Turning, she surveyed the room – most of the girls lay on their beds, tumbling into drug-hazed dreams. The small brunette was still awake, huddled on a bed in the far corner. She plucked at her dressing gown's hem, as though she couldn't stay still.

Gretchen walked back to the girl's bed. 'What happened to Monika? Who shot her?'

The girl's face was still soft with baby fat; she couldn't be any older than Gretchen. 'I don't know.' The words came out hard and angry. 'The police don't seem to care. Not even Monika's parents do – she hadn't spoken to them in years.' She swiped at the tears on her cheeks and nodded at the other girls. 'We were on the stroll when it happened.'

On the stroll . . . Surprise stopped Gretchen in her tracks.

All of these girls were prostitutes. Did this lodging house only accept boarders who worked in that profession? She remembered Frau Fleischer's comment about sending her to a doctor, and nerves coiled in her stomach. Frau Fleischer must think she was a prostitute, too. She'd have to get out of this place soon, before they figured out that she wasn't.

Stay for Daniel, she reminded herself and sat on the girl's bed, the mattress rustling under the added weight.

'What's your name?' she asked.

'Birgit.' She rubbed at the white dust coating her nostrils.

'What happened that night?'

Birgit flicked a silver lighter into life and fed the end of her cigarette into the flame. She took a long drag. 'A car pulled up. A fellow got out of the backseat. It was Monika's best customer's car. I was so curious because he'd never shown himself before.' The words tumbled out as though she was eager to talk about that night. 'Monika wouldn't ever tell me his name, although I begged. I thought at last we were going to meet this fellow, and then he called out, "Fräulein Junge!" and she turned and said, "Who are you?"' Birgit shuddered, hugging her knees to her chest. 'He pulled out a pistol and shot her in the head. She didn't make a sound. She just fell to the ground and didn't move.'

So Monika Junge hadn't known her killer. He hadn't been a jealous boyfriend or a regular customer, but someone sent with the express purpose of murdering her. She and Daniel had been right: this killing was important. Why it was, she could not yet begin to guess.

'This customer must be behind Fräulein Junge's death,' Gretchen said. 'But since she didn't recognize her killer, the customer couldn't have been the man who shot her.'

Clearly, it had been a carefully planned assassination. But why murder a lowly prostitute? Had she merely been a convenient victim, someone whose murder would go largely unnoticed? An easy crime to blame Daniel for? By February 28, the day of Monika's death, the National Socialists had known that Daniel was back in Munich. With Hindenburg as president and the Enabling Act not yet passed, Hitler's power was very limited. He must have realized that he needed a legal-looking reason to have Daniel executed.

But the scenario didn't unspool neatly like a ribbon. If the National Socialists had only wanted to pin a murder on Daniel, they would have killed an anonymous person in the street. The murderer, though, had known Fräulein Junge's name. She'd been the intended target. Her death, and Daniel being blamed for it, had been the proverbial two birds killed by a single stone.

14

DANIEL WAS STILL WAITING ACROSS THE STREET WHEN
Gretchen sneaked out twenty minutes later. His eyes burned
into hers as she hurried across the road. Up and down the
snow-dusted avenue, boys bent over games of jacks as girls
skipped rope, chanting a nursery rhyme to the steady *thwack*
of the rope hitting the ground. Daniel grabbed her hand and
pulled her into a passageway between the soot-stained houses.
Here the walls slumped toward each other so precariously
that they blotted out the weak strains of winter sunlight, and
the children's shrieks faded.

As quickly as she could, she told him everything she had
learned, ending with the part she knew would upset him: she
had asked to tag along with the rooming house girls tonight,
to see if the customer drove past. Daniel shook his head, but
she plowed on before he could interrupt.

Her offer had been refused – Frau Fleischer had said she
couldn't work, or even accompany the other girls as she'd
hoped, until she'd been checked over by a physician and
registered with the police. Prostitution might be legal in Berlin,

the Frau had advised, but the profession had rules that were well worth following. After all, she'd added, if a customer caught a venereal disease from a prostitute, he could sue her in court for causing bodily harm. The landlady had cackled, saying Gisela – Gretchen had nearly started before remembering her false name – could enjoy a rare night off.

'Which means I'll be alone tonight in the rooming house,' Gretchen said, 'We might not have such a chance again.'

Daniel nodded in instant comprehension. 'You said Frau Fleischer had Monika Junge's lockbox in her office. Maybe there's something inside that can help us figure out why she was killed.' He paused, his brows furrowed in thought. 'There's a men's hostel down the street. It looks poor, so perhaps they'll be too eager for my money to ask for my papers. I'll reserve a bed there for myself, so I can be nearby.'

He touched her face, as if he was about to kiss her, then seemed to change his mind and stepped back, his hand falling to his side. Gretchen tried to ignore the stab of disappointment. *He's miserable in England*, she reminded herself. And she couldn't imagine wanting to live anywhere else. Perhaps it was for the best if they distanced themselves from each other – even though the absence of his touch was a pain so bright and sharp, it took her breath away. She had to pause before she could speak.

'Tonight I'll open the front door when the coast's clear, so keep a watch on the house,' she said at last. 'Get a tool of some kind from a hardware store, if you can. We'll need it to break into the office. And here's some money – you'll need it for the hostel.' She gave him a few bills, which he took without a word, his cheeks slightly flushed.

'I'll see you tonight,' he said. 'Stay safe.'

They separated at the street. Back in the bedroom, the girls were asleep, and Gretchen sat on her bed, wrapping herself in the blankets Frau Fleischer had provided. Snow had started falling again. As she listened to it hissing on the windowpane, she traced in her mind the little she had seen of the rooming house's layout: the front hall, flanked by a parlor on the right, a dining room on the left, presumably with the kitchen behind. Frau Fleischer's office was probably off the parlor, close to the chimney, so she could stay warm while going over the account books.

Most likely the office was kept locked, but Gretchen doubted the mechanism was too complicated for her to pick. She had plenty of experience because Papa had taught her how when she was little.

Sitting on the bed, surrounded by the girls' shallow breathing, her old memories reared up: inching down the unheated stairwell with Papa in the middle of the night, trying not to stumble in the darkness, keeping a lookout while he fitted a thin pick into the cellar door lock. Watching as he twisted the tool back and forth until the tumblers fell into place.

Steady hands, delicate wrists, he used to say, his teeth shining white as he tried to smile. They would grab handfuls of coal from the bins in the basement; it was intended for their building's furnace, but Papa always said nobody would notice the few missing pieces they needed to heat their kitchen stove. Gretchen would giggle because that was what he wanted, but her shame made her insides hot. Her big, strong papa, who made shoes and had fought so hard in the war, was a thief.

Had he been as wicked as Hitler? Or had he been a simple man, so enthralled with his war comrade 'Adi' that he had wanted his son to become his copy? What did it say about *her*, to have a monster or a fool for a father? Hitler would proclaim that blood and birth were inescapable bonds, but Alfred would tell her that she was her own person. She prayed Alfred was right.

At six o'clock, Frau Fleischer rang the supper bell and everyone trooped down the stairs into the dining room. Gretchen sat between Birgit and the redheaded girl. Back at the boarding-house in Munich, she'd eaten in the kitchen with Mama and Reinhard, and now she found herself as shy as if she sat at a fancy restaurant and wasn't sure of her table manners.

She soon discovered that she needn't have worried; suppers at the rooming house were noisy, raucous affairs, with girls reaching over one another's plates for the bread basket and chattering loudly. Some of them talked about going to the arcade at the Haus Vaterland tomorrow afternoon. One of the girls said she wanted to try the new tearoom on the Geisbergstrasse, which brought howls of laughter and jeers that she only wanted to see the Chinese businessmen who preferred it, because they were reputed to be big tippers, and what would her beau say?

'Do you have one?' Birgit asked Gretchen.

Gretchen started. She'd been thinking of her revolver, which she'd left rolled in a blouse in her suitcase. She'd wanted to bring it with her, but none of the other girls had carried their pocket-books downstairs. 'One what?'

'A beau.' Birgit reached for her glass of beer.

'Yes,' Gretchen said automatically, then thought of what she and Daniel had said to each other by his parents' house. She picked at her bread, miserable. 'I don't know.'

Birgit laughed. 'Either you do or you don't.' She speared a green bean and waved her fork. 'I don't have a beau, and it's much easier that way. Nobody to worry about but myself. Nobody to fuss at me about my job.' She chewed while the others chattered and giggled around them. 'You look new to all this, so let me give you some advice: it's better being alone.'

The words echoed in Gretchen's head throughout supper. She smiled while the girls teased her about her modest clothes and unpainted face, and nodded as they said they'd help her get herself fixed up properly before work tomorrow night. Afterward, as they congregated in the front hall, smoking and talking as they slipped on hats and coats, Gretchen watched them from the parlor.

Better being alone . . . Was that true for her and Daniel? Since he was so unhappy in England, should she insist that he make another life for himself somewhere else, where he could find a real reporter job and friends? Maybe it was cruel to tie themselves together when he had nothing in Oxford except for her. She wished she knew what to think, how to feel. This suspension in midair was agonizing.

The door banged shut, the chatter stopping as abruptly as if a switch had been turned off. Gretchen snapped back to the present. For a moment, she stayed still, listening to the building settling. Nothing. No footfalls on the stairs, no voices calling, no toilets flushing. Frau Fleischer must be ensconced in her room for the night. It had to be now.

She turned off the gas parlor lamp, so the Frau wouldn't come down to investigate why the lights had been left on. With measured footsteps, she crossed the front hall. The prostitutes had extinguished the gas wall sconces when they'd left – apparently Frau Fleischer was as stingy about utility bills as Mama had been at the boardinghouse – and the room was a black hole. She moved cautiously until her fingers brushed the cold brass of the front door handle. It turned easily in her hand.

Lights glowed in the windows of the decrepit stone and brick buildings opposite. Across the avenue, a few men in peacoats shuffled past, the burning tips of their cigarettes red dots in the darkness. No cars coasted across the cobblestones, and there was no sound except for the whistle of wind. It was an ordinary winter night.

A lone figure jogged toward her and passed through a square of gold thrown on the ground by a window. Daniel.

He ran up the front steps and together they crept across the hall. In the parlor, the sofas and chairs were little more than massed shadows. Gretchen could trace the rectangle of the chimney, dark and straight against the whitewashed plaster walls. Beams from a passing car's headlamps swept through the room, sparkling on a brass doorknob in the far corner. Frau Fleischer's office.

Daniel twisted the handle, then shook his head. 'Locked.'

Crouching, Gretchen studied the door. A common handle and a keyhole. This should be easy. She almost smiled when Daniel took a slender lock pick from his coat pocket.

As she slid the tool into the keyhole, Daniel moved closer, ready to dash into the office the instant the door was open. Carefully, she worked the pick back and forth, concentrating on the rasp of metal on metal.

Steady hands, delicate wrists, said Papa's voice in her head. She leaned forward, twirling the pick in a slow circle until its tip caught on the locking mechanism. Barely daring to breathe, she pressed down and heard the tumblers click.

'Good work.' Daniel eased the door open. He pulled something out of his pocket and clicked it on. The flashlight's yellow circle skimmed the small box of a room: a plain wooden desk, a single chair, a dented filing cabinet. A few framed photographs dotted the walls: men sitting at a sidewalk café and smoking cigars, a couple standing on a car's running board with their arms around each other's waists, a group of dark-suited fellows playing cards.

A creaking sound froze Gretchen in place. 'Daniel, did you hear that?'

But his flashlight was trained on the photographs.

'The rings,' he gasped.

Gretchen followed his gaze. The men in the final picture sat around a large table, cigarettes dangling from their lips, smoke misting the air. They held their cards close to their chests. Each of them sported a band inlaid with a shiny stone – probably a diamond – on their left pinkie fingers.

Daniel spun to face her. 'Did any of the prostitutes or the landlady have diamond rings?'

'Frau Fleischer does.' She couldn't understand why he sounded so urgent.

'How big was the stone?'

'Huge. But why—'

'We must get out of here immediately,' he interrupted, seizing her hand with his good one. He pulled her out of the office. Somewhere she heard the creaking sound again, but close enough this time that she recognized it – a floorboard whining under someone's weight.

They raced into the parlor just as the unmistakable pop and fizzle of gas lights flaring into life sounded from the front hall. As a yellow glow flickered and grew, a black shape dashed through the entryway straight toward them.

Gretchen stumbled backward, her heart surging into her throat. Nearby, she heard Daniel cursing and wrenching the pick free from the lock.

The shape flew at them, sharpening into the bone-thin, black-dressed figure of Frau Fleischer. She carried an ancient-looking shotgun. Gretchen let out a harsh cry as the landlady swung the weapon up and jammed it against her forehead.

'Don't move,' Frau Fleischer snapped. 'The men will deal with you when they arrive. I telephoned them as soon as I heard the front door open *after* my girls had already left. Now if you so much as breathe, I'll blast your head off.'

15

GRETCHEN DIDN'T DARE MOVE. HER EYES STAYED ON Frau Fleischer, who glared back, unblinking. Her hand holding the gun was steady. Gretchen didn't feel the shotgun shaking, only its cold barrel pressing into her temple.

In the sudden hush, she heard Daniel's ragged breaths behind her, and then his low growl. 'Let her go.'

'Who the devil are you?' Frau Fleischer demanded. 'This girl's pimp? And how dare you sneak into my office! Looking for business secrets, were you? Well, you'll see how we deal with rivals trying to horn in on our territory!'

Business rivals? Did Frau Fleischer think she and Daniel belonged to a competing prostitution ring? She cursed herself for leaving her revolver upstairs.

'I'm sure we can come to an agreement of some sort.' Daniel sounded cool. His hand brushed Gretchen's as he stepped forward, but she didn't risk looking at him because the shotgun was still held against her head. 'We're not trying to harm your business.'

'You must think I'm softhearted or stupid.' Frau Fleischer

snorted. One-handed, she fished in her skirt pocket and pulled out a cigarette. She rolled the white cylinder between the fingers of her left hand. 'I'm neither.'

Moving only her eyes, Gretchen scanned the parlor. There had to be a way out of here.

The gas lamps had been turned on low, gilding the room with glimmers of gold. There were a couple of shabby brocade sofas, a few spindly wooden chairs, a wireless on a stand in the corner. The doorway was easily twenty or thirty paces away. They would never make it.

'We don't wish to infringe on your territory,' Daniel said. 'We're investigating Fräulein Junge's murder. We wanted to see her lockbox, that's all.'

The Frau's eyebrows rose. 'No one cares about our poor Monika's murder except us. Besides, you're too late. Some SA men came for it last week, the day after she was killed.'

Gretchen's pulse leapt. Why would SA men, instead of the police, retrieve Fräulein Junge's possessions unless they were somehow involved in her death? Beside Gretchen, Daniel sucked in a breath. He must have wondered the same thing. She stayed silent. The shotgun was pressed so insistently on her temple that the twin circles of the muzzle ground into her skin.

The front door burst open, blasting cold air into the parlor. Men's voices mingled together. Their footsteps crossed the hall, stopping at the entryway. Three men peered in.

They were youngish, perhaps in their early thirties, and wore black suits and bowlers. Gold and diamond bands winked on their pinkie fingers.

'What's this about?' the tallest man asked. He aimed a contemptuous look at Gretchen and Daniel. 'These are just a couple of kids.'

'Kids or not, I caught them breaking into my office,' Frau Fleischer said. 'They were looking for Monika's lockbox.'

The men exchanged swift glances. 'We'll bring them to Iron Fist Friedrich,' one of them said. 'He'll know what to do.'

Iron Fist Friedrich . . . Who was he? Terror closed Gretchen's throat.

The men seized her and Daniel, pushing them through the front hall and down the steps. A black Mercedes idled at the curb. A bearded man sat behind the driver's wheel, picking his teeth with a pocketknife. Several paces away, a group of men stopped to watch, speechless and unmoving. Nobody was going to help them.

Gretchen was shoved inside the car so hard that she half fell, half landed on the backseat. She pushed herself upright. One of the men, smelling of cigarettes and beer, slid in beside her. Frantically, she searched for Daniel – they were pushing him into the backseat, too, and his eyes met hers, wide and confused – and then another man got in behind him, so she and Daniel were hemmed in on either side. The doors slammed shut, and the car started with a lurch, its tires slipping in the snow as it took a corner too fast, heading toward whatever awaited them.

Gretchen stared out the window, searching for a chance to escape. The car had crossed the Spree River, shining silver in the darkness, and was driving west along Unter den Linden. She recognized the street's line of lime trees from photographs.

The avenue was at least two hundred feet wide and jammed with stone buildings – jewelry stores, silver shops, apartment buildings, and fine hotels. Ladies in silk and furs and men in tuxedos hurried along, laughing, their steps the unsteady stagger of the inebriated. In the street, gleaming private automobiles and taxis glided past. No National Socialist flags dripped down the fronts of buildings; no shouts or running footsteps sounded through the closed car windows. They had entered a world made of satin and velvet.

Lights from the passing streetlamps flashed over the faces of the men sitting with her and Daniel. Grim, hard, alert. The one wedged between her and the door watched her. His grip on her arm was so tight, the blood thundered in her veins under his fingers. There was no way she could wrench herself free, fling the door open, and throw herself out.

'Where are you taking us?' Daniel's voice cut through the silence.

'You'll find out soon enough,' the driver said. 'I'd shut your mouth, if I were you. Iron Fist Friedrich doesn't like people who ask questions.'

Gretchen risked a look at Daniel. He managed to smile at her, but his face was pale. His left arm was pressed against her; through the layers of their clothes, the muscles of his arm contracted. Fear and fatigue must be taking a toll on his old injury.

Through the window, she saw the Reichstag rising up on her left like a phantom. They couldn't be going there. Not to Berlin's seat of government, where Hitler now presided with President Hindenburg. *No.* She couldn't see Uncle Dolf again. She heard someone wheezing for air and realized it was herself.

The Reichstag was set in an open plaza. Its pale sandstone walls looked ghostly at night. Two-hundred-foot-tall towers stood at each of its four corners. When she was younger, she had studied its photograph in her history textbook, thinking it looked like an Italian castle.

Now it was a darkened shell. Its numerous windows were black, its walls streaked with soot. The famous glass dome was completely gone. The place looked like an abandoned building.

They can't be taking us there, she told herself even as her chest grew tight. This was ridiculous: National Socialists didn't use nicknames like 'Iron Fist'. Whoever they were dealing with, it wasn't Party men. Besides, Hitler was living a few miles south of here at the Chancellery. She wouldn't see those wild blue eyes again, focusing on hers and pinning her in place. She wouldn't hear that low, sinuous voice, chiding her for being stupid enough to fall in love with a Jew, then rising to an out-of-control shriek as he screamed that he would punish her for her betrayal. *Please*, she thought, laying a hand over her heart, begging it to slow down. Dimly, she realized the men were staring at her, and Daniel said sharply, 'Stop the car. Something's wrong with her.'

But the Mercedes shot across the Spree, pushing farther north. Gretchen sagged against the seat in relief. They weren't taking her and Daniel to see Hitler. She could withstand anything, as long as she didn't have to see him again.

Daniel's hand brushed her leg. 'Are you all right?' he asked quietly.

Before she could reply, the man beside Daniel growled, 'No talking!' She gave Daniel a smile she hoped looked reassuring.

The streets narrowed and the fine buildings changed to crumbling brick tenements. Communist flags hung in some windows. Gretchen wondered at their owners' boldness, for surely displaying support for the Communist Party after the Reichstag fire was an invitation for an arrest or a beating. Dilapidated factories rose up and fell away, their windows shuttered, their chimneys cold. They were in the slums.

The car rumbled over a bridge, pulling to a stop beside a sign reading NEW JOHANNES CEMETERY. Tiny white head-stones dotted the ground, nearly indistinguishable against the snow.

Beyond the cemetery, pine trees speared toward the star-sprinkled sky. There was no one in sight. A fresh mound of dirt marked the spot where someone had recently been buried: a pile of brown in a sea of white. This was an ideal place to conceal another body – all their captors had to do was dig up the newly turned dirt and throw her and Daniel into the hole. Nobody would know they shared this grave. Was this – a quick death in a deserted cemetery – what lay ahead of them? Gretchen had to press her fist over her mouth so she wouldn't scream.

'Let's go.' The man sitting beside her opened the door and got out.

As she scrambled outside, the frigid air hit her face like a slap. She'd left her coat at the rooming house, and the wind blew right through her skirt and silk blouse. She shivered.

Beneath her feet, the ground felt frozen; she could imagine how hard the gravediggers must have worked to make a deep enough hole. Beyond the bridge, she picked out the slum's sagging roofs and narrow chimneys, silvered by starlight. So far off. There was no way she and Daniel could make a run for it and find help. They were on their own.

16

THE TWO MEN STOOD BESIDE HER, THEIR RIGHT HANDS raised, moonlight shining on their revolvers. Daniel climbed out of the car. His hat must have fallen off for he was bare-headed now, his dark hair disheveled. His eyes met hers and he mouthed, *Don't worry*. His face looked so calm. Was he trying to protect her again? Or did he know something she didn't?

The automobile roared off, leaving the four of them alone in the snow-covered cemetery.

'What are we doing here?' Daniel asked.

'We're waiting.' The tall man looked incredulous. 'Did you really imagine we would take you to our hideout? You won't find out its location so easily. Friedrich will be brought here to deal with you instead.'

'There's been a misunderstanding.' Gretchen hugged her arms around herself to keep warm. 'Please, you must believe us—'

'Quiet!' The stocky man spun toward her and slipped in the snow, falling to his knees. The first fellow reached down to help him, and Gretchen saw her chance.

'Run!' she shouted at Daniel.

She raced across the field, dodging the headstones. She could hear Daniel's footsteps crunching in the snow behind her – she thought she heard him yell, 'Wait!' but that didn't make any sense – and she ran on. Ahead the pine trees stretched along the horizon, a black mass in the starlit darkness. She plunged into the woods, moving so fast that the tree trunks were nothing more than a blur. Her breath heaved in her chest. Somewhere behind her an automobile engine purred, but she didn't look back.

Daniel darted between the trees on her left. Behind them came the crash of branches breaking. She glanced over her shoulder. The men were rushing into the forest. Her foot caught on something, and her mind only had time to register that it was a tree root before she fell forward into the snow. She tried to scramble upright, but something was digging into her back, holding her down – a knee, she realized as she pushed against the weight – and then hands closed around her wrists and yanked her arms up, behind her back, immobilizing her. The cold snow burned her cheek.

She screamed, 'Daniel, keep going!'

The man's knee lifted, and she was dragged upright. The bearded driver glared at her – she'd been right when she'd thought she'd heard a car engine, she realized. Another man stood behind her, holding her by the wrists. She was going to die. She saw it in the men's faces.

She was shaking, but the convulsions seemed distant, as though they belonged to somebody else and she was watching from a distance. This couldn't be happening. She was trembling so hard that she had to lock her jaw to keep her teeth from chattering.

Two of the men melted into the darkness, searching for Daniel. *Keep running*, she thought at him, wishing she could magically push her words into his brain. He had to get out of here. She couldn't bear it if he was captured.

'Come,' the man clutching her wrists said. With his foot, he shoved at the back of her knee so her leg nearly buckled beneath her, the motion forcing her forward.

Dully, she walked out of the forest. Her legs felt so stiff that they nearly folded beneath her a few times. Snow had wetted the front of her blouse. She could feel goose bumps rising from her skin. The muffled sound of footfalls in snow reached her ears. She turned to look behind her. Daniel was weaving between the trees, shouting, 'Stop! Don't hurt her! Let me take her place!'

He was willing to sacrifice himself for her sake. Even though he must know his return wouldn't make any difference.

The two other men appeared behind him, grabbing his arms and marching him closer. As he passed Gretchen, he murmured, 'Trust me.'

She had never trusted anyone more. She nodded, even though she didn't understand what he meant.

They were led back in the direction from which they had come. A man leaned against the black Mercedes parked in the lane beside the cemetery. As he pushed himself off the car, he straightened to his full height – he was at least six feet and built like a wall. An unbuttoned leather greatcoat flapped over his three-piece suit. He looked to be about thirty-five. Beneath his black bowler hat, his eyes were expressionless as they flickered over Daniel, then her. This must be Iron Fist Friedrich. She saw no feeling in his face at all. They could hope for no mercy from him.

'These kids are the reason I've been called away from a dice game?' Friedrich's voice sounded like bits of gravel rubbing together. He slipped a cigar from his coat pocket and flicked a lighter into life, the orange flame hooding his eyes.

'They look like a couple of scared rabbits, hardly business rivals.'

Gretchen's guard tightened his grasp on her wrists. 'Not just business rivals, Friedrich. They're lovers. The boy came back for her.'

'Indeed.' Friedrich raised an eyebrow. Then he jerked his chin at Daniel. 'Strip him to the waist. Get your whip,' he added to the bearded man. Gretchen started to gasp, 'No,' but Iron Fist Friedrich went on.

'This gives me no pleasure,' he said to Daniel. 'But we must hold fast to our rules. And you've broken the most sacred code of all – interfering with a competitor's business affairs.' He nodded at Gretchen. 'Let's see what stuff his girl's made of.'

'Beating me isn't necessary.' Daniel sounded composed, but his pulse throbbed in his throat, where his collar had come undone. 'I can't be one of your rivals, and I'll prove it.'

Two men removed Daniel's overcoat. He put up his good hand, holding them off, and they waited, their arms tensed, ready to grab him if need be. Daniel gazed at the ground while he took off his shirt and undershirt. Shivering, he stood in the snow, stripped to the waist. It had been so long since Gretchen had seen his injured arm bared that she had to swallow a moan. She had forgotten how shocking its appearance was. A long scar extended from his left shoulder to the elbow, from where the London doctor had cut his arm open to examine the damaged tissue. His arm looked pitifully thin compared to his muscular right limb.

A murmur of surprise rippled among the men.

A flush spread up Daniel's neck. Still, he didn't look at Gretchen, but stared at the snow, his body shaking with cold. She saw goose bumps dimpling the hard ridges of his chest. The way he hung his head tore at her heart. She wished he

148

could understand that his scars made him even more beautiful to her.

Friedrich circled Daniel, studying his upper torso. 'What happened to you? Were you born like this?'

'Does it matter?' Daniel sounded bitter. 'Isn't it enough to know that none of your competitors would want me in their ranks? I can hardly provide muscle, can I?'

Friedrich laughed. 'A smart mouth on this one!' He gestured for Daniel to put his shirt on. 'I like your spirit. Get in the car. If you tell me everything I want to know, then my men won't have to beat your pretty girl.'

Gretchen raised her chin. She'd been beaten before, when Reinhard had discovered that she'd snooped in his room. Nothing these men could do to her would compare to how she'd felt that night, her eye swollen shut, her lips split, her knees and hands scraped from being flung to the floor. *I'm not afraid*, she told herself for the thousandth time.

Daniel's eyes flashed onto Gretchen's. 'You're safe,' he said softly. 'These are *Ringverein* men.'

She stared at him in confusion. Wrestling clubs? What on earth did athletic organizations have to do with anything?

Friedrich pitched his half-finished cigar into the snow, where it sizzled out. Together, he, the driver, and Daniel walked to the car. Gretchen watched them go, her mind spinning.

The Mercedes trundled across the bridge and back into the slums, leaving her alone with these three stone-faced men. They grabbed her arms and marched her over the bridge and down into the narrow, empty streets. The windows in the shabby brick tenements were dark, and none of the chimneys spiraled smoke into the sky. Several houses down, a cellar door opened and closed, letting out a blare of jazz music. A bar, perhaps. The avenue was silent except for the skittering of a dog's toenails on the pavement. The beast slunk past, thin and mangy.

Where were they taking her? Was Daniel all right? He'd said they were safe with these fellows, but why would he think that?

The men brought her to a street corner. The sign read ZWINGLISTRASSE, but it meant nothing to her. A single street-lamp cast a pale glow over the surroundings: endless crumbling tenement buildings, no cars, a few Communist banners pasted in apartment windows. Where *was* she?

A Mercedes glided to a stop beside them. Friedrich got out, then Daniel. Relief exploded in Gretchen's chest. She had to force herself not to run to him.

'According to this boy,' Friedrich said to his comrades, 'he and his girl wish to solve our Fräulein Junge's murder.'

They murmured, obviously surprised, but Friedrich silenced them with a flick of his gloved hand. 'The boy has satisfied my curiosity for the moment. Put them upstairs.'

'But then they'll know where we keep our hideout!' a man objected.

Friedrich looked annoyed. 'Don't question my authority! Take them upstairs immediately.' He stuck a new cigar in his mouth and studied Gretchen through the haze of smoke. 'We'll begin the test tomorrow.'

Gretchen didn't dare ask what he meant. Silently, she followed the men into a brick building. They guided her and Daniel through a lobby and up a stairwell, twisting around until they reached the fourth floor and there were no more stairs to climb. She had expected a corridor lined with doors, like in an ordinary apartment building, but there was only one door. Presumably this hideout took up the entire story.

They led her and Daniel through a rabbit's warren of small rooms, dark and empty except for tables and chairs. They pushed them into another room. Gretchen glimpsed

150

white plaster walls before the door slammed shut and a key rasped in the lock. She and Daniel were alone.

He placed his hands on her shoulders, peering into her face.

'I had to tell this Friedrich fellow the truth,' he said. 'As long as he understands we want to solve the murder of one of his employees, we're safe. I had to give him our real names. He'll have his men look into our backgrounds, and Gisela Schröder and Leopold Schmidt have no pasts. I'm sorry,' he added when she shrank back, her heart in her throat. 'I know you'd prefer that we remain anonymous. But *Ringverein* men despise the National Socialists. You don't have to worry about them betraying us.'

'What do these men want with us?' she whispered, afraid they might be listening on the other side of the door. 'Why do you call them *Ringverein?*'

'*Ringverein* are what they're called, but not what they are.' Daniel ran his hands over the walls and shook his head. 'These are rock solid.'

She joined him. Her damp blouse still stuck to her back, but the pain had dulled to a steady ache. The plaster walls were smooth, unadorned by decorations or pictures, and the floor was linoleum crusted with dirt. A room off a kitchen, perhaps, since wisps of heat pushed through a wall, possibly from a stove. Moonlight filtered through the single barred window, stretching lines of white across the room.

'The *Ringvereine* are shrouded in secrecy.' Daniel shook the bars in the window. 'But I know a little. They started about forty years ago, when the Berlin underworld began to organize itself into clubs that were originally set up like workers' unions. The first was dedicated to its members' physical fitness through wrestling, so the name has stuck all these years.'

151

Gretchen pressed her ear to the wall, listening for any indication that there was someone else in the apartment. From far off, footsteps tramped back and forth. At least one man had remained to guard them. 'The Berlin underworld? You mean organized crime?'

'Yes. Before I finished Gymnasium, I used to visit the *Berliner Zeitung am Mittag's* office, begging for a job.' He turned away from the window, half smiling at her. 'Not that they were interested in hiring a student. But I did pick up information from the crime reporters – you're shaking,' he interrupted himself.

Quickly, he strode across the room. 'You should get out of these wet clothes.' He started unbuttoning her blouse with his good hand. For an instant, Gretchen stood still. The sensation of his fingers through the thin fabric of her shirt was feather-light. Never before had he dared to touch her so intimately. Not even when they were traveling together to England, staying in rundown hotels, lying in the sheets and kissing each other breathless.

Now, everywhere he touched, her skin turned to flame. She sucked in a shaky breath. The sound seemed to startle Daniel, for he stepped away, his hands falling to his sides. He cleared his throat.

'I beg your pardon.' His voice was stiff.

'It's all right, I mean, I wasn't expecting—' Gretchen stammered. Her face felt hot. Before she could figure out what to say next, Daniel turned his back to her and slid off his coat. He held it out to her without looking.

'Here, you can wear this once you've taken off your things. It should keep you warm.'

'Thanks.' This new awkwardness between them felt so foreign. Maybe this morning, before she'd learned how unhappy he had been, they could have laughed about his boldness. Now she didn't know what to say to him. Judging by the rigid line of his shoulders, he felt as uncomfortable as she did.

Flushing, she peeled off the blouse and skirt, then the stockings, slip, and brassiere. She laid the sodden clothes on a chair by the window and grabbed the coat from Daniel's outstretched hand. It still held the heat from his body. She put it on gratefully, letting its warmth wrap around her. She fumbled for something to say to cut the silence.

'How do you know these men are part of a *Ringverein?* Did Friedrich tell you in the car?'

'He didn't have to.' Daniel sank onto a mattress lying in the corner. Gretchen sat down beside him. The makeshift bed was covered with a couple of thick, musty blankets. 'It was the diamond rings in the photograph that clued me in,' he continued. His voice was now matter-of-fact, his face hidden by the darkness. She couldn't guess how he felt about unbuttoning her blouse. Did he regret it? Her cheeks burned.

'*Ringverein* men get rewards for their years of service,' Daniel said. 'Gold signet rings, diamond rings, gold watch fobs, that sort of thing. Only men can be members, so Frau Fleischer is probably a widow who wears her late husband's ring.'

Gretchen remembered the diamond had been set in a thick band, like a man's ring.

'How can we trust these men?' She cast a nervous look at the door. 'We're locked in and entirely at their mercy.'

'We're far safer with them than with the National Socialists. These *Ringvereine* live by a strict code of honor. They're rarely violent and they don't kill, as a rule. They won't permit murderers or sexual criminals to join them. And they protect their members as though they're part of the same family. If we can convince Iron Fist Friedrich that we truly

153

want to solve the murder of one of his prostitutes, I believe he'll move heaven and earth to help us.'

'Then why did you become so frightened, back in Frau Fleischer's office?'

'I panicked.' He sounded embarrassed. 'I've never met a *Ringverein* man before. I don't think there are any in Munich, or I'm sure I would have come across them when I was working at the *Post*. I'd rather not get us mixed up with the criminal underworld, but it's too late now. And they could be powerful allies for us. After all, we have the same enemy.'

That Gretchen understood. For years, she'd heard Hitler promise his supporters that he would crack down on crime if he was elected. Since the end of the Great War, crime rates had skyrocketed, and voters had welcomed his pledges. *The criminal underworld is a Jewish-Communist conspiracy*, he used to thunder during speeches. *Criminality is hereditary and stamped into these men's subversive natures. They are subhumans*.

For so long, she had believed him. But Iron Fist Friedrich hadn't killed them, although he easily could have. He had even sounded reluctant when he'd thought he would have to beat answers out of Daniel.

'What's this test we're supposed to have tomorrow?' she asked.

He sighed. 'I have no idea. But there's nothing we can do about it now. We should try to get some rest.'

They slid under the blankets, Gretchen still wearing his coat. It had been so long since she had lain beside him in bed. She heard the steady exhalation of air through his nose; heard the feathers in the mattress sigh when he shifted onto his side. He was so close. If she moved her hand an inch, she would touch him. But she didn't. Instead, she closed her eyes. Somewhere, across the Spree River and down the Wilhelmstrasse, stood the massive Chancellery building. Hitler was in there. Perhaps pacing because he was an insomniac and sometimes walked his bedroom for hours before sleep claimed him. Only a few miles separated them.

I'm not afraid, she thought through gritted teeth as her heart began to race. She curled onto her side and willed her mind to black.

17

GRETCHEN'S CLOTHES HAD DRIED DURING THE NIGHT. She changed into them while Daniel stood with his back to her, although she half wished he wouldn't act so chivalrous and would sneak a glance at her, as he had when they'd shared hotel rooms on their way to England all those months ago. She still remembered the way her skin had prickled with awareness when she'd caught him, and how he had flashed his lopsided grin and turned away.

Daniel insisted that she keep his coat, and she was glad of its warmth as they explored their surroundings again. Part of her wondered if she should bring up the talk they'd had outside his parents' house yesterday, but it seemed pointless to discuss whether they had a future together when they might not have a future at all.

Dawn had washed the room white. There was no furniture, save for a chair and the mattress on the floor; it was more of a prison cell than a room. Through the window, Gretchen saw brick tenements across the street. Beyond them, smoke from nearby factories spiraled into the sky. Men and women in threadbare coats streamed out of the houses, holding their children's hands, perhaps on their way to church.

Something lay on the ground by a building's front steps, a dark shape against the snow. Gretchen pressed her nose against the glass to see better. It was a dog and lay without moving; probably it had starved or frozen to death during the night. She doubted it would last long on the street – someone would be desperate enough to take it home and cook it. The Whitestones and their well-stocked kitchen seemed like a dream, inhabitants of a world she had thought up. She pushed them out of her head before her memories brought her to tears.

Daniel joined her at the window. 'We're in Moabit. It's Berlin's worst slum. It's also a Communist stronghold, which is a point in our favor. Right now we're surrounded by the National Socialists' biggest enemies.'

Nerves clenched in Gretchen's stomach. If those men trundling to church knew that she had once been one of Hitler's favorites, what would they do to her? Automatically, she touched the swastika charm on her necklace – she'd forgotten she was wearing it. She yanked so hard on the chain, the links broke. She opened her fist to see that the charm had imprinted itself on her palm. Six little slashes that used to shape her life. How skillfully Hitler had taken the ancient sun symbol and made it his own – as he had once made her mind his, too. She shoved the broken necklace into her skirt pocket, resolving to throw it away the first opportunity she had.

The door opened and one of the men from last night entered.

'Lavatory break,' the man said, gesturing with his pistol for Gretchen to follow him.

She hesitated, reluctant to leave Daniel. But none of these men had hurt them yet, and without her revolver, she had no choice but to follow the *Ringverein* fellow. He marched her through a parlor jumbled with card tables and sagging sofas into a bathroom, to her relief.

In the spotted glass, she barely knew her face: pale, exhausted, framed with a tangle of unfamiliar brown hair. After she was led back to the room, and Daniel had returned from his trip to the lavatory, the man brought them a tray with hard rolls, cheese, and hot coffee. He waited while they ate in silence, then took the tray and left, locking the door behind him.

Gretchen couldn't stay still. What was going to happen to them? What was this test Iron Fist Friedrich had mentioned? Yesterday, she would have leaned her head on Daniel's shoulder, taking comfort from his solid presence. Today, the new distance between them felt too great. She paced back and forth, her shoes crunching on the dirty linoleum.

Daniel sat on the mattress, head hanging, hands braced on his knees. He was tired and nervous; she could see it in the way his knuckles whitened. But he still gave her a smile of encouragement when their eyes met. Everything in her yearned to go to him, to press her lips to his smiling cheek. But she couldn't bring herself to move.

The door opened again. Iron Fist Friedrich stood in the entryway, considering them sternly. Today he wore a pinstripe suit. A gold watch chain gleamed over his vest. His pale brown hair was brushed straight back from his forehead.

'It's time to prove yourselves.' He gestured for them to leave the room. 'Welcome to the hoodlums' court.'

Friedrich led them into a room crammed with about forty men all in black, some in sweaters and trousers, others in suits, their faces obscured by swirling cigar smoke. In silence, they sat on chairs or leaned against walls, watching Gretchen and Daniel as they were escorted to the table at the head of the room.

As Gretchen stared at the sea of hardened faces, Friedrich's words made sense: she and Daniel were being put on trial for their supposed robbery attempt last night, and the *Ringverein* men would be their jury.

Blindly, she reached for Daniel's hand. He squeezed her fingers, the pressure pitifully light, and she realized she had grabbed his wounded hand. She let go.

'Honesty is prized and respected within our circle,' Friedrich said. He stood beside Gretchen. 'For those who don't know, Frau Fleischer caught these two breaking into her office. Herr Cohen insists that he and his girl were only looking for information about our Fräulein Junge's murder. Let's see if he was clever enough to tell the truth. Detective Chief Superintendent Gennat?' He turned to an overweight man sitting in the first row of chairs.

Detective? Gretchen's surprise must have shown on her face, for Friedrich explained, 'Superintendent Gennat is the head of the Berlin Homicide Division, and a long-standing friend. We maintain order in the streets in our territory, and in return the superintendent respects our right to conduct our business enterprises.'

Gretchen's heart gave a hard knock against her ribs. Then there was no one they could trust completely, not even one of the top detectives in the city. She and Daniel were completely alone.

Gennat had a long, heavy face topped by a thatch of dark hair woven with silver. His eyes flashed over Gretchen and Daniel. 'Herr Cohen is indeed wanted for Fräulein Junge's murder,' he said in a rumbling voice. 'As the two detectives in charge of the case are dedicated National Socialists, however, I don't give much credence to their conclusions. Crime solving must be based on evidence, not politics, but sadly, owing to the current situation, I'm saddled with those two incompetent fellows. Fortunately for Herr Cohen, however, the only photograph we have of him is a couple of years old and he looks quite boyish in it. By all rights, I ought to haul him in, but his actions aren't those of someone who's guilty. Only an innocent man would come to Berlin to exonerate his name.

'Fräulein Müller doesn't have a file at my department,' Gennat continued, but Gretchen shivered, knowing it didn't matter whether or not she was wanted by the police. If Hitler found her, he would order her killed and Daniel executed. She could already feel a pistol jammed against the back of her head and see Daniel's neck pressing into the wooden bar of the guillotine. One instant, and they would be gone.

'Daniel,' she gasped out. Before them, the men muttered to one another, discussing Gennat's information. Daniel clasped her hand, his weakened fingers linking with hers. She held on as though his hand were a life preserver.

'Thank you, Superintendent,' Friedrich said. 'I assume we can depend on your discretion?'

Gennat lumbered to his feet. 'Yes. But if I find out this young lady and man are guilty, I'll need to bring them in. For now, they're your responsibility. I hope they're worth the trouble.'

'I think they might be.' Friedrich's smile was sharp. He nodded at his underlings. 'Escort the superintendent out, won't you?'

Two of them stood and ushered the detective from the room. Once the door had closed behind them, Friedrich turned to Gretchen and Daniel, his face a tense mask. Gretchen's chest burned as she tried to draw in a breath. What was he going to do to them?

'As you all know, the Nazis have pledged to stamp us

160

out,' he said. The room was so quiet Gretchen could hear chattering voices in the street, the cheerful sound so jarring that she started. 'They say we're subhumans – that we're wicked and beyond redemption.'

The men muttered angrily, and Friedrich raised his hands for silence.

'Now they've gone after one of our own. They must be the ones who killed our Fräulein Junge; there's no other reason some SA men would have taken her lockbox. Some of you in the room know what a sweet young woman she was. Caring to her friends, ambitious in her plans to become an actress someday. She deserved to live a long life.' He firmed his lips into a line, as though struggling to maintain his self-control.

'Herr Cohen tells me,' he went on in a low voice, 'that if we can prove the Nazis killed our Fräulein, the scandal could ruin them forever.' He nodded at Gretchen and Daniel. 'As Herr Cohen has shown himself to be both honest and an enemy of the Nazis, I propose we join forces with him and his girl and investigate our Fräulein's murder.' A grim smile twisted his lips. 'We can avenge Fräulein Junge's death and rid ourselves of our opponents once and for all.'

A hush fell. The men sat motionless, scrutinizing Gretchen and Daniel. What could they possibly be thinking? Had Friedrich convinced them?

One man's arm slowly rose. 'I agree,' he said.

More arms went up, and more, then more, until Gretchen was confronted with a forest of arms. She and Daniel smiled uncertainly at each other. Friedrich thumped the table with the flat of his hand.

'It's settled!' he announced.

The men milled about, talking and smoking, while Friedrich leaned closer to Gretchen and Daniel. 'All *Ringverein* recruits must prove themselves by completing a challenge before we offer membership – impossible for you, naturally – or our protection and help, which you'll have if you accomplish this task.'

Daniel shot him a wary glance. 'What do we have to do?'

Friedrich stubbed out his cigar in an ashtray, looking pensive. 'I haven't decided yet. Now get back into your room until I'm ready to deal with you again.'

'Thank you,' Daniel said quietly. 'You've been more than fair.'

Friedrich barked out a laugh. 'I've been your savior, and don't you forget it. If you two had stayed out in the open much longer, I'm sure the Nazis would have tracked you down. We're not so naive to pretend that we don't know what they would have done with you.'

Gretchen's throat went dry. He was right; he had kept them alive, and they were beholden to him. But what price would they have to pay?

18

GRETCHEN HAD THOUGHT THAT FRIEDRICH WOULD BE eager to begin the investigation, but he didn't return to their room that day. No one did except for a man who brought them trays of food at mealtimes and escorted them to the lavatory. As she was guided through the cigar-scented rooms, Gretchen studied the activities from the corner of her eye: a handful of men in cheap suits, playing cards and dice, and a couple poring over accounts ledgers. They fell silent when she passed, and none of them looked at her.

By the morning after the hoodlums' court, she was ready to scream with frustration. She listened to the minutes ticking past on her wristwatch – minutes they couldn't afford to lose if they wanted to solve Fräulein Junge's murder before the Enabling Act was approved. Today was the thirteenth, which meant they only had ten days left.

After her lavatory trip, the man guided her to a different room, where Daniel was waiting for her. It was a proper bedchamber, with a bed in a brass frame, a bureau holding a chipped blue-and-white water basin, a hooked rug on the floor, and wallpaper striped brown and gold. On the foot of the bed lay their two suitcases. Daniel was already going through his. He shot Gretchen's guard a wary look.

'Why is Iron Fist Friedrich having us shut up in another room?' he asked. 'We should be out investigating Fräulein Junge's murder right now!'

'Friedrich is very busy,' the fellow snapped. 'He oversees dozens of enterprises and is responsible for well over one hundred men. Consider yourselves fortunate that he's spending any time on your harebrained scheme.'

'Harebrained?' Daniel looked shaken. 'Then he doesn't believe that exposing Fräulein Junge's killer could ruin the National Socialist Party – and get rid of some of your toughest enemies?'

The fellow shrugged. 'He believes it, but he's far too clever to put all his eggs in one basket. He's ordered us to assist in your investigation, but we can't assume that it'll be successful. In the meantime, we must look after our business, Herr Cohen. Friedrich will send for you when he's ready.'

He shut the door. Gretchen flew to her suitcase, letting out a soft cry of relief when she saw her false papers lying inside, on top of the pile of her neatly folded clothes. She riffled through her things. Her revolver wasn't there, but someone had tucked her purse in the suitcase. It still held the envelope with the Whitestones' money. She looked at Daniel in surprise.

'They returned all of the money. Everything except the revolver, but that would have been too much to hope for, I suppose.'

'I would have been shocked if they'd taken your money – given their strict code of honor.' Daniel flashed her a grin. 'This is a sign. They've accepted us. We're part of them now.'

Gretchen dropped the silk blouse she'd been holding. 'What if they want us to commit crimes, too?'

164

'I'll do whatever I have to in order to survive and bring down the Party.'

'Are those the sorts of things my father told himself?' She folded the blouse, needing to keep her hands busy. 'He'd promise me that it was all right to steal coal from the building furnace because we needed it for our stove. He'd say that we should hate Jews because they grew fat off our misery.' She blinked away the tears in her eyes. 'It's such a slippery slope. You begin with one little lie, and the next one gets bigger and easier, and then the next, until you don't even know anymore what's real and what's false.'

Gently, Daniel put his good hand over hers, stilling her nervous fiddling with the blouse. 'You're not your father. You're *not*,' he said when she shook her head. How could he know how hard she'd had to fight her former ways of thinking when she'd never told him? The shame had always stopped her.

When she'd first moved to England, sometimes she had missed her old hate. Back when she'd been Uncle Dolf's darling, she'd wrapped herself in it like a coat, and felt warm and protected. Safe. Without it, she had been stripped bare. Vulnerable and aching in the cold.

Hate had made her life easy. Hitler had taught so carefully. Any of the wrongs done to her could be traced back to Jewish or Communist hands. A poor exam mark meant her teacher didn't approve of her political beliefs; a slight from friends on the playground meant the Jewish students had turned their classmates against her. Nothing was her fault.

Love was so much harder, messy and complicated and confusing. A minefield full of unexploded bombs that she must step carefully between. Walking through that field toward Daniel, though, had been worth it. She'd rather have the pain and pleasure of love than the comfort of hate.

165

'The difference between your father and us is we won't ever lie to ourselves,' Daniel said. 'Yes, we're going to work with criminals. But I wouldn't change things. Not if it means that Friedrich will help us. Stopping Hitler matters more than anything else.'

Keeping their hands linked, he guided her onto the edge of the bed, where they sat together, so close their knees touched. 'I can't stop thinking about Aaron.' His voice was ragged. 'He died alone in the hospital for *nothing*. And my colleagues – stuck in jail or who knows where because they dared to write the truth.' His thumb traced a circle in her palm, the same careless gesture he used to make when they sat in the flickering darkness of a movie theater in Oxford. The familiar motion pulled a lump into Gretchen's throat. Those days, and their old, uncomplicated relationship, seemed as though they belonged to another life.

For a moment, Daniel was quiet. 'When I was a kid,' he said at last, 'I used to get excused from religion class at school. The three other Jewish boys in my class and I would sit in the hall until the lesson was over. Nobody ever teased us. It wasn't until a few years ago that everything began to change for me, when the National Socialist Party started getting popular in Berlin.'

He paused. Gretchen waited, sensing he had more to say.

'The boys I'd been friends with for years started avoiding me,' Daniel said. 'Or mocking me to my face. One of my teachers made me and the other Jewish students sit in the same corner. He called it "Jerusalem". My father didn't get any more promotions at work.'

He glanced at her. There was a hesitance in his expression that she hadn't seen before. 'I've never told you this. It happened the year before I graduated. I was planning to attend Berlin University. I wanted to become a physicist.'

He smiled a little as Gretchen started. 'I know. It doesn't sound like me. I was different then. Anyway, I was walking home when my best friend, Otto, came up to me. He was wearing a Hitler Youth uniform. I started to tease him because he looked so ridiculous. And he – he punched me in the face.'

Gretchen gasped. 'Oh, Daniel!'

'No, please, don't say anything or I don't know if I can finish.' Daniel stared at the pool of lamplight wavering on the floor. 'I didn't know what to do. I just looked at him. And he said, "I had to do it. They're watching me." I saw some of our classmates in Hitler Youth uniforms, watching us from behind a bush. They'd wanted him to prove his loyalty to them, I guess. I didn't say anything. I just left. After supper that night, he showed up at my house to practice boxing in our cellar, as if nothing had happened. He wanted us to secretly remain friends. Because he liked me but he was ashamed of me. And that made me ashamed of myself, too.'

Gretchen's heart felt so full that she didn't know if she could contain it. Her beautiful Daniel, who kept handing her pieces of himself. Even those that humiliated him. Despite the new awkwardness between them, he wasn't afraid to share each part with her.

'I'm not ashamed of you,' she said fiercely, her hands tightening on his. 'Everything about you makes me proud.'

Finally he looked at her. His face calm, his eyes quiet. 'Thank you. I'm not ashamed anymore. But it took me a long time to get to this point. After Otto hit me, I knew I couldn't pretend anymore that things weren't changing. I started going to newspaper offices after school. I thought if I could become a reporter and write about what was happening to my people, then I could help to stop it.'

His voice broke. 'But nothing the other reporters and I did seemed to do any good. Now they're gone, with no one left to speak for them. *So* many people are gone. Dead or jailed unjustly because of Hitler. That's why I'm willing to do anything to prove the National Socialists killed that woman. I'll steal and I'll lie, if that's what it takes. But if the Enabling Act passes . . .' He took a deep breath. 'I'm afraid nothing will stop Hitler.'

He reached forward, brushing a strand of hair from her face. His smile seemed tired. 'This fight needn't be yours. You've got your papers and money. Why don't you go back to England? You deserve to have a good life.'

'I'm never leaving you,' she told him. For a moment, they looked at each other. He wanted her to leave; she saw it in the sadness in his eyes. 'But . . . what happens if we manage to get out of Germany? You said you won't go back to Oxford.'

He sighed. 'I can't. I don't know where I'll go. Wherever it is, it won't feel like home unless you're there.' He stroked the side of her face, his touch feather-soft. 'But I don't want to take you from the only real family you've ever had.'

Gretchen swallowed hard. How could she remain with Daniel and not hate him for taking her from the Whitestones and her planned career? How could he return to Oxford and not despise her for condemning him to a dead-end job and loneliness? There were no answers, at least none she could find.

'Besides,' he added softly, 'I have nothing to offer you.' His face twisted and he looked away. 'I've lost everything. My family, my home, my work. My fellow Jews are being beaten in the streets, and I can't help them.'

She'd never seen him look so depressed before: his eyes damp, his shoulders hunched, his face drained of color. 'Oh, Daniel!' she said. 'I understand how you must feel—'

'How can you possibly understand?' he interrupted. 'You've gained so much while I've only lost—' He broke off.

Suddenly, in every unhappy line of his face, she saw what he had stopped himself from saying: their relationship may have ripped her out of her old life, but she'd gained a loving family and a stable home.

And it had cost him everything. The family he loved so much, the work that had given his life meaning. The pretty home in Waidmannslust, the sense of community and faith he'd felt when he'd walked into his temple on Friday nights.

For a long moment, they stared at each other. She noticed the hollows in his cheeks, the stiff lines of his shoulders, as though he were holding himself tightly together.

'I'm so sorry,' she said. 'I never meant for any of this to happen to you.'

'It's not your fault,' he said quickly. The Adam's apple in his throat bobbed as he swallowed hard. 'Gretchen, I love you so much. No matter what.'

'I love you forever.' The words felt razor-sharp, scraping the inside of her throat. She looked at his left hand hanging at his side, the damaged fingers curled in their habitual position. How she loved those fingers. And the wasted muscle between the bones of his hand. The skinny wrist, the rigid lines of his forearm, the long scar. Every part of him. She didn't know how she would bear it, if someday she couldn't hold that injured hand again. Couldn't feel his fingers jerking in hers, and both curse the pain that plagued him and be proud of it, because it was proof of his bravery. A sob rose in her chest. She didn't want to live without him. But she also didn't want to stay with him and watch their love harden into resentment.

He cupped her face in his hands. 'I cannot give you forever,' he said softly. 'In my faith, we don't focus on the afterlife, but on our actions in the here and now. I don't even know if I believe that there's anything beyond this world. But I promise I'll love you until the day I die.'

Then he kissed her. His lips on hers were as light as a breath. And she couldn't stop the horrible thought that his touch felt like a farewell.

PART THREE
THE FIRST OF HUMAN QUALITIES

Courage is rightly esteemed the first of human qualities,
because, as has been said, it is the quality which guarantees
all others.
—*Winston Churchill*

19

IN THE KITCHEN THE NEXT MORNING, GRETCHEN FOUND the guard sitting at the table, flipping through the morning papers. The dark-haired girl from the Fleischer Rooming House sat next to him – Birgit, she remembered. Today she was dressed as simply as Gretchen in a pleated skirt and sweater set. She flashed Gretchen a cheerful grin and bit into a piece of toast slathered with jam.

'Good, you're finally up,' the *Ringverein* man said, his pale eyes meeting hers over the top of his newspaper. 'Have something to eat. Then you and Birgit need to go to Friedrich's apartment. She'll show you where it is. He wants to speak with both of you.'

'Where's Daniel?' she ventured to ask. He had been gone when she'd awoken a few minutes ago.

The fellow tossed the paper onto the table. 'At the bar down the street. There was a brawl last night, and he's helping with the cleanup.'

She wanted to ask why Daniel had been sent to work at a bar, but the hardness in the man's face stopped her. Uneasily, she sat and tried to choke down some ham and cheese with hot rolls and butter.

When she had finished, she fetched her coat from the bedroom and hurried outside with Birgit. Up and down the street, men streamed from the brick apartments, clutching sandwiches wrapped in waxed paper, their workday luncheons no doubt. Children skipped along to school. Over the roofs of the buildings, smoke from nearby factories sent black plumes into the winter-white sky.

Gretchen sneaked a glance at Birgit. When they'd talked at the rooming house, she'd seemed kind. Maybe she would answer some questions.

'I don't understand,' Gretchen said as they cut over to the next street. 'Why do they have Daniel working at a bar?'

'The bar is under our control,' Birgit said.

'So . . . Rings run businesses?'

Birgit laughed. 'No. I suppose it must be all right to tell you, seeing as you're staying at our hideout. We offer businesses protection in exchange for jobs. Each Ring has its own territory in Berlin. We keep criminals and other *Ringvereine* from robbing or causing trouble at the restaurants, nightclubs, and businesses in our area. In return, loads of fellows in our Ring work as bouncers or porters at our bars and restaurants. I fancy Friedrich is hopping mad about the fight in his bar last night. His men are supposed to prevent that sort of damage from happening.'

She huffed out an impatient breath at Gretchen's uncertain expression. 'We're not a bunch of killers. Mostly the men operate fraud schemes and loan shark businesses. Everybody pushes drugs, of course, mostly cocaine.' She fished a packet of cigarettes out of her purse, holding it up in invitation. Gretchen shook her head.

'Stealing is our bread and butter, though,' Birgit went on

174

in an unconcerned voice as she lit a cigarette. 'That's why safecrackers are at the absolute top of the Ring hierarchy. Pimps are at the bottom, and I'm afraid that we girls don't even rate a spot. Women aren't allowed to become members, you see. We're the prostitutes, wives, or girlfriends. Nothing more.'

Gretchen's head was whirling. 'Do you like it?' She wished she could snatch the words back as soon as they came out, but Birgit just laughed.

'Most of the time it's ghastly dull, but the pay's decent. I could only find work a few days a week as a telephone switchboard operator at Wertheim's, so I need the extra money. Working for this Ring is better than how I started out – I used to walk the Friedrichstrasse and the Kurfürstendamm with the other independent girls. After a customer gave me a black eye, I decided I wouldn't mind sharing a cut of my earnings in exchange for some protection, so I offered my services to *Schweigen*.'

She dragged on her cigarette, then blew out the smoke in a steady stream. As they walked, Gretchen watched the wind carry the smoke away. 'What's *Schweigen?*'

'The name of our Ring.' Birgit sounded proud. It was an appropriate name, Gretchen thought, for it meant to keep silent, and she imagined such an organization depended upon its members' discretion to survive.

'Friedrich has worked hard to make our Ring one of the most well run in Berlin, and to make sure we're connected throughout northern Germany,' Birgit went on. 'We belong to a parent group called the *Norddeutscher* Ring and have brother Rings in Dresden and Hamburg. If I wanted to, I could move to either of those cities and find a job, because those Rings would be expected to take care of me. See how well organized Friedrich is? Ah, we're here. This is his apartment.'

175

She pointed at a brick building on their left, then caught sight of something in the distance and stiffened. Gretchen followed the line of her gaze. At the far end of the street, a car had appeared. Up and down the avenue, men stopped walking, their shoulders tense, their heads swiveling as they watched the car drive past. Along the sidewalk, children continued hurrying to school, laughing, oblivious to the red automobile careering down the road. Its tires rumbled over the cobblestones, sounding loud in the sudden silence.

The car slammed to a stop a few yards from Gretchen and Birgit. Automatically, Gretchen shrank against the wall of the nearest building. What was happening?

The car doors sprang open. Men scrambled out, about five or six of them. They wore the brown uniforms of the SA. In their hands, they clutched truncheons.

Had they found her? Gretchen scanned the street, searching for a place to hide, blood roaring in her ears. Some of the factory men pulled on the children's hands, pointing at the tenements and shouting to go inside. Others remained frozen on the sidewalk, staring at the SA men. Beside her, Gretchen heard Birgit curse under her breath.

The SA men strode to the nearest shop. As she watched, they raised their truncheons high, then smashed them down on the darkened shop's windows. The glass shattered.

'Break everything in sight!' one of the men shouted.

Comprehension flashed through Gretchen's mind. It was a *Strafexpedition*, an excursion made by National Socialists into a Jewish or Communist neighborhood to punish the people who lived there. She'd heard Reinhard and his old comrades laugh about them too often to doubt what would happen next.

The SA men were going to rip the street – and everyone in it – apart.

Gretchen raced up the front steps of Friedrich's building and tried to open the door. Locked. Next to her, Birgit knocked on the door again and again, whimpering.

'Let us in!' Gretchen shouted. 'Friedrich, please!'

She looked back. Along the avenue, children and men ran to their apartments. The SA fellows had finished smashing the first shop's windows and had started on the next one. 'Communist swine!' they shouted.

Birgit pummeled the door with her fists. Another moment and the SA might notice them, two girls alone in the street. Gretchen couldn't imagine what they would do to her and Birgit. Whenever Reinhard and his friends had started talking about the girls they found during their *Strafexpeditions*, one of the boys would interrupt and tell her to leave, saying some things weren't fit for her ears.

'Stop! These are our homes, our businesses! Please!' A lone man walked toward the SA fellows, his hands outstretched in supplication. The street was almost empty now, the other residents hidden inside their apartments.

'Friedrich!' Gretchen pounded on the front door. 'Let us in!'

Behind her, someone screamed. The SA fellows had surrounded the man in a circle, lashing him with their truncheons. Through the kicking legs, Gretchen could see him crumpling to his knees, his arms wrapped protectively around his head.

The door opened so unexpectedly that she fell inside. Hands gripped her arms and held her upright. She looked up into Friedrich's furious eyes. He let her go and yanked Birgit inside, then slammed the door shut. He turned and headed up the stairs.

'Come,' he said.

Closed doors lined the second-floor corridor. Friedrich

opened the nearest one and ushered her and Birgit inside. The parlor was crammed with furniture: an overstuffed flowered sofa, chairs upholstered in pink velvet, a heavy wooden table. Warmth hit Gretchen in the face. She hadn't felt such heat in days.

'Were you hurt?' Friedrich asked. The concern in his voice surprised Gretchen, and she could only shake her head. 'Good,' he went on. 'Sit down, both of you.'

She and Birgit sank onto the sofa. From the entryway opposite, three little girls peered into the room.

'Papa,' the smallest said, 'aren't we going to be late for school?'

'There's some trouble outside.' He smiled at her. 'We'll wait for it to end before you leave. Back to your bedroom, all of you, and tell Mama to wait, too.' He glanced at Gretchen. 'I prefer not to involve my family in my business affairs.'

'Of course.' She didn't know what else to say. It was so difficult to reconcile this image of Iron Fist Friedrich as a family man with the tough criminal. 'There's a man being beaten outside,' she said. 'Perhaps you and your men . . .' She faltered under his unblinking gaze.

'Perhaps my men and I could rescue him?' He sounded sarcastic as he dropped into a chair. 'Yes, we might fight the SA off this time. But they'd only come back with more men and more weapons. I stick my neck out for my people and nobody else, Fräulein.'

Gretchen's disgust must have shown on her face because he snapped, 'Do you imagine this is how I want to live? How any of my men prefer to support their families? We do what we must to survive.' He sighed. 'Once I was in the army, but after the war ended . . .'

He said nothing more but Gretchen understood, for she'd heard Hitler complain about the military's pitiful circumstances

178

often enough. *Scores of demobilized soldiers have been released from the army, unskilled except in fighting, desperate for work*, he'd shouted. As much as she hated to agree with him, she knew he was right on this point: after Germany had surrendered in the Great War and her military had been capped at 100,000 troops, thousands of ex-soldiers had returned home without any job prospects.

'That's why you joined the *Ringverein*,' Gretchen said to Friedrich. 'To provide for your family.'

He looked her hard in the face, then nodded, as if she'd passed a test. 'Yes. Now I want to hear more about our Fräulein Junge's murder. I've already spoken to Herr Cohen about it, the other night in the car, which is why he's making himself useful at the bar this morning,' he said to Gretchen, surprising her again. She wouldn't have imagined that a top criminal would feel the need to explain himself to anyone.

'I don't know any more about it than Herr Cohen does,' she told Friedrich.

'On the contrary.' He gave her a grim smile. 'You spent years within the Nazis' inner circle. You know how they work. Your insights could prove invaluable.' He turned to Birgit. 'Tell me about the night Fräulein Junge died. Every detail.' He sat back in his chair, steepling his fingers.

'It was an ordinary night.' Birgit's voice shook a little. She bit her lip, but pushed on. 'We were walking along the Tauentzienstrasse, waiting for customers, when a gray Mercedes pulled up. It was Monika's favorite customer's car. I wanted to peek inside and see him, but I didn't dare. One time I tried, but all I could see were scarlet-colored seats before Monika scolded me off. This time, a man got out of the backseat and said her name. She turned around and asked who he was. He didn't say anything; just shot her in the head. We all ran to her, but she was already dead.'

Something rustled in the back of Gretchen's mind. A gray Mercedes with a scarlet interior was highly unusual; she knew that much from having to listen to Hitler's endless monologues about cars over the years. Why did that automobile sound familiar? Party men tended to drive black cars, except for Hitler during their years together, of course, when he'd been chauffeured in a red Mercedes—

Hitler. The recollection hit her like a punch to the chest. She knew who owned that car. She'd listened, bored, as Hitler had raved about the marvelous motorcar he'd bought as a gift. Almost two years had passed, but she remembered how jealous his comments had made her feel. The Müllers had been loyal to Uncle Dolf for years, and all he'd ever bought them were chocolates, tea, and cheap trinkets.

But for this man, who'd fled from Germany after the disastrous shoot-out in which Papa had been killed and who at the time had only recently returned to the country, Uncle Dolf had bought a car. A wonderful machine, Hitler had said, the only one made of its kind with a gray exterior and scarlet seats. It had been exhibited at a motor show in Berlin, and he'd had to have it for one of his most trusted men.

'It's Minister Göring's car,' Gretchen breathed. According to Daniel's journalist friend, Herr Delmer, Göring had begun infiltrating the Berlin police force with SA and SS troops. She struggled to pull together the scraps she knew about him. He was the new Minister of the Interior, so all of Prussia's police divisions fell under his jurisdiction. After Hitler, he was the most influential National Socialist in the country.

Friedrich shot her a sharp look. '*Hermann Göring* was Fräulein Junge's customer? You can't be serious! The fellow's one of the top Nazis. Besides, it's common knowledge that he's romancing an actress in Weimar.' He sucked in a breath. 'Maybe he had Fräulein Junge killed to keep her a secret.'

180

'That can't be,' Gretchen said as a picture rose in her mind: having tea in the back garden of Göring's fine villa in the Obermenzing suburb when she was a little girl. His wife, Karin, lying in a lawn chair, sickly, yet still lovely. Göring smoothing her hair back from her fine-boned face, his tone gentle as he asked if she needed a blanket or another cup of tea. He had loved her with a devotion Gretchen hadn't seen in many other men. 'He wouldn't cheat on Frau Göring when she was alive, and I can't imagine him cheating on this woman in Weimar. Unless he's changed completely since I knew him.'

Friedrich jumped to his feet and walked the room. Beside Gretchen, Birgit dabbed at her eyes with a handkerchief.

'I don't understand,' Friedrich burst out. 'If Göring was seeing Fräulein Junge, why kill her? Why go to the trouble of sending someone else to shoot her in the street from a car that could be tied to him?'

'Hitler likes his subordinates to be upstanding family men.' Gretchen fumbled for reasons. 'Perhaps Göring had Fräulein Junge murdered to maintain his reputation.'

'Then strangle her in an alley!' Friedrich shouted. 'Dump her body in a canal! Don't shoot her in the head in full view of her friends!'

He kicked a chair across the room. It crashed into the wall and fell onto its side. Gretchen couldn't move. She had seen that kind of rage before – from both her brother and Hitler. She knew how unpredictable it could be.

But Friedrich braced his hand on the wall and hung his head. 'I beg your pardon,' he said at last. 'Fräulein Junge was under my protection, and I failed her. I keep thinking of her, bleeding to death in the street like an animal.' He rubbed his eyes, clearly exhausted.

His words pushed a button in Gretchen's brain. He was right; the murderers had disposed of Fräulein Junge as though she were no more than a dog. But they'd killed her clumsily, driving to the scene in Göring's personal automobile and shooting her in front of dozens of witnesses.

That didn't speak of callousness, but desperation.

'Göring must have wanted her eliminated immediately,' Gretchen said. 'So he sent a man to kill her where he knew she would be at that hour of the night. If he was afraid of their relationship being exposed, he would have had her killed discreetly. But he needed her dead right away. Which means she must have known something,' Gretchen realized. 'And he wanted her silenced before she could tell anyone.'

Friedrich raised his head, his dark eyes locking on hers. 'I think you're right.' His tone was so deceptively soft that the hairs on the back of Gretchen's neck rose. 'Let's get Göring into our territory and find out for certain. Our Ring's annual ball is in four nights' time. That spoiled, overgrown child won't be able to resist an invitation, especially since he must know that the top members of the police force always come. We'll ply him with drink until he's ready to tell us anything.' Friedrich's grin was quick and angry. 'Let's see how he likes being on our turf, for a change.'

20

THE NEXT THREE DAYS SETTLED INTO A STRANGE NEW rhythm. During the day, *Ringverein* men drifted in and out of the hideout like shadows, dropping off payments and loot to one of the fellows who hung about the parlor, tallying numbers in a ledger or playing dice if there was nothing to do. Gretchen realized that no one seemed to live at the hideout. It was a place for them to store the Ring's earnings and stolen goods or congregate for meetings. Every night, a different man took turns sleeping in one of the bedrooms, presumably to watch over the Ring's money and her and Daniel.

The men themselves were quiet and polite. They all had nicknames – Bloody Hans, Muscles Gebhard – and they dressed in cheap pinstripe suits and bowler hats, like down-at-the-heel clerks, or in black sweaters, trousers, and hobnailed boots, like street toughs.

Despite her frustration at having to wait so long before the gangsters' ball, especially with the Enabling Act looming on the horizon, Gretchen found herself fascinated by the *Ringverein* men, for they were so unlike what she had expected.

The ones who worked as bouncers, bartenders, and porters at the establishments under the Ring's protection seemed proud to have respectable jobs, boasting to her that they earned steady wages.

Some of the men who worked as thieves and safecrackers asked her to demonstrate her lock-picking skills, and once she'd broken into the parlor, they'd burst into a round of applause, saying it was a pity she wasn't a man and could join them properly. Daniel had watched from the sofa, his eyebrow raised, looking as though he was struggling not to laugh.

Gretchen had smiled, but the wooden floors she walked on felt like shifting sand. These criminals stole and ran insurance scams and kept their gazes on her face, not her body. They talked about blackmail schemes and discussed the funeral expenses and pension plan for a fallen comrade's widow and children. This Berlin was a city of smoked glass, where every reflection seemed distorted. The kindest people she'd met were criminals and prostitutes. Nothing made sense anymore.

She didn't have much time to puzzle it over, though, for she was kept busy running to the bakery for poppy-seed cakes or rye bread, or to the delicatessen down the street for liverwurst and salami. Friedrich liked the kitchen to be well stocked, she was told, for any of his men who might stop by and be hungry.

Daniel had chores, too: cleaning the bar in the mornings before it opened, mopping the floors or unloading casks of beer. The work must have felt endless, as he had to do everything one-handed, but when she asked him about it, he merely shrugged, looking exhausted.

At night, they went to a bar in the central part of the city, close to the National Socialist Party's elegant new Berlin headquarters on the Vossstrasse. Lots of Party men went there for a drink, and Friedrich thought Gretchen and Daniel might pick up gossip about the SA men who'd taken Fräulein Junge's lockbox from the rooming house. He sent a couple of his newest recruits to accompany them, explaining that the National Socialists might recognize his more experienced men – after all, the *Schweigen* Ring and the Party had been bitter enemies for over a decade.

Gretchen hated going to the bar. Every minute she sat on a stool, sipping a beer and chatting up the SA fellows leaning over their drinks, she feared might be her last free one, even though on a rational level she knew that it was highly unlikely any of these men would know her face. When she'd been Hitler's pet, she'd been well known among his followers in her hometown, but the Berlin and Munich National Socialists had always revolved on separate axes. Still she couldn't stop the knots from tying in her stomach or her eyes from straying to the front door, half expecting to see Hitler there. Foolish, she knew, for as chancellor he probably didn't have the time or inclination for evenings at bars, especially since he didn't like to drink alcohol.

They learned nothing from the barroom fellows except idle chatter: Chancellor Hitler had declared that the Reichstag fire was a Communist conspiracy and was giving daily speeches, warning of the international 'red menace'; the Party had shut down the Karl Liebknecht House, Berlin's Communist headquarters, and flown swastika flags from the building. A few boasted to Daniel about what they'd done on the night of the fire: they'd been ordered to arrest Communist Party members, dragging hundreds of men from their homes and driving them to SA barracks to beat them. Daniel had grinned and clapped them on the back, saying he wished he could have seen it, but later, he'd sat in the little bedroom with Gretchen, holding his head in his hands, saying that the thought

185

of all those innocent men kidnapped from their beds made him sick.

Gretchen wished she knew how to comfort him. Once she would have wrapped her arms around him, but now she sat at his side, murmuring platitudes. Soon enough, if they were lucky, they would establish his innocence or get out of the country. Either way, they would probably leave each other's lives, so Daniel could find a new home where he could be happy. As for her, she didn't see how she could ever be happy again. With or without him, her future yawned wide like an empty hole. So she found herself uncertain what to say or how to help him.

Time was moving too fast; only six days remained until the Reichstag convened to vote on the Enabling Act. Even now, Göring and his subordinates might be manufacturing evidence against Daniel and bribing witnesses to testify. People who would claim that they'd seen Daniel step out of the gray Mercedes and shoot Fräulein Junge in the head. The men who could have proven that Daniel had been in Munich at the time of the murder were probably in jail or had gone into hiding to evade arrest.

If he was caught, it would be easy to convict him. Göring had always been an ambitious man, and arranging Daniel's arrest, trial, and execution would be quite a feather in his cap. In her nightmares, Gretchen could see Daniel walking toward the guillotine, his face pale and resolute. Resting his neck on the wooden bar while the executioner stood beside him. Then the sickening whistle of the blade as it flew down.

The gangsters' ball couldn't arrive quickly enough to suit Gretchen. Friedrich had said that she and Daniel could attend, agreeing that since Göring hadn't seen Gretchen in years he likely wouldn't recognize her. There weren't any other National Socialists who would come. Whatever information Friedrich pried out of Göring, she prayed it would help them track down definitive proof of Daniel's innocence. Something that Herr Delmer could publish in his English newspaper and use to push Hitler out of the Chancellery. But they had to get the evidence soon. Before Hitler's control seeped into every aspect of the government and police departments. Before the trap swung shut.

The night before the ball was the Ring's weekly meeting. Gretchen and Daniel were in their bedroom, waiting for it to be over so they could try out a different National Socialist – frequented bar. Although they sat inches apart on the edge of the bed, Gretchen felt as far from him as if they were in different rooms. If only he would give her one of his old careless grins, or she knew the right words to say to shorten this distance between them.

Through the door, she heard the rumble of Friedrich's voice.

'Light Fingers Matthias was seen drunk in public. Three marks' fine. Matthias, that's the last time, or I'll have to take your membership pin, do you understand?' He plowed on without waiting for a response. 'How's the insurance scam coming along – what's the meaning of this interruption?'

'I beg your pardon,' gasped a girl's voice. Gretchen sat up, startled. It was Birgit. 'But Frau Fleischer wanted me to tell you straightaway – she knows who took Monika's lockbox. His photograph was in a newspaper. He was shown with Chancellor Hitler.'

Gretchen's and Daniel's eyes met. *This is it*, he mouthed, and she nodded, her heart racing. At last, they had something tangible to go on.

'Who is he?' Friedrich's tone was cold.

'The paper didn't mention his name.' Birgit sounded

apologetic. 'It showed a picture of Hitler making a speech. This fellow was one of the SA men surrounding the podium.'

Daniel dashed from the room into the parlor, Gretchen following close behind. The room was so full of black-clad men, leaning against the walls or sitting on chairs crammed together, that there was no space for her or Daniel to walk. They stood in the doorway, squinting to see through the wall of cigarette smoke. Friedrich swung around to look at them.

'These meetings are private affairs,' he growled, but Daniel shook his head.

'I know how to find out the man's name.' He glanced at Birgit, who was twisting her hands together anxiously. 'What newspaper was it? And what did the SA fellow look like?'

'*Berliner Tageblatt.*' Birgit bit her lip, thinking. 'Tall. He was wearing an SA uniform, of course. And he was standing on the ground directly below Hitler on the stage, if that helps.'

'Give me a minute.' Daniel ran into the corridor. Gretchen heard the clicking sound of the telephone earpiece being picked up. Daniel's voice floated back into the silent parlor, where everybody seemed to be holding their breaths. 'Herr Delmer? It's Cohen. Listen, did you see today's *BT* edition? Good. Who's the tall SA fellow right below Hitler in the photograph? . . . You're certain? . . . All right, thanks, I owe you a favor. Yes, again.'

He slammed the earpiece down and raced back into the room. 'He's Helmut Weiss, one of Hitler's new bodyguards. My friend said that Hitler's delivering a speech at the Sportpalast tonight and Weiss is sure to be there. If I leave right now, I should be able to get there early enough to talk to him and nip out before Hitler comes in. Hitler always likes to keep the crowd waiting for a few minutes. That's all the time I should need.'

'How the devil do you propose tricking one of Hitler's

bodyguards into telling you anything?' Friedrich surged to his feet, his chair scraping over the floorboards. 'You've got guts, I'll grant you that, but you're not a miracle worker.'

'I won't need a miracle.' Daniel's eyes were dark and determined. Gretchen's heart sank at the sight – he was resolved to do this incredibly dangerous thing. 'When I was a reporter in Munich, I talked to dozens of Party men. I know how to get information out of them. *Trust me*,' he added when Friedrich said nothing.

'Very well.' Friedrich sighed. 'I hope you know what you're doing, Herr Cohen. Birgit, you'll go with him, so you can show him which fellow Weiss is. I'm afraid my recruits already have an assignment to break into a watch repair shop tonight, and the rest of us are far too recognizable to show up at a Party speech.'

Gretchen's heart thundered in her chest. There was no way she wanted Daniel going without her. But she could still feel the heat of Hitler's hands as he lifted hers to his lips to kiss. In her mind, she heard the deep cadence of his voice, the words slow at first, then speeding up until they rushed forward like a freight train and she'd had to hold on for dear life. *You're a child, my sunshine, and can't understand yet the dangers that the Jews pose to our nation. They poison us from within . . .*

She looked at Daniel, who was talking quietly with Friedrich, and the pressure in her chest eased. Despite everything that had come between them, he was still her Daniel, straightforward and loyal and true. She couldn't let him go alone, and the danger would be minimal as long as they left before Hitler arrived.

She found her voice. 'I'm going, too.'

Daniel spun around to stare at her, shaking his head. Her hands clenched into fists at her sides, but she said steadily,

'You forget that I grew up surrounded by Party men – I know how to handle them, too. I want to help.'

Then he smiled at her, such a clear, grateful smile that she could almost pretend the uneasiness between them didn't exist.

They took an omnibus across the river. It dropped them off on the Potsdamerstrasse and they walked down the street toward a massive white building with the black letters BERLIN SPORTPALAST spelled across its front. Lights blazed from its windows. The indoor stadium was set back from the road, and cars rolled along the pavement, disgorging fashionably attired Berliners, the ladies in furs, the men in camel-hair coats. Others, modestly dressed in rough jackets or plain dresses, strolled in from the street.

Gretchen and Birgit walked on either side of Daniel. None of them spoke. Gretchen shoved her hands in her coat pockets, so nobody could see how badly they were shaking. Hitler might be here already, sitting in a back room, sipping mineral water and waiting for the moment to make his grand entrance. Or he was being driven through the city, staring out the window at the buildings sliding past, reviewing his planned words in his head.

He won't see you, she promised herself. Daniel had been right when he'd said that Hitler liked to keep the crowds waiting for a few minutes. They'd talk to the SA man Weiss and slip out before Hitler entered. Still, her stomach was roiling.

They joined the groups swarming inside and entered a cavernous room. Enormous swastika banners hung from the ceiling. Hundreds of folding chairs had been set up in rows across the floor, which Daniel had explained during the bus ride lay beneath an ice rink or a bicycle arena on other occasions. A main aisle ran between the rows of seats; it was lined with poles topped with National Socialist standards – carved metal swastikas surrounded by garlands, with silver eagles perched above.

Hundreds of people, perhaps as many as a thousand, walked to their seats, chattering with one another. The sight took Gretchen's breath away. She'd been to the shabby Circus Krone in Munich countless times to watch Hitler talk, but back then the audience had usually consisted of a few hundred people. She had sat in a position of privilege in the front row, so close she could see the sweat pearling on Hitler's forehead and hear the rasp of his voice. It had been nothing like the spectacle unfurling around her now.

'That's him,' Birgit whispered. 'Third from the left.'

A wooden stage had been erected at the stadium's far end; it contained a dozen chairs and a podium. SA men ringed the stage, their feet wide apart, their arms folded behind their backs, ready to spring forward and drag out hecklers. The fellow who Birgit had indicated was burly and blank-faced. Gretchen suppressed a shudder. Just the sort of brainless hulk that Hitler preferred for his SA troops.

'Let's go. Remember to follow my lead.' Daniel wove between the crowds, Gretchen and Birgit following. They stopped a few feet away from Weiss. Birgit fished her compact out of her purse and peered into it, pretending to fuss with her appearance, a ruse they had agreed upon during the bus ride. Gretchen fiddled with her wristwatch, trying to look bored. From the corner of her eye, she watched Daniel amble toward the stage, straining to hear him above the song blaring from the loudspeakers. He looked relaxed, his hands in his pockets.

'Big crowd tonight,' he said to Weiss, who grunted. 'I don't suppose you'd be willing to give me a quote or two? I've got to turn in an article tonight to my editor or he'll have my hide. They're terrible taskmasters at the *Berliner Zeitung*.'

Weiss grunted again. 'Filthy rag. Owned by a couple of Jews.'

'Well, we'll see how long they can hold on to it.' Daniel flashed him a grin. 'My boss has been giving me a rough time ever since that girl got killed in the street a couple of weeks ago – maybe you heard about it. Monika Junge? Shot in the head?'

Weiss shifted. 'You'd better find a seat. The chancellor should be here any minute.'

'We've got time yet.' Daniel stepped closer to Weiss, giving him a conspiratorial smile. 'Take pity on me, will you? My boss is convinced that Fräulein Junge's death is some sort of cover-up, no matter what I say to him. I've got to come up with a scoop tonight or he'll sack me.'

'Your boss is a fool,' Weiss snapped. 'That's your scoop.'

'A fool?' Daniel grinned wider while Gretchen watched, her heart in her throat. *Be careful*, she thought at him, but he continued talking. 'Come now! You can't say something like that without backing it up.' He raised an eyebrow. 'I heard you fellows took the girl's possessions. Sounds significant to me.'

Weiss leaned closer to Daniel, his face hard. 'Tell your boss to drop the story. There's nothing in it. I know – we were looking for the girl's diary. Her diary!' He snorted in open disgust. 'What sort of task is that for me and my men? We didn't even find it. Stupid waste of time.'

'Thanks,' Daniel said cheerfully. 'I'll convince him to find another pet story.'

Whistling, he strolled away. Birgit looped her arm through Gretchen's and they followed him, skirting the rows of chairs while Gretchen's thoughts spun. What secrets were hidden in Fräulein Junge's diary? And, most important of all, where was it now?

192

Most people had sat down, talking quietly with one another. Several yards away policemen in dark blue uniforms guarded the entrance; Gretchen wondered if they were expecting trouble tonight. It was hardly her concern, though. A few more minutes and they would be out of this place.

The German anthem started up. People stood, turning to look at the back of the stadium. Their arms whipped up in the National Socialist salute.

'Sieg Heil, Sieg Heil!'

That was the signal that Hitler was entering the room. Gretchen let out a half-strangled gasp. They were too late. They couldn't reach the doors and slip outside before Hitler came in. If they tried to leave, they'd attract the attention of the hundreds of people in the stadium.

The apology was clear on Daniel's face. There was nothing they could do.

She would have to see Hitler again.

Everything in her went hot, then cold, at the thought. Dear God, what if he recognized her? Or she couldn't control her fear and burst into frantic sobs as soon as she heard his voice? *I can't do this*, she thought, but the chorus of *Sieg Heils* had risen to a roar. Hitler was coming, and there was nowhere she could run.

Daniel grabbed her hand and tugged her toward a row of seats. She stumbled after him, her knee connecting with the back of a chair. Dimly, she was aware of pain flaring up and down her leg, but she barely felt a thing. She stood woodenly. As if lifted by an invisible string, her arm rose automatically in the Nazi salute. On either side of her, Daniel and Birgit raised their arms, too.

The shouts of *Sieg Heil* filled the air. Through the crush of bodies, Gretchen had to strain to see a figure striding down the aisle. He looked to be about average height and wore a brown Party uniform with a red swastika brassard on his right arm. The sloping line of his shoulders was instantly familiar. The blood in her veins turned to ice.

It was Hitler.

21

AS HE CAME CLOSER, HIS IMAGE SHARPENED INTO FOCUS.
His face still held that half-starved look she remembered so
well. Beneath the stadium's harsh lights, his cheeks looked
pale and paper-thin. Above them, his electric blue eyes were
focused on the stage ahead. Brilliantine glistened on his brown
hair. The lips that used to kiss her hands were tight lines now
– exactly how she recalled he used to set his mouth before
launching into a speech, as though he had to hold the stream
of words inside. His mustache was the same dark smudge.
He didn't look as though he'd changed at all.

She shrank back and ducked her head, blood roaring in
her ears. All it would take was one glance, and Hitler would
recognize her. She and Daniel would never escape. On all sides
they were surrounded by Party members who wouldn't hesitate
to kill or beat them.

Through the strands of her hair, she watched Hitler
approach her row. *Please don't look, please don't look*, she
begged silently, staying motionless, fearing the slightest movement would catch his eye. As he neared, she glimpsed his

uniform – a suit jacket and matching khaki-colored trousers. It was finer than anything she'd seen him wear before. Back in the old days, he'd usually worn a blue serge suit, much mended, but of which he was terribly proud.

Then he swept past her, and her legs turned to water. She grabbed the chair in front of her for support. Ahead, he climbed the steps to the stage. The thousand or so people were screaming now. '*Sieg Heil, Sieg Heil!*' Hitler looked down at them sternly, then saluted them. The people shouted louder. '*Heil, Heil!*'

Hitler raised both of his hands. The crowd immediately quieted and sat down. Mechanically, Gretchen sat, too. *There are a few hundred people between us*, she told herself. *I'm not afraid.*

It was a lie. The pressure on her chest was so heavy she feared she was going to pass out. Daniel's good hand found hers and gripped it hard.

'The great epoch for which we have waited for so long is finally upon us,' Hitler said. The loudspeakers magnified his voice so it sounded as though there were dozens of Hitlers speaking all around the stadium in unison. Gretchen wanted to cover her ears. He sounded different; there was a scratchiness to his voice that she hadn't heard before. Perhaps he'd damaged his throat by screaming so much during speeches, as her mother had warned him.

'Germany has awakened,' he continued. 'For years, our great nation has struggled against the perils of democracy, of parliamentarianism, of Communism. Those political systems pledge freedom, but their promises are illusory.

'The Communists' goal is the destruction of all non-Jewish nations.' Hitler shook his fist in the air. Gretchen remembered seeing him practice the same movement while Papa nodded admiringly. The whole thing was nothing more than

196

a carefully orchestrated performance. 'The Communists' cowardly act of setting fire to the Reichstag was a God-given signal that a new epoch in German history is upon us! Through all of the Communists' assaults, we have remained steadfast and strong. The virtue that has sustained us is bravery. That is what will assure us of our eventual victory!'

With each word, he spoke faster and louder until he was almost screaming. He leaned over the podium, clutching its sides, strands of sweat-dampened hair hanging over his forehead. His face had turned bright red. The audience roared its approval.

'Beat the Red Front to pulp!' a group of men in SA brown shouted from a few rows behind Gretchen. It was the same rallying cry she'd heard during countless speeches over the years, after Hitler had warned the audience about the dangers their strongest political opponents, the Communists, posed. Once she had shouted those words, too, convinced that Communism was like a foul disease stretching across the Russian steppes to infect so many European countries. Now she understood why Hitler hated the Communists so much: they were strong and they were in his way.

Hitler raised his hand, signaling that he wanted silence. A hush fell over the crowd. 'Communism,' he said slowly, 'is the product of Jewish minds. The time has come at last to expose the Communists as the foul Jews and cowards that they are! Germany awake!'

'Germany awake, perish the Jew!' the audience chanted back. It was the same phrase Gretchen had heard and parroted when she was younger, little realizing the meaning behind it. Not understanding that Hitler was saying that if Germany wanted to survive, then its Jews had to die.

Daniel's hand tightened on Gretchen's. His expression was calm, but the way his fingers grasped hers told her how furious and helpless he must feel. He looked at her, a muscle clenching in his jaw, and she tried to smile, hoping he realized what she was trying to tell him: she didn't believe the lies anymore. He smiled faintly back.

When the speech ended, Hitler strode out while the music was still playing, his old trick to avoid his supporters who might want to haggle over points he'd made. Gretchen's heart pounded when he approached her row, but again, he didn't look at her, only straight ahead. It was his custom, Gretchen knew, his way of disconnecting slightly from his audience, so he could seem above them. But what if he happened to glance her way? He would recognize her, she knew it. The hair dye and cosmetics wouldn't fool him.

He was coming closer, so near she could see flakes of dandruff dusting his shoulders, white flecks on brown. Her heart surged into her throat. *Don't look, don't look*, she begged. She tried to tear her gaze away, but she couldn't keep herself from staring at him. Even now, she felt herself as drawn to him as a moth to an open flame. There was something impossibly mesmerizing about him – something glittering and powerful, a lightning strike that dazzled the eyes long after it had sizzled into nothingness.

He was only a few feet away now. Her arm, raised in the salute, shook from the effort of holding it aloft. Soon he would see her. He must.

But he passed her row, his eyes still focused in the distance. She sagged in relief, letting her arm fall, her fingers curling around the back of the chair in front of her for balance. Around her, the audience broke into little clumps, talking about those wretched Communists. Daniel placed his hand on the small of her back, jolting her. She followed him and Birgit to the exit. It took all of her self-control not to push people out of the way and race from the hall.

They caught an omnibus at the corner. It was crowded, and Daniel insisted that Gretchen and Birgit take a seat together while he sat at the only other empty spot, among a cluster of drunkards singing 'Mack the Knife'.

'So he's your "sort-of" beau?' Birgit nodded at where Daniel sat at the back of the bus. 'What's sort-of about it? He's rather gorgeous. You ought to lay claim to him before someone else does.'

Heat rushed into Gretchen's cheeks. 'It's not that simple. There's no way we can stay together and have everything we need to be happy.'

Birgit rolled her eyes. 'Of course you can't have everything. Why the devil did you think you could?'

Gretchen opened her mouth to reply, then shut it in surprise. Was Birgit right? Was it impossible for any one person to have each of the pieces she needed to make her existence whole? She and Daniel had already sacrificed so much for each other's sake. How could she give up the Whitestones, the first proper family she'd ever had, or Daniel, his cherished career, and not watch their love warp into loneliness and anger? Tears pricked the backs of her eyes. It was impossible.

'I'll give you some advice, though Lord knows you prob ably won't want it.' Birgit settled back in the seat, all the merriment gone from her face. 'I grew up very poor – there were seven of us in a one-room apartment. I left school as soon as I could, four years ago when I was fourteen. I wanted to help support my family, so I've done – well, you know what I've done.'

Her usual confident manner was gone, her voice soft and hesitant. 'Monika was a lot like me. She came from a rich family in the Charlottenburg district, but she'd left home when she was quite young, too.' The corner of her mouth pulled up, a flicker of a smile. 'She wanted to be an actress, you see,

199

and her parents thought that was beneath her. So she supported herself however she could while she went on auditions. I don't think she ever landed a role. She got so discouraged. That's when she turned to cocaine. I – I need it, too. To help me forget what I have to do at night.'

She pulled a handkerchief from her purse, but her eyes remained dry. Gretchen shifted uncomfortably. 'Birgit, you don't need to tell me any of this, if you don't want to—'

'I want to so you can understand,' Birgit interrupted fiercely. 'You have something beautiful with him and you're ready to throw it away because it isn't easy. I saw how he looked when you said you wanted to go to the Sportpalast with him. As though he'd been punched in the stomach. As though he'd do everything in his power to protect you.'

In her lap, she twisted the handkerchief into a rope. 'Monika would have done anything to have a man look at her that way. Lord knows she tried to find a man who loved her so deeply.' She let out a shuddering breath. 'But he had her killed instead. And I . . . I'll never find a decent boy who can overlook what I have to do.'

Gretchen couldn't help thinking of Geli and Eva. Had they, too, been desperate to find a man who loved them? Was that why Eva had carved herself down into someone Gretchen barely recognized?

Slowly, she became aware of Birgit's stare. She didn't know what to say to her. 'I'm sorry,' she said at last. 'I had no idea how difficult your lives were. And I do love Daniel. So much that I'm willing to give him up, if that's what it takes for him to find a place where he can be happy. If he goes back with me, he won't be able to find work and he'll be miserable,' she added in a low voice. 'I can't bear to have him abandon his career for me. I'd rather be without him than cause him any unhappiness.'

200

'Oh.' Birgit let out a heavy sigh. 'That's true love, then, what you have. And I'm the one who's sorry.'

She rested her arm over Gretchen's shoulders, drawing her closer. They sat in the jostling bus, their heads touching, just as Gretchen and Eva used to do when they were little and sharing secrets. Gretchen closed her eyes and let a few tears slide out from under her lids. It was too much – the possibility of losing Daniel, seeing Hitler again, reliving the old memories of Eva and her family.

Tears wouldn't change anything. She opened her eyes. Through the window, she watched the Tiergarten rise up. The massive park seemed frozen under a layer of snow. Little lamps flickered among the trees like dozens of fireflies, the tiny gold orbs reflecting off the snow so the ground glittered. Figures walked the pathways, moving from the shadows into the light from the lanterns and back again. They reminded Gretchen of the trapped souls in Dante's *Inferno*, never fully in the dawn or the dark but caught somewhere in between. Like Hitler. She shivered and looked away. He wasn't here. But she could have sworn she heard the low cadence of his voice and smelled his scent of toothpaste and sugar.

Back at the hideout, Daniel was jubilant. 'That fellow Weiss walked right into my trap!' he told Friedrich, who had stopped by in between rounds of some of the nightclubs under his protection. 'He said they were looking for Fräulein Junge's diary, but didn't find it.'

Friedrich tapped his fingers together thoughtfully. 'Which means it's still out there somewhere. And we'd better find it first. I can't imagine where she would have kept it, if it wasn't in her lockbox. We'll see what I can pry out of Göring at the ball tomorrow night.' He thumped Daniel on the shoulder.

'Excellent work, Herr Cohen. You and your girl should get some rest. Tomorrow night will be a long one.'

Grinning, Daniel took Gretchen's hand and they walked to the bedroom they shared. Behind them, Gretchen heard the front door open and close; Friedrich was gone, and the only other occupant of the darkened apartment was tonight's *Ringverein* guard. The place was so quiet, she could imagine that she and Daniel were alone.

'Are you all right?' he asked. 'After seeing Hitler?'

She tried to nod, but tears filled her eyes instead. 'He looks the *same*,' she burst out. 'After what he did to Papa and Reinhard – he should feel *something*! I used to think he felt emotions so keenly. When I was little, I remember how he'd become so angry or depressed, sometimes for days at a stretch. But now he seems to go on and on and on without feeling a thing.' She took a shuddering breath, swiping at her eyes with the back of her hand. 'He ruined my family, and he doesn't care.'

Daniel wrapped his good arm around her. 'No, he doesn't. I'm so sorry, Gretchen.'

She pressed her face into his neck, her body shaking with sobs.

'Oh, Gretchen.' Daniel sounded desperate. 'Please don't cry. I can bear anything except your tears.'

He held her closer and kissed her cheek. Her heart started hammering. She had missed this – the feel of his mouth on hers, the sense that they were sharing a breath. Without thinking, she reached up just as he bent down and their lips met. The room seemed to fall away, and the thunder of Hitler's voice in the stadium; the tight ache in her throat; the tinkle of glass as SA men smashed shop windows; the swastika banners snapping in the breeze; and police wagons rumbling over the cobblestones in Munich. All she felt was the heat of his mouth and his hands, rubbing up and down her arms.

She kissed him back, on the mouth, the soft skin of his temple, the curve of his neck, until the tension had melted from her body and all of her muscles felt as warm and liquid-smooth as honey. Through her blouse, his hand caressed her back with his fingertips, his touch sending shivers down to her toes.

'My Gretchen,' he murmured, his lips a breath away from hers.

His voice snapped Gretchen back to the present. She pulled away from him. Daniel's eyes flew open. The moonlight painted his cheeks with silver, showing the surprise on his face. 'What's wrong?'

'I – I can't kiss you. Not when things feel so uncertain between us.' She looked away from his stricken expression, biting her lip so she had a different pain to concentrate on.

He embraced her, pressing his cheek against hers. 'We'll figure things out,' he said into her hair. 'I promise.'

'How?' she said. 'There are no solutions for us.'

'I don't know.' There was such sadness in his voice that tears rose to her eyes again. 'I just don't know.'

She stood in his arms, listening to his heart beat in rhythm with hers, a steady thump as regular as clockwork. Wishing she knew if she had the rest of her life to hear that reassuring sound or only days, if they proved his innocence and parted forever. Wondering if tomorrow night's gangsters' ball would bring them closer to the answers they sought – and push them further apart.

The next night, they took a taxi across the Spree to the Hotel Adlon, where the Ring's annual ball was being held. They spoke little, and what they said was formal and polite, the conversation of acquaintances. Fatigue had left the inside of Gretchen's mind as gray and sluggish as a puddle of rainwater.

203

Several times during the night, she had woken with a hammering heart, trying to hold on to the lingering wisps of her dreams. Hitler's voice, low and laughing, and the taste of sugar on her tongue were all that remained. As she had burrowed under the blankets again, she wondered why she felt as though she was forgetting something.

Now, as she sat beside Daniel in the taxi, he looked tense, his fingers tapping on his thigh. *Five days*, Gretchen thought. That was all that remained until the Enabling Act was brought to a vote before the Reichstag. They were running out of time.

As they alighted on the sidewalk, Gretchen caught their images in the cab's back window. They were almost unrecognizable, even to her eyes. Members of the *Ringverein* had lent them clothes for the evening. Daniel wore a tuxedo, a white silk scarf around his neck, his slicked-back hair hidden by a top hat. Gretchen had rouged her cheeks and painted her lips red. With her short hair curling around her face, she looked like a flapper – so unlike the girl in childish braids that Hitler had known. Her gold column dress and black sequined wrap glittered in the glass before the taxi pulled away into the traffic streaming up and down Unter den Linden. It seemed like a dream that they had been driven down this street as prisoners of the *Ringverein* just seven nights ago. Today she'd even been given her revolver back – yet more proof that these *Ringverein* men were people of their word, and an uneasy trust existed among them. Gretchen carried the Webley in her black evening bag. Its weight was comforting.

'Ready?' Daniel asked.

'Yes,' Gretchen said, but nerves knotted her stomach. Together, she and Daniel crossed the pavement toward the massive hotel. They had been there once before, months ago, when they had met Herr Professor Forster, who had treated her father and Hitler at the end of the Great War and admitted that he had diagnosed Hitler as a psychopath.

The hotel looked different at night, its dozens of windows blazing with golden light. A long striped awning extended from its entrance to the street, to protect the beautifully dressed men and women slipping out of taxis and private automobiles. Elaborate lanterns on either side of the front doors illuminated the bronze plates beneath etched with the words 'Hotel Adlon.'

They joined the guests filing inside. The lobby reminded her of the illustrations she'd seen of Bavarian palaces. The yellow marble pillars stretched to the ceiling high overhead. Everywhere dark and white marble gleamed, and porters in pale blue peaked caps whisked guests' bags into the elevator.

She and Daniel followed the line of men in top hats and tails and women in evening dresses into the ballroom. At the entrance, she paused for an instant, dazzled by the spectacle. Chandelier lights threw glittering squares of gold across the room. Swing music cascaded from the orchestra's bandstand, a quick, sinuous rhythm of brass and drums. At a glance, Gretchen guessed there were about two hundred people crammed into the ballroom. Couples spun around the dance floor, the ladies' gowns blurring into a long smear of red and blue and silver, the men's tuxedo tails swirling. For an instant, she wished she and Daniel could join them, dancing and laughing as if they hadn't a care in the world.

Don't, she told herself sharply. There was no sense in wanting things that couldn't possibly happen. Her eyes squinted to see through the cigarette-laced air. Along the ballroom's edges, a couple dozen *Ringverein* men and their girlfriends or wives stood, smoking, drinking, laughing so loudly that the sounds of their merriment cut through the music. Diamonds sparkled around the women's necks, and the men's hair gleamed with pomade. She recognized many of the fellows from the hideout, although they looked drastically different in their tuxedos.

Long tables, laden with silver platters of hors d'oeuvres, had been set up along the room's perimeter. Gretchen had never seen such food – oysters in the shell, finger sandwiches, caviar, paper-thin crackers. It was hard to fathom that across the Spree there lived people who subsisted on horse meat and lung soup that cost a measly sixty pfennigs a bowl.

With Daniel's hand on the small of her back, Gretchen wove between the guests, searching for Hermann Göring, but there was no sign of him. He'd accepted Friedrich's invitation immediately, but perhaps he'd changed his mind about attending. She tried to ignore the ache of disappointment. *He'll be here,* she promised herself. The lure of gourmet food and the social cachet of attending a gangsters' ball would be too much for him to resist.

They sat at a table jammed against the wall. Daniel hadn't used the hat check, as he wanted his things nearby in case they needed to leave suddenly, so he set his hat and walking stick on a chair. Gretchen laid her wrap over them.

'That's him.' Daniel's hand gripped her arm. 'At the entrance.'

She peered between the dancing bodies. A hugely overweight man in a tuxedo stood by the doorway. Surprise stole her voice. There was no question it was Göring; even from this distance she recognized his icy eyes and fair hair glistening with brilliantine. But the face she'd remembered as long and aquiline had grown broad and florid. The once-trim figure was now buried in rolls of excess flesh. She'd heard he'd gained weight after he'd been shot in the putsch with her father, but she'd had no inkling he was so transformed.

As she watched, Friedrich ambled over to Göring. Though the music and raised voices made it impossible to hear what

206

they said, she saw them shake hands and laugh. A National Socialist and a *Ringverein* man, sworn enemies, chuckling over a shared joke. She shook her head in disbelief. Daniel had warned her that Berlin's freewheeling atmosphere was another world from provincial Munich, but she hadn't really understood until this moment.

'Let's get closer so we can listen.' Daniel's voice was a warm murmur in her ear. 'Friedrich said he might want to duck away and ask you for advice on how to handle Göring.'

'Very well.'

They skirted the edges of the dance floor. A group of men, red-faced with drink, staggered into them. Gretchen lost her grip on Daniel's hand. She spun to look for him, but all she saw was a line of girls about her age, blowing out rings of cigarette smoke or gulping champagne. One was chattering about the new trapeze act at the Wintergarten; another was whining that she only had three marks, not nearly enough for a packet of cocaine.

She tried to slither away from them, but they were packed so tightly together that there was no pathway to ease herself through. The girls' elbows knocked into her back as they gestured, complaining that it was simply too ridiculous that you couldn't buy cocaine for less than five marks these days. Gretchen turned, searching for Daniel, and found herself facing a National Socialist Party pin, a white circle rimmed with red and intersected by a black swastika, pinned to a jacket lapel. Her heart surged into her throat. Göring was the only National Socialist in attendance – the only person who would wear such a button. She let her eyes travel up to the man's face and the blood in her veins cooled to ice. It was him.

Please, please don't remember me, she begged silently. He smiled blandly at her. 'What a pleasure to see a delicate flower among weeds. How do you do, Fräulein?'

'Very well.' She heard the words coming out of her mouth automatically. What would Alfred tell her to do? The image of Göring and Hitler sitting on her family's threadbare sofa rushed back to her, Göring in a finely tailored suit he couldn't possibly have been able to afford, Hitler in a worn blue suit and brown leather vest and shoes with a hole in the bottom. *Appeal to his vanity*, she thought, and somehow she pulled her lips into a smile she prayed looked natural. 'I'm a great admirer of yours, Minister Göring.'

'You're a Bavarian!' he exclaimed, and she cursed her accent. 'You've come a long way from home.' He guided her toward the bar and held up two fingers at the bartender. Gretchen glanced at the labels on the bottles: Clicquot, Mumm, Heidsiek, Roederer, four different types of champagne alone. She'd never seen such extravagance. 'What do you think of our great city?'

This question she knew the answer to; most National Socialists followed Hitler's lead and despised Berlin, calling it a cesspool of corruption and depravity. 'It's awful.'

Chuckling, Göring took the champagne flutes from the bartender and handed her one. 'It's not as bad as that.' His voice was light and kindly. 'Berlin's music and theaters are marvelous.'

The response startled Gretchen so much that she took a sip to give herself time to figure out what to say. How could she handle this fellow? A National Socialist who didn't jump onto the Party bandwagon was more of a challenge than she had anticipated. Through the fog of cigarette smoke, she saw Daniel moving toward them from several feet away, and she shook her head slightly. He stepped back, his face tight, his gaze trained on her face.

'So you say you're an admirer of mine?' Göring asked. Above his glass, his eyes met hers – they were as she remembered, a sharp bright blue, like a lake frozen solid. 'I confess I'm surprised. I thought you *Ringverein* types weren't interested in politics.'

She went hot all over at her blunder. What in heaven's name could she say to him? Just then a loud voice boomed close behind her. 'Minister Göring! You see I've left my sickbed to join you! If it hadn't been for Chancellor Hitler and the wretched tin can he calls an airplane, I wouldn't have succumbed to the flu in the first place! But no, he must make speeches in three separate cities in one day. Twelve hours in an airplane – pure misery!'

Gretchen stilled. No. It was impossible. The newcomer sounded exactly like Ernst Hanfstaengl, the Party's foreign press chief, who had watched her grow up and who had been her boss at the National Socialist headquarters. But he still lived in Munich with his wife and son – didn't he? *Oh, God.* Please let it not be him! There was no way he wouldn't recognize her.

She had to get out. Now.

'Fortunately, you had excellent accommodations for your recovery.' Göring laughed. 'Fräulein, may I present Herr Hanfstaengl? He has been a guest at my palace for several weeks.'

She kept her head down, letting her curls slide forward to curtain her face. 'A pleasure,' she muttered. 'Please, excuse me – some fresh air—'

She started to move away, but Göring's hand clapped down on her shoulder, anchoring her in place.

'I'm gratified to make your acquaintance.' From the corner of her eye, she saw a dark blur: Hanfstaengl bending forward in an elaborate bow. 'Yes, Minister Göring has been kind enough to let me stay with him until I can find proper lodgings for my family. And I've been grateful for his offer or else

209

I'd be stuck in that monstrosity where Herr Hitler lives! Why, the hideous place is symbolic of everything that's been wrong with the government since the war ended. Did you know the riots used to be so bad that they constructed a secret passage from the attic running all the way to this hotel, so that the chancellor could escape in emergencies? What a shambles our government has been! But that will all change.' He barked out a laugh. 'Herr Hitler plans to have the passage walled up. He won't need it.'

'Fascinating,' Gretchen murmured. What could she do? If she ran, they'd wonder why and might chase her. If she looked up . . .

'Shut your mouth, can't you, Hanfstaengl?' Göring hissed. 'Need I remind you where we are? Ah, there's our host coming toward us. Behave yourself.'

Göring's hand slipped from her shoulder. This was her chance. She slid her eyes to the left and saw Daniel pushing through the masses of people to get to her. She held up her hand, hoping he understood that he needed to stay back. Since Göring wanted him caught for murder, surely he'd acquainted himself with Daniel's criminal file – and photograph.

'Pardon me,' she muttered and plunged into the crowd, weaving between the tightly clustered people, her heartbeat thundering in her ears.

'Wait a minute,' she heard Hanfstaengl say behind her. 'There's something familiar about that girl.'

She started to move forward just as a hand fastened on her wrist and whipped her around. Motionless, Hanfstaengl stared down at her, a towering figure almost six and a half feet tall. He looked the same: a long face with a lantern jaw, wiry hair falling over his forehead, wide shoulders. Several feet behind him, Gretchen glimpsed Göring, who had already turned away to chat with someone else.

Hanfstaengl raised a trembling hand to push back the hair hanging in his eyes, as though he needed to see better. 'My God,' he said.

He had recognized her.

22

GRETCHEN COULDN'T LOOK AWAY FROM HANFSTAENGL'S face. *'Please,'* she whispered while all around them guests laughed and danced and drank. He wouldn't betray her, would he? Not after all the years they'd known each other. He'd watched her grow up.

Hanfstaengl's hand gripped her shoulder; his fingers felt hot through her dress's strap. His face had settled into a grim expression she'd never seen before. 'You stupid child,' he snapped. 'What sort of game do you think you're playing? Surely you must know what will happen to you if Herr Hitler knows you're in Berlin.'

'Please,' she said again, 'Herr Hanfstaengl, if you ever cared for me at all, don't tell anyone I'm here.'

He glared down at her. 'Of course I won't; I don't want you to die, you lovesick fool. I suppose you came to Berlin for your Jew.' Before she could figure out how to reply, he grabbed her hands and pulled her onto the dance floor so roughly that she stumbled and fell against him. He smelled of cologne and hair cream. 'Did you know he's wanted for murder?' he growled into her ear, yanking her into his arms and clapping a hand on her waist. 'That's the repellent creature you've destroyed your life for. Now dance. Laugh. Act as though you're having a good time.'

'He didn't do it,' she started to say, but Hanfstaengl flicked a hand dismissively, silencing her. A band had woven around her chest, drawing tighter until she could scarcely breathe. Automatically, she began to move in Hanfstaengl's arms. Through her gown, his fingers dug into her waist. She still carried her pocketbook, and they had to clutch it awkwardly between their clasped hands.

As they whirled across the dance floor, the other guests blurred into an endless series of colors: black, gold, red, lavender, blue, silver, green. Somewhere among them she caught Göring and Friedrich, chatting, their postures relaxed, and a few feet from them, Daniel, looking pale and intent. She shook her head at Daniel again, hoping he would continue to stay back. Hanfstaengl might care enough about her to let her go, but he would have no compunction about turning Daniel in to the police.

As she and Hanfstaengl danced, her mind worked furiously. He had mentioned Daniel being wanted for murder. It was possible he knew more. And this might be her only chance to find out. She looked up at Hanfstaengl and forced a smile. 'Surely you realize that's nonsense about Herr Cohen. He isn't stupid enough to kill anyone, especially Minister Göring's mistress.'

The shot had hit home; she saw the muscles along his jaw tighten. 'How do you know that?' As usual, he didn't wait for an answer, but plowed on. 'She was no mistress. Only a plaything to take his mind off his loneliness. He hasn't been the same since his wife died. And don't you dare insinuate that Göring had anything to do with the girl's death,' he warned, pulling her closer into his arms, his schnapps-scented breath washing over her face. 'On the last day of her life, he only saw her for a few minutes. Lord knows why he bothered. No doubt she was pestering him for attention again. Göring's innocent – he didn't have a spare instant to shoot the girl.'

Hanfstaengl twirled her around. There was something about his words that didn't make sense, but she couldn't snatch hold of what was bothering her. The other dancers whirled past, their steps clumsy from drink. Nearby, a man slipped and fell to the floor, laughing so hard that he couldn't get up. Other men hauled him upright by the armpits, saying it was time he switched to coffee – and she realized. *Time.* That was what was wrong with Hanfstaengl's story. Why would Göring have spent any time, even a few minutes, with Fräulein Junge on what must have been an extremely busy day for him, when he was dealing with the aftermath of the Reichstag fire? Whatever the reason for their meeting, it must have been urgent.

Hanfstaengl drew Gretchen close to him again. She leaned back in his arms, trying to smile at him in her old playful way. 'Well, I haven't been able to find Herr Cohen to ask for his side of the story. By now he's probably in Austria.' She kept her tone light. *Stay back, Daniel*, she pleaded silently. 'What does Minister Göring say about his last day with Fräulein Junge?'

Hanfstaengl's face tightened with irritation. 'He was terribly cut up by her death and had nothing to do with her murder. He keeps saying at least her last day was a happy one because—'

He broke off, looking startled. 'What an idiot I've been! I need to go.' He released her and took a few steps away, then spun to look at her, his expression tinged with sadness. 'You must leave Berlin at once,' he said gently. 'Herr Hitler despises you, and if he knew you were back, he would stop at nothing to run you to ground. Forget your Jew. Go back to wherever you've been hiding all this time – if not for your sake, then for your father's. He didn't sacrifice his life so you could throw yours away.'

She didn't know how to reply. As much as she longed to tell Hanfstaengl the truth about her father's death, she knew he would never believe it and her words would only infuriate him. Before she could beg him to stay and explain more, he had left the dance floor and was heading toward Göring, who was sipping champagne. She scanned the crowds for Daniel; he still stood near Göring. When their eyes met, she jerked her head at Hanfstaengl's retreating figure and he nodded in instant comprehension. He sidled closer to Göring, and as Gretchen watched him, she silently urged him not to let Göring catch sight of his face.

She slipped to the edge of the ballroom. Through the swirl of dancing bodies, she could see Hanfstaengl reach the bar and bend down to talk to Göring. Daniel stood a few feet away with his back to them, watching the couples waltzing past. Göring slammed his glass down on the bar. His face had gone red. He turned and pushed his way between the guests toward the entrance, Hanfstaengl on his heels. Where were they going? What had Hanfstaengl figured out?

Daniel rushed through the throngs toward her. 'Hanfstaengl remembered that Fräulein Junge had gone to her parents' house on the day she died,' he murmured in her ear. 'But she'd been estranged from them for years. Göring said that he remembered picking straw out of her hair when he picked her up that afternoon. She must have been in her parents' stables.'

'Why would they care that she went there?' Gretchen whispered. Between the dancers' bodies, she spied an overweight man raising the conductor's baton – it was Ernst Gennat, the chief superintendent of the homicide department. The *Ringverein* men had said it was customary for the highest-ranking policeman in attendance to conduct the orchestra's last number. In a few minutes, the room would be flooded with people trying to leave. 'Maybe she'd reconciled with her parents. Or—'

'Or maybe she hid something in the stables,' Daniel interrupted urgently. 'Remember that Weiss said they were looking for her diary? Maybe she concealed it at her parents'.'

Gretchen's pulse leapt. Daniel could be right. Which meant that Göring was sending his men to the Junges' house at this very second. They had to get there first.

A taxi carried them to the Charlottenburg district. At the hotel, they had asked the clerk at the front desk for the city directory. Listings for the name Junge had filled several pages, and in desperation, Gretchen had dashed into the ballroom to find Birgit, who had told her that Monika's father was named Ulrich and he lived somewhere on the Hardenbergstrasse. Armed with that information, locating the house number in the directory had been easy, and Gretchen and Daniel had run outside to the line of taxis idling at the curb.

A sharp rain had begun falling by the time they passed an enormous temple on the Fasanenstrasse. Gretchen had expected the shabby synagogues she was accustomed to seeing in Munich, built in backyards, sheltered from pedestrians' eyes. Through the icy needles, she saw a stately and ornate stone building that stood right on the street. The builders' boldness in constructing such a structure in plain view stole her breath in shock.

Then the car rolled on. Outside the window, rain washed the street black. Large houses lined the avenue. There was no trash in the gutter, no loud music, no prostitutes or drug pushers lurking on the corner, no flash of bloodred banners. She and Daniel had reached another world.

The taxi glided to a stop. Gretchen paid, grateful that Friedrich had returned the Whitestones' money to her. She and Daniel scrambled out of the taxi.

For an instant, they stood on the pavement, listening. Nothing. Only the patter of rain, washing away the thin layer of snow, and the purr of the taxi's engine as it drove off. If Göring had sent his underlings to the Junges' house, they hadn't arrived yet.

'Let's go.' Daniel nodded at the narrow driveway next to the Junges' house. Gretchen crept after him into the darkness, wincing when loose gravel crunched under her shoes. Rain trickled down her bare arms. She shivered. She'd forgotten her wrap in the ballroom, and Daniel had left his hat and walking stick.

They sneaked past the house. Trees, black outlines in the night, dotted the backyard. The yard sloped down to two bulky shapes, presumably the garage and the stables. Gretchen thought she heard the whicker of horses.

They cut across the yard, breaking into a run. The snow- and rain-soaked grass was slippery under Gretchen's heeled shoes. She nearly fell, grabbing Daniel's arm for balance. He hissed in pain, and she let go instantly.

'Your arm! I'm sorry.'

'It doesn't matter.' Daniel pointed to a shiny padlock hanging from the stable door. 'Think you can pick that?'

As she bent to examine it, tires screeched from the street. Car doors slammed and boots thudded across the pavement. Gretchen's heart clenched. Göring's men had arrived.

Daniel cursed. 'There's no time.' He whipped off his scarf and wound it around his hand. 'Stand back,' he ordered, then punched through the window next to the door. The glass broke with a faint tinkle.

Several jagged shards remained, but Daniel brushed them off. He wriggled through the opening and dropped from sight.

Gretchen looked over her shoulder. Streetlamps backlit the men rushing down the drive, but she recognized their SA caps. Had they seen her?

Fear made her move quickly. She seized the bottom of the window frame and hauled herself up. The opening was narrow, but she managed to squeeze through and fell to the floor below. She threw out her arms to catch herself, landing so hard that her hands smarted.

She scrambled to her feet. A row of stalls stretched along one wall; on the other Gretchen saw hooks laden with harnesses. The horses shifted in the stalls, straw rustling under their hooves. The smell of manure, mixed with oats, assailed her nose.

'Daniel!' she said as loudly as she dared. 'They're coming!'

He was staring at the stalls. An engraved plaque had been nailed to each of them. CHESTNUT, SUNSHINE. These must be the horses' names. MAVERICK, LOVER.

'Lover!' Daniel whispered. 'This is where she hid the diary, it must be!'

They raced to the stall gate. The horse reared up on its hind legs, whinnying. It kicked its front legs and Gretchen pulled Daniel away. 'We can't go in there! He'll trample you!'

The stable doors banged back and forth. The men must be pulling on the padlock chain.

'It's too late!' Gretchen hissed. 'We have to go!'

Daniel didn't seem to hear. He leapt up and grabbed at Lover's plaque. It came loose from its wooden post with a scream of nails. Something small and dark was stuck beneath the plaque. It had been pierced through by a nail. Daniel

218

wrenched it free and threw the plaque to the floor, where it landed with a metallic clang.

'The window's been broken!' a man shouted from outside. 'Somebody's already in there!'

Gretchen and Daniel flung themselves at the back door. It swayed but didn't give under their combined weight. Probably it was padlocked from the exterior.

'Take this.' Daniel thrust the object into her hand – a small cardboard box, she saw now – and he shoved his hand, still wrapped in the scarf, through the window. The glass shattered. Tiny crystalline flecks hit Gretchen's shoulders.

'Someone's trying to get out the back!' one of the men yelled.

Daniel boosted her into the opening. Pieces of glass pricked her dress, but she kept pulling her body through. Below, the wet ground gleamed palely with snow and rain and ahead loomed a tall brick wall. She heaved herself out the window.

She landed on her knees. In an instant, she was up and pushing the box into her dress's bodice, so she could have her hands free. She sprang as hard as she could at the wall. Her fingers grasped the top, the rough brick scratching her palms. Gritting her teeth, she held on and pulled herself up.

She heard Daniel jumping into the grass behind her. Behind her, men shouted, their voices and footsteps growing louder as they rounded the stables. Gretchen peered into the darkness beyond the brick wall and flung herself off the ledge.

23

THE IMPACT JOLTED HER SO HARD THAT THE BONES IN her knees crunched. Daniel landed beside her. Together, they raced up the sloping yard, nearly slipping in the snow. A darkened outline loomed up ahead: another big house, unlit at this late hour.

Gretchen looked back over her shoulder. Nothing except apple trees. No bobbing flashlights, no angry shouts.

'They're not following us,' she managed to gasp out.

Daniel kept running. 'They're probably hoping to cut us off at this street. Hurry!'

They raced down the driveway and into an empty road. The rain was falling harder now, and the fine houses opposite wavered behind sheets of water. Around a corner, a car's headlamps, two misted yellow circles, appeared in the gloom.

'They're coming!' Gretchen whispered.

'We can't hope to outrun them.' Daniel glanced around the street. 'Come on.' He grabbed her hand, pulling her toward the nearest house. They skidded to a stop next to the front steps. Gretchen risked a look over her shoulder. Through the wall of rain, the car's headlamps glowed as it slowly rolled down the avenue.

Daniel braced his good hand on the railing and kicked at the wood planking that formed the bottom sides of the porch. The wood broke with a vicious crack. Daniel kicked again and more pieces of wood splintered, leaving behind a small hole. The darkness beneath the porch yawned like an open mouth.

'Get in,' Daniel panted, and Gretchen didn't hesitate. She wriggled through the hole. On her hands and knees, she crawled forward to give Daniel room to get inside. The ground felt soft and damp. She tried to sit up but knocked her head on the porch floor, white-hot pain bursting at the top of her skull. Gritting her teeth, she didn't make a sound.

Daniel lay beside her in the shadows. He let out a sudden piercing cry and curled into a ball. Gretchen crawled toward him. 'What's wrong?' she asked.

'My arm,' he gasped out. 'It feels like it's about to explode.'

She had seen this happen a few times before, when his damaged nerves turned to flame and he writhed in agony, moaning. Pain attacks, he called them. They usually lasted a few minutes. And he was always loud during them – crying out in torment.

Her heart clutched. 'Daniel, you *have* to be quiet.'

'I – I don't know if I can,' he choked out. He had gone white to his lips; the only spots of color in his face came from his eyes, which were dark and feverish. He was making noises low in his throat, like a wounded animal.

From the street sounded the rumble of an automobile. Göring's men were coming.

Gretchen touched Daniel's arm. Under her fingers, the muscles rippled, as though something alive were moving beneath his skin. Then they contracted, stiffening until they

221

felt like metal. Daniel groaned. The breath came quick and hard through his nose.

Tires thudded over the cobblestones, the sound muted by the rain. The low purr of the car's engine died. There was the metallic wrenching sound of car doors opening, then the click of boots on the pavement.

'They can't have gone far,' a man shouted.

Gretchen's and Daniel's eyes met. *I'm sorry*, his seemed to say. He clapped his good hand over his mouth, trying to stifle his moans.

Frantically, Gretchen looked around, but she could barely see anything in the darkness. Her wrap, which she could have used to muffle Daniel, was still at the ballroom. There had to be *something* she could use. She ran her hands over the dirt, even though she knew it was hopeless.

Footsteps sounded on the pavement a few feet away. They were so near. If Daniel couldn't hold back his cries anymore, they would definitely hear him. Gretchen scrabbled in the dirt. Nothing. She glanced at Daniel.

A wave of pain hit him – she could tell by the way his entire body stiffened – and he bit down on his lip so hard that he drew blood. It trickled down his chin in a long line. He didn't make a sound.

'Nobody here!' a man called from the street. 'Let's get going.'

Car doors slammed and its engine growled to life. Gretchen listened to the automobile slide away, its tires shushing in the rain. When she couldn't hear them anymore, she crawled back to Daniel's side. His face was dead-white, and sweat had stuck strands of his hair to his forehead. Gretchen fumbled for a handkerchief in her purse, using it to mop Daniel's face. His eyes focused on hers, dark and steady, but neither of them said a word. The car might return. The seconds lengthened, endless and quiet. There was only the icy patter of rain on brick. No whoosh of tires on pavement, no tramp of jackboots, no shouts.

At last she spoke. 'Are you well enough to go?'

'I'll manage.' He rolled to his hands and knees, wincing when he put weight on his left hand. In that instant, Gretchen wanted nothing more than to take his poor hand in hers, press her lips to his palm. But she didn't know how to cross this strange distance between them. Besides, she had to protect herself. If they managed to escape from Germany, there was no telling where Daniel would end up and how far from each other they would have to live. She had to start disentangling herself from him, or she was afraid she'd never be able to. Loving him and losing him was better than staying with him and hating him for taking her from the Whitestones and her planned career. But the prospect still felt like a vise around her chest, squeezing until she couldn't draw a deep enough breath.

Daniel crawled toward the hole in the porch wall. 'We'd better get to the hideout and open the box.'

Gretchen pulled it from her dress. She didn't say what she was certain they were both thinking: the diary, if that was what was inside, might have cost Fräulein Junge her life.

They took another taxi back to the hideout. An exorbitant expense, but it couldn't be helped; they could hardly board the late-running S-Bahn trains in their ripped evening wear. Gretchen held the cardboard box tightly on her lap as the car wended the long streets. The box was so small it fit in one of her hands and was dotted with raindrops. If only she could open it, but she didn't dare under the driver's curious gaze.

They left the taxi on a side street near the Spree River and took another, and then a third, hoping to cover their tracks this way. At the hideout, they changed out of their soaked clothes and into the men's flannel pajamas that the *Ringverein* guard provided; apparently, they kept a supply of nightclothes for the members who took turns sleeping there. Gretchen still felt cold to the bone.

The *Ringverein* man had gone to the kitchen to telephone Friedrich, leaving Gretchen and Daniel alone in the parlor. Daniel opened the box, the wet cardboard coming apart in his hands. Inside lay a small book covered in red-and-white-checked cloth. The diary. Gretchen's pulse throbbed unevenly with excitement.

They flipped through the pages. The short entries had been written in a sloping hand. After skimming through the first few, Gretchen remembered that Friedrich had said that Fräulein Junge had been an aspiring actress. She'd been a real person with career plans and dreams.

Nineteen thirty-two rushed past: auditions Monika had gone on and roles she'd lost to other actresses, cold nights on the stroll, afternoons lost in cocaine-fueled dreams, yearning to break free from the drugs but coming back to their oblivion again and again. Over the winter, the entries changed.

> *I bungled the audition, of course, for my head ached so badly I could scarcely remember my lines, let alone say them with the proper feeling. But it hardly matters! A most wonderful man stopped by the theater. I recognized him at once - I doubt there's a soul in Berlin who doesn't know his face, and I was thrilled, for he's known to be a great lover of the theater and could nudge my career forward. Afterward, he invited me to go on a drive.*

*Naturally I refused, for I can't waste an
evening when I should be making money.
But he was most persistent, and in the end
I agreed to go with him the following
afternoon.*

Daniel raised an eyebrow. 'The romance begins.'

From then on the pages were full of Hermann – Gretchen
nearly started at seeing Göring's first name, for she remembered
his love for titles and grandeur, and when she was a little girl
she'd had to address him as Captain, not Herr. Fräulein Junge
and Göring had taken long drives to Potsdam, talking about
art in the backseat, far from curious eyes. They'd sneaked into
the Wintergarten after the lights had gone down, and watched
trapeze artists swing below a star-flecked blue ceiling.

By last month, the tone had changed:

*Hermann says he wants companionship,
not romance! For so long, I've thought
his love for his late wife stopped him
from touching me. He would ask instead
that I fill his head with my silly chatter.
As though I were no more than a child.
I understand now. He's lonely, and so I
would do for company. But he doesn't
want me. He has a woman in Weimar.
An actress, so perhaps she isn't quite a
lady, but she must be better than I am.
A Cabinet man mustn't be seen with the
likes of me, I know.*

The page was dotted with sepia-toned circles. Tears, most
likely. Gretchen touched the wrinkled spots on the paper. Poor,

troubled Monika. It had taken her so long to realize that she was nothing more than a sweet voice to break the silence. *Like Eva*, Gretchen thought. Would her friend ever figure out that she was nothing more than a toy to Hitler?

Daniel turned the page, shaking his head. 'Fräulein Junge has started complaining,' he said. 'Now she's become a liability to Göring.'

The final entry was dated 28 February 1933 – the day after the fire, Gretchen recalled, probably written a few hours before Monika was killed. Almost three weeks ago – and two weeks before Gretchen herself had arrived in Germany.

I've just spoken with Hermann, Monika had scribbled.

> *He telephoned the rooming house to cancel our luncheon date. Isn't that like a man! Wanting you only on his timetable. He was in a foul mood, muttering something about a nosy fireman, Heinz somebody-or-other, and saying he was exhausted since he'd spent the whole night shuttling between his ministry office and the Reichstag, to keep track of the fire's progress. Poor Hermann. As angry as I get sometimes, I really must make more allowances for him. He has many responsibilities and they weigh on him heavily.*
>
> *I need to hide this book, so none of the other girls can read it. They're all curious about Hermann. I caught one of them trying to get into my lockbox last week. She said she only wanted to borrow my silver bracelet, but I know she wanted*

226

to see this diary. I'll put it in the stables. Mama and Papa don't care a pin about the horses, and they'll never know I went by the house. When I'm done there, I get to see Hermann this afternoon! He rang me again a few minutes ago, saying he wanted to talk to me about our phone conversation this morning, and he can spare me fifteen minutes. He'll pick me up in his car.

The entry ended there. Daniel flipped through the diary's remaining pages, but they were blank.

Gretchen's mind swam. A secret girlfriend. An indiscreet comment about a nosy fireman. A fifteen-minute-long meeting to discuss an earlier phone conversation. An assassination in the street hours later. Each a link in the chain winding back to the night when fire had blazed through the Reichstag.

She found her voice. 'Fräulein Junge wasn't killed because she was an embarrassing companion for Göring.'

Daniel's eyes flashed onto hers. 'She was murdered because she knew Göring was angry with a fireman. The question is – why did Göring say this fireman was nosy? What did the fireman know about the arson attack that Göring didn't want him to?'

For a moment, they were silent. Outside in the street Gretchen heard the rattle of paper trash pushed by the wind, and from the stairwell the creak of footsteps. Friedrich, probably, eager to talk to them.

The enormity of this discovery made her heart race. What did this fireman know? Had he stumbled across evidence that the National Socialists were behind the blaze and had set up their despised political opponents to take the blame? Had he suspected that the Dutch Communist arrested on the scene was a patsy?

'Do you realize what this means?' Daniel said. 'The National Socialists aren't only guilty of murder – they must have been involved with the fire! If we can prove it, the Party won't be able to recover from the scandal. Hitler's career will be over.' He grinned and leaned forward to kiss her, then seemed to catch himself and sat back. Quickly, he looked away. There was a sudden ache in Gretchen's throat that she couldn't swallow down.

The hideout door whined open. Footsteps raced across the hall, stopping at the parlor entryway. Friedrich braced his hand on the doorframe, his eyes bright with reflected lamplight. He still wore his top hat and tails from the ball.

'What have you found out?' he asked. 'My man said you thought it was important.'

'It's a secret far greater than any we could have guessed.' Daniel held out the diary to Friedrich. 'It looks like Fräulein Junge was told something she shouldn't have been about the Reichstag fire. You must have heard the rumors that the fire couldn't have been set by the Dutchman they found on the scene, since he's half blind. Maybe they're right, and the National Socialists really are the ones behind everything. There's only one person in Berlin who might know the truth and be willing to tell us – a fireman whose first name is Heinz.' He paused. 'We must do everything in our power to find him.'

24

FOR THE NEXT HOUR, GRETCHEN AND DANIEL DISCUSSED the diary's contents with Friedrich, going over and over Fräulein Junge's comment about the inquisitive fireman. Daniel said it was common knowledge that an underground tunnel connected Göring's palace and the Reichstag because the two buildings shared a central heating system. Before the Socialist and Communist newspapers had been shut down last week, many of them had reported the fact, speculating that Göring had sent SA men through the tunnel to set the blaze. The tunnel was reached through a doorway next to Göring's porter's lodge and ended in the Reichstag cellar.

Gretchen remembered Hanfstaengl's careless words at the gangsters' ball about secret passages causing trouble for the Party. She had assumed he meant the passage connecting Hitler's Chancellery with the Hotel Adlon. But he must have also meant the tunnel beneath Göring's palace.

There was so little they knew about the fireman: a nick-name – presumably 'Heinz' was short for 'Heinrich' – and he must work at a station close to the Reichstag, or he wouldn't have been on the scene that night. Friedrich was confident his men could track down the fellow, for they were experienced at locating men who didn't want to be found: gamblers who'd skipped out on bets, borrowers who'd defaulted on a loan. If the fireman was still alive and in the city, the *Ringverein* would find him.

Finally Gretchen and Daniel crawled into bed. Her thoughts were spinning, but the instant she closed her eyes they silenced like leaves after a windstorm, and she sank into sleep.

She was sitting cross-legged on the floor in Uncle Dolf's rented room. Cakes frosted with eagles and swastikas had been stacked everywhere: the linoleum floor, the top of Hitler's bookcase, and on a writing table.

Hitler sat on the edge of his bed, his face pale and haggard. He wore a white shirt without the attached collar, suspenders, and carpet slippers. Strands of hair fell over his forehead. Gretchen had never seen him so disheveled.

Papa sat in the middle of the room, cradling an iced cake like a baby. Concern was etched into his face. His mouth was open, as if he was about to speak—

Gretchen shot up in bed, her heart thundering. *Just a dream, just a dream*, she reassured herself, but she knew it wasn't.

She remembered that afternoon in Hitler's old bed-sitting-room, for it had been the last of his birthdays that she had celebrated with her father, as he had died seven months later. During that first horrible winter without him, she had often recalled that day, wishing she could freeze it like an insect in amber because it had seemed so perfect. Her and Papa and Uncle Dolf, stuffing themselves with cake, then trooping out to the old piano in the entrance hall when Hanfstaengl had shown up with flowers.

Hanfstaengl had played *Die Meistersinger* while Hitler marched back and forth, conducting an invisible orchestra. She had tagged along after him, mimicking his every move until finally, flushed and laughing, they rested on the floor, and she had leaned against him, smelling his familiar scents of sugar and sweat-dampened cotton.

Shuddering, she scrubbed her face with her hands, as if she could clean away the memory. Why had she dreamed about it – and about that particular instant in the room Hitler used to rent on the Thierschstrasse, before he had moved into his posh apartment? That had never been the part she had chosen to remember when she had run through that afternoon in her mind.

She knew what Alfred would say: the subconscious often hid secrets within dreams. Was her mind trying to tell her something?

Outside, church bells were ringing – it was Sunday, she realized, the nineteenth of March. Four days until the Reichstag session. Her stomach dropped. They had so little time left.

The bedroom door burst open. She whirled, her hand at her throat. Daniel bolted up in bed. Friedrich stood in the entrance, clad in a leather greatcoat and bowler hat. Today he carried a blackjack, which he tapped lightly in his gloved palm.

'Get up,' he barked at Daniel. 'My men have learned the fireman's identity. His name is Heinz Schultz. He works night shifts out of the Linienstrasse fire station, but he hasn't been seen in about three weeks. Since a few days after the fire, in fact.' He slipped the weapon into his coat. His smile was quick and predatory. 'If he's home, I'm sure he'll talk to us. And if not . . .' He patted his pocket. 'I can be very persuasive.'

25

HEINZ SCHULTZ LIVED IN AN APARTMENT ON THE Nollendorfstrasse. Shabby stone buildings lined the street. Even at the early eight o'clock hour, lamps burned in the cellar shops. Store windows were crammed with tarnished silver pots and broken furniture: wood chairs missing an arm, tables with uneven legs, lamps with ripped shades.

The cheap smells of horsemeat and stopped-up drains permeated the air. Gretchen skirted dirty-faced children playing jacks and families trudging to church services. A few men clustered on the corner, rags in their hands, a bucket of water at their feet, ready to leap forward and wash car windshields for a few groschen. A couple of rangy mutts skittered across the street, slipping on the icy cobblestones. Last night's rains had washed away the snow, leaving the roads frozen.

Gretchen saw desperation in the men's lined faces and the children's thin cheeks and the dogs' matted fur. Years of hunger and unemployment had ground everyone down to shadows. She doubted any of them cared who had set the Reichstag on fire or about politics in general; they were too concerned with finding

232

the next mouthful of food, the next lump of coal, the next pfennig. Uncle Dolf had always said that was how the Jew prospered, like a weed in the heart. Growing when others were too burdened with their own survival to notice.

He had lied, Gretchen thought, rage sweeping over her. That was how *he* grew.

Number 19's front door was unlocked, its lobby unlit. Friedrich took the stairs two at a time, his leather greatcoat flapping about his ankles, Gretchen and Daniel rushing after him. Four closed doors lined the third-floor corridor.

Friedrich knelt before the second door and inspected the lock. 'It's been broken into. See the scratches around the keyhole?' He rattled the knob. 'Someone's locked it again.' Without waiting for a response, he inserted a metal pick into the lock, jerking his wrist once. The tumblers clicked and the door swung open. Clearly he'd earned his position as the top *Ringverein* member – Gretchen had never seen a lock picked so fast.

Inside, the curtains had been drawn and the lamps left unlit, so walking into the parlor felt like walking into unbroken blackness. As Gretchen's eyes made out the humped shadows of furniture, a horrible smell reared up. Something foul, like fruit gone rotten, magnified a thousand times. She fell back, struggling for fresh air.

'I know that stench.' Friedrich dashed through a door in the wall opposite, presumably into the kitchen or bedroom.

Daniel held out his arm, blocking Gretchen's way. 'Stay back. You won't want to see this.'

Gretchen didn't have to ask why. There was nothing else it could be: a body long dead. She breathed through her mouth, trying not to imagine the corpse beyond the door, bloated and disfigured by time.

Blinking, she waited for her eyes to adjust to the dimness.

Friedrich staggered back into the room, holding a hand-kerchief over his mouth. Sweat had pearled on his forehead.

'It's bad,' he gasped. 'A man, lying in pajamas on the bed. I couldn't tell any more than that – the body's too badly damaged. I'll go down to the lobby to telephone the police.'

Then they were too late. The fireman's secrets about the blaze had died with him. Gretchen struggled to swallow down her disappointment. There had to be another way to find the information they needed.

Then Friedrich's other words registered. She stared at him.

'The *police*?' Daniel asked. 'Surely they're among the last people we should contact?'

Friedrich wiped his handkerchief over his damp forehead. 'I'll speak to Superintendent Gennat, naturally.' Gretchen remembered the heavyset detective from the hoodlums' court as Friedrich added, 'We must be quick before any of the neighbors notice we're in here. You two search the parlor while I telephone. Maybe you can find something to explain what happened to Schultz. You'd best keep your gloves on. Gennat will be sure to dust for fingerprints.'

The urgency in his voice told Gretchen there was no time to ask questions. She held her hand over her mouth, trying to block out the horrific odor.

Pale slivers of light shone through the curtains. Daniel moved to open them, but Friedrich said, 'No. We must disturb things as little as possible. You'll have to work in the dark.'

He hurried from the apartment. Gretchen rushed to the parlor table while Daniel looked through the writing desk. She yanked open drawers, riffling through the contents. Nothing except for a couple of issues of *Vorwärts*, the Social Democrat paper. So the fireman hadn't been a National Socialist – the Party couldn't have depended on his silence or loyalty, if he had discovered something incriminating.

234

The flash of glass on the wall caught her attention: a framed photograph, showing two young men, dark-haired, smiling and squinting into the sun, wearing firemen's uniforms. Heinz Schultz, presumably, and a brother or cousin – the similarities in their faces were too pronounced for them to be anything except relatives.

'I've found a letter.' Daniel held up an envelope and a slip of paper. 'Written to Heinz and Gunter, both of this address, from their mother.'

Brothers, then, and roommates. An idea occurred to Gretchen, and she slipped the photograph from its frame. Written on the back were the words, *Gunter (left), and Heinz (right), at Linienstrasse fire station, October 1929*. She studied the image. Gunter was at least six inches shorter than Heinz.

The door opened, and Friedrich came inside. 'Gennat's on his way. Find anything?'

Gretchen slid the photograph back into its frame and hung it on its nail on the wall. 'Maybe. How tall was the body in the bedroom?'

'Short. Perhaps five three, at the most. Why?'

'It could have been Gunter, not Heinz.' Gretchen's pulse jumped with excitement. 'The men looked so alike, the killer could have made a mistake and murdered the wrong brother. Heinz might still be alive.'

'What's this about brothers?' Friedrich stuffed his handkerchief into his pocket.

She started to explain, but he waved her off, saying they could talk outside in the clean air. They checked over the parlor, making sure they had left everything precisely as they had found it. The stench had grown so overpowering that Gretchen's eyes watered.

In the corridor, Friedrich closed the door behind them.

'No sense locking it as Gennat will be the next man to enter,' he said. 'What else can you tell me?'

'It was quick,' Daniel said, and Gretchen nodded, thinking of the tidy parlor. 'There was no evidence of a struggle, at least in the front room. So either the victim knew his killer and wasn't afraid of him or it was the work of a professional.'

Tires squealed from the street.

'That must be Gennat now,' Friedrich said. He led Gretchen and Daniel into the street, where an enormous, dark six-seater Daimler sat at the curb. A patrolman in a blue cape was opening its trunk, and Superintendent Gennat stood on the sidewalk, surveying the apartment building. He had heavy pouches of skin under his eyes, perhaps a remnant of last night's late festivities.

Friedrich leaned against the car, pulling a cigar from his coat pocket. 'Before you ask, Gennat, no, the fireman had no dealings with my crew. We suspect his brother is the dead man.'

'Indeed?' Gennat raised his eyebrows. 'And what were you doing in their apartment at what is for you the ungodly hour of nine o'clock?'

'Searching for answers,' Friedrich said smoothly. 'The fireman might know about our Fräulein Junge's murder. You'd best watch yourself, Superintendent, or I'll be after your job.'

Gennat laughed as he rummaged through the car trunk. It was enormous and packed with all sorts of materials: bottles of chemicals, searchlights, cameras, tape measures, rolled-up maps, and dozens of tools from diamond cutters to pickaxes. As Gennat opened a small black leather bag, the sort doctors used for house calls, Gretchen glimpsed the silver flash of surgical instruments inside. She'd never seen such a bizarre assortment of things.

236

The detective must have sensed her interest, for he smiled at her. 'This is the first crime car in the world, Fräulein. I designed it myself.'

'And the most famous car in Berlin.' Friedrich puffed his cigar, gray curls of smoke wreathing his face. 'It's called Gennat's Toboggan.'

Gennat hefted his medical bag. 'You'd best get moving, unless you fancy being locked up.' Through the hum of traffic, Gretchen heard the far-off wail of a police siren. Her legs tensed, ready to run. She glanced at Daniel as he flipped up his coat collar to hide the lower half of his face.

'Let's get out of here,' he said.

They walked fast, heads down, saying nothing. Behind her, she heard a police car screeching to a stop, then the low murmurs of Gennat's and the patrolmen's voices. Footsteps rang on the iced-over cobblestones, growing louder as they got closer.

She looked back. It was only Friedrich, hurrying to join them and pitching his half-finished cigar into the gutter. When he reached them, no one spoke. They kept moving, gazes trained on the grimy pavement, but she didn't feel as though she breathed until they boarded the S-Bahn to carry them across the city, back into Moabit.

26

'SUPERINTENDENT GENNAT WILL LET ME KNOW THE
identity of the dead man as soon as he has it,' Friedrich said
when they returned to the hideout. 'But I think it's already
clear that he must be the fireman's brother. I'm going to send
several of my men to track down this Herr Schultz. Some will
go to the fire station to pick up gossip from his colleagues,
and the rest will go to bars near Schultz's apartment. You'll
both need to stay here.'

Relief washed over Gretchen. After the horrors of the
fireman's apartment, she wanted nothing more than to stay
inside the hideout. She didn't know if she could have managed
to go back outside, where she might bump into another
National Socialist from the old days. The next one she met
probably wouldn't be as sympathetic as Herr Hanfstaengl.
She shuddered, thinking of the dead body in the bedroom.
She knew too well how they dealt with their enemies.

'Let me go with them,' Daniel said quickly. Gretchen
clasped his wrist in warning, wishing he would be quiet. She
didn't want him to go. But he didn't seem to notice her touch

and said, 'I'm experienced at ferreting out information from sources.'

'I know you are.' Friedrich paused at the door to the parlor, looking back at Gretchen and Daniel. She dropped his wrist. 'But I want you to remain here for now. Fräulein Müller would attract too much attention – no *Ringverein* works with ladies. As for you, Herr Cohen, I'm afraid you'd never pass as one of my men.' He smiled slightly. 'You're a bit *too* well-spoken, aren't you?'

'I can put on an act,' Daniel protested.

'I've made my decision,' Friedrich snapped. 'I'll have word sent to you once we have news. Take a nap. You couldn't have had much sleep last night.'

Then he was gone, the door slamming behind him. Gretchen was suddenly aware of how quiet the hideout was. No voices from the other rooms, no footsteps or snap of cards on a table or dice rattling in a cup. She was alone with Daniel. And she had no idea what to say to him – or how to combat the desperate sadness she saw in his eyes when he looked at her.

'I'm going to get some rest.' She hurried to their room before he could say anything.

For a moment, she sat on the bed, staring at the floor-boards with unseeing eyes. The stench of the dead body was still in her nostrils; with every breath she took, she inhaled more of the rotten meat smell. Her stomach roiled. Heaving, she forced her head between her knees, feeling the blood rush from her head.

Dimly, she heard a door open and close, then footsteps come toward her. Daniel. She recognized his quick tread. His hand touched her back. 'Gretchen? Are you ill?'

'The body.' She couldn't stop shivering. 'I can still smell him. He must have been in there for days.' Her voice thickened.

239

'Alone, with no one noticing or checking on him. Soon Superintendent Gennat will have him identified, and the police will contact his family. And shatter their lives.'

Her eyes stinging, she looked up at Daniel. 'I know how they'll feel. As though the world should stop rotating or the sun shining or the rain from coming down. When those things do happen, they won't be able to believe it. Because they'll think that the world should be different, now that their loved one has been killed. But the world won't be different. *They* will.' Her voice cracked. 'That's how I felt after Papa died – was murdered,' she corrected herself. 'I remember waking up the next morning and being so angry that the sun had risen just like always. It didn't seem fair that life should go on if he wasn't there anymore.'

Daniel sat down next to her. His eyes were steady on hers as he said, 'That's how I feel about you. As though the whole world would go dark without you in it. On the ride back from Herr Schultz's apartment, I couldn't stop thinking how I would feel if something happened to you. And how fragile life is. All the time it probably took to kill that man in the apartment was one second. An instant to pull a trigger and extinguish a life.'

She couldn't breathe. What was he trying to say?

He moved close. She breathed him in until the stink of the dead body was gone, and all that was left was Daniel.

'I don't want to live without you,' he said. 'Life is so short and so precious, and I don't want to waste another second of it wondering how you feel about me or what's going to become of us. I love you. If anything happened to you, the world would stop for me. I would *want* it to stop because I can't go on without you. Please, Gretchen.'

He looked so unlike his usual confident self, his face open and vulnerable, that she stared at him. Many times in the past

240

he'd said he loved her. But never with such an aching intensity in his voice or pleading in his eyes. She realized that he was handing another piece of himself to her – a defenseless part he hadn't let her see before.

'We can work everything out,' he said in a rush. 'I'll live in Oxford. I don't mind. I can convince my editor to give me my old job back. Assuming we get out of here alive,' he added with a slight smile. Then he looked at her and it slipped away. 'Gretchen, I can find a way to be happy,' he said quietly. 'Even if I'm working as a society reporter again. But I can never find a way to be happy if I'm not with you.'

Something golden and warm spread through her chest and then down her arms and legs until all of her was tingling with it. He loved her. Despite everything that should have pulled them apart, he still loved her. And she loved him. Maybe that was all that needed to be true. They didn't need to have the answers now. What mattered was whether they were willing to seek them out together. If she and Daniel somehow escaped from Germany, they could find a compromise. Even if it meant living apart for a few years while she stayed with the Whitestones and finished her schooling and he got a newspaper job elsewhere. She knew he would wait for her. And she would wait for him. As long as it took, she would wait for him.

She smiled. 'I want to be with you, too, no matter what. We can figure out a compromise. I'll always love the Whitestones, but even if I don't live with them, I can still visit them. I *need* to be with you. Everything else – families and jobs and schooling – we'll find a way to have them, too. It won't be perfect, but I don't care. All I know is that a life without you would be a half life. I love you, Daniel. Every part of you.'

As he smiled, his face softening with relief, she put her hands on his shoulders. Through his suit coat, she touched the corded muscles of his right shoulder, the boniness of his left. She blurted out the first thing that came into her head. 'I love your scar.'

Daniel had been bending down to kiss her, but he jerked away, looking startled. 'What?'

'Your scar,' she repeated. She ran her hand down his arm, feeling the raised ridge of puckered skin. 'I know you hate it. But every time I think about it, it reminds me how brave you are. How you don't give up. It makes me so proud of you.'

The muscles in his neck worked as he tried to swallow. 'Really?'

'Really,' she said, and he caught her face between his hands and kissed her so hard on the mouth that her head spun. They drew back, grinning at each other. He lifted an eyebrow in the familiar gesture she liked so much. It usually meant a joke was coming.

But he surprised her by saying, 'You're the only one for me. The only one, Gretchen.'

She wrapped her arms around his shoulders and held him close, half laughing and half crying at the relief of his touch as he kissed her again. She kissed him back until she couldn't breathe. Could barely think except for one clear thought piercing her consciousness: kissing Daniel felt exactly like coming home.

When Daniel pulled back, he rested his forehead on hers. The heat of his skin pulsed into hers, and she couldn't stop smiling, savoring the sensation of her lips throbbing from their kisses.

'We'd better stop before we can't,' Daniel said, sounding reluctant.

'Would that be so terrible?' Gretchen asked.

His laugh rang out as her cheeks went hot. 'I certainly don't think so. But . . . you're special. You deserve more than a dingy room in a hideout.' He kissed her gently. 'You deserve the best of everything. I wish I could give that to you.'

'You already have,' she told him, her heart pounding at her boldness. 'You're the best of everything.'

His smile was softer than she'd ever seen it. He kissed her on the mouth, on both of her cheeks, on the warm skin of her throat until all of her body was alive and thrumming from his touch. Grinning, he stretched himself out on the bed. Gretchen lay down beside him, resting her head on his chest and listening to his heart beat into her ear. It was the most beautiful sound she'd ever heard. He was alive and here with her. As long as that was true, she knew she could handle anything. She listened to the slow inhalation of his breath; felt the arm holding her turn to lead and fall onto the blanket.

She smiled and peeked at his face. Relaxed and quiet in sleep, so unlike the way he looked awake: his mouth moving quickly as though it struggled to keep up with the pace of his thoughts; his eyes often narrowed and focused. Wonderfully complex and imperfect and impatient and sarcastic. Her Daniel. Still smiling, she closed her eyes and slept at last.

The next morning, Superintendent Gennat telephoned Friedrich to confirm that the body in the apartment had been Gunter Schultz's, the younger brother of the fireman they sought. Which meant that Heinz might still be alive.

Friedrich ordered a couple of his men to return to the bars around Herr Schultz's apartment, once night had come and the establishments had opened. Someone needed to question Schultz's neighbors, too, he added. Perhaps one of them had seen something.

'I can go,' Daniel had jumped in.

Friedrich shot him an annoyed look. 'My men are pretending that Herr Schultz defaulted on a gambling debt and that's why they're looking for him. Nobody will give them a second glance. You, Herr Cohen, as I've already told you, can't possibly pass as one of us. You'll wait here until I figure out how you can be useful again. That will be all.'

He and the three *Ringverein* men left. Gretchen watched Daniel, sensing his frustration in the way he paced the parlor. *Three days*, she thought, but didn't speak it aloud, knowing it would make Daniel feel worse. Today was the twentieth – which meant they had three days until the Reichstag voted on the Enabling Act and Hitler assumed dictatorial powers. She didn't see how they could possibly prove that the National Socialists had had Fräulein Junge killed to cover up their responsibility for the Reichstag fire. They didn't have enough time.

She sank onto the sofa and covered her face with her hands. From another room, she heard the steady ticking of a clock. Ticking down minutes they didn't have.

Unbidden, the image of Hitler in his old bed-sitting-room, surrounded by birthday cakes, rose in her mind. She hadn't had time to puzzle over the dream, but now she wondered again why she had had it. What was her subconscious trying to tell her?

She fetched a piece of paper and a pen and sat at the table. Alfred had taught her a technique he used on his patients to coax forth their repressed memories. He had based it on Freud's free-association method, in which patients were encouraged to say whatever came into their heads, without censoring their thoughts. Often this technique opened a back door into people's memories. It might help her now.

Taking a deep breath, she imagined again the scene in Hitler's room: him slumped on the bed, surrounded by cakes, and her father starting to speak to him. She wrote down the first word that occurred to her: *cake*. Then the next – *taster*.

244

Her fingers flew over the page as more words popped up in her thoughts. *Poison. Reporter. Blood. Smoke. Lies.*

She stopped, studying the words, the black slashes of them on the white paper. Slowly, she set down the pen.

The trick had worked; bits of the afternoon had flown back to her. The ugly parts, before Hanfstaengl had arrived. At first, Uncle Dolf had been afraid that some of his birthday cakes might have been poisoned, moaning that he had so many enemies. She had offered to sample the cakes for him, like the king's tasters she had learned about in school, and he had burst into delighted laughter. *My little glutton!* he'd said, patting her cheek. *Very well, we'll have some. Which do you want to try first?*

Once they had begun eating, he and Papa had talked in low voices about Herr Gerlich, who had wanted to meet with Hitler to discuss his plans to improve Munich's economy. She had forgotten that Hitler and Gerlich had met a few times that year; they'd been friendly with each other until Hitler had tried to overthrow the city government in the putsch in which her father had died. Gerlich had declared Hitler couldn't be trusted, and they'd been bitter enemies ever since. Her throat tightened. These days, Gerlich was trapped in Munich's city jail, and she didn't imagine that Hitler would ever approve his release.

Focus, she ordered herself. Worrying about Gerlich wouldn't help him. She glanced at the next words on the list. *Blood. Smoke.* She could hear Hitler's voice in her head, murmuring that he hoped Gerlich was as credulous as the public. *They'll swallow anything if it's repeated often enough*, he had said, clapping her father on the shoulder. *Like blood and smoke, eh, Müller? The truth doesn't matter. Only the appearance of it.*

Then had come the part she didn't want to remember:

245

Quite right, her father had replied. *Misdirection is the best tool in our arsenal, Adi.*

There was a bitter taste in the back of her throat. She already knew that her father hadn't been the good-hearted man she'd once imagined him to be. But the proof of it still hurt. Blinking hard, she tried to make her thoughts cold and rational. What had Hitler meant when he had mentioned 'blood and smoke'? She considered smoke, swirling, dark and heavy, concealing what was truly there. Blood, red and thick, the essence of life. The symbol of racial purity, in Hitler's opinion. And death.

She frowned. Hitler had said that he didn't need to tell the truth; he merely needed to appear as though he did. He had sounded as if he were planning on deliberately misleading others. Like setting fire to Berlin's seat of government, a terrorist attack reported all over the world, and then blaming your strongest political opponents for it. Misdirection, as Papa had said.

'Daniel,' she said shakily, and he whirled to face her, his eyes narrowed in concentration, 'I think I've remembered something important.'

Once she had told him about the memory, he sat with his head bowed for a moment, thinking. 'It doesn't prove anything,' he said at last. 'But it shows Hitler's state of mind.'

Gretchen nodded in instant comprehension. 'He's not afraid to fool the public to further his own goals. The fire was the perfect opportunity to frighten everybody so much that they didn't complain when he suspended civil liberties.'

'And it sets him up to assume absolute power when President Hindenburg dies.' Daniel sounded grim. 'We have to stop him before the Enabling Act is passed.'

They spent the rest of the day in the hideout, waiting for news. Gretchen sat bolt upright on the sofa, too nervous to

246

move. Daniel must have walked five miles, he crossed the parlor so many times. The *Ringverein* guard who sat at the table, tallying columns in the account books, kept shooting them wary looks but remained silent.

For supper, they choked down a couple of sandwiches with potato salad that Gretchen had been sent out to get from the delicatessen down the street. As she and Daniel were filling the sink with hot water to wash the dishes, the telephone shrilled from the corridor. They froze, straining to hear the *Ringverein* man's muttered conversation.

He appeared in the kitchen doorway. 'Friedrich wants to speak to both of you straightaway. He's at the bar down the street – Herr Cohen, you know the one, it's where you've helped out in the mornings.'

'Thanks.' Daniel dashed from the room, Gretchen close behind him. This had to be the news they'd been waiting for. They grabbed their coats and hats from the bedroom, flinging them on as they raced down the stairs and outside.

Night had laid itself across the city like a blanket. At this hour, the Zwinglistrasse was deserted except for a couple of skinny dogs and a handful of drunkards, weaving along the pavement. Gretchen and Daniel hurried past them.

The bar took up the cellar of a large brick building on the corner. They wound down the steps into a gray dimness and the slurred voices of the inebriated. A handful of men and women in much-mended clothes slumped over their drinks at the bar. Behind the long counter, a woman in a flowered dress poured potato vodka into water-spotted glasses.

At a table in the corner, two girls sat with a couple of young men, laughing uproariously over a shared joke. Gretchen realized with a start that one of them was Birgit. She smiled at Gretchen. Maybe this was her night off – did prostitutes even have those? Gretchen wondered – or she was with a customer.

'Pardon me,' Daniel said to the woman behind the counter. 'We need to speak with Iron Fist Friedrich.'

'Office in the back,' the woman muttered.

'Thank you.' They went to the corridor at the opposite end of the barroom. It was paneled in dark wood and flanked with a few closed doors. A frosted glass panel with the word OFFICE painted in black stood on their left. Daniel knocked.

'Come in,' called Friedrich's voice. He stood when they entered, waving at a couple of battered wooden chairs. They sat down. Knives twisted in Gretchen's stomach and she clutched her purse, feeling the revolver's reassuring shape through the leather. What had Friedrich's men found out? Had they finally found the clue that would break open the case?

'One of my men has just stumbled across a piece of luck.' Friedrich dropped into a chair. 'Heinz Schultz's neighbor returned from visiting a relative today, and she had most interesting information. She said she saw Schultz leaving his apartment a day or two after the fire. He was carrying a folded-up canvas camping tent.' Friedrich tapped his fingers together, the diamond in his pinkie ring catching the lamplight. 'She hasn't seen him or his brother since.'

That made no sense. The fireman had to be mad to go camping in March in Berlin. During the day, the temperature rarely rose above twenty or thirty degrees, and at night it plunged toward the zero mark. *Mad*, Gretchen realized, *or desperate*.

Daniel gasped. 'He must have gone to the Kuhle Wampe.' He glanced at Gretchen, adding, 'It's the largest tent camp for the homeless in the city. Countless people live there on the shores of the Müggelsee. During the winter, they stay in shelters, so the place should be deserted now.'

'That's my guess as well.' Friedrich ground his cigar into an ashtray. 'Let's go. I have a car waiting—'

He broke off as a thunderous cascade of footsteps drowned him out. It sounded as though a dozen people or more had rushed down the steps into the barroom.

'Police!' several men's voices shouted. 'This is a raid! Everyone, hands where we can see them!'

Gretchen couldn't move. Through the walls, she heard women screaming and the splintering crash of wood hitting the ground. Glass shattered. The police must be throwing tables and chairs and drinks onto the floor.

She surged to her feet. 'We have to get out of here!' Another minute and the police might come into the office and see her and Daniel . . .

'These raids happen all the time.' Friedrich waved a dismissive hand. 'I'll throw some money at them, and that'll be the end of it.'

He strode from the room. As one, Gretchen and Daniel crept to the half-open door and peered into the corridor. She could see nothing except a lamp bracketed on the wall. From the barroom, more glass broke. Men's and women's shouts tangled together into an indecipherable wall of sound.

'Get these people to shut up!' someone yelled. 'I want *order*!'

It was Hermann Göring. Gretchen clutched blindly at Daniel's arm. 'This isn't a raid!' she hissed. 'Göring's here!'

Daniel pulled her back into the room and closed the door gently. Fear had tightened his face into a mask. His gaze skittered around the room. Gretchen looked, too: a desk, a cabinet, a table, four chairs. And the small rectangular window, turned black by the fullness of night. It was so high up that the top of its frame reached the crease between the wall and ceiling. The window wasn't even two feet wide; she didn't know if they could squeeze through.

'The table.' Daniel nodded at it. 'If we move it under the window, we should be able to hoist ourselves up.'

'But what about Friedrich? He's out there and so are those poor people. Birgit's there!' she remembered, her heart lurching. 'We have to do something.'

Daniel took a decanter and glasses off the table and set them on the floor. 'We go out there and we're dead.'

He was right and she knew it. They could only hope to save themselves. She cast an anxious look at the door, thinking, *I'm sorry, Birgit*. She seized one end of the table. Together, they carried it across the room. As quietly as they could, they set it on the floor beneath the window, and Daniel ran a hand over his injured arm. His left-hand fingers were spasming uncontrollably; she could imagine how much his effort to carry the table had cost him.

Through the closed door, there were more screams and shouts from the barroom. Then Gretchen heard the sickening smack of nightsticks meeting flesh. Was Birgit being beaten, too? Her stomach wrenched as she thought of her friend falling to the ground, her arms wrapped protectively over her head.

'How much will it cost to send you lot away this time?' Friedrich shouted above the din. The barroom silenced as if a switch had been thrown. 'I confess, I'm surprised to see you here, Minister Göring. After we met at the ball, I fancied we had become friends.'

Daniel clambered onto the table. It wobbled under his weight.

'Take him into the corridor,' Göring ordered.

Daniel fumbled with the window's hand crank. Slowly, the panel eased open.

Footfalls tramped down the corridor, stopping outside the office door. *Don't come in*, Gretchen pleaded silently. The door shook in its frame as a body slammed against it. Gretchen had to bite her lip so she didn't scream. *Friedrich*.

Daniel waved Gretchen closer. *Come on!* he mouthed at her.

She climbed onto the table. Under her added weight, it started wobbling and Gretchen felt herself losing her balance. God, the racket it would make, if she fell to the floor! She jumped back to the floor and the table righted itself.

From the corridor, Göring spoke again, sounding breathless. 'You shouldn't have sent your men to the fireman's apartment tonight to talk to his neighbors. That was foolish. Did you really imagine it would escape my notice?'

Gretchen braced her hand on the wall for balance.

'You loathsome coward!' Friedrich growled. 'I know what you did to Fräulein Junge. Perhaps you think you're innocent because you sent someone else to do your dirty work. But your hands are just as bloodied.'

'Shut your mouth!' Göring yelled. 'Somebody, shoot him! Why do you hesitate? Shoot and I will protect you!'

Gretchen thought of the revolver in her purse. What could she do? It sounded as though there were a couple dozen police and SA men out there. She couldn't possibly shoot them all.

A sharp report echoed up and down the corridor. Something heavy fell. She recognized the sound, for she had heard it before: a tangle of limbs collapsing to the floor. Friedrich had been shot.

27

FOR A HORRIBLE INSTANT, GRETCHEN STOOD FROZEN ON the table. There was no cry of pain from the corridor, no plea for mercy. Nothing but the creak of leather. A pistol being returned to its holster, perhaps. Friedrich must be dead. The thought pushed the air from her lungs. In one instant, the trigger pulled and a life extinguished, just as Daniel had said. It seemed too quick. Too easy. Murder should be harder than a split-second decision and a bullet.

But it had happened; Friedrich was gone; she could tell by the sudden hush from the corridor, broken only by the men's panting breaths. She thought of the little girls she'd met in Friedrich's apartment, with light brown hair and shy smiles. Her throat tightened. Friedrich might have been a criminal, but he had cared about his employees and had wanted to support his daughters and wife. And he had been kind to her and Daniel, in his way.

Daniel's hand gripped her arm. She saw her own horror reflected in his eyes.

We have to go, he mouthed at her.

His words broke through the haze in her mind. Jerkily, she nodded. There was nothing they could do for Friedrich. The most they could hope for was finding a way to escape themselves. She grabbed the window ledge and hauled herself up.

From the barroom, the fights had started again, men shouting and punching, fists plowing into skin, glass breaking. Footsteps sounded from the corridor, fading as they retreated toward the bar. Göring shouted about getting a morgue wagon.

She wedged herself into the window's narrow opening. Her shoulders scraped the edges, but her head was through. The space was so tight she couldn't take a breath. Glancing sideways, she saw the window opened into a long, brick-lined alley.

Daniel grasped her waist and pushed hard. She wriggled forward until her arms were free, then curled her hands around the icy cobblestones, straining to pull herself through. Her arms shook from the effort. She pulled again and burst free from the window. She fell about an inch to the cold ground, landing so hard that a white-hot ache exploded in her knee.

She scrambled upright and yanked on Daniel's arms as he emerged from the opening. His weakened left limb trembled under her grip. She pulled harder, her fingers digging into the rough wool of his coat.

Then he was out, sprawling across the cobblestones, white-faced and cradling his injured arm. He jumped up. Together they crept to the mouth of the alley and peered into the street. There were two police cars parked at the curb. All of her felt numb except her knee, which throbbed.

There were no policemen in the street; they must all be inside. She and Daniel would have to be quick before the officers came back outside. By unspoken assent, they ran out of the alley. Together they sprinted through the darkness toward the hideout to warn whoever might be there.

The hideout was quiet when they arrived. The lamps had been left off, and a dozen men moved by the illumination from the flashlights they carried. Little yellow circles bobbed around the parlor as they scooped jewelry into leather bags or stacked bills and coins in suitcases. Nobody spoke.

'There's been a raid at the bar—' Daniel started to say, but a fellow cut him off.

'We know. One of our men managed to slip out and warn us. We were working at the nightclub one street over, so we were able to get back here quickly. We need to set up a new hideout, in case the police come here. Get your things and get out. There's nothing more we can do together.' He fastened the buckles on a suitcase. 'And for pity's sake, don't turn on any lights. We don't want to alert anyone who might be watching that we're in here.'

Gretchen swallowed hard. 'Friedrich—'

'Is dead,' the man interrupted, his tone harsh. He grabbed the suitcase and hurried toward the door, pausing at the entrance to glance back at them. 'We've already heard. He was a fair man, and his widow and children will be cared for. But I'm in charge now, and I say we abandon the investigation into Fräulein Junge's death.'

'Even if it could ruin the National Socialists?' Daniel burst out.

The man sent him a cool look. 'We Rings have never cared a toss about politics. I'd like to see the Nazis chased from Berlin since they've chosen to make us targets. But I need to protect my men and our livelihood more. We have to save our own skins.' He gave them a brusque nod. 'Good luck to you.'

254

He slipped out the door. None of the other men looked at her or Daniel; they were too focused on collecting their loot.

They rushed into their bedroom. Their bags lay on the floor by the foot of the bed. Fortunately, they'd never unpacked. They grabbed their suitcases, Gretchen clutching hers so hard that its handle bit into her hand.

In the parlor, none of the men seemed to notice as they left. They raced down the stairs. One thought drummed over and over in Gretchen's head: *Get out, get out, get out.*

As they followed the twists of the stairwell, they ran into someone who was coming up. Gretchen stumbled back, her heart in her throat.

It was Birgit. She was pale, but looked unhurt. Her coat flapped open over a pale pink dress and she wore heels, not her working girl leather boots. She was breathing so hard she could only gasp out, 'Friedrich – they killed him – Minister Göring and a bunch of SA men—'

'We know, we were at the bar,' Daniel broke in. 'We were hiding in a back room. How did you get out? Weren't they going to arrest everyone?'

'I don't know! Minister Göring told us to get out. I came straight here. I wanted to – I wanted to . . .' Birgit faltered. Tears poured down her face. 'They shot Friedrich. Like he was *nothing.*'

'It's horrible,' Gretchen said. 'But, Birgit, we have to get out of here *right now.*'

Birgit grabbed her arm. 'You want to damage the National Socialists, don't you?' At Gretchen's impatient nod, she said, 'Then take me with you. I'll do whatever you want. Just give me the chance to hurt the men who killed Friedrich and Monika.'

'Fine, but come on!' Daniel dashed down the rest of the stairs. Gretchen and Birgit clattered after him.

At the door, they peered outside cautiously. Curious onlookers had gathered on front steps or peered through windows. Customers streamed up the bar steps into the Zwinglistrasse. They rushed off in different directions, heads down, silent. But free. Gretchen couldn't understand it.

Daniel walked quickly down the street, away from the bar. She and Birgit had to break into a jog to keep up. As they neared the corner, she glanced back. A police wagon was lurching to a stop in front of the bar. It must have come to transport Friedrich's body to the morgue. Dead because he'd cared enough about Fräulein Junge to try to find out what had happened to her. Something broke through the shock fogging her brain, and she had to swallow a sob.

She whipped her head around and kept running. The next street was dark except for the streetlamps, whose bulbs hung like misted pearls in the gloom. From within the tenements, lights blinked on and anxious faces appeared at the windows. Gretchen ducked her head to avoid the people's probing gazes. She realized that her hat had fallen off at some point and she must look strange, rushing bareheaded through the street. Hunching her shoulders, she looked down, letting her hair fall forward to curtain her face.

'Where should we go?' she asked.

'We have to get out of Moabit. Göring and his men will probably begin patrolling the streets any minute.' Daniel sprinted down the sidewalk, Gretchen and Birgit close at his heels. He nodded at a faded Communist banner hanging above a wooden door. It must be a bar; Gretchen had seen plenty of Bavarian banners of blue and white dangling outside beer halls and cafés in Munich. 'They might have a public telephone in there, and I need to make a phone call.'

'To whom?'

They reached the bar, and Daniel paused with his hand on the door, his chest heaving. 'Tom Delmer.' He glanced at Birgit. 'He's a journalist friend of mine. He can help us get to Heinz Schultz, if he's hidden at the Kuhle Wampe.' He looked back at Gretchen. 'Herr Delmer might have valuable information for us, too. Remember? He said he was with Hitler in the Reichstag while it burned.'

They took the S-Bahn to the Köpenick district, sitting nervously, their suitcases at their feet. Gretchen touched the revolver through her purse, needing its comforting presence. As long as she had it, she didn't feel so helpless.

Beneath the squeal of brakes along the track, she heard the thud of Friedrich's body, over and over. She saw his little daughter smiling at them in the parlor, her high, childish voice asking if she was going to be late to school. Gretchen's chest felt as though it were on fire.

Friedrich would get no justice, of that she was certain. Göring would claim Friedrich had been shot while resisting arrest. A justifiable death, the report would conclude, then be put away to molder in a filing cabinet.

And now she, Daniel, and Birgit were alone, without the *Ringverein's* protection. She shuddered and thought of the people back in the bar, bent over their drinks, quiet until Göring and his subordinates had arrived. Now that she'd had time to think about it, his decision to let the customers go made sense. He must have realized there would be a public outcry if he ordered a mass roundup of law-abiding people, whose arrests he couldn't blame on politics or criminal acts. Those men and women had been lucky tonight. Who knew how long it would be before Göring could arrest whomever he liked and no one would dare to protest?

Daniel laid his good arm across her shoulders and drew

her close. 'I know,' he said quietly. 'It's awful. Nothing will ever make it right.'

She rested her head on his chest, feeling the train's jostling vibrate through his body and into hers. She thought of all the deaths that Hitler and his men were responsible for: her father and brother, Friedrich, Daniel's cousin Aaron, countless political opponents who had been knifed in the street or bludgeoned in alleys. So many lives and so much waste. And although the train car was stiflingly hot, she felt as though she would never be warm again.

28

HERR DELMER MET THEM AT THE STATION. WHEN DANIEL started to speak, he cut him off and hustled them toward a cream-colored Opel he said he'd borrowed from a friend. The Kuhle Wampe was too far to walk to, and the fields and forests were easy to get lost in at night, he added as he started the car. They'd done the right thing by asking for his help.

The Opel crept from the curb into oncoming traffic. There were few automobiles on the road, and Gretchen had to bite her lip so she didn't snap at Delmer to go faster. In the back-seat beside her, Birgit looked out the window with dull eyes. Gretchen recognized the signs: Birgit was in shock. She reached over and squeezed Birgit's hand. Birgit started.

'What were you doing in the bar tonight?' Gretchen asked.

'I took the evening off and was on a date.' Birgit smiled faintly. 'Some date, huh?'

'Herr Cohen, what's this about?' Delmer asked. 'You said so little on the telephone.'

'We suspect a fireman has been hiding out at the tent camp since the Reichstag blaze,' Daniel said.

'What the devil does a fireman have to do with Fräulein Junge's murder?' Delmer demanded.

'We think the fireman knew something incriminating about the fire, and Minister Göring slipped up and mentioned him to Fräulein Junge. She was killed in order to keep her quiet. If we can find the fireman and prove the National Socialists set the fire, then we could destroy them forever.'

Delmer sighed. 'More conspiracy theories? Haven't the National Socialists and the Communists done enough mudslinging to make you heartily sick of the fire by now?'

'The fireman's brother was murdered,' Daniel said. 'Probably by a professional. The brothers looked alike and lived together. It's possible the killer made a mistake. We think the fireman came home, found his dead brother, and disappeared because he knew they'd return for him. Whatever he knows, it's important.'

Delmer shot Daniel a sharp look. Then he punched the accelerator. The car raced down a deserted lane surrounded by fields. Ahead, Gretchen saw the ragged black shadows of pines against the night sky.

'You were at the fire,' she said to Delmer. 'What did you see?'

'I was outside the Reichstag five minutes after the blaze broke out,' Delmer said. He spoke in the same clipped tone Daniel used when he was relating past events, and Gretchen wondered if all reporters had the ability to assemble their thoughts into a coherent story at an instant's notice. 'A cordon had been erected around the building, and no one was allowed past it. When Hitler's motorcar arrived, I rushed after him, and was just quick enough to attach myself to the fringe of his entourage as they went up the Reichstag steps. Later I learned that Hitler had come straight from a dinner party, where Herr Hanfstaengl had called him with the news that the Reichstag was burning.'

Hanfstaengl! So he was mixed up in this mess, too. Gretchen felt a stab of disappointment. Somehow, she'd hoped he wouldn't get sucked into the Party's dirty dealings. *Think, don't feel*, she commanded herself. At the gangsters' ball, Hanfstaengl had mentioned that he was staying at Minister Göring's palace – the same palace that was connected to the Reichstag by an underground tunnel. What might Hanfstaengl have seen that night while the Reichstag turned to flame less than two hundred yards away?

Starlit fields flashed past. The car shuddered from the effort of going so fast. Delmer tapped the brake.

'Göring met us in the lobby,' he said. 'He'd been working late and had come directly from his office at the Prussian Ministry. He was shouting that the fire was undoubtedly the work of Communists. The police had already arrested one of the incendiaries, but Göring promised there were bound to be more.'

The trees loomed on the horizon, a tangled mass of black. Between their trunks, Gretchen glimpsed the silvery gleam of water. It must be the Müggelsee. Almost there now.

The car barreled along the road. Daniel stared at Delmer. 'What else? Hitler must have done something.'

'Our group went to the part of the Reichstag that was still in flames,' Delmer said. 'Firemen were working frantically with hand pumps. Never have I seen such fury on Hitler's face. He screamed, "God grant this is the work of the Communists! You are witnessing the beginning of a new era in German history. This fire is the beginning."'

Gretchen's mind whirled. She had suspected the National Socialists had set the fire themselves, so they could declare a state of emergency and pave the way for Hitler to assume dictatorial powers someday. And so they could frame the Communists for a terrorist act. But Hitler had sounded as

261

though he hadn't known who had started the blaze – although he *hoped* it had been the Communists.

His words sounded like those of an innocent man.

Confusion hampered Gretchen's tongue. She wanted to ask Delmer more questions, but her thoughts were spinning too fast. Was it possible that Hitler hadn't ordered the burning of the Reichstag? Then what had Herr Schultz discovered that had angered Göring so deeply – and had led him to have Fräulein Junge silenced before she could mention it to anyone?

The car slowed down. Delmer's eyes met Gretchen's in the rearview mirror. 'That's not all. When we went to inspect the burnt-out Session Chamber, Hitler flew into a rage. He screamed, "Our enemies will be destroyed! All Communist deputies will be hanged!"'

Gretchen frowned. That couldn't be right. Over the years, she'd heard Hitler harangue his opponents many times. But always in an eloquent stream of words, carefully vague so he could incite his supporters to violence while distancing himself from their brutal acts. That was how he kept his hands clean. He never would have spoken so plainly in front of men who weren't his faithful followers, and certainly not a foreign correspondent for a British paper.

Unless . . . unless Hitler had been caught off guard and had said the first things that came into his head. No carefully rehearsed speeches, just immediate rage. And he would have been surprised only if he hadn't planned the fire himself. None of the National Socialists would have dared to do it without his blessing.

Perhaps they had been looking at this all wrong. The papers had reported that the Dutch arsonist was half blind, so they had assumed that his poor eyesight would have prevented him from working alone. But what man could be better prepared to run through the Reichstag in pitch blackness than one who was

262

accustomed to moving in the dark? Had Schultz discovered that a single man, not the Communist Party, had been behind the blaze, thus putting himself in danger?

If the Dutchman had set the blaze on his own . . . then there was no Communist conspiracy. No reason to declare a state of emergency. No reason to pass the Enabling Act. And no reason to put dictatorial powers within Hitler's grasp.

This was a secret well worth killing for.

The rumble of tires on grass pulled Gretchen out of her thoughts. Delmer was parking the car alongside the road. 'We're here.'

As Daniel and Delmer got out, Gretchen hesitated, peering through the window at the closely clustered pine trees. The waters of the Müggelsee shone between the black trunks. What if the National Socialists were even now creeping through the forest toward the tent camp? They had known that Friedrich's men had questioned Herr Schultz's neighbor. Had they spoken to the same woman and figured out the significance of Schultz's camping tent?

The car engine ticked as it cooled down. There were no other automobiles on this lonely road, no figures moving among the trees. Gretchen left the car, nearly slipping on the ice-hardened grass. Birgit slithered out after her.

Daniel had paused at the edge of the forest to look at her. Beneath his fedora, his eyes looked worried. 'Are you all right?'

'Fine,' she lied.

He laid his hand on her cheek, the sensation of his cold fingers jolting her. He must have forgotten to put on his gloves. 'You and Birgit should stay in the car. If you feel like you're in danger, start driving and don't turn back.'

She would never leave him. 'I'm coming with you.'

His smile seemed sad. 'I wish I could protect you from this—'

'Hurry up!' Delmer whispered.

They plunged into the forest. Gretchen glanced behind her to see Birgit following them, a flimsy stick in her hand as a weapon.

The branches of the pines formed such a dense canopy overhead that Gretchen couldn't see the light of the stars. She moved as quickly as she dared, her hands outstretched for possible obstacles. In front of her, Daniel's and Delmer's footsteps crunched on pine needles and the water lapped on the shore. She heard something else that sounded like laundry snapping on the line.

The trees thinned. Between the pines, Daniel and Delmer stood motionless, their heads cocked as if listening. Gretchen stopped beside them.

Several feet ahead, the shore began, a strip of sand stretching out to the icy lake. Under the last line of trees, a handful of simple wooden posts had been screwed into the ground. A few strips of black-and-white-striped canvas flapped from one of them. The tent camp had been dismantled for winter, as Daniel had said. The shore stood silent and empty.

Except for a flash of white beneath the trees, on the forest's outskirts. Gretchen touched Daniel's hand and pointed to the left. He nodded, his eyes narrowing. Then he crept forward, Delmer a pace behind.

Gretchen fished her revolver out of her purse.

'Gretchen,' Birgit gasped. 'What are you doing?'

'Shh.' Gretchen made a cutting motion with her free hand, and her friend subsided into silence.

Quickly, she wove between the trees after Daniel and Delmer. She stepped with her knees braced for the recoil's impact, as Hitler had taught her. Her finger on the trigger was steady. Blood thudded in her ears, and the sound of her breathing seemed as loud as an ocean's waves battering the shore. She took tiny sips of air, trying to be quieter.

As they neared the flicker of white, it sharpened into a canvas tent strung between two trees.

The fireman's. It had to be.

The tent had been pitched under the final cluster of pines, and its flaps hung open, showing there was no one inside. The patch of sand directly in front of the tent was crisscrossed with footprints. Someone – perhaps several someones – had been here, recently enough so their marks hadn't been erased.

They were too late.

The sudden crack of a twig seemed as loud as a gunshot. Gretchen jumped and scanned their surroundings, her heart pounding. A half-dozen yards away, along the curving shore-line, several shadowy figures emerged from the curtain of trees. They moved so fast, she caught only their outlines, but that was enough to recognize the distinctive shapes of their knickers and caps. They were SA men. Silver glinted in their hands; knives, maybe.

The men charged across the shore toward them. For an instant, Gretchen stood rooted to the spot, feeling her heart thud in her chest. All she could think over and over was *no*. Even as her mind seemed to be frozen, though, her arm raised her weapon. She squinted. Ten men, at least. There were too many of them to shoot; by the time they got within range, she'd only be able to squeeze off a couple of shots before the others reached her and wrestled her gun away.

Daniel shoved her hard between the shoulder blades. 'Run!'

She turned and raced into the forest. The pines whipped past, skinny lines of black and green; they would provide no protection for her to hide behind. She kept running, her breath crashing so hard in her ears that she couldn't hear how close the SA men were. She didn't dare look back.

She raced between the pines, dodging and weaving, praying her uneven movements would keep her off target if the SA had pistols. A low-hanging branch hit her in the face, but she didn't even feel it.

From the corner of her eye, she caught a dark blur falling to the ground. 'Gretchen!' cried a girl's voice.

Birgit. She looked beseechingly at Gretchen. 'My ankle,' she gasped.

Gretchen grabbed Birgit around the waist and hauled her to her feet. 'Come on,' she panted. Birgit draped her arm across Gretchen's shoulders and they half ran, half hobbled through the woods, finally bursting through the last line of firs. They struggled forward, stumbling on the ice-encrusted grass. Birgit started to fall again. Gritting her teeth, Gretchen yanked her up.

Directly ahead, Delmer's car sat beside the road. They staggered toward it. Gretchen flung the back passenger door open. She pushed Birgit inside, throwing herself after her, half falling across the seat. She heard a wrench of metal as someone ripped open the front door – she bolted upright and saw it was Delmer – and jumped in. The car started with a throaty rumble and shot forward, its tires skidding on the grass for an instant until they reached the smooth pavement of the road.

Beside Delmer, the front seat was empty.

PART FOUR

TORCHLIGHT

Whoever lights the torch of war in Europe can wish for
nothing but chaos.
—*Adolf Hitler*

29

'WHAT ARE YOU DOING?' GRETCHEN SCREAMED AT Delmer. 'Daniel's still back there!'

'Do you think I don't know that?' he snapped. 'He didn't run. He stayed behind to fight them.'

She whipped her head around. Through the rear window, she could see the trees, and beyond them, the dark shapes of men ranged in a circle, their arms raising again and again as they hit at something on the sand. *Daniel*.

'We have to go back!' Gretchen yelled. 'We can't leave him there – he'll be killed!'

'We can't! They'll kill us, too.'

As Gretchen watched, several SA men broke away from the circle around Daniel and plunged into the forest, running toward them. They were shouting something – it sounded like 'Stop!' – but they were too far away for her to hear them clearly. The men rapidly shrank as Delmer's automobile shot down the road.

'Turn the car around!' Gretchen lunged over the front seat, trying to grab for the steering wheel. 'We have to help Daniel!'

'Sit down!' Delmer barked. Keeping one hand on the wheel, he reached and shoved her away, his fist connecting with her shoulder, then her neck, so hard that she lost her breath and fell back into her seat. 'Do you want us to die, too? Because that's what will happen if we return.'

She tried to reply, but her neck ached where he had pushed her, and she started coughing instead, tears coming to her eyes. She sucked in a lungful of air and felt it burning as it traveled down her throat. Birgit stared at her, white-faced.

'I can't leave him!' Gretchen gasped out.

'You go back, and you'll be dead, and you won't be able to help him at all,' Delmer said. He drove so fast that the tires squealed on the road. Through the windows, the trees streaked past, an endless haze of black. He glanced at her, his eyes wild. 'I'm sorry.'

'Stop the car. I'll get out.' She would have to be close, within at least fifty yards of the men, if she wanted her aim to be accurate. She looked down at the gleaming metal of the gun and knew she couldn't possibly hit all of the SA men before some of them reached her. It didn't matter. She would shoot as many of them as she could, providing a distraction so Daniel could get away.

'I won't send a young girl to her death!' Delmer cried.

She grabbed the door handle and pushed. It was hard to open; the car was barreling so fast down the road that the wind pressed on the door like an iron weight, and she had to strain with all of her might. The door opened a foot. She leaned out a little. The wind tossed her hair over her face, so she saw the road rushing below through a screen of brown strands. The car was going too quickly; there was no way she could jump out without breaking her legs, forced to lie, help-less, along the road until someone found her.

She screamed in frustration and slammed the door closed. 'Please,' she begged Delmer. 'I have to go to Daniel.'

Delmer glanced at her. 'Do you think Herr Cohen didn't know what he was doing? *He never ran*. He sacrificed himself to save us. To save *you*, I should say. You won't help him by going back; you'll only sign your own death warrant.'

'No!' Gretchen shouted. 'Please, *please* stop!'

Birgit's arms came around her, trying to hold her in place as she thrashed, desperate to get out of the car. But Delmer kept driving. He didn't look at her.

'I'm sorry,' he said, and she heard the grief in his voice. 'We can't go back.'

Her thoughts seemed to be made of ice; all she could think over and over was Daniel's name, and she heard Delmer's voice as though from far away. She pushed Birgit off and twisted around to look through the rear window again. She couldn't see Daniel and the SA men anymore, just the silvery waters of the Müggelsee and the dark mass of the forest. Then the car rounded a curve in the road, and they were hidden from her, too.

The car ride into central Berlin was silent. Gretchen sat slumped in her seat, watching the farm fields of the Köpenick district flash past with dull eyes. Her hands held onto the revolver so tightly that they had begun to ache, but she couldn't loosen her grip.

This isn't real, she told herself. But she looked at her hands, white-knuckled on the Webley, and her wool overcoat falling gently over her legs, and the cracked leather seat of the automobile, and she knew that what she saw was real; she wasn't trapped in another nightmare. Daniel truly had been captured.

Slowly the farmland turned into rows of apartments and

shops. The eastern edges of the city's heart rose around her: shabby structures of stone, streaked with soot; streets whose gutters were choked with trash and snow darkened by tires. The car slid to a stop at the curb and Delmer turned to look at her and Birgit, his expression serious.

'I'll go to a friend of mine at the British Embassy first thing in the morning,' he said. 'Perhaps there's something he can do, given that Herr Cohen lived in England for the past year and a half. It's doubtful,' he added as Gretchen raised her head to stare at him, hardly daring to hope. 'He's a German citizen, so the British can't lay claim to him. But I'll do what I can.'

She nodded. It was something, at least. She wanted to curse him for not turning the car around; she wanted to climb over the seat and shake and slap him, but she saw the agony on his face. Part of her understood that he had had to make an impossible choice, and she couldn't hate him. She swallowed over the dryness in her throat and said, 'Thank you.'

'There are a few lodging houses on this street,' Delmer continued. 'You two should stay together tonight.'

'I want to go back to my rooming house.' Birgit's voice was shrill with anxiety.

Delmer shook his head. 'Not a good idea after what happened to your Ring tonight. You ought to go under for a bit. I'll come by in the morning after I've gone to the British Embassy. Try to get some rest. There's nothing more we can do for now.'

Gretchen nodded mechanically. She got out of the car, carrying both her and Daniel's suitcases. Each of her movements felt painfully slow, as though it took several minutes for her body to respond to her brain's commands. Her legs felt wooden as she forced them forward, following Birgit down the street.

The avenue was dark and deserted; she heard nothing except their footsteps echoing on the sidewalk. There was a lodging house halfway down the block, a skinny stone building with unlit windows. She stood on the front steps and watched without interest as Birgit rang the bell. It seemed as if everything was happening to another person; she had separated from her body and stood off to the side, observing.

Birgit had to ring the bell a second time before an irritated-looking man in a belted bathrobe opened the door.

'People with any sense are in bed at this hour,' he grumbled. As they slipped inside, Gretchen looked over her shoulder to watch Delmer's car drive away. He waved to her, but she could not make her hand wave back.

In the lobby, the man got out the guestbook for them to sign. Gretchen had to write slowly and carefully so she didn't scribble *Gretchen* by mistake. Once she'd written *Gisela Schröder, Nuremberg* and she and Birgit had shown the fellow their papers, he led them upstairs to a cell of a bedchamber.

The instant he left, Gretchen looked for something to barricade the door. There were no chairs, only an old wooden bureau, so she dragged that across the floor, heedless of the racket it made. Birgit watched her, rubbing her wrenched ankle. Still in her coat, Gretchen slid down the wall to sit. The iciness of the floorboards seeped through her clothes, but she couldn't bring herself to care. Nothing mattered, now that Daniel was gone.

Tears burned in her eyes. *Gone.* What a weak word to cover a multitude of horrors. It was no use prettying up the truth: Daniel was as good as dead. The SA must have gotten to Heinz Schultz first and taken him away somewhere or beaten him senseless, then set up several men to keep watch on the tent and capture anyone who arrived seeking the fireman. If they had recognized Daniel, they'd want to know how much he had uncovered about Fräulein Junge's murder and they'd be frantic to know where she was. Capturing Hitler's former little pet would be quite a coup for them.

Daniel might survive for a day or two, while the SA tried to torture answers out of him. He would hold out for as long as he could. She could imagine the sort of agony that was in store for him. Burned with cigarettes until his arms were a patchwork of blackened flesh. Dunked face-first into a pail of water and held under while he thought his lungs would explode. Whipped again and again, the skin of his back splitting apart into deep troughs of blood and severed muscle.

No one could withstand such pain for long. Eventually, he would die or he would break. Even the second option meant death; they would kill him once he was no longer useful. And she had absolutely no idea how to help him.

She covered her face with her hands and sobbed. The floorboards creaked as Birgit sat down beside her.

'I'm so sorry, Gretchen,' Birgit said. She wrapped her arms around Gretchen's shoulders and pulled her closer. Gretchen pressed her face into Birgit's shoulder and wept. *Daniel*. She still felt his hand on her back, pushing her toward the trees. *Run*, he had shouted at her, but he had stayed. Sobs caught in her throat. He had sacrificed himself to save her.

In sudden frustration, she slipped from Birgit's arms and surged to her feet to pace the room. How dare Daniel? He deserved to live, more than anyone else she'd ever met. He should be working at a first-rate newspaper, writing the stories that he thought everyone needed to read, exposing the lies that he despised so deeply. He should be able to stop by his family's house for Sabbath evening supper and tease his sisters about their beaux. He should be able to live freely *here*, in his own country that he loved.

As abruptly as the anger had consumed her, it drained

away. She sagged onto the mattress and started sobbing again. Now she heard how loud she sounded, though, so she muffled her mouth against the pillow. Her tears trickled into the flowered pillowcase, making the dampened fabric stick to her face.

She cried until she felt empty. Then she lay on her back and stared at the ceiling. Birgit sat on the edge of the bed, watching her with anxious eyes, but Gretchen couldn't summon the energy to say anything to her.

Her thoughts drifted to the time she and Daniel had left Munich and run out of money in Switzerland, where they had taken menial jobs to earn enough to pay for their passage to England. In their hotel, she had rested her head on his chest, listening to the steady thump of his heart. Beyond the window, the waters of Lake Lucerne had glittered in the autumn sunlight.

'What if we stayed here forever?' she'd asked him. 'Just you and me, hidden away?'

He'd laughed. 'We'd both die of boredom within a month. We're city people, Gretchen. Besides, we need to get you to the Whitestones. From everything you've told me, Herr Doktor Whitestone sounds like a good man. And he said he'd like you to stay with his family, if you were ever in trouble.' His hand had rubbed her shoulder. 'You deserve to have a real family.'

'What about you?' She'd shifted in his arms so she could look into his face. 'What do you want?'

He'd looked serious. 'I can't ever have two of the things I want the most – my family and my job. But I'll find another newspaper post, I'm certain of it. I'll only be unhappy if I feel useless.' He'd ruffled her hair and smiled. 'Don't look so upset. We're together and we're alive. That's what matters most.'

Now Gretchen's throat tightened. He *had* felt useless in

England, and miserable and alone, while she had moved in with her new family, content and secure for the first time in her life. And she hadn't realized it. If only she could unwind the clock, so they could be in England together again. Or to yesterday morning, when she'd lain beside him, listening to him breathe. She wished she could hold on to that moment forever. Feeling the warmth pulsing from his body, smiling because they had told each other they could solve the obstacles keeping them apart.

A sob rose in her throat but she choked it down. Thank God she had told him that she loved him, before he had been taken from her. He knew how she felt. She repeated the thought over and over, clinging to it like it was a life preserver and she was swimming in storm-tossed seas. He would die, knowing she loved him. It was the last gift she would ever be able to give him.

'Gretchen?' Birgit sounded desperate. 'Please say something. I need to know you're all right.'

Her voice dragged Gretchen back to the present. She sat up, pressing the heels of her hands into her eyes, stanching the tears that threatened to return.

'I'm fine,' she said for Birgit's sake, although it couldn't have been further from the truth.

She crossed the room and twitched aside the curtain to look at the street below. Still deserted. No cars, no policemen walking their beat, no SA fellows prowling past. Daniel was somewhere out there: in a prison cell, perhaps, or the dank cellar of an SA barracks, where nobody would object to a prisoner's torture.

Calm, calm. She rested her forehead on the glass and took three deep breaths, focusing on the sensation of air filling her chest. She moved back from the window, letting the curtains fall into place.

What could she possibly do? There was no one she could go to for help; the *Ringverein* men were scrambling to save themselves and reassemble their organization, and the police force was under Göring's jurisdiction and had been invaded by his men. She didn't dare go to the Cohens' house – her heart twisted at the thought of them. They had no idea what had happened to their son; they might never know. She couldn't go to them for help, for now that the National Socialists knew for certain that Daniel had returned to Berlin, they might have the house under surveillance, expecting that his allies could drop by. She couldn't telephone the Cohens either or telegram the Whitestones, since there were no longer any secure lines of communication throughout Germany. Except for Delmer and his pessimistic offer, she was alone.

'I have to help him,' she said aloud.

'You mean, *we* have to,' Birgit said.

Gretchen started. She had been so wrapped up in her thoughts, she had forgotten that Birgit was there. Sitting on the edge of the bed, Birgit watched her, white-faced but determined.

'You don't need to,' Gretchen said quickly. 'Going after Daniel will be dangerous—'

'I know.' Birgit's eyes burned into Gretchen's. 'Those men killed Friedrich and Monika. They shot them without a second thought. We both know what will happen to Daniel if we don't get him out.'

A wave of gratitude washed over Gretchen, swamping her so that she couldn't speak for a minute. 'Thank you,' she said at last. 'I have no idea where to begin.'

'Well, we can't do anything tonight. Herr Delmer will have news tomorrow, and we can figure things out from there.'

Gretchen nodded woodenly. She knew that Daniel would live through the night. The SA would torture him, but they'd be too eager to learn the information he knew to kill him immediately. Daniel could withstand tremendous pain, thanks to the months he'd spent coping with his arm injury. He knew how to build a wall within his mind, isolating it from his body.

Stay strong, Daniel, she thought, wishing he could somehow magically hear her. *Hold on*.

Because no matter what, she was coming for him.

30

MORNING DAWNED GRAY AND COLD. TWO DAYS UNTIL the Reichstag session when the Enabling Act was up for a vote, Gretchen thought automatically. She rolled onto her side, seeking the warmth of Daniel's body. Her hand skimmed his arm, and she frowned. Something was wrong. She didn't feel his puckered scar through his pajama sleeve, but the harsh scratchiness of wool.

She bolted upright. Even as she saw Birgit, still asleep, wearing one of Gretchen's sweaters over yesterday's frock, the knowledge crashed down on her like a wave: Daniel was gone.

She had to put her hands over her mouth so she didn't cry out. *Don't fall apart,* she ordered herself. Daniel deserved more than her tears.

Quickly, she slipped from bed and dressed in a black skirt and red sweater set. After she'd washed in cold water in the basin, she combed her hair and brushed rouge over her cheeks. In the mirror, she almost looked normal; only the tightness around her eyes betrayed her tension. Satisfied, she turned away. It was important that she appear ordinary, so nobody would give her a second look.

Although she longed to do something, *anything*, she sat in a chair while Birgit got up. When Birgit returned from the lavatory, white dust surrounded her nostrils. Gretchen said nothing. A part of her longed for the escape of cocaine, too, but Daniel needed her to keep her wits.

In silence, she and Birgit waited for Herr Delmer to show up. From the street, she heard the bells of the Church of St Nicholas ringing the hour. Eight o'clock. Maybe somewhere in Berlin, Daniel was waking up to a new day, too. Or he'd been kept awake all night by his captors as they whipped him—

Stop, she begged herself, pushing the images of a bloodied Daniel out of her head before she screamed. He was alive and she would get him out. She couldn't let herself think anything else.

It was half past nine before the lodging house proprietor knocked on their door, mumbling that they had a gentleman caller downstairs. Delmer; it had to be – no one else knew they were here. Gretchen and Birgit snatched up their coats and pocketbooks and rushed to the front hall. Delmer stood in a corner, his downcast expression telling Gretchen imme-diately how his errand had gone. She tried to ignore the ache of disappointment. Wallowing wouldn't do Daniel any good.

'I'm sorry,' Delmer said. 'My friend said there's nothing the British Embassy can do since Herr Cohen's a German citizen. I'll do my best to investigate more, but I'm not opti-mistic about our chances.'

She had expected this answer, but hearing it still hurt. Somehow she managed to thank him and watch him leave without crying. Then she and Birgit nodded grimly at each other. They had stayed up for hours last night, figuring out a plan. Their first step may have ended in failure, but the second could still work.

Together, they slipped outside, scanning the buildings for a restaurant or a tearoom. They found a café a block over. Inside, it smelled of coffee and sausage. Gretchen's head felt light from hunger, but she ignored the small tables and headed to the public telephone hanging on the wall by the lavatories in the rear. Birgit stood next to her, lighting a cigarette.

Before Gretchen dialed, she glanced around the room: a half-dozen tables were occupied, but everybody was concentrating on their food and talking with their companions. With sweating hands, she lifted the receiver. When the operator asked how to direct her call, she had to clear her throat before she could say police headquarters.

A brisk-sounding man's voice sounded in her ear, informing her that she had been connected with the criminal police division. 'I need to speak to Superintendent Gennat,' she said, turning away from the diners and speaking quietly. 'It's urgent.'

'Name?'

Thank God she'd anticipated the question! 'Tell him we met through a mutual acquaintance – Friedrich. He'll understand.' She hoped.

'One moment.'

She listened to the whistling and clicking sounds of the call being rerouted. 'This is Gennat,' a familiar gruff voice boomed down the telephone wires. 'I know who you are, and I can guess why you've called.'

'I'm not sure how much I can say – should we meet?' Gretchen asked.

'This line's secure, if that's what you're worried about. I got the news first thing this morning. Friedrich Walter is in the morgue and his death has been listed as justifiable homicide. According to the paperwork, he tried to attack the police and SA officers who were conducting a raid on a bar under his protection.' He spit out the words as though they tasted foul.

Gretchen's cheeks burned with shame. In her fear over Daniel's fate, she'd forgotten about Friedrich. 'That's not all that happened last night. My' – she hesitated, not daring to say Daniel's name over the line, despite Gennat's reassurances that it was safe – 'my young man was captured by the SA. Is there anything you can do for him?' She held her breath.

'He's been arrested?' Gennat sounded furious. She heard papers rustling. 'I've had no notification that he was picked up and by all rights, I certainly should have since he's wanted by my homicide division.' He hissed out a breath. 'It was the SA that took him? You're certain?'

The image of the brown-uniformed men, surrounding Daniel and hitting him, rose in her mind. Shakily, she said, 'I'm certain.'

Gennat cursed. 'I'll do everything in my power to track him down and have him transferred to my jurisdiction. That's the best I can do for you. I can't understand it,' he burst out in frustration. 'The different police departments have always worked so well together, but ever since Minister Göring started adding his own men to our force, I feel as though people are throwing roadblocks in my path. Apprehending a murder suspect without alerting me is inexcusable. Ring me in a day or so and I should have more to tell you.'

'Very well. Thank you.' Slowly, Gretchen replaced the receiver. She was shaking so hard that she had to grind her teeth together so they wouldn't chatter. Transferring Daniel from the SA to the criminal police would only be exchanging a quick death for a gradual one. Göring would make sure that Daniel was tried and found guilty of Fräulein Junge's murder; within months, he would be guillotined.

She'd been so certain that Gennat would help but now she realized that, as Daniel had already been captured, there was nothing Gennat could do except lay claim to him. If he tried to arrange for Daniel's release, Göring and his men would accuse him of corruption, and possibly have him removed from his post. The best she could hope for from Gennat was information about Daniel's location, but that might not come soon enough. Her heart twisted. Daniel could be dead before Gennat found him.

'People are staring,' Birgit murmured in her ear. 'Let's sit down and have something to eat. You look ready to collapse.'

Dazed, Gretchen let Birgit guide her to a table and order for both of them. In silence, they waited for the food to arrive. Gretchen stared so hard at the red and white checks on the tablecloth that they blurred together. What was happening to Daniel right now? How badly was he hurt?

When the waitress set their bowls of pea and ham soup down, Gretchen's stomach churned. How could she possibly eat when Daniel must be going hungry?

Birgit shoved a spoon into her hand. 'Eat,' she said firmly. 'You're no good to him if you faint from hunger.'

Reluctantly, Gretchen dipped her spoon into the bowl. The broth warmed her and when it was gone, she had to admit that she felt a little better. In low murmurs, she explained to Birgit what Gennat had said.

'I'm afraid I don't have any more ideas,' Birgit said, looking miserable. 'Is there *anyone* else we could ask for help? Someone who might know where Daniel's being held?'

Gretchen hesitated. There was one person – Herr Hanfstaengl. He hadn't turned her in when he'd seen her at the gangsters' ball. As a houseguest at Minister Göring's palace, he might be privy to top-secret information. Doubtless, he'd be furious if he saw her again, though, for at the ball he'd warned

283

her to leave Berlin, and she knew he would hate that she'd disregarded his orders. Maybe he would even be angry enough to hand her over to Göring's men.

For Daniel's sake, she was willing to take that chance.

Alone, Gretchen followed Birgit's directions to the nearest S-Bahn stop and took a train across the city. At the café, they'd argued about Gretchen's plan – Birgit had wanted to accompany her to see Hanfstaengl, but Gretchen had been adamant that it was too dangerous. Her years of friendship with Hanfstaengl might keep her safe, but he had no connections to Birgit. If he realized that she was part of the *Schweigen* Ring or was trying to help Daniel, he might feel compelled to turn her in.

She got off at the stop for the Wilhelmstrasse. The long avenue was lined with plain white government buildings. In the middle of a Tuesday morning, the pavement was clogged with civil servants and burghers, hurrying to and from meetings, and the street teemed with the usual motley assortment of vehicles: streetcars, pale yellow omnibuses, private automobiles, bicycles.

To her left loomed the Chancellery, Hitler's new home. Her gaze was drawn to it as relentlessly as a magnet, even though she didn't want to see it.

The Chancellery was a massive block of stone set back from the street. As Gretchen passed it, she couldn't help looking at its dozens of windows, flashing gold from the winter sunlight, and wondered if Hitler was standing at one of them now, peering at the street below and mentally writing the speech he would give when the Reichstag convened the day after tomorrow.

Or perhaps he was chatting with his usual favored companions, his adjutants and bodyguards, indulging in one of his pet topics and telling them the exact dimensions of each room in the Chancellery. She could remember him doing the same with her family when he'd moved into his posh apartment in Munich; for weeks afterward, he'd delighted in telling her how tall and wide his splendid parlor was, and she'd pretended that she didn't already know the measurements since he took such pleasure in discussing them.

Her heart started pounding. They were so close again. Had he already been told that Daniel had been captured? Had he smiled when his adjutants brought him the news, or had he become incensed, railing against reporters like Daniel who criticized him in the papers until he'd slumped, exhausted, in a chair and rested his head in his hands, as she'd seen him do on the occasions when he'd let his temper get the best of him? She knew that no matter what he ordered done to Daniel, his conscience would not utter even a whisper.

She rushed past the Chancellery. Each sound jolted her heart – the snapping of swastika banners in the breeze, a car backfiring a block away, the click of her heels on the pavement. Ordinary noises. Not the rich timbre of Hitler's voice, shouting for her to stop. He wouldn't find her. He *wouldn't*.

A building of pale stone rose on her left; she almost stopped before recognizing it as the presidential palace from a photograph in her old history textbook. She pushed on until she saw Minister Göring's home up ahead, instantly identifiable from another picture in her schoolbook. As Reichstag Speaker, Göring lived in an official residence, a gloomy box of a building with a mansard roof. From across the street, she watched the house and waited. Sooner or later, Hanfstaengl would have to arrive or leave.

Minutes stretched on. She hopped from foot to foot to warm her numbed toes. A group of men in suits sauntered past, a couple of them sliding curious glances at her. She ignored them.

Eleven o'clock came and went, and it was nearly half past twelve when the palace's front door opened and someone jogged down the steps. Even from this distance, she recognized the man's awkward gait, as though his oversized limbs were being jerked about by invisible strings. It was Hanfstaengl. And he was alone.

He reached the street and headed south, his shoulders hunched under his belted trench coat. She watched the traffic, gauging the distance between the automobiles, taxis, and streetcars before she darted between them. When she got to the opposite side, she saw that Hanfstaengl was a few yards ahead and she ran to catch up to him.

'Herr Hanfstaengl,' she said breathlessly, 'please, I need your help.'

He whirled around. 'Gretchen! What the devil are you still doing here?' His hand gripped her wrist and he yanked her into the shadows between two buildings. 'Have you lost your mind? Do you want to end up in prison? You need to get out of Berlin!'

'I can't leave.' Tears thickened her throat. 'Herr Cohen has been captured by Minister Göring's men. I have to help him. Maybe you can find out where they're keeping him—'

'Listen to yourself!' Hanfstaengl snapped. 'You're giving up your life for the sake of a Jew!'

She looked at him: his long face contorted in a scowl, his lips pursed in anger. It was no use fighting with him; there was nothing she could say that he would agree with. Alfred's advice came back to her – psychology could be her best form of protection. She hated the thought of manipulating Hanfstaengl into doing what she wanted, but it couldn't be helped. Nothing mattered more than rescuing Daniel.

'I've been foolish,' she said. The words tasted like soot in her mouth. 'But I can hardly be expected to know better, can I, without my papa to guide me? And surely you understand how love can transcend boundaries?'

He made an annoyed sound in his throat. 'I married an American, not a Jew, and I need hardly remind you that I'm half American myself.' He sighed and scrubbed his ham-sized hands over his face. 'Forget your Jew,' he said quietly. 'There's nothing you can do for him now. Leave this place and do something worthwhile with your life that would make your father proud. You've made mistakes, but I can't see the point of punishing a child like you for poor decisions when you haven't finished growing up yet.'

She barely heard his advice, seizing onto his earlier words instead. 'What do you mean, there's nothing I can do for him now? What do you know?'

Sighing, he let his hands fall from his face. His grave expression was so unlike him that he was almost unrecognizable. Something icy trickled inside Gretchen's mind. And she knew suddenly, desperately, that she didn't want to hear what he had to say.

'No,' she said, but Hanfstaengl bent down so he could look into her eyes.

'I hate to have to tell you this,' he said.

A dull buzzing sounded in Gretchen's ears. She shrank from Hanfstaengl, willing him not to say the words, because saying them would make them real, but he kept talking.

'I just spoke to Minister Göring on the telephone,' he said gently. 'Gretl, you must brace yourself.'

'No!' she started to scream but Hanfstaengl cut her off.

'He's gone, Gretchen. Daniel Cohen was shot to death this morning.'

31

TIME SEEMED TO STOP. FOR A LONG MOMENT, GRETCHEN stared at Hanfstaengl, unable to understand what he had just said. She noticed tiny details about his appearance that she hadn't seen before: a dark patch of stubble on his jaw that he had missed with his razor, strands of silver inter-woven with his brown hair, the wrinkles between his eyebrows. Part of her mind understood what she was doing: she was latching onto insignificant trivialities because they were easier to comprehend than what she had been told.

Finally she found her voice. 'You're lying.' Her voice came out in a shaky whisper.

'It's the truth.' Hanfstaengl's eyes met hers, unblinking. 'Minister Göring said the boy was a troublemaker and a criminal, and it was in Germany's best interests to have him executed immediately.'

His words hit Gretchen like a pail of water. *Dead.* She wouldn't believe it. Daniel was alive and he was fine and she would find him. Fury surged through her, and she flung herself at Hanfstaengl, pummeling his chest with her fists.

'I don't believe you!' she shouted. 'You're a liar!'

He grabbed her wrists, holding her in place. 'Don't be a fool! Do you want everyone in the street to look at us?' Still holding her by the wrists, he pulled her into an alley where the shadows were so thick that she could only see his outline and the whites of his eyes gleaming in the darkness. He released her, breathing hard.

'He's dead, Gretl.' His tone was no longer gentle, but flat. 'Need I remind you that Cohen was a wanted murderer? Minister Göring may have acted harshly, but he did what was necessary to protect our city. As far as I'm concerned, he did you a favor. Now you can get out of Berlin and settle someplace safe. Build yourself a proper life with the right sort of companions.'

She barely heard him. 'You must have made a mistake – maybe you misunderstood Minister Göring or he was making a joke.' With each word, her voice rose higher and higher until she was practically screaming.

Hanfstaengl gripped her shoulders and shook her. '*Listen to me*. Minister Göring was very clear. He said the Jew Cohen was found last night. As a dangerous killer and a political subversive, his very existence threatens Germany's stability. Ordinarily, Göring would have turned Cohen over to the police, but we're living in dangerous times. We have to fight our enemies with every ounce of our strength. I might not have made the same decision that Göring did, but I understand his reasoning. He did what had to be done.'

Gretchen saw the weary sorrow in Hanfstaengl's face. His eyes never left hers; he didn't look away or fiddle with his coat buttons or hum under his breath, any of the things he did when he was nervous. He was telling the truth. He believed every word he said. Daniel truly was dead.

She couldn't speak. She gazed at her hands and her skirt;

they seemed to belong to someone else. Tears filled her eyes, blurring the cobblestones until she saw them through a sheen of water.

Hanfstaengl patted her shoulder. 'Calm yourself. I know you fancied yourself in love with Cohen, but he was a Jew and a killer and so far beneath you that I can't believe you gave him a second look. You may be sad for a day or two, but eventually you'll see that this was for the best. You're free of his bad influence. I wish you could come back to us, but I'm afraid it's too late for that. You'll have to start over somewhere else.'

She didn't want to start over; all she wanted was Daniel. 'I don't—' she began to say, then had to stop because her chest burned so badly that she couldn't talk. Taking a deep breath, she tried again. 'I don't understand.' She had to speak carefully so her voice didn't careen out of control. 'Wouldn't Minister Göring want Daniel kept alive so he could get information out of him?'

Hanfstaengl shrugged. 'He said that Cohen didn't seem to know anything.'

Tears trickled down Gretchen's cheeks. She had been so certain that Daniel would be able to withstand torture without spilling any of his secrets. What she hadn't realized was that he could feign ignorance so convincingly that his captors had believed him. His silence had cost him his life. And he had done it for her. She knew it deep in her bones. He had wanted to protect her, so he hadn't told them anything. In the end, he had died for her.

Although she tried to push the image away, it rose in her mind: Daniel, lying in a crumpled heap on the floor of a jail cell, blood pooled on either side of him. His eyes glazed, his face slack. His body a shell.

She made a noise deep in her throat, but she couldn't say a word.

'Come now,' Hanfstaengl said quietly. His hands cupped her elbows, steadying her. For an instant, she stood, swaying a little, before she stepped away from him. With shaking hands, she wiped her face. The lines of stone and mortar in the alley wall looked too clear, as though her eyesight had suddenly strengthened. She stared at the sliver of sky between the two buildings, willing the tears to stay back.

'What are they going to do with' – she could barely force the words out, but she had to know – 'with Daniel's body?'

Hanfstaengl's eyebrows lifted in surprise. 'I have no idea. Does it matter, at this point?'

'He should be buried by sunset. It's important in his religion.' She realized what she was saying and hysteria bubbled in her chest, threatening to break loose in peals of wild laughter. What was she thinking – suggesting the National Socialists ought to bury Daniel in accordance with his faith, as though they cared a toss about their Jewish victims?

Besides, he'd been executed illegally. They would be eager to conceal his body. Most likely, they'd dig a grave for him in an abandoned field or forest on the outskirts of Berlin, where no one would ever find him. She wouldn't even have the luxury of visiting his grave.

Hanfstaengl was talking, but she didn't hear him. She clutched her purse, so that she had something to hold onto, her fingers curling over the bulge of her revolver. If only she hadn't run but had stayed to shoot those men instead . . .

Knowledge blazed through her brain like a line of fire. She knew what she had to do. She could give Daniel's death meaning. That could be her last gift to him, not her declaration of love.

She would punish the men who had murdered him.

'I beg your pardon,' she interrupted Herr Hanfstaengl. 'Where was Daniel killed? I deserve to know,' she added when he hesitated, looking unsure of himself. 'Give me that much at least.'

'I really shouldn't say—'

'I want to know what his final moments were like,' Gretchen snapped. When Hanfstaengl remained silent, she stepped closer to him, trying to smooth out the anger in her face. Hanfstaengl would want her to act submissive and contrite, she knew. She'd let him think that was exactly how she felt. For Daniel's sake, she would lie to everyone. 'I promise, I'll leave Berlin straightaway if you'll tell me. I only want to know what sort of place he was in – and if he suffered very much.'

'It would have been a clean death,' Hanfstaengl said hastily. 'Göring was a military man, and I'm certain he would have insisted on a quick kill. Your Jew wouldn't have been in pain.'

Gretchen prayed he was right. The thought of Daniel, bloodied and bruised, enduring hours of torment before they finally shot him was more than she could stand.

'Thank you,' she said. 'What about' – she paused, steadying her voice, hoping Hanfstaengl didn't notice her eagerness – 'what about the place where he was held?'

'It's the cellar of a trade union office building,' he said. 'The SA recently shut it down and took over the place.'

Berlin probably had dozens of trade unions, and it could take her days to find out which ones had been closed by the National Socialists. She needed more information, but she couldn't let Hanfstaengl suspect what she was planning.

'Please tell me the street. Just so I can walk by and pay my respects. Then I'll leave, I promise.'

Hanfstaengl's eyes focused on hers with lightning intensity. 'You swear it?'

'Yes.' The lie slid off her tongue.

Sighing, he said, 'Fine. It's on the Lange Strasse. It's in a poor neighborhood, so mind you keep watch on your pocket-book. Now that's all I know, and if I talk with you much longer, I'll be late for luncheon with Herr Hitler at the Chancellery. You know how impatient he gets.'

She nodded and he rested his hand on her cheek, in his old familiar manner. Tears pricked her eyes. He still loved her enough to touch her – even though he must believe she'd been contaminated by Daniel and the so-called Jewish virus. His hand fell away, and she stood on tiptoe to kiss his cheek.

'I'll never forget your kindness to me,' she said.

His smile was sad. 'God keep you safe, Gretchen.'

She watched him walk out of the alley into the sunlight. He turned to the left, and then he was gone. For a long moment, she stood still, carefully blanking her mind so she could go out into the street and not break down in tears. She would not let herself think about Daniel. Only one thought would guide her actions now.

Revenge. She would destroy the men who had killed Daniel. Thanks to Hanfstaengl, she knew where to find them.

Again, she clutched her purse, feeling the weight of her revolver. She allowed herself a small smile. She would hunt down those men and make them pay. Hitler had taught her too well for her to miss.

32

BIRGIT WAS WAITING FOR GRETCHEN WHEN SHE
returned to the lodging house. 'Well?' she demanded, rocketing
off her chair, swiping at the dust ringing her nostrils. 'What
did your friend say?'

Grief swamped Gretchen, and she couldn't speak. Shaking
her head, she closed the door. With the slow, automatic movements of a sleepwalker, she slipped off her coat and gloves.
Then she sat on the bed, covering her face with her hands,
trying to close herself into her own world.

'Daniel's dead,' she said. With dull eyes, she stared through
her fingers at the cream-colored bedspread. She wished she
could surrender to the relief of tears, but she was wrung dry.
'Minister Göring had him shot this morning.'

'Oh my God!' Birgit tried to embrace Gretchen, but she
eased out of her friend's arms.

'Please don't,' Gretchen said. 'I'll be all right as long as
nobody touches me.'

She couldn't explain this sudden need to feel separate and
isolated from everyone else; all she knew was that if someone

showed her kindness, she would shatter. Turning away from the hurt in Birgit's eyes, she added, 'There's nothing more we can do. You ought to go back to Frau Fleischer's rooming house.'

'I won't leave you alone.' Birgit sounded shaky. 'How can the National Socialists hope to get away with this? With killing Monika and Friedrich and now Daniel?'

'Because the National Socialists are taking over the police.' Gretchen's tone was so harsh she didn't recognize it. 'Our country's disappearing in front of us, and we can't stop it. The best thing you can do for yourself is return to your life. I'll be fine. Don't worry about me.'

'What are you going to do?'

There was no way that Gretchen would tell her the plan she'd devised. It was too dangerous, and anyone who took part in it probably wouldn't survive. For herself, she didn't care. She was ready to die for Daniel's sake. Her only regret was that the Whitestones wouldn't know what had happened to her. She wished she could spare them the agony of wondering about her fate. But this had to be done. She wouldn't let Daniel's death go unpunished.

She realized that Birgit was watching her, waiting for an answer. 'I'm going back to England,' she said quickly to cover up the awkward silence. 'Daniel would want me to be safe.' That, at least, was true. 'Please, Birgit, go home.'

'I'm not sure I should go back to the rooming house.' Birgit bit her lip. 'No doubt the National Socialists are keeping a close eye on my Ring. You know how they want to stamp us out – sooner or later, they'll strike.' She turned to Gretchen. 'You're truly returning to England?'

Gretchen got up and washed her hands in the basin on the bureau, so she could hide her face from Birgit. 'Yes. It's for the best.' She sounded breathless even to her ears.

'Maybe this could be my chance to get out of Berlin. I could go to one of the Ring's brother groups in Dresden or Hamburg. Maybe they can get me a job as a nightclub hostess. It'd be a vast improvement over what I've got here. And I've always wanted to live by the sea.'

'Good. That's settled then.' Gretchen pulled a few bills from her purse and stuffed them into Birgit's hand. She wouldn't need them anymore. 'This should be enough to pay for a train ticket to Hamburg. You should leave straightaway. Don't go back to the rooming house, if you think it might be dangerous.'

'I can't take this.' Birgit tried to return the money, but Gretchen clasped her hands behind her back.

'I've got plenty to get me home,' Gretchen lied. 'You've been a true friend to me. I'll always be grateful to you for wanting to help Daniel.' She blinked away tears, forcing a smile. 'You deserve to make a good life for yourself.'

Birgit flung her arms around Gretchen's neck. 'I can't thank you enough.'

'You don't have to.' Gretchen hugged her back. The contact didn't break her, as she had feared, but felt warm and soothing. 'You'd best get going.'

'I'd better get my things from the rooming house – oh, what does it matter?' Birgit laughed, although tears glittered in her eyes. 'I barely own anything, and this way I can make a fresh start.'

She put on her hat and coat, then paused at the door to look at Gretchen. 'Daniel was a good person. I hope that comforts you. After Monika was murdered, it made me feel better to remember what a sweet girl she was.'

Gretchen swallowed against the emotion welling in her throat. 'He *was* good. The best person I've ever known.'

Birgit embraced her a final time, then slipped out the

door. Motionless, Gretchen listened to her heels clack down the hallway and away from her. For several minutes she sat on the bed, listening to the sounds of the building: the low hum of a jazz tune from a room upstairs, a toilet flushing, voices from the lobby downstairs. Through the window, she glimpsed the sun, a gold coin turning to white as clouds floated across it. The world was continuing to rotate, like it had after her father's murder. It was the same, but she was different, just as she had told Daniel when she'd tried to explain how the death of a loved one tore a hole in one's life.

But Daniel's execution wasn't merely a hole; it was an abyss. And she didn't want to climb out of it.

Memories streamed through her head: dancing with Daniel in a nightclub, memorizing the way the golden chandelier light reflected in his eyes, bewildered because he had seemed so human, utterly unlike the monster she'd been taught to expect; peering through a train window with Daniel, bloodied, dirty, and exhausted, watching a tiny Swiss village appear in the valley below them; and feeling Daniel's lips brush her cheek as they stood on a ferry deck and the white cliffs of Dover rose above the blue-gray waters of the English Channel. *We made it*, he'd said. *I knew we could do it, as long as we were together*, she'd replied.

She sagged onto her side and sobbed. How could he be dead? He'd been the most *alive* person she'd ever known, laughing and loud and confident. It seemed impossible that he could be gone.

In her mind, she traced the curves of his face. His mouth would be silent now, his eyes dulled, the broad chest that she loved to rest her head on no longer rising and falling. One instant, one snap decision, and he was dead, just like Papa and Reinhard.

297

Unsteadily, she got to her feet. She needed something of his, just one small thing to hold on to. She went through his suitcase. A pair of trousers. Two white shirts, a navy suit jacket. Socks, one with a hole in the heel. A comb, a toothbrush. A spiral-bound notebook. She flipped through it, but the pages were empty. Of course. Daniel hadn't written anything down, in case the book fell into the National Socialists' hands. Now she wished he hadn't been so cautious. She would give anything to see his untidy hand-writing again. She loved the way he wrote her name: the messy loop of the G blending into the r. He wrote exactly as he talked: quickly, the words running into one another when he was excited.

Burying her face in his shirts, she breathed in his light, clean scent. This was all that was left of him: a couple of garments and an unfilled notebook. It wasn't enough. Nothing here indicated that he had been a fearless reporter, a brother, a son, a friend. And the love of her life. Sobs shook her shoulders.

Finally, she sat up, mopping her face dry with his shirt. The sky had turned the hard blue of twilight. She must have lain on the floor for an hour or two, clutching his clothes. It felt more like minutes.

She went to the window, peering down into the street painted navy and black by the descending dusk. It was too dark for her to see clearly enough to shoot accurately. She would have to wait until tomorrow to go to the old trade union building. She knew exactly what she would do: she would surprise the men there and kill them. It didn't matter if they were the ones who had shot Daniel. They worked at this secret execution cellar, and so they were all guilty.

Her traitorous stomach growled and she frowned. How could she be hungry when Daniel was dead? She didn't want to feel anything anymore, not even something as simple as hunger.

Ignoring the cramping in her belly, she crawled onto the bed. Holding Daniel's shirt to her chest, she inhaled his scent and lay quietly, waiting for morning.

33

GRETCHEN FORCED HERSELF TO EAT BREAKFAST THE NEXT day. The rolls and cheese tasted like ashes, but she choked them down anyway. She'd be useless if she didn't keep her strength up.

The Lange Strasse was a quiet street lined with dilapidated brick and stone buildings. A man she passed pointed out the former trade union house to her; it was a three-story structure whose windows looked like black rectangles, empty and unlit. *One front door*, Gretchen thought as she studied it from across the street. Presumably a back door, too, but the front would be her best bet; the back courtyard could be bordered by walls or a fence, making it difficult for her to get in and out. Not that she was concerned about escaping. She already knew that her chances of getting away were low.

For several minutes, she pretended to flip through the newspaper she'd swiped from the lodging house lobby, studying her surroundings from the corner of her eye. Up and down the avenue, children streamed from their apartment houses, chattering with one another as they headed to school.

A gleaming black automobile coasted to a stop in front of the union building. As Gretchen watched, two men in SA uniforms got out and jogged up the front steps. *Daniel's killers.* They might not have pulled the trigger, but they worked at this place. They all had blood on their hands.

Her heart felt as though it was being squeezed in someone's hands, tighter and tighter until she thought it would burst. *Calm down,* she ordered herself. She started to let her mind empty, then stopped. This was one of the concentration tricks Hitler had taught her. *It doesn't matter,* she thought fiercely. She didn't care what she had to do, or whose advice she had to take – not as long as she could get revenge. Once again, she forced her mind to go blank, her vision sharpening until all she saw was her target, the two brown-clad backs of the SA officers. She pulled out her weapon.

A group of little boys charged past her, giggling.

Gretchen dropped the revolver into her purse. What the devil was wrong with her? She'd been so carried away that she'd forgotten the street was swarming with schoolchildren. Leaning against a wall, she waited for her pulse to slow. Across the street, the trade union's front doors closed behind the men. She'd missed her chance. She couldn't go inside – into a building whose rooms and corridors she didn't know, with too many places where the men could hide from her.

Cursing to herself, she huddled into her coat and resigned herself to wait.

Over an hour passed before the doors opened again. Gretchen swept the street with her gaze: deserted except for a couple of housewives down the block, gossiping on a building's front steps. It was time. She pulled out her revolver, hiding her hand between the folds of her coat.

Two SA men emerged from the building. They stood on

either side of a man in a dark suit, gripping his arms tightly. Slowly, the three of them started down the steps. The man in the middle moved gingerly, as though he was in pain. He tripped, his head jerking forward and his hat falling off. As he looked up, Gretchen could see his face clearly.

Shock slammed into her. It was the fireman, Heinz Schultz.

Why in heaven's name was he still alive? She'd been certain that the National Socialists would kill him as soon as he was captured. They would only keep him around if he had something that they wanted. Which meant . . . whatever incriminating secret he knew about the Reichstag fire, he must not have shared it yet with the National Socialists, or he would have been coming out of that building as a corpse.

Her plans unspooled like thread. She could free Herr Schultz and find out his secret. Then she could tell it to Herr Delmer and he'd have it published in his British newspaper, just as Daniel had wanted. Whatever this fireman knew, it must be a threat to the Party's reputation. Perhaps it would be enough to convince President Hindenburg to order Hitler expelled from office, or would forever disgrace the National Socialists. This would be her revenge, not merely on the men who'd killed Daniel, but on the entire Party. It would be a far better tribute to Daniel. He would be so pleased.

Squinting, she raised her gun and bent her knees slightly, so the Webley's recoil wouldn't knock her backward. One of the men's voices carried to her; he was saying something about his son. Her hands started shaking. They were real people, with families. She couldn't do it. She couldn't kill them.

She would have to hurt them instead. She aimed. The rest of the world melted away until all she saw was one of the SA men's hands, raised as he gestured to his companion. She fired.

He screamed and fell to his knees. Clutching his bloody hand in his good one, he moaned, 'Help me!'

'What—' the second SA man started to say, turning toward him. Gretchen didn't hesitate. She aimed at his right knee and squeezed the trigger. His body jerked. Blood instantly seeped through his trouser leg. Screaming, he grabbed at his knee and sank to the ground.

Herr Schultz stood between the two men, looking from one to the other, obviously dazed.

'*Run!*' Gretchen shouted at him. 'Herr Schultz, come with me right now!'

Limping, he hurried across the street toward her. She snatched a quick impression of him – black hair, dark eyes, tattered suit, a match to the photograph she'd seen in his apartment – and she grabbed his hand, pulling him with her. Together they raced down the street, away from the SA men who were still screaming behind them.

34

THEY RAN FOR SEVERAL BLOCKS UNTIL SHE SPOTTED AN alley and dragged Schultz into it. He sagged against the stone wall, breathing hard, his gaze never leaving her face.

'Who are you?' he gasped.

'Never mind that.' Gretchen glanced over her shoulder at the mouth of the alley, but no one was walking past; they were alone. 'You know something about the Reichstag fire. I need to know what it is. *Now*,' she added when he hesitated and she plunged her hand into her purse for her revolver.

His throat constricted, but his voice was steady. 'I nearly died to keep it safe from the Nazis. I'd hardly tell you.'

'I want to use it to destroy them!' She gritted her teeth in frustration. How could she convince him that they were on the same side? 'My friends and I went to your apartment. We saw what they did to your brother. We tracked you down to the Kuhle Wampe, but we were too late. They' – the words stuck in her throat – 'they killed my best friend.' It was the strongest description she could think of for Daniel, far better than the weak-sounding 'beau', because he had been her dearest friend, the twin of her heart. 'I know what kind of people they are. I *shot* them to free you.'

For a moment, he stared at her. Up close, she saw that he had a black eye and a couple of his teeth were missing. He held himself tightly, as though he was in pain, and both knees of his trousers had holes in them.

The distant wail of sirens cut through the air, but he and Gretchen didn't move. Then he nodded, as if satisfied. 'I hid Göring's first report on the fire. I haven't told anyone about it until now.'

Gretchen shot him a suspicious look. 'How the devil did you get Göring's report?'

'I was inspecting the Session Chamber to determine what accelerants had been used when Minister Göring came in with another man. They were arguing about the second man's press communiqué on the fire.'

'Tell me what they said,' Gretchen demanded. 'Every word.'

Schultz took a deep breath. 'The man said he had based his report on the official findings of the police and fire brigades, but Göring said it was rubbish. He started writing on the paper, then threw it to the ground and shouted that he would dictate his own report to his secretary and have that distributed to the news agencies instead. As soon as they were gone, I read the report.'

'What did it say?'

'That there was only one arsonist – the Dutchman they captured on the scene.'

Gretchen sucked in a breath. Her suspicions had been correct – the fire hadn't been the result of a Communist or National Socialist conspiracy. No wonder Göring and his men were so desperate to silence Herr Schultz. If the report went public, everyone would find out that the National Socialists had known the arson attack had been the act of one deluded individual and the Enabling Act wouldn't be passed tomorrow, keeping legislative powers out of Hitler's hands.

She raised her head to gaze at Herr Schultz. Why hadn't the SA men killed him when he'd been in their custody? Once he was dead, their problems about the fire disappeared with him. Unless the report was still out there somewhere and they needed to get their hands on it . . .

She grabbed the front of Herr Schultz's coat. 'Where's the report? Don't bother lying to me,' she warned as he opened his mouth. 'They only would have kept you alive if they needed you to tell them where it is.'

'You're right,' he said quietly. 'I hid it behind the burnt wall panels in the Session Chamber. I didn't dare take it out of the Reichstag, in case my fire chief ordered us searched to make sure we hadn't stolen anything. I had the foolish notion that I could retrieve it later and sell it to a news agency. When I returned home from my next night shift and' – he broke off, tears shining in his eyes – 'and found my brother murdered, I realized the Nazis had figured out what I'd done. His death was either a mistake or a warning. So I went to the tent camp and prayed they wouldn't find me.' He wiped at his eyes with dirt-stained fingers. 'And, of course, they did.'

Gretchen's hands fell from his coat. Her pulse pounded in her head, such a rapid rhythm that she felt incredibly light, as though she were no longer tethered to this world and might float away. Because she knew exactly what she had to do – and how to destroy the National Socialist Party. She would break into the ruined Reichstag, retrieve the paper, and deliver it to Herr Delmer. He would have the truth about the Reichstag fire published in his newspaper, and soon everyone would know that the National Socialists had known all along that the arson had been committed by one person. The only conspiracy had been the Party's attempt to convince the public that they were in imminent danger from more Communist attacks and whip them into such a panic that they wouldn't object to the Enabling Act's passage. They had deliberately misled the public, just as Papa and Hitler had discussed all those years ago at his birthday celebration.

'Thank you,' she said to Herr Schultz. She gave him a couple of bills from her dwindling supply of the Whitestones' money. 'You won't be able to get over the border without papers, but maybe you can start a new life in another city.'

He stared at the money. 'Why are you giving me this?'

She didn't answer. But she knew she wouldn't get out of Berlin alive, and money would be worthless to her. Once the report was made public, Herr Hanfstaengl would probably guess she had done it and tell the others about her. As soon as Hitler knew she was in Berlin, he would have every train, bus, and car leaving the city searched. She'd never be able to escape. After they had captured her, they would bring her to him. He would want to see her one last time before they killed her. Part of her didn't care. Daniel's death had drained all the color from the world. She didn't want to lead a gray life, drifting through the years. And she needed his death to matter. He couldn't have died in vain. She wouldn't let that happen.

Another part of her, though, was so terrified that she could barely breathe. *I can handle this*, she told herself. She could face Hitler again, knowing that she had avenged Daniel. He was worth any price.

'You'd better get going,' she finally said, evading Herr Schultz's question.

'Thank you. A thousand thank-yous, Fräulein.' He kissed her hands.

She watched him leave the alley with dry, aching eyes. Then she slipped out into the street and walked fast, keeping her head down, trying to look like an ordinary girl, hurrying because she was late for school or running errands for her mother, while in the distance police sirens continued to shriek.

Back at the lodging house, Gretchen sat by the window, watching clouds scud across the sky and thinking about ways to break into the Reichstag. When images of the SA men, writhing in agony on the ground, flashed through her mind, she took deep breaths and blanked her thoughts, keeping the memories at bay. She wasn't sorry, and she would do it again. But she couldn't help wondering if she was turning into her father. Lashing out and hurting others because she was hurting.

The difference between your father and us is we won't ever lie to ourselves, Daniel had said.

Tears surged into her eyes. No, she wouldn't lie to herself. She had shot those men, and she was glad. If they suffered one-tenth of the pain Daniel must have felt, then it was worth it.

Her thoughts turned back to the Reichstag. Although the building was no longer being used, she imagined that watchmen patrolled it. The best way to get inside was probably through the tunnel that ran from Göring's palace to the Reichstag cellars. Its doorway was next to the porter's lodge, she remembered Daniel saying.

How could she sneak onto Göring's grounds and into the tunnel without being seen? The minister and Hanfstaengl might be home, or the half-dozen servants that surely worked there. Frowning, she paced the small room. She'd crossed it several times before the answer hit her and she almost smiled. Of course! Tomorrow afternoon the Reichstag was scheduled to convene at its temporary location in the Kroll Opera House. Göring, as Reichstag Speaker, would attend and no doubt Hanfstaengl would be at his foreign press office, eagerly awaiting word on the Enabling Act's passage so he could forward the news on to foreign correspondents. The servants would be busy cleaning, or readying the palace for a dinner party to celebrate the Enabling Act. There would be no better time for her to creep in, undetected.

That night, she got into bed again with Daniel's shirt in her arms. No matter how many times she buried her nose in his garment, she caught only a whiff of his scent. So much of him was gone, in just two days. Soon she would have nothing left of him but memories.

She felt as though she had a glass ball in her chest, shimmering and fragile, and if she breathed too deeply, she would shatter it. Lying on her side, she took small sips of air, clutching Daniel's shirt tightly.

Every time she closed her eyes, his image pressed against her lids. Grinning at her in good-natured impatience as they sat in a crowded tearoom, his least favorite place in Oxford because of the fussy lace doilies and what he saw as the tedium of lingering over scones and tea when he would have far preferred to be doing something, anything. His gaze steady on hers as she talked about Thomas Mann's *The Magic Mountain*, listening without interrupting while they walked in the fields behind the clinic, and whenever she stumbled over her words, unaccustomed to respectful silence from a male, he had encouraged her with a smile. And Daniel as she had seen him last: white-faced, his jaw set, stepping carefully across the sandy lakeshore. She could still feel his hand on her back, shoving her forward, and hear his voice shouting at her to run.

Tears streamed from her eyes. She couldn't help remembering what he said to her once, when they'd been escaping from Munich all those months ago: *Gretchen, don't you realize by now I would give up everything to be with you?*

He had, she thought as she swiped at her eyes. He had given everything, his very life, for her sake.

Now it was her turn.

She spent the morning in her bedroom, emerging only for breakfast and luncheon at a cheap café and to buy a flashlight at a hardware shop the next block over. The Reichstag was probably kept unlit, since it wasn't being used, and she couldn't waste time fumbling in the dark.

When nearby church bells chimed two, she checked her appearance in the tarnished mirror: She looked ordinary in her black skirt, white blouse, and maroon cardigan – Daniel's favorite. She slipped on her gray wool coat and exited the room, leaving her and Daniel's suitcases at the foot of the bed. Whatever happened to her next, she doubted she'd need them. She carried her purse, though, her fully loaded revolver and the lock pick Daniel had bought to break into Frau Fleischer's office concealed inside.

Everything seemed like a dream: Berliners strolling the streets, chattering cheerfully to one another; automobiles gliding past; streetcars rumbling along. Gretchen felt as though an invisible bubble separated her from everyone, muffling the sounds of their voices and the blare of car horns.

By the time she reached Göring's palace, the sky had turned to white behind a wall of clouds and the air carried the sharp bite of an approaching snowfall. A long, wide driveway ran past the building, stretching back to the garages and courtyard. There was no sign of anyone. It had to be now. Gretchen raced down the driveway.

On the right, she saw a small outbuilding – the lodge for the porter, she guessed. Praying he was out on his rounds, she darted to a wooden door at the side of his lodge. It was locked, but an instant's work with her pick solved that problem.

She slipped inside, glimpsing a set of steps leading down before the door shut behind her, enclosing her in a pocket of black.

She switched on the flashlight. Its tiny circle of illumination guided her down the steps. At the bottom, she found herself in a long, brick-lined passage. Shining electric lights had been installed along the walls at periodic intervals. Clicking off the flashlight, she started forward.

Something hard and flat shifted under her feet, then fell back into place with a loud clank.

She froze. The floor was lined with loose steel plates. Every step she took would sound deafening.

Keep going, she told herself. The noise might not carry up the stairs and through the closed door.

She continued walking, the plates thunking underfoot. Each groan of metal clenched her heart. The tunnel seemed to run in a straight line; but underground, without the landmarks of buildings or the sky, it was impossible to tell which direction she traveled or how far she had gone. After a few minutes, she caught sight of a closed door ahead. As she got closer, she realized it was a massive door made of iron.

It was locked, so she fitted the pick into the keyhole, wiggling back and forth until she heard the tumblers click. She pushed the door open, a wave of musty air washing over her.

She walked a short distance before she found another iron door. Again she picked the lock and kept going. Every few minutes, she encountered another locked iron door and wanted to scream with impatience. This was taking too long. She looked at her wristwatch. Almost four o'clock. Had the Reichstag session ended? Was Göring arriving home right now?

She raced through another doorway and found that the

passage branched into two. This place was a maze! Stifling a cry of frustration, she chose a direction at random and hurried on, the steel plates clunking with every step she took. She found another iron door and picked its lock, then pushed through again, into a place of darkness and silence. The door clicked shut, cutting off the sharp gleam of light from the tunnel. For an instant, she stood still, listening with all of her might. Nothing. Only unbroken blackness.

She let out a breath of relief. This must be it. She had made it to the Reichstag cellar.

35

GRETCHEN TURNED ON THE FLASHLIGHT. BY ITS WEAK beam, she could see that she was in a narrow passageway. She hesitated, thinking. The moment had come. All she had to do was go up the stairs, find the press report in the Session Chamber, and track down Delmer to give it to him. The morning edition of his English paper would blast the news that the National Socialists had known all along that the fire hadn't been a Communist conspiracy and had deliberately whipped up the public's fear so they could pass the Enabling Act – and put dictatorial powers in Hitler's grasp. Hitler would be ruined, the Party disgraced. She didn't see how they could overcome the scandal.

As for her, she could flee from Berlin as soon as she gave Delmer the report. There might be enough time for her to sneak over the border using her false papers. But she couldn't bring herself to care what happened to her. Nothing mattered except exposing the truth and finishing the work that Daniel had started.

Thinking of him made her hands shake, causing the yellow

beam from the flashlight to bounce around the passageway. She couldn't let herself fall apart now. Resolutely, she wiped her mind blank and began walking, turning, then turning again as the passage seemed to double back on itself. For a sickening instant, she thought of mice in a maze.

But she kept walking until the passage split into two. At the T-shaped intersection, she hesitated, sniffing the air. To the left, it smelled fresher, which meant a door was probably nearby. She set off in that direction.

For several minutes, she walked the passage, hearing nothing but the shuffling of her footsteps. When she rounded a corner, she saw the dark shape of stairs winding up to the first floor. Relief arrowed through her. She wasn't trapped down here. She rushed up the steps. They seemed to go on forever, and the muscles in her legs burned.

The door at the top of the stairs was shut. She turned off the flashlight, fearing a watchman might be on duty. Then she eased the door open and stepped through.

Here the blackness was so heavy she had to move by feel. As she inched forward, she trailed her hand along the wall. It felt like plaster and had buckled and scorched from the flames' heat. The air stank of smoke and mildew. Beneath her feet, the carpet felt spongy, as though it had absorbed water from the firemen's hoses and hadn't dried out properly.

For a moment, she stood still, listening, but all she heard was the relentless silence. The place seemed empty. She switched on the flashlight, sweeping its beam around the room she had stepped into.

It was a massive lobby. If any cleanup had been attempted after the fire, she could see no evidence of it: the wood-paneled walls were blackened, and curtains hung in soot-stained shreds. An unlit chandelier hung so precariously from a half-melted chain that she feared it would crash down at any moment.

Arrows written in chalk had been scrawled over the walls. The arson investigators' markings, she guessed, for they must have traced the direction the arsonist and the fires had traveled.

Frowning, she tried to remember the little she knew of the building's layout, from the articles she'd read about the fire. The Session Chamber was to the left of the lobby.

As she entered the room, she froze in shock. She had assumed the newspaper accounts had exaggerated the damage the blaze had caused – after all, in England she'd read that the Reichstag had burned to the ground, yet the building seemed mainly intact – but this room was a ruin.

The cavernous, high-ceilinged chamber was a tangle of burnt wood. Tables and chairs had been shrunk to spindly skeletal remains, and the walls were warped and blistered from heat and water. The ceiling was gone. Overhead, the sky had turned the pale gray of pewter. She remembered that the Session Chamber's famous glass dome had saved the building from further destruction: the glass had cracked, then shattered apart, shooting roiling masses of smoke into a sky flickering red from flames. The sudden enormous hole in the ceiling had acted as a natural chimney, sucking fire and smoke upward into the night.

Hopelessness swept over Gretchen as she surveyed the mess. How could she find the report in this wreck of a room? The task was impossible.

Well, she'd never locate it if she didn't get started. She ran her hands over the walls, squinting for the white flash of paper concealed behind a loose panel. Snowflakes drifted through the empty ceiling, hitting her shoulders, pressing dampness into her skin and making her shiver.

For several minutes, she worked methodically, finishing one section and moving on to the next. By now the Reichstag session was probably over, the Enabling Act passed, and the deputies on their way out to celebrate. Göring might come into his foyer at any second.

Laws can be repealed, she promised herself, working faster, yanking down panels, the heat-weakened wood giving easily in her hands. Somewhere behind her, a hissing sound cut through the air. She stopped, trying to identify where it had come from, but all had gone silent again.

She ripped another panel down and stared as a white piece of paper fluttered loose from it and drifted toward the floor. This had to be the report. She let out a half-gasping laugh. *I did it, Daniel*, she thought, tears spurting into her eyes. *We've got them, at last.*

Her hands were shaking so badly that the paper crackled as she picked it up. By the glow of the flashlight, she saw that about twenty lines of type filled the page. According to the heading, this was an official press communiqué compiled by a Herr Sommerfeldt. At nine p.m., she read, a fire had been discovered in the Reichstag by a passing civilian, who in turn notified the nearest policemen. When the police brigade entered the Reichstag minutes later, they found a man running in the Bismarck Hall. He was carrying a Dutch passport and fire-lighters, small tablets used to spark wood or coal fires. He was taken immediately to the Brandenburg police station.

In blue pencil, someone – obviously Minister Göring – had scribbled all over the report. The words 'a single arsonist' had been crossed out and Göring had written over them 'ten, perhaps twenty men'. Near the end, he'd added, 'Clearly the terrorist attack was the signal for a Communist uprising.' A large *G* that presumably Göring used in lieu of a full signature had been scrawled across the bottom.

All the evidence she needed was right here.

Her heart throbbed against her ribs. Tonight Herr Delmer would wire the story to his paper, and when the morning

316

edition appeared, the truth would come out at last. The German public would be furious at having been duped; there would be an outcry and the Enabling Act would be repealed. Hitler's career would be over.

Even with tears running down her face, she couldn't stop smiling as she slipped the paper into her coat pocket. *We did it, Daniel*, she thought. *When they find me, I only hope that somehow I can be with you again.*

She picked her way over the debris-covered floor. As she reached the door leading into the lobby, she heard the hissing again. This time she recognized the sound: it was the slithering whisper of shoes on water-logged carpet.

Someone was outside the door.

Blood started pounding so loudly in her ears that she could hear nothing else. She ran from the door, stumbling over piles of burnt furniture. The far wall had fallen into shadow – she didn't even know if there was another exit – but she charged toward it, nearly tumbling over a chair lying on its side. She jerked herself upright, gasping at the wrenching in her knee. Behind her, the door burst open.

She looked back. Several men were running toward her. They wore the brown uniforms of the SA. Frantic to get at her gun, she scrabbled at her purse's clasp and looked up just in time to see a man fling himself at her.

They fell together to the floor. Gretchen landed hard on something that felt like broken chair legs; the impact shoved the air from her chest, and all she could do was wheeze for breath. The man's face pressed against hers, his stubble rough on her cheek, the scents of linen and tobacco swirling around her.

She pushed at him, but his body lay heavily on hers, his hand closing around her neck. She pulled desperately at his fingers, but his grip didn't loosen. Her vision narrowed to a pinprick.

'That's enough,' someone said. He sounded as though he were underwater.

The man released Gretchen's neck, and her hearing roared back. She heard herself gasping and coughing. Tears smarted her eyes. She rolled onto her hands and knees. Gray patches obscured her vision. Wildly, she ran her hands over the floor, searching for her purse. It had to be here, somewhere.

'Get up,' a voice snapped.

Shakily, she rose. Gray dots receded from her vision, and she saw that an SA man stood in the doorway, staring at her. He was unfamiliar: middle-aged, his expression flat, his eyes icy. One hand held her purse, which he gave to another SA man. Gretchen tried to ignore the lurch in her stomach. Now they had her gun.

'How did you know I was here?' The words tumbled from her mouth before she could stop them.

'The steel plates in the tunnel,' the man replied. 'The porter heard you from his lodge and summoned us. Minister Göring will be very interested to know why a girl sneaked through his tunnel to the Reichstag.'

Two SA men jerked her arms behind her back. Nothing felt real, as though she had split into two selves – the girl standing in the ruined room, and someone else standing to the side, watching. This couldn't be happening. She had failed. Now nobody would know the truth about the fire, and she would be dead by dawn. She bit the inside of her mouth so she wouldn't make a sound.

Another SA man patted her down. He grinned when he found the report in her coat pocket and handed it to the man who seemed to be in charge. As he scanned it, his eyebrows lifted. 'Well, now we know why you broke in here.' He shoved his face into hers, so close she smelled his tobacco-scented breath. 'Who told you where to find this report?'

She said nothing. All of her muscles tensed for the punch she knew was coming.

The man slapped her across the face, so hard that her ears rang. 'It was the fireman, wasn't it? Were you the one who helped him escape? You shot two of my best men! I ought to have you ripped limb from limb right here!'

The ache in her cheek dulled to a steady throb. She pictured Daniel: his lopsided grin before he threw his head back in laughter. *I'm coming to you*, she thought. *I won't be afraid.*

Faintly, she heard the SA man panting, as though struggling for control.

'Take her out of here,' he said at last. 'I'll get word to Minister Göring.'

She didn't fight the three men as they marched her outside and down a long flight of steps. There was no use. They had won.

Two black automobiles were parked in the Königsplatz below, cockeyed, as though their drivers had jerked to a sudden stop. The guards pushed her into the nearest car's backseat. She sat, sandwiched between two of them, their bodies so close their knees ground into hers.

The driver sped them across the square. When she glanced in the back window, she saw the other car gliding in the opposite direction, carrying the lead SA man on his way to Minister Göring.

A young-looking fellow put his lips to her ear. 'Why'd you break in? Are you a filthy Jew?'

His words couldn't touch her; nothing could now. She stared at her hands clasped in her lap. Somehow they didn't look like her hands, and she stretched her fingers, noting the way her tendons flexed. Soon she wouldn't witness the miracle of blood and sinew responding to her thoughts. Soon she wouldn't feel anything at all. A sob rose in her throat. She swallowed it. She wouldn't give these men the satisfaction of her fear.

The car coasted to a halt. Gretchen peered through the window at the rows of apartment houses. Her heart seemed to stop for an instant. She recognized this street: it was the Lange Strasse, where the captured trade union building was located.

They weren't simply going to kill her. They were going to torture her first.

'No!' she gasped as the men took her arms, pulling her outside into the darkened street. She twisted in their arms, but their grips were too strong. 'Please!' she cried, even though she hated herself for begging them. A quick, clean kill she could face, but she didn't want to be reduced to tears and blood until finally she couldn't stand the pain anymore and told them everything, said anything they wanted her to say, just to make the agony end.

They dragged her up the stairs and into an unlit lobby. Her legs trembled so badly that they almost collapsed beneath her.

'Hurry up!' the men growled at her and pulled her along the corridor until they reached a closed door. One of them opened it and they yanked her down the concrete steps. She squinted in the dimness. A couple of bare lightbulbs hanging from the ceiling flickered in and out of life. She saw a dirt floor, four cinderblock walls, a couple of chairs. In a corner of the room, a man lay huddled into a ball on his side, his face curled into his chest, his hair falling forward and shielding him. Silver handcuffs winked at his wrists and were attached to long chains that had been bolted to the wall.

The man lay still. His dove-gray woolen overcoat was streaked with dirt, his dark hair matted with blood. He had crossed his arms protectively over his chest. One of his hands was twitching.

Gretchen couldn't move. She knew those fingers and the injury that made them convulse.

It's impossible, she thought as the men shoved her so hard that she fell to her knees. As she stared at the man on the floor, scarcely daring to hope, to breathe, one of the SA men strode past her, bent over the man's body, and grabbed him by the hair.

'Look, Jew, we've brought you company,' the SA man said, laughing.

The man raised his head. Through the tangle of his hair, his eyes met hers and all the air seemed to go out of the room. It was Daniel.

36

GRETCHEN COULD ONLY STARE AT DANIEL. HE COULDN'T be real. She was imagining him. It was her brain's way of protecting itself from the horrors to come. Part of her mind registered the cold dirt of the floor under her legs and hands, but the rest had blanked to a cool whiteness. This couldn't be happening. Daniel couldn't be alive; Hanfstaengl wouldn't have lied to her. She was hallucinating.

She drank in the sight of Daniel, though, unable to look away from him. Both of his eyes were bloodshot. One only opened a slit and was surrounded by a purplish-black bruise. Blood had dried on the corner of his mouth. A rust-colored streak stretched from his ear to beneath his collar. Dirt, possibly from having his face shoved into the floor again and again, had left a film of gray on his skin. When he raised his hands to push his hair out of his eyes, the chains around his wrists clanking, two of the fingers on his left hand hung at awkward angles, the knuckles swollen. They must have been broken.

Shock tightened his face. His eyes burned into hers, but he didn't say a word.

The room seemed to shrink, gray cinderblock walls pressing in on her until she could no longer breathe. *He's dead*, she told herself. She couldn't let herself hope that he was real. Somehow, she had to be dreaming. She was vaguely aware of the SA man holding Daniel's hair saying something; she saw his mouth moving, but she couldn't hear what he said over the buzzing in her ears.

The men gripping her arms hauled her upright and marched her across the room. She stood motionless as they fitted handcuffs on her and pulled on the chains linking her restraints to the wall, making sure they held.

The blackness receded, the room sharpening into focus again. Daniel was still there, crouched on the floor, his gaze trained on her face. She shook her head, as if to clear it, but he remained. She curled her hands into fists, letting the fingernails dig into her palms, hoping the pain would break through the fog in her head. His image never wavered. Something seemed to explode under the left side of her ribs, and she let out a choking gasp.

He was real.

Warmth burst in her heart, flooding her rib cage and down her arms and legs until all of her body felt tingling and alive. Tears rose to her eyes, and she smiled so hard she thought her face would crack. She couldn't form a coherent thought; all she could do was repeat his name in her head, and she opened her mouth to say it out loud.

Daniel shook his head slightly, and she understood at once, biting her lips to keep herself silent. They mustn't let the SA men figure out that they knew each other. They would use the information against them – taking turns torturing each of them in front of the other until one of them shattered and told them everything.

The men clattered upstairs, leaving her and Daniel alone in the flickering darkness.

They crawled toward each other. The chains tightened, holding them in place, a foot from each other. Gretchen stretched out her hand, desperate to touch him, and he reached for her. The tips of their fingers brushed. The feel of his warm skin, even for an instant, was enough to flood Gretchen's eyes with tears. He was real, and he was alive, and he was with her.

'Herr Hanfstaengl told me you were dead,' she said hollowly. 'Minister Göring ordered you to be shot.'

'I changed his mind.' Daniel's voice sounded weak. 'It doesn't matter – are you hurt? Did they' – his face twisted – 'did they touch you at all?'

'No,' she said quickly, and he let out a shuddering breath, bowing his head.

'I'm so glad you were spared that.' He was crying. 'Oh, Gretchen, I'd give anything for you not to be here. I've seen them kill two men this week. They took them apart, piece by piece. By the end, they were begging to die, just to be put out of their misery.'

He blurred behind a sheen of her tears. 'We're together,' she managed to say through her clogged throat. 'When I thought you were dead, all I wanted was to see you one more time.' Somehow she smiled. 'I'm getting my wish.'

'I love you so much.' He looked up. His tears had cut lines through the grime on his cheeks, so she could see the soft skin beneath the dirt. 'I'd hoped never to see you again – because that would mean you were safe. What happened? How did you end up here?'

As quickly as she could, she told him the events of the past three days. When she reached the part about freeing Herr Schultz yesterday, she faltered in confusion. Why hadn't he told her that Daniel had been imprisoned alongside him? The answer came to her before she could ask it: she hadn't mentioned Daniel to him, and he hadn't known who she was, so he hadn't guessed that Daniel was important to her.

While she talked, they remained on their hands and knees, stretching out their right hands so they could press their fingertips together. She closed her eyes, savoring the comforting sensation of his fingers on hers.

After she finished, she opened her eyes to see Daniel gazing at her intently, as though he was memorizing each one of her features. 'I wish I'd never met you,' he said through cracked lips. 'If it wasn't for me, you'd still be safe.'

'Don't you dare say such a thing!' She was suddenly furious. 'If we hadn't met, I would still believe every lie Uncle Dolf told me. I would' – her voice wobbled – 'I would have become a monster. You saved me from that.'

Everything in his face seemed to crumple. He lunged toward her, but his chains pulled him back so hard that he lay on the ground for a moment, gathering his strength.

'Thank you,' he said after a moment. 'It means the world to hear you say that. I was afraid you'd hate me for bringing you into danger. And I wouldn't have blamed you in the least.'

'I could never hate you.' The ludicrousness of her statement struck them at the same time – because she had hated him, just as he'd hated her when they'd first met – and they smiled at each other. Then Gretchen glanced at their surroundings again: dirt floor, solid walls, a bucket in the corner, no sign of food or beds. This was where Daniel had spent the last three days, being beaten and watching men die. The smile slipped from her lips. 'How have you managed to survive this long?'

Daniel got up, sitting cross-legged on the ground. 'Göring showed up the other day – I'm not sure when, I've lost all track of time in this place – and he told the guards to shoot me. Said I was worthless. I made up a crazy story about

325

Fräulein Junge being alive and someone looking like her having been shot instead. I told Göring that Fräulein Junge had been hidden by a rival *Ringverein*. I gave him the name of a fictitious Ring, saying they controlled the Wedding district, and he went off to investigate. Since then, he's come back a few times, saying I'm a filthy liar and I deserve to be killed immediately, and then I make up more details and he sends his men to look into it further.'

Gretchen remembered how quickly he'd come up with a story when they were leaving the train at Dachau, and she shook her head in admiration. 'I don't know anyone else who can think so fast on his feet.'

He sighed. 'I couldn't make up a tale to get me out of here. Oh, Gretchen, I'm so sorry you've wound up in this place. I—' He broke off as the cellar door creaked open and footsteps thundered down the stairs. Three of the SA men were back, their hands on the knives and guns at their belts.

'Get up,' the one in charge growled at Gretchen. Her mouth went as dry as sand.

'Where are you taking her?' Daniel demanded.

Gretchen had thought the man would hit Daniel for asking, but he grinned instead. 'The Chancellery. Herr Chancellor Hitler was most curious when Minister Göring told him about the break-in at the Reichstag. He wants to meet this would-be girl thief.'

She closed her eyes as they unlocked her handcuffs. It was going to happen – what she had feared for the past eighteen months. She would have to see Hitler again.

The instant they saw each other, he would recognize her. Of that, she had no doubt. She could already picture his blue eyes blazing in fury as they surveyed her, his old sunshine, the race traitor. She might survive the night, if he wanted to prolong her torture. But she was going to die, and soon. She

326

had become an inconvenience to him, like her father and brother had. What would death be like? The fields of wild-flowers and angels her childhood priest had preached about, or a void of blackness and silence? Dear God, she wasn't ready to find out. Her legs started shaking so badly they threatened to buckle beneath her.

'If you're taking Gretchen, then you'll have to take me, too.' Daniel's firm voice cut into her thoughts and her eyes flew open. He had gotten to his feet and stood, hunched in pain. 'I put her up to sneaking into the Reichstag. It's my fault.'

'No!' Gretchen cried. 'It isn't true!'

'It's over, Gretchen,' Daniel said gently. 'It doesn't matter if they know who we are, not if they're taking you to see Hitler.' He gave her a small smile. 'I don't want you to have to go there alone.'

Her eyes filled with tears. Even now, in their final moments, Daniel was thinking of her. 'Thank you.'

The men looked at one another and shrugged. 'If the boy has a death wish, it's none of my concern,' the one in charge said. 'Bring them both.'

They were led outside to a car. The sun had set long ago, and the sky had turned black. In silence, they drove through the long streets. Gretchen peered around the SA man sitting between her and Daniel, so she could look at him. He smiled a little and mouthed *I love you*. She realized, with a lurch of her heart, that he was saying good-bye to her. She mouthed the words back.

These really were the last minutes of her life. She stared at Daniel, drinking him in, the bruise around his eye, the dried blood at the corners of his mouth, the uncombed knots of his hair. He had never looked better to her. And she knew, with a terrible, burning desperation, that she didn't want to die.

Not now, with Daniel still alive. But there was no way out that she could see. They were trapped.

The car coasted to a stop. On her right, the Chancellery loomed, an enormous slab of pale stone shining in the darkness. The sound of the car doors opening was so loud that she winced. The men took her and Daniel by the arms again, pulling them outside into a courtyard where the wind scraped over her face so hard that tears rose to her eyes.

The men gripping her arms ran toward the building and she was forced to keep pace or be dragged on the ground. They burst inside, but before she could look around to get her bearings, the men were running again, hurrying her and Daniel through a maze of darkened, high-ceilinged rooms. The air was rank with the odor of stopped-up drains. Beneath her feet, the floors felt soft and rotted.

The men took them upstairs to a long, dimly lit corridor lined with closed doors and told them to stand against the wall. As they waited side by side, Daniel's hand touched Gretchen's, the barest brush of his fingers on hers. Soon, she knew, she would never feel his hand again. She was too terrified to make a sound.

One of the men knocked on a door.

'Yes, what is it?' called a voice from within the room.

Hitler. Gretchen would know that deep, melodic tone anywhere. Her legs buckled and she started sliding down the wall. One of the men jerked her upright so hard that her arm burned. She stared straight ahead with unseeing eyes.

'I've brought the Reichstag thief and Herr Cohen to you,' the man called back. 'Herr Cohen says he ordered her to break into the Reichstag, so I thought you would want to see them both.' He hesitated, glancing over his shoulder at her and Daniel. 'They seem quite devoted to each other, Herr Chancellor Hitler.'

328

There was a pause. Through the walls separating them, Gretchen imagined Hitler standing up, surprise creasing his forehead, a slender, white hand smoothing the front of his shirt. He must have guessed it was her. He would want a moment to himself, so he could arrange his thoughts and wipe the shock from his face. He would need to be in control of his emotions when she was sent into his office.

Daniel slid down the wall, clutching his left arm, moaning.

'What's wrong with him?' a guard snapped.

'He's having a pain attack.' Gretchen strained against her captor's grasp. 'It's from an old injury. Please let me go to him!' She saw the confusion in their faces and said, 'He's helpless when he's like this. Please!'

'He's a cripple,' one of the guards said. 'I saw – we had him stripped to the waist yesterday. His left arm's deformed. We have nothing to fear from him.'

Daniel slumped to the floor. His closed eyes fluttered, then focused on her. And he winked. Gretchen stilled in bewilderment. What on earth was he up to?

'That's Fräulein Müller,' Hitler called. The door muffled his voice, so she could not hear the emotion in it. 'Send her in alone. I'll deal with the Jew next.'

'Very good, Herr Chancellor,' the guard said. He opened the door. She swiveled in his grasp, trying to get one final look at Daniel, but the guard shoved her forward. She stumbled into the office. The door clicked shut behind her. She peered into the dimness, her heart racing.

'Hello, Uncle Dolf,' she said.

37

⌒⌒

A SINGLE TABLE LAMP HAD BEEN LIT, LEAVING MOST OF
the room in shadow. Hitler stood behind a desk. The lamplight
gilded him with gold, softening the face she knew so well. He
didn't look at her, but flipped through some papers.

One glance at him was enough to turn her insides to ice.
She couldn't move. *Step closer, don't show him you're afraid,*
she ordered herself, but she was frozen in place. All she could
do was stare at him.

He looked smaller, or perhaps she had grown. He wore
the plain brown Party uniform he'd taken to donning regularly
during her final months in Munich. Half-moons of sweat
darkened his armpits, probably from the effort of making
speeches all afternoon during the Reichstag session. Up close,
she could see the hollows in his cheeks had begun to fill out.
Maybe the years of gorging himself on desserts were catching
up with him.

As usual, he had slicked his hair back with pomade, but
several strands had worked themselves loose and flopped over
his forehead. He smoothed them back, then raised his gaze

to meet hers. His eyes reminded her of the sparks flying from the streetcars' cables, shooting bits of blue fire in the darkness. Under their force, she was powerless to move.

'You will address me as chancellor,' he said in a low, quiet tone. He sounded calm; his face carefully scrubbed clean of emotion. As always, he had hidden himself from her – she could not guess what he was thinking.

Panic wrapped like a band around her chest and pulled tight, blocking off her breathing. Gray spots danced in front of her vision. She was going to pass out, right here, while he watched her with a bored expression. She couldn't fight him. He was too strong for her. He always had been.

She bowed her head, gulping in air so she didn't faint. 'As you wish, Herr Chancellor Hitler.'

The air was so cold that it pressed through her stockings into her skin. She had to will herself not to shiver. Beneath her feet, the warped floorboards dipped so that she stood off balance. She stepped forward onto a flatter section of floor and raised her head. Hitler was staring at her with undisguised horror.

'Your hair,' he murmured. 'It's turned *brown*. The Jewish virus . . .'

She fought the wild urge to laugh. Naturally Hitler would think she'd been infected by Daniel's touch. And he would be afraid to touch *her* for fear he would be contaminated, too. The thought gave her pause. Could she use this to her advantage?

Hitler leaned across the desk, glaring. 'You're foolish to have imagined yourself in love with a Jew. After all that I taught you! Every day pure-blooded Aryans suffer while the inferior parasites thrive. What we have to do is create a new master race of men who, unlike you, won't allow themselves to be guided by the false morality of pity.'

She barely listened; it was the same tired rhetoric she'd heard for years. Instead she stood meekly, hands clasped in front of her, scanning the room without moving her head. The chamber was so dark that she could only make out the humps of tables and chairs to the side, presumably where Hitler sat with his adjutants or cabinet ministers. His desk was covered with a tidy stack of papers and a tray holding a glass and a bottle of clear liquid, probably his favorite mineral water. Beside it was a silver dish filled with hard candies embossed with swastikas.

Unblinking, Hitler stared at her, waiting for her to speak. Beg for forgiveness, most likely, and start crying. She wanted to shout at him that she'd never ask for his pardon, but when she opened her mouth, she found that she couldn't say a word. From the corner of her eye, she caught a flicker of movement. With a massive effort, she tore her gaze from Hitler's. At his side, his right hand clenched into a fist and then relaxed, over and over.

She recognized the gesture – when he was upset, his right hand would contract uncontrollably. He might pretend to be nonchalant in her presence, but now she knew how agitated he truly felt. Was there a way to exploit his emotions to help her and Daniel? She didn't see how; they could never hope to escape from Hitler and his armed guards. Her thoughts turned to Daniel. Why had he winked at her in the corridor?

The room had gone so silent she could hear Hitler breathing rapidly. His eyes traced her face as he said, 'You've grown into such a stubborn, willful girl. What a delight you were when you were a child! Unspoiled and lovely. Now you've made a ruin of your life. And all for the love of a *Jew*.'

He spat out the last word and reached for his water glass. As he drank, the muscles in his neck worked. Somehow the sight sickened her. He set the glass down with a thump.

'We can dispense with the formality of the trial that Göring had his heart set on for your Jew,' he said. 'Goring will be disappointed, but it can't be helped.' He smiled to himself when he said Göring's name, his voice warming. Then his face hardened again. 'Your Jew will die tonight. My men will take him down to the coal cellar. The ceiling's high enough for them to string him up. I'm told that using piano wire instead of rope prolongs the torture, so we'll be sure to try it. You will watch.'

Her eyes were wet. *Stop crying*, she told herself as Hitler wavered in front of her. *This is the reaction he wants. He's playing games with you.*

He continued talking, but she barely heard him. Why had he mentioned Göring's name with such easy affection? It made no sense. Shouldn't he have been furious with Göring for slipping up and mentioning the fireman to Fräulein Junge? For changing the official press communiqué in Herr Schultz's presence? The Hitler she'd known would have been enraged, and had Göring dismissed or demoted immediately. Why hadn't he? What was she missing?

She interrupted his tirade. 'Minister Göring has been indiscreet. I'm surprised you've tolerated his mistakes.'

'Göring has a valuable talent,' Hitler snapped. 'The man has one of the finest minds in the world when it comes to aerial combat. He has ice in his veins – he's not afraid to do what needs to be done.'

A chill raced up Gretchen's spine. She understood: Hitler would need Göring's aerial abilities if he planned on going to war. All of the speeches she'd listened to over the years, the dinnertime conversations, the chats over tea, everything Hitler had said he would do to make Germany great again had been carefully crafted lies. He didn't want to pull Germany out of this pit of unemployment, inflation, and crime. He wanted to force her into battle.

Hitler's daring in telling her something so incriminating bewildered her. As they gazed at each other, his eyes were flat. He didn't care that he'd spilled one of his secrets, she realized, because he knew there was no one she would be able to tell. Because she was going to die.

She wrapped her arms across her chest, trying to hold herself together. But she would speak. Hitler deserved to know that she'd seen through him.

'That's why you wanted the Enabling Act passed.' Her voice seemed loud in the hushed room. 'So someday you can go to war without needing the Reichstag's approval. You must believe they'd never consent to another war. And you need Göring to oversee the air force – that's why you excused his blunders.

'You must have realized quickly that the fire was the act of one person. But the opportunity was too perfect to pass up. It was easy to convince people that the fire was a Communist conspiracy. Once President Hindenburg dies, absolute power can be yours—'

'That's enough,' Hitler interrupted, sounding eerily calm. 'The Enabling Act passed overwhelmingly this afternoon, and I see no reason it should ever be repealed. Unfortunately, it's quite true that Hindenburg's health is failing. I'd be surprised if he survives the year.'

He ran a hand down his brown shirt, smoothing imaginary wrinkles. His tic had faded away, his hand had relaxed, the fingers hanging loose and pliant. A smile tugged on his lips. She understood why his irritation had vanished: she was powerless. He had won.

The unfairness of it all nearly choked her. She glared at Hitler, but he was flipping through the papers on his desk again, his expression unconcerned. Nothing ever seemed to touch him. He had ripped her family apart, and he didn't care. Even more, she suspected he hadn't noticed what he had done to them. Everything he held turned to ash. And he deserved to know it.

'You destroyed my family,' she ground out between her teeth.

Still, he skimmed through the papers, never looking up. A sudden rage filled her, so red and heavy that she couldn't contain it. He *would* listen to her.

'You ruined Geli's life!' she yelled. 'You did something to her, I'm sure of it, and that's why she killed herself.'

Hitler's head snapped up. 'Don't you dare speak her name,' he said slowly. Only the paper rustling in his trembling hand betrayed his emotion. 'You have no right to mention my princess.'

Then he firmed his lips, as though determined to keep inside the words he longed to say. Gretchen slumped in disappointment. The rein he'd always had on his self-control was as tight as ever. She would die, and he would remain unpunished. Her and Daniel's deaths would have no meaning. Somehow, that seemed the worst of all. She made a noise deep in her throat but couldn't say a word.

A thump and a muffled oath sounded from the corridor. Hitler frowned. 'What was that?' His hand strayed toward the desk drawer. For a weapon, Gretchen suspected – in the old days in Munich, he'd never left home without his pistol, cartridge belt, and whip, and though he didn't wear a gun holster tonight, she was certain he had his Walther nearby.

Hitler's office door shook in its frame, as though something heavy had been thrown against it. Daniel and the guards must be fighting. Suddenly, Gretchen understood why he had winked at her – he'd been pretending to be suffering from a pain attack, so the SA men would let their guards down, and he could take them by surprise. Which meant it was up to her to get out of this room alive and back to him.

'I'm sure it's just the SA fellows having a bit of fun,' she said, her mind working furiously. If she ran, Hitler would shoot her before she reached the door. How could she get away from him?

Hitler didn't answer, tapping his fingers on the desk. The tic pulled on his left cheek, his eyes stone above the rippling flesh, just as he had looked the last time she'd seen him. The thought hit her with lightning swiftness: she had escaped from him before by making him so enraged that he lost control. Instead of summoning his nearby adjutants and her brother to deal with her, he'd begun ranting, giving her precious seconds to dash through his apartment's foyer and fling open the front door.

This was how she could get away before he shot her to death – she had to infuriate him to the extent that he rushed to attack her, leaving the weapon forgotten in his desk. How could she push him over the edge?

From the corridor, somebody shouted. Hitler jerked open his desk drawer.

As she took a step back, he looked at her sharply. 'Don't move.'

Her heart pounded against her ribs as she raised her hands in surrender. How could she trick him into losing control? The advice he'd given her over the years rushed through her head in a confused jumble. She snatched hold of some of the words: *hate's more lasting than dislike*, he'd said to her so many times. *If you can't be loved, then you ought to be hated, so people will feel strongly about you. Anything's preferable to indifference.*

Instantly, she knew what to do – she had to pretend that he meant nothing to her. 'Herr Chancellor Hitler, all those years we spent together, you thought I cared about you. But I was kind to you because I felt sorry for you – you seemed alone and friendless, without a proper career or family of your own.'

He stilled. Above his undulating cheek, his eyes were as cold as chipped glass.

Her mind flashed back to the story her mother had told her in Dachau, about Hitler's father teasing him when he found him clad in a bedsheet, after taking off his clothes to wriggle through the window and run away. 'Your father must not have loved you either. Didn't he call you the toga boy?'

His eyes bulged. 'Who told you that?' he demanded, rushing around the desk toward her. 'You vile child!'

She turned and ran.

'Disgusting Jew lover!' he yelled. Behind her, she heard his footsteps thudding on the floor and the harsh rasp of his breathing. She raced toward the door. On the other side, men shouted and a volley of shots sounded.

'Daniel!' she screamed, her fingertips brushing the door-knob – almost there – she was turning it—

Hands seized her shoulders and spun her around. Hitler glared down at her. Rage had turned his face red, and perspiration had darkened the hair hanging over his forehead from brown to black.

'Don't you understand who I am?' he shouted. 'The hand of Providence has always protected me! Over and over during the Great War, men in my regiment died all around me but I lived – because I was meant to! And now Providence has brought you back to me. I'll have you killed right now. I'll take you to the cellar myself!'

Before she could wrench herself free, he drew his hand back and cracked her across the face so hard that her vision went black.

For an instant, there was nothing but the flare of pain in her cheek. Then her sight flooded back and she saw Hitler again, still standing in front of her, one hand gripping her shoulder, the other raised to strike her a second time. Behind him, she glimpsed the outline of the desk in the half darkness. Easily thirty paces away. He'd never get to his pistol in time.

She stretched her hands behind her, groping blindly for the doorknob. Blood welled in her mouth – her teeth must have cut the inside of her cheek. Her fingers brushed cold brass. The doorknob. She was almost free.

'Thank you,' she said to Hitler. The effort to speak sent a dull ache pulsing through her jaw, but it was worth it to see his face slacken with confusion.

'What—' he started to say as she twisted the doorknob and stepped back. The last thing she saw before she slammed the door shut was comprehension flash over his features and his mouth open in a furious shout.

38

IN THE CORRIDOR, DANIEL AND AN SA GUARD WERE struggling over a gun. All Gretchen could see was their arms jerking as they each held onto the weapon, trying to pull it free. They didn't speak. The air was filled with their grunts and panting.

Three guards lay on the ground, moaning, clutching their thighs, blood coursing between their fingers. A gun was still clipped to the youngest-looking fellow's belt. Gretchen started to reach for it, then looked back at Daniel and his assailant. Their bodies were too close for her to shoot; she might hit Daniel instead. She wrestled a truncheon free from the young man's belt instead and raced to where Daniel and the guard were fighting. Without hesitating, she smashed the truncheon onto the guard's head. He crumpled instantly, the gun in his hand.

'Let's go!' Daniel yelled.

Together they dashed down the corridor. The entrance to the stairway loomed up ahead, a tiny rectangle in the dimness. Gretchen was running so hard, each footstep jarred her burning jaw. The entrance was only a few feet away. Behind her, she heard the click of a door. She glanced over her shoulder.

Hitler stood in his office entryway, his chest heaving with labored breaths. Something silver glinted in his hand – a pistol. He swung his arm up and aimed. She heard the click of the hammer being pulled back.

'He's going to shoot!' she screamed.

They raced through the entrance to the stairway landing. There was a popping sound, then the splintering of wood as a bullet buried itself into the wall behind them.

'Where are the rest of my guards?' Hitler screamed. 'Somebody, get the Müller girl and the Jew! I want them dead!'

As they skidded across the landing, Gretchen heard the thunder of footsteps coming up the stairs, right toward them.

'More guards,' she breathed.

'Upstairs.' Daniel turned and started running up the steps.

'We can't get out that way!'

'Yes, we can!' His sharp tone left no room for argument.

She dashed after him, tossing a glance over her shoulder. Hitler stood in the corridor, screaming at his guards, red-faced and furious. He wouldn't chase them, she knew; he was far too careful with his personal safety to run after them into the darkness. His eyes met hers for an instant, and the iciness in them stopped her heart for a beat. She kept running, and he was gone from sight, his ragged voice reaching up the staircase after her, shouting for his guards.

Here none of the wall sconces had been lit, so Gretchen felt as though they were racing up a steep hill at night. Where could they possibly be going? Did one of these stairway landings lead to a corridor that might provide another route out of this building? How could Daniel know which to take—

And then she remembered: there was a secret passage in

340

the Chancellery attic that led all the way to the Hotel Adlon. Hanfstaengl had said so at the gangsters' ball, and she'd later told Daniel. They might actually get out of this place after all.

Abruptly, the stairs stopped. There was nowhere else to go but down a corridor. They raced into the yawning blackness. Daniel flung open the first door they came to, its rusty hinges groaning in protest.

'It's the attic,' he said breathlessly. 'Come on.'

They stepped inside, closing the door softly behind them. Maybe the guards wouldn't guess where they'd gone, and they could earn themselves a few more minutes to get away.

In here, the darkness felt like a wall. Gretchen stepped forward, her toes bumping into something solid. A stair. Bracing her hand on the wall for balance, she hurried up the steps, moving by feel alone. She heard Daniel panting beside her.

She raised her foot, meeting nothing but empty air. She brought her foot down and slid it forward. It was a flat floor. They must have climbed into the attic itself. Gretchen spun around blindly, her arms extended, reaching for the slope of a wall, the hardness of a door, anything.

To her left, something creaked. A door. Daniel must have found it. She rushed toward the sound. Faintly, she could make out Daniel's outline. He was gesturing at her to hurry.

She stumbled through the opening. Here the air was musty and hot. She flung her arms out and they knocked into walls. Such a narrow space. This had to be the secret passageway. Heedless of the dark, she raced forward, the floorboards groaning underfoot. She kept her hand on the wall, following the passage's curves. Where were they now? The next building was the Foreign Office, but beyond that, she had no idea. Behind her, Daniel's ragged breathing crashed in her ears.

She smacked face-first into a wall. She was so anxious she didn't even feel the impact. In an instant, she and Daniel were running their hands over the wall – there it was, the cold metal of a doorknob – and together they yanked the door open and she raced through first.

This passage was as dark and twisty as the previous one. There was no sound beneath them. Presumably whatever ministry building they were in, it was closed down for the night. Faintly, she caught the now-familiar rasp of a door's hinge. The guards had found the door to the attic.

They kept running. They reached another door. Gretchen bumped into it so hard she was breathless. Daniel ripped the door open. His hand rested on the small of her back, urging her on, and she raced forward into the endless black. In the distance, the guards shouted something unintelligible. They must be gaining on her and Daniel. She surged forward in a desperate burst of speed.

She careered face-first into another wall. Her lips were on fire, but she ignored the pain, touching the wall all over, searching for another doorknob. Blood, hot and coppery, dripped from her mouth onto her chin. She'd split her lips open.

There was no doorknob. They must have come to the end of the passage. She tried to speak and had to spit out blood; the inside of her mouth still throbbed from Hitler's punch. 'The hotel—'

'We must be in the Adlon's attic,' Daniel panted. 'Come on!'

The darkness made it impossible to make sense of their surroundings. She bumped into furniture – chairs, bedside tables, lamps with the shades missing. This must be where the hotel staff stored extra or broken supplies.

Nearby, she heard Daniel stumble. 'Here are the stairs!'

She ran toward his voice. Below them shone slivers of gold – it must be the light from the downstairs hallway showing around the spaces where the door hadn't fitted properly in its frame. The four lines of light were all the illumination they needed to race down the steps. They barged through the door into a brightly lit corridor. The sudden glare dazzled Gretchen's eyes. She raced on, starbursts exploding before her as her vision adjusted.

A back staircase spiraled below them. Together they ran down. The steps were empty, thankfully; guests must take the elevator. Gretchen risked a glance over her shoulder. Nothing yet. But the guards must be on their way.

She whipped her head around to face front. The stairs wound down and down until they reached another corridor. Daniel pushed through the door at its end, and Gretchen saw the polished marble of the lobby gleaming ahead of them.

Without a word, they charged toward it. Bellboys in gold braid and guests in suits and silk frocks stared at them. The man behind the reception desk shouted, 'You ruffians stop this instant!' but they kept going, making for the massive front door.

A porter in pale blue opened it for them, his movements automatic, his expression startled as they pounded past him and onto the sidewalk, skidding to a stop to get their bearings. Up and down Unter den Linden cars crawled the clogged thoroughfare, and along the pavement men and women in fancy evening dress strolled and chatted. Lights blazed from the fine hotels lining the avenue.

'This way.' Daniel nodded toward the left.

They walked fast, not wanting to draw attention by breaking into a run. Everyone they passed, Gretchen imagined turned to look at them. Up ahead, the golden statues atop the Brandenburg Gate gleamed in the night. They were close to the entrance of the large park known as the Tiergarten.

They reached the edge of an open plaza. Daniel glanced at Gretchen. 'We'll cut through the Tiergarten to the Zoo Station. It's a train stop on the other side of the park. In a few minutes, we can be on our way out of the city.'

Hopelessness washed over Gretchen. 'They took my purse. We can't pay for train tickets.'

'We'll hide in the lavatory when the conductor checks tickets. Then we can figure out our next step.'

Sirens wailed behind them. Gretchen couldn't stop herself from looking back. Three police cars swarmed down Unter den Linden, screeching to a halt in front of the Hotel Adlon. Officers scrambled out of the cars. One yelled, 'The station just radioed in! Roadblocks are being set up across the city!'

'Good!' another shouted back. 'Guard the entrance!'

The men disappeared inside, leaving one behind at the front door. Gretchen and Daniel looked at each other. His face had drained white.

'Keep going,' he said shakily. 'We'll hide in the Tiergarten until we decide what to do.'

There was no escape. She knew Hitler too well to doubt what he would do next: he would have every train, every bus, every automobile leaving the city searched. They would never get out of Berlin.

Her legs felt wooden with fear. Somehow she kept walking across the square toward the park entrance. A few men hustled past, but they didn't look in their direction.

Each step she took, she wished she could run. But two fleeing figures would draw curious eyes. She and Daniel kept walking. They reached the gate's pillars, and finally Daniel started to run. She fell into step alongside him and they raced into the blackness stretching across the park.

The snow-scattered grass feathered out in all directions, intersected by walkways and riding paths. Gretchen had hoped for the oblivion of darkness, but as they moved deeper into the Tiergarten, she saw little lamps flickering from the trees. People strolled the paths, arm in arm, talking quietly.

Gretchen and Daniel kept off the paths, trying to stay in the pockets of shadows between the trees. Her legs shook with exhaustion. It had been hours since she'd had anything to eat or drink, and she knew it was sheer adrenaline that kept her moving. When she stumbled over a tree root, Daniel stopped running and put a steadying hand on her arm.

'Are you all right?' He touched her split lips. Even the light pressure of his finger made her cringe in pain.

'Yes,' she said. 'What about you?'

His expression darkened. 'I'm fine,' he said, though his abrupt tone told her he was anything but.

'There's no way out of the city,' she said, wrapping her arms around herself, shaking in the cold wind. 'Hitler will have every vehicle searched. Even private automobiles . . .' She trailed off.

Daniel stared at her, his eyes dark and narrowed. Gretchen practically felt electricity leaping through the air between them.

Because there *was* one car in the city that no policeman or SA officer would dare to stop. The most famous automobile in all of Berlin – Detective Chief Superintendent Ernst Gennat's Daimler, the Toboggan.

39

THIRTY MINUTES LATER, GRETCHEN AND DANIEL WAITED at the southwest corner of the park near Zoo Station. The rattle of locomotives along the tracks carried on the harsh wind. Plumes of smoke curled across the sky, gray on black. The occasional shuffle of footsteps sounded on the sidewalk as a weary traveler or burgher returned home, and each time, Gretchen shrank against Daniel. He kept his good arm around her shoulders, leaning down to say, 'It can't be much longer. He said he would come.'

She nodded, searching the darkened street for the glistening curves of Gennat's Daimler. Back in the park, they'd cleaned Daniel up as best they could; she'd wetted her handkerchief with snow and wiped the blood and dirt from his face and hands. Nothing could be done about the unnatural angle of his broken fingers or his bloodshot, blackened eyes, but he looked like someone who'd been in a bar brawl, not a boy on the run. His appearance would have to pass muster, because she had refused to leave him alone in the park to telephone

Gennat at police headquarters. Wherever they went from now on, they went together.

They had found a café with a public telephone down the street from the park, and Gretchen scrounged a couple of coins out of her skirt pocket – not enough for train tickets, but plenty to make a call. She had been terrified that Gennat might want to bring Daniel in – after all, when she'd gone to him for help, he'd said he would try to track Daniel down and have him placed within the homicide department's custody – but it was a risk they had to take. There were no other options left.

Daniel had insisted on being put through immediately to Superintendent Gennat. He'd refused to tell the officer on telephone duty who he was, just as Gretchen had a few days ago, saying instead to mention 'Friedrich' to the detective. The *Ringverein* man's name had worked again; within a few minutes, Gennat had come on the line. Daniel had said they had met through Iron Fist, and he and his companion had found themselves without transportation.

There had been a long pause. Then Gennat had said in his sandpaper voice, 'I shouldn't like to refuse a favor from the friends of a fallen friend. Particularly *innocent* friends.' He laid such emphasis on the word that Daniel's shoulders sagged in relief. 'Tell me where to meet you.'

Which was why they had been standing outside the Tiergarten for the past half hour, afraid to talk. Gretchen kept looking at Daniel, as if he might disappear if she didn't keep her gaze on him constantly. He smiled at her, and she leaned her head on his shoulder, savoring the sensation of his bones and muscles through his coat. He smelled of blood and sweat and unwashed skin. But he was alive. Whatever horrors he'd been through, they'd find a way to cope with them together.

The wind blew little pieces of trash across the street. Somewhere a door opened and shut, releasing a blare of jazz music. A man strode past, clutching a briefcase. Gretchen peered into the road, nerves clenching her stomach. Gennat was taking too long. What if he didn't come, or worse, arrived with a squadron of brownshirts?

The harsh glare of a car's headlamps hit her in the face. As she blinked, struggling to see clearly, an automobile purred to a stop at the curb. Gennat's Toboggan.

He had come, as he had promised. Tears of relief burned in Gretchen's eyes.

The overweight detective heaved himself out of the passenger's seat. 'Hurry! Into the trunk!'

Gennat's driver jumped out, wearing a patrolman's dark blue uniform and helmet. He opened the trunk, gesturing for Gretchen and Daniel to climb in.

There was no time to think. Daniel pushed the medical bags, rolled-up maps, and boxes of tools to one side, and Gretchen clambered inside. She lay down, curling herself into a ball. For an instant, Daniel's body blocked the stars as he climbed in, then the car settled as he lay beside her. The driver slammed the trunk shut, enclosing them in the dark.

As the car started with a lurch, Gretchen rolled into Daniel. The edge of a box dug into her back, and she heard glass bottles of chemicals clinking together.

The car sped down the street. The tires rumbled over the asphalt, such a quick revolution that the sound became a relentless blur.

Daniel's good hand found hers and squeezed. She squeezed back. They would escape to England. She promised herself nothing less. The evidence they'd needed to prove the truth about the Reichstag fire might have been destroyed, but she'd learned something equally valuable: Hitler planned to start a war. And he didn't want anyone to know it yet. She had no idea what to do with his secret, but together she and Daniel would figure out something. And they'd find a way for both of them to be happy in England, just as they had promised each other.

The car whipped around a corner on two wheels. Gretchen slid into Daniel, feeling his arm encircle her. They lay crushed together along the edge of the trunk until the car righted itself. Bruised and aching, Gretchen inched herself back into her old position. She rested on her side, staring up into the impenetrable dark, the tips of her fingers touching Daniel's.

When the car finally stopped, Gretchen's and Daniel's bodies were so cramped that they had difficulty scrambling out of the trunk. The patrolman had parked on the side of a country road. Long fields stretched out, the tall grasses sighing in the wind. The noise and light of Berlin seemed far away.

Gennat stood with his hands in his pockets, his expression remote. 'We're right outside Leipzig,' he said. 'This car's too distinctive for us to stop within the city, but you can walk to the train station. Get on the first train available, and whatever you do, don't turn back.' He pulled a few bills from his wallet and gave them to Daniel. 'This ought to get you to the border.'

Daniel shook the detective's hand. 'Thank you. There's no way we can repay you for what you've done.'

Gennat sighed. Moonlight touched his face, highlighting the hollows beneath his dark eyes. 'Escape and fight, and that will be payment enough for me.' He nodded in the direction of a line of buildings, black walls against the night sky. 'You'd better start walking.'

'Thank you.' Gretchen wished there were better words to express the depth of her gratitude. But Gennat seemed to sense it, for he smiled at her for the first time and tipped his hat.

'Good-bye,' he said and got into the car. The automobile swept in a wide semicircle across the road, then shot back toward Berlin, its taillights fading to dots.

A hard wind blew across the fields, rustling the long grasses. Daniel touched Gretchen's shoulder. 'Let's get moving,' he said.

They walked for a moment in silence before she ventured, 'How can we possibly get out of the country? We don't have identity papers. And what if the border agents are on the lookout for us?'

Daniel smiled. 'We have something else that Hitler doesn't know about. Allies,' he added before Gretchen could ask. 'Remember that the *Schweigen* Ring has brother gangs in Dresden and Hamburg? We'll ask for their help. According to their code of honor, they never refuse a colleague in need. Maybe they can forge papers for us, help us come up with decent disguises. They must know how to do that sort of thing.'

She almost laughed. It was brilliant and simple – and it would never occur to Hitler.

'You're right,' she said. 'Birgit left a couple of days ago for Hamburg. We can go there. She'll vouch for us. And we can take a boat to England.'

They walked along the road lined with long fields lit by the silvery gleam of the stars. Gretchen strained her ears, but she heard nothing: no rumble of tires, no squeal of sirens. Only the steady tramp of their footsteps.

Daniel grabbed her hand and kissed her palm. 'I never thought I'd see you again.' His voice broke, but he smiled at her.

'I was terrified for you, Daniel. It must have been so awful for you in that place.'

He looked down. 'It was like a nightmare,' he said at last.

'They kept a few of us chained in the cellar. When I wouldn't talk, they – they beat one of the other prisoners in front of me. Every time they hit him, they said it was my fault. That I could stop it at any time, if only I would tell them why I'd been on the shores of the Müggelsee.'

A muscle clenched in his jaw. 'That man's screams – by the end, he didn't even sound human anymore. Those SA men made me hate everything. Myself for letting them torture that prisoner. Them for hurting him. Even him, for making me feel guilty.' He let out a shaky breath. 'I – I don't think I can talk about this any more.'

'It's all right.' She gripped his hand, wishing it was true, but he shook his head.

'It never will be.' Tears glittered in his eyes. 'We *failed*. That poor man is dead. The Enabling Act passed, and Hitler's still chancellor. I'll never be able to see my family again. I'll always be known as a murderer.' He swallowed hard. 'And there's nothing we can do to fight the National Socialists. They're too strong and there's too many of them. The best we can hope for is to get out of here alive.'

'Maybe not.' Gretchen's excitement felt like a light glowing inside her, steady and warm. 'Do you remember that English politician you told me about? The one who said that Hitler wants war?'

Daniel shot her a wary glance. 'Winston Churchill.'

'He's right. Hitler accidentally let it slip when I was in his office. He *is* planning on waging a war, and he doesn't want people to know. If we can get to England and warn Mr Churchill, maybe he can find influential people who'll listen to him.'

'How do you know – wait,' Daniel interrupted himself. 'There's no time now. You can tell me later.' He flashed her the old confident grin she'd missed so much. 'There's still work we can do.'

351

Gretchen knew there were people they might never see again: her mother, Daniel's parents and sisters, Eva. And there were secrets forever lost to them, such as which of Göring's underlings had pulled the trigger on Fräulein Junge and who had shot Herr Schultz's brother. But they knew why the victims had died, the truth about the fire, and Hitler had revealed more than he'd intended. It would have to be enough. Together, they walked toward the twinkling lights of Leipzig.

THREE MONTHS LATER

THE SKY HAD LONG AGO TURNED BLACK WHEN Gretchen and Daniel reached the Whitestones' house. Night's first stars tossed silver onto the brick building, so she could make out the darkened bedroom windows on the second story. The lace curtains she and Julia had hemmed last summer still hung in her room. They hadn't redecorated her bedchamber. Her throat constricted with swelling emotion. Perhaps, even after three and a half months of silence, they hadn't given up on her.

She stood next to Daniel at the side of the lane, glancing over her shoulder at the taxi's taillights fading into red pinpricks in the distance. The June breeze, warm and smelling of summer, swished through the grass. With every breath, Gretchen felt her heart lifting. They had done it at last; they had made it back to England.

After taking a train from Leipzig to Hamburg, they had stayed there for weeks, lodging first in a flophouse where the proprietor cared more about Gennat's coins than their lack of identity papers. They made splints for Daniel's broken fingers from handkerchiefs and a leather-bound book they

353

bought from a secondhand shop, Gretchen sawing the cover apart with a knife she'd stolen from the flophouse kitchen.

For a couple of nights, they'd skulked around bars, listening to gossip until they'd learned which establishments were under *Schweigen's* brother Ring's protection. They had gone to the closest nightclub and asked to meet with the *Ringverein* head, explaining they had been Iron Fist Friedrich's associates.

The *Ringverein* had accepted them, but they'd had to earn their boat tickets to England. They had worked at a nightclub in the Ring's territory: Daniel as a porter, Gretchen as a hat-check girl alongside Birgit. They had wept and embraced each other when they saw each other again. Birgit had been bubbling over with excitement: the money was lousy, but it paid for a bed and meals in a rooming house, and it was a different world from grappling with strangers in the dark.

After each shift, Gretchen and Daniel counted their coins, deducting the amounts needed for rent, *Ringverein* dues, and false identity papers. Every time Gretchen saw brown or black Party uniforms in the street, her heart clutched, but no one gave her a second look. She had dyed her hair back to its natural blond – she'd been certain that Hitler had told his men to be on the lookout for a brunette, since he would believe that the 'Jewish virus' had turned her hair brown permanently. Daniel had colored his hair black. Wearing cheap, secondhand clothes they'd found in a thrift shop, and several pounds lighter because they'd rather save their money than spend it on food, they had looked little like themselves.

When they finally had enough money, one of the Ring's forgers made their new passports. The next morning they sailed for Dover. As the white cliffs rose above the churning gray waters of the channel, Gretchen had breathed deeply for the first time in months.

Once they had disembarked, they went straight to a post

office so Daniel could send a telegram to his parents: *The Lion is safe in his new lair. He hopes you will join him.* He'd left it unsigned. Though he said nothing as they stepped outside into a lightly pattering rain, she knew how desperately he wished his family would leave Germany. But there was no telling what they might do, or what lay before them if they remained in Berlin.

Gretchen and Daniel had taken the first train to Oxford. Now she stood in the lane with Daniel, studying the house and gardens rising before them in the darkness, her heart racing. What if the Whitestones didn't understand that her silence had been an attempt to protect them? What if they were angry and turned her away?

Daniel's hand found hers. 'Don't worry. They love you.'

'Let's go in,' she said, her voice catching. Together, they climbed the porch steps. Gretchen eased the front door open and listened to the classical music, click of knitting needles, and scratch of pencils on paper drifting from the parlor. Her little brothers must be drawing, Julia making another wobbly scarf, Alfred sitting back in his favorite chair, eyes closed, lost in the music.

Her throat was so thick she couldn't speak. 'It's us!' she choked out at last.

For an instant, there was no sound except the radio. Then voices shouted, 'Gretchen! Daniel! Thank God!' and footsteps rushed toward them. Gretchen stood by the front door, smiling so hard her face ached as Alfred, Julia, and the three boys raced into the hall. She glimpsed a jumble of wide-eyed faces before Julia swept her into an embrace, shaking and sobbing. Gretchen hugged Julia back, inhaling the soft scent of her lily perfume.

Then Julia released her, and Alfred surprised her by overcoming his usual reserve and kissing her cheeks. He held her hands, beaming down at her despite the tears filling his eyes. Looking at him, Gretchen's heart seemed to fill her chest until it pressed against her ribs. *This is what a family feels like*, she thought, smiling until she caught sight of Daniel, standing off to the side, his hands in his pockets, his head downcast.

Something tightly wound inside her seemed to break. She ran to him, flinging her arms around his shoulders, drawing him close for an instant before letting go and turning to face the Whitestones.

'I'm sorry,' she said, her voice cracking. 'All I've wanted for months was to come home to all of you. But I won't live without Daniel. He can't stay in Oxford, because he's known here under his real name. We – we couldn't prove his innocence,' she faltered.

Alfred studied them, his expression grave. 'Boys,' he said in a tone that brooked no argument, 'upstairs. Now. Your mother and I need to speak with Gretchen and Daniel.'

Sighing, Colin, Andrew, and Jack dragged themselves upstairs, sending pitiful looks over their shoulders. Alfred and Julia ushered Gretchen and Daniel into the kitchen, where Julia put on a pot of tea to boil and fixed them sandwiches, saying that they both looked far too thin. As they ate, the whole story tumbled out.

It took nearly an hour. When they finished, Gretchen stared at the tile floor, its pattern of white and yellow squares blurring together as she blinked back tears. She thought of gentle Herr Gerlich, dragged off to jail, and Daniel's old colleagues at the *Munich Post*. Friedrich, who had died because he'd cared about what had happened to an employee. The deluded Dutch arsonist, sitting in a cell, waiting for his trial to begin. The hundreds of Communists and journalists who'd been imprisoned, and the anonymous men who were even now being tortured in the trade union cellar. So many people had already been lost.

She knew she and Daniel had been fortunate. Her heart, though, ached so badly that she could not take a deep enough breath, and her head felt light from the lack of air. She had to tell the Whitestones that she and Daniel were here to say good-bye and that they had to move on to another place, where they could be anonymous and safe.

She saw by the sadness in Alfred's and Julia's faces that they understood what she needed to tell them, without her saying a word. Tears burned in her throat as she said, 'I'm sorry.'

'It seems to me that there may be another solution,' Alfred said slowly. 'Daniel, you said that you want to tell Mr Churchill about Hitler's intentions to start a war someday. I could arrange for you to see him – I know his cousin slightly, as he lives nearby and has often supported the clinic over the years. Why don't you tell Churchill your own story? He may not be an influential politician anymore, but he's a prolific writer and an avowed anti-Nazi. Perhaps there's something he can do for you.'

Daniel hesitated. 'What if he decides to alert Hitler's government about my whereabouts? I'm a wanted murderer, after all.'

'Nonsense,' Alfred said. 'You've been out of the country, so I suppose you wouldn't know – Mr Churchill recently gave an impassioned speech before the House of Commons, warning that Hitler will stir up pogroms and Jewish persecution in Germany. It's clear he despises the man. You couldn't find a more sympathetic ally.'

Daniel shot Gretchen a wary glance. Giving him a smile that she hoped looked encouraging, she took his good hand in hers. 'Very well,' he said at last, but his tone was despondent. 'It's worth a try, but I don't see how he could possibly help me.'

Gretchen didn't see how, either, and had to blink back tears. They may have managed to get to England, but there was nothing here for Daniel except for her. He had no job prospects, no references; he couldn't even live under his own name. As his grip on her hand tightened, she couldn't help thinking that this might be one of the last times she got to see the Whitestones before she and Daniel had to move on to somewhere else.

Two days later, a taxi dropped Gretchen and Daniel off in a country road in front of a brick house. She supposed it looked like a typical rural estate, for she knew little about such things. Its owner, however, was anything but typical: this was Mr Churchill's home, Chartwell, outside the village of Westerham in Kent. Although he had agreed to meet with them, thanks to Alfred's machinations, Gretchen was afraid he wouldn't believe them.

As they crossed the large lawn, she glanced at Daniel. By the grim set of his face, she could tell he was worried.

'It will be all right,' she said, trying to keep her tone light. 'We're together again, and that's what matters most.'

He nodded, but didn't reply. Together, they strode toward the front door. On the house's south side rose a redbrick wall, and between the wall and the great house lay an orchard of fruit trees and a grass tennis court. To the north, she caught the watery gleams of a swimming pool and a pond where black swans glided along the surface. She and Daniel had entered a different world from Berlin's long, gray streets. The silence of the tranquil countryside felt so alien that Gretchen looked about uneasily, but she saw no hidden threats, only a small, black goat snorting in the orchard.

A butler answered their knock and escorted them into an enormous study. Out of habit, Gretchen took it in with a glance, noting the windows and doors in case they needed to get out quickly. Above a mahogany desk hung an old-fashioned painting of a man she supposed was Churchill's father, Lord Randolph. Bookcases were crammed with leather-bound volumes, and a couple of rich Turkish carpets covered the floor. It was the sort of place she would love to sit in for hours, reading.

A middle-aged man in a dark suit entered the room. Wispy white hair covered his head, and his face had the delicate pallor of a redhead's. The pugnacious thrust of his jaw identified him as easily as if he had introduced himself, for Gretchen had seen the same expression in her history textbook, on the chapter about the Great War. It was Mr Churchill.

'My cousin tells me that you have important news about Germany,' he said in a clipped, upper-class accent.

'We have uncovered some secrets about Mr Hitler,' Daniel replied in his careful English.

Mr Churchill regarded them thoughtfully, unsmiling. Then he waved at a couple of striped chairs, muttering for them to sit. He stood at the window, stroking a bronze cast of a woman's hand lying on the sill. 'Very well. Go ahead.'

It took only a few minutes for them to explain the real background of the Reichstag fire and the reasons Hitler had wanted the Enabling Act passed. By the time they had finished, Churchill was pacing the room.

'I knew it!' He punched the air with his hands. 'That accursed Hitler is preparing for war!' He shot them a fierce, unblinking look. 'Unfortunately, there's no proof I can use to convince anyone else. But you're right, and I know it. I must work harder than I ever have in my life,' he said to himself, 'to get myself back in a more powerful position.'

Daniel rose. 'Respectfully, sir, you'll need help.'

Churchill shot Daniel a sharp look. 'I see,' he said slowly. 'You wish to volunteer your services to me, don't you?' As Gretchen watched, silently begging Mr Churchill to accept, he shook his head and sighed.

'Mr Cohen,' he said, sounding regretful, 'you're very young. You've undergone experiences no one should have to. It's time you let yourself live a real life again.'

'How can I?' Daniel's eyes were dry, but his jaw was

clenched so hard his words ground out between his teeth. 'I'll never get another newspaper job. I have nothing, not even my name. Daniel Cohen is known as a killer.'

'Why, I was a wanted man once myself.' Churchill's face creased into an unexpected smile. 'Oh, yes,' he said when Gretchen and Daniel stared at him in surprise. 'When I was a young soldier fighting in the Boer War, I escaped from a prisoner-of-war camp. They put a price on my head. Mr Cohen, there's no shame in being a wanted man when you're innocent.'

'Please, Mr Churchill.' There was a desperate note in Daniel's voice. 'I have dedicated the last two years of my life to investigating the National Socialists. I could be a great help to you.'

'I have no doubt that your intimate knowledge of the political situation in Germany will prove invaluable to me,' Churchill said. 'If it's agreeable to you, I would like to consult with you often.'

Daniel nodded, looking deflated. It wasn't enough, but it was something, Gretchen thought. 'I would be glad to help you in any way I can, sir.'

'I know Hitler better than anyone else in England,' Gretchen said, flushing under Churchill's appraising look. 'I'll tell you anything about him that you want to know.'

'There may come a day when I'll call upon both of you for assistance,' Churchill said. He smiled slightly. 'Mr Cohen, I saw your face when you talked about your newspaper work. You love it. If you like, I can arrange for you to get a job at the *Times* in London. You'll most likely start at the bottom of the pile,' he warned. 'But it's one of the best papers in the world.'

Daniel's eyes went wide. He opened and closed his mouth twice before he could speak. 'Thank you,' he said at last and clasped Mr Churchill's hand. 'I gladly accept. I'd be honored to work there.'

'Oh, Daniel!' Gretchen gasped. It was better than anything she'd let herself hope for.

'I'll have it arranged within the next day or two,' Churchill said. 'You'll have to come up with a new name, naturally, but it had better be German as I doubt you can fool anyone with your accent. I know just the man in London to put together new identity papers for you. Yes, yes, you said that you already have false papers,' he said when Daniel started to speak. 'But this time, you may pick your own name. What a chance you're getting! You have the opportunity to reinvent yourself precisely how you'd like to be, rather as I suspect Miss Whitestone has already had a chance to do. Now you'd best get yourselves home.' He smiled, such a kind, open smile that Gretchen felt tears prick her eyes. Hitler had never looked at her so gently. 'Take pride in your despicable enemies because it means you've stood up for your beliefs.'

Back outside, they waited by the lane for the taxi that the butler had called for them, to take them to the train station so they could return to Oxford. Daniel's smile slipped away. 'I'm not asking you to come to London with me – I know you want to finish your schooling, and you deserve to live with a family that loves you. But . . . do you think . . . someday . . .' He trailed off, uncertain.

She stepped closer to him. Their quick breathing and the far-off hum of bumblebees and braying goats filled her ears. But everything fell away when she put her hands on his shoulders, feeling the corded muscle of his right, the sharp ridge of his left, two of the many parts of him that she loved so much.

'You're worth waiting for,' she said. 'London's only sixty miles from Oxford. You can visit on your days off, and I'll come on school holidays. It won't be long before I graduate. London has loads of excellent universities, and I'm sure I'd like living there, too. I can't stay with the Whitestones all my life,' she said when his eyebrows lifted in surprise. 'Sooner or later, I have to make my own way. And I want it to be with you. Forever.'

He traced her lips with his finger. 'Forever,' he murmured, smiling. 'You know I can't give you that. But I promise I'll love you for that long.'

'Sounds perfect to me.'

She stood in his arms under the shade of a poplar tree, letting her thoughts turn to her father and brother, becoming part of the earth. Her mother, alone in the marshlands; Eva, dead-eyed in the park; and Geli, lifeless on her bedroom floor. All of them lost because of Hitler. She would never stop mourning her family or wondering what sort of man her father truly had been. But she had made her own choices. She had wanted to love, and that had made all the difference.

Daniel leaned down, pressing his lips lightly on hers. She kissed him back, tasting the warm honey of his mouth. Her Daniel, straightforward and passionate, as clear as sunlight on water, nothing like the misted corridors of Hitler's mind. As they kissed, she couldn't help but remember how much she had once wanted to hate him. The first time they'd met, he'd seen her defend a Jewish man from her brother and his comrade, and she had been terrified that word of her traitorous actions would reach Hitler. She had been so afraid that the loss of Hitler's friendship would crush her; that it would end everything in her life that she had thought was good and true. Now, as she pulled back from Daniel and smiled at him, she knew it hadn't been the end.

It had only been the beginning.

Author's Note

CONSPIRACY OF BLOOD AND SMOKE IS A BLEND OF FACT and fiction. Although Gretchen and Daniel, their families, the Whitestones, the Schultz brothers, Monika Junge, Iron Fist Friedrich, and the *Ringverein* members are fictitious, the other characters were real people and the story revolves around real events. Please note that this section contains several spoilers, so read no further if you haven't finished the book!

The Reichstag fire is one of the most mysterious events in Nazi history. For the next thirty years, many people believed it was the result of either a Nazi or a Communist conspiracy. It wasn't until Fritz Tobias's groundbreaking and meticulously researched book, *The Reichstag Fire*, came out in the early 1960s that opinions began to change. Today it is commonly believed that a single man was responsible for the terrorist attack.

The bare facts are these: on February 27, 1933, a twenty-four-year-old half-blind Communist Dutchman named Marinus van der Lubbe set fire to the Reichstag. He was arrested on the scene and confessed. Hitler took advantage of the ensuing panic to convince President Hindenburg to suspend major civil liberties. On March 23, the Reichstag passed the Enabling Act, effectively voting itself out of existence. Dictatorial power now lay in Hitler's grasp.

In late 1933, van der Lubbe went on trial. Reporters from around the globe flocked to the highly publicized event. The Dutchman was found guilty of arson. Four other Communists who had later been arrested were all acquitted, fueling many people's suspicions about the fire's origins. Today the prevailing opinion is that the additional men were innocent and had been framed by the Nazis in an attempt to make the fire look like a Communist scheme. On January 10, 1934, van der Lubbe was executed by guillotine. As German tradition of the time demanded, his executioner wore a top hat, evening dress, and white gloves.

The secret passages in this book really existed. The underground tunnel connecting Göring's palace with the Reichstag became a source of embarrassment to the Nazis – for years afterward, the rumor persisted that Göring had sent a group of SA men through it to set the fire. The passageway running from the Chancellery's attic to the Hotel Adlon was walled up when Hitler had his new home renovated in the mid-1930s.

Hindenburg died during the summer of 1934. Hitler rolled the offices of president and chancellor into one and became known as the 'Führer'. He never repealed the Enabling Act, so technically Germany operated under a state of emergency throughout the Nazi regime.

The attack on Daniel's cousin was inspired by real events. Those who failed to salute Nazi parades were often beaten in retaliation. Foreigners, unaware of the custom, were most at risk. In 1933 alone, more than a dozen Americans were attacked, and the US State Department considered issuing a travel advisory warning Americans not to visit Germany.

One of the reasons for the Nazis' electoral successes, which is largely unknown today, was their tough stance on organized crime. Since criminal rates had skyrocketed after the end of World War One, Hitler's pledge to wipe out the *Ringvereine* was welcomed by many voters. In November 1933, Göring's Prussian Ministry of the Interior enacted a decree for 'the application of preventive police detention of professional criminals'. Scores of *Ringverein* men were arrested and placed in concentration camps. The Nazis rationalized the roundups by claiming that *Ringverein* men were *Untermenschen*, subhumans whose criminality was part of their very natures. Although there were occasional criminal cases involving *Ringvereine* throughout the 1930s, the organizations were mostly stamped out during the first years of Hitler's rule. The fictional *Schweigen Ringverein* in this book is based on several real-life Rings, including the notorious gangs *Immertreu* (Ever Loyal) and *Felsenfest* (Rock Solid).

The cellar where Daniel is held by the SA is based on the makeshift torture centers that brownshirts set up in the basements of recently captured train union offices. The abandoned powder factory, which Gretchen sees when hiking through the Dachau marshlands, later became the site of the Nazis' first concentration camp. Approximately two hundred Communist, *Reichsbanner*, and Socialist leaders were the camp's first inmates when it opened in late March 1933. The *Reichsbanner* was a paramilitary force composed of members of various political parties. Originally, the camp was overseen by a detachment of policemen from Munich. In April, however, Heinrich Himmler placed the camp under SS control. A sadistic reign of terror ensued. Dachau operated until the end of World War Two and was used primarily for political prisoners.

The 'toga boy' incident in Hitler's childhood is true. In a rare moment of candor, Hitler himself told the story to

Hanfstaengl's wife. He really did eat swastika-stamped candies, called *Lutschbonbons*, like the ones Gretchen sees on his desk. He could shoot snowballs apart, too, an ability he once demonstrated in front of an astonished foreign correspondent. Because he kept thwarting death, he believed he was protected by divine providence, just as he tells Gretchen during the scene in his office. There were at least forty-six known attempts on his life, but it's possible there were many more. The ideas he expresses in this book are based on his early speeches and his autobiography *Mein Kampf*.

Eva Braun remained Hitler's mistress until the end of her life. She attempted suicide at least three times, the first being the incident she describes in this book to Gretchen. Her final try was successful. On April 30, 1945, one day after Hitler and Eva were married, knowing Germany's surrender was inevitable, they committed suicide together. He shot himself through the head and she took cyanide. Hitler had been terrified that his body would be desecrated, as Benito Mussolini's had been, and had ordered their corpses to be burned. His adjutants carried out his final request. Hitler's and Eva's bodies smoldered in the Reich Chancellery garden as Russian tanks rolled into Berlin.

Hermann Göring, the Prussian Minister of the Interior, really did rewrite his assistant's official report of the Reichstag fire and distribute his own version to news agencies. What Gretchen read in the paper hidden within the Reichstag – and the changes Göring had made in blue pencil – are based on the real-life initial press communiqué. For the purposes of my story, however, Göring berated his assistant, Martin Sommerfeldt, in the Session Chamber, not in his Prussian Ministry Office, where the dressing-down actually took place.

Göring's one-of-a-kind car, a gray Mercedes with scarlet seats, was given to him by Hitler during the spring of 1931.

In 1935, Göring married an actress, Emmy Sonnemann, in a lavish ceremony. Hitler served as the best man. During World War Two, Göring commanded the *Luftwaffe*, or air force. Their initial successes were so stunning that Hitler rewarded Göring with the title of 'Reich Marshal'. Göring eventually became the second most powerful man in Nazi Germany.

After Germany's surrender, he gave himself up to the Allies. He became 'defendant number one' during the trials of major Nazi war criminals in Nuremberg. He was found guilty of the four indictments against him, including war crimes and crimes against humanity, and was scheduled to die by hanging. On October 15, 1946, hours before his execution, Göring committed suicide by taking cyanide. To this day, no one knows exactly how he got the poison capsule. Once the other defendants were executed, all eleven bodies were burned in a Munich crematorium in the presence of American, British, French, and Russian officers. The ashes were poured into the dirt of an unidentified country lane, to prevent the men's graves from becoming shrines.

Ernst 'Putzi' Hanfstaengl, the Nazi Party's foreign press chief, really was Göring's palace guest during this story's time frame. He eventually fell from favor. In 1937, Göring ordered Hanfstaengl parachuted into Spain, in an area where a civil war was taking place. Hanfstaengl believed Göring's command was a death sentence, although Göring later maintained it was a practical joke. Hanfstaengl fled from Germany in disguise, settling in England until war broke out and he was interned as an enemy alien. In 1941, he was sent to a camp in Canada and offered his services to his old college friend from Harvard, American president Franklin Delano Roosevelt. For the rest of the war, Hanfstaengl was kept in secret in a country house in northern Virginia, where he wrote reports for the American government on the inner workings of the Nazi regime. After the war, he resettled in Germany. He died in 1975.

Ernst Gennat, the Detective Chief Superintendent of Berlin's Homicide Division, was one of the most famous detectives in German history. He revolutionized forensic science and created the world's first crime car, Gennat's Toboggan. In all, Gennat solved 298 murders and coined the phrase 'serial murderer'. He regularly attended gangsters' balls. He never joined the Nazi Party, and he died in 1939.

Fritz Gerlich, a courageous anti-Nazi journalist, was personally arrested on March 9, 1933, by Max Amann, the head of the Nazi publishing business. For several months, Gerlich was kept in 'protective custody' in a Munich jail. He was later sent to the concentration camp at Dachau, where he was murdered during the summer of 1934. The only notification his widow received of his death was his pair of trademark round spectacles, splattered with blood, in the mail.

Many *Munich Post* reporters were also taken into custody during the mass arrests of March 9, including Edmund Goldschagg, a young reporter nicknamed the 'Prussian Nightingale' for his elegant writing style. He was later drafted into the army and eventually saved the life of a Jewish woman during World War Two. Goldschagg and my father, who was a reporter when he was a young man, inspired me to create the character of Daniel Cohen.

Sefton 'Tom' Delmer, the foreign correspondent for a British newspaper, got into the burning Reichstag by walking in with Hitler's retinue. He witnessed Hitler's reaction to the fire, including overhearing Hitler's fervent wish that the blaze was the work of a Communist conspiracy. During the war, Delmer relocated to England. There he engaged in a series of 'black radio' programs meant as a form of psychological warfare against Germany. As a result, he earned a top spot on the Nazis' list of people to be arrested and handed over to the Gestapo, if Germany invaded England.

Winston Churchill, the 'benchwarmer' politician and writer, was largely viewed as a has-been in 1933. In April, he delivered a speech before the House of Commons, warning of the possibility of Jewish persecution and pogroms in Germany. Few people wanted to listen to him. Convinced that Hitler was dangerous, Churchill assembled a group of experts who advised him on the shifting situation in Germany throughout the 1930s.

In 1940, Churchill became Britain's prime minister. He later said he felt an overwhelming sense of relief, because now he could finally begin to do the work that had to be done to defeat Hitler. The two men never met but despised each other. They came within yards of each other on a World War One battlefield, and in 1932, Hanfstaengl tried to arrange a meeting between them in Munich that never came off after Churchill questioned Hitler's hatred for the Jews.

Churchill served as prime minister for the majority of World War Two. His refusal of a truce with Germany enraged Hitler, who had wanted to avoid fighting a war on two fronts. Churchill's brave, energetic, and optimistic leadership during the war has become legendary. In the 1950s, he served a second term as prime minister. He was awarded the Nobel Prize in Literature and is the first person to have been made an honorary citizen of the United States. Upon his death in 1965, Queen Elizabeth II granted him the honor of a state funeral. The 'has-been' who endured years of political exile is now widely regarded as one of the greatest leaders of the twentieth century.

Selected Bibliography

Adlon, Hedda. *Hotel Adlon: The Life and Death of a Great Hotel*. Translated and edited by Norman Denny. New York: Horizon Press, 1958, 1960.

Bartoletti, Susan Campbell. *Hitler Youth: Growing Up in Hitler's Shadow*. New York: Scholastic, 2005.

Berben, Paul. *Dachau, 1933–1945: The Official History*. London: The Norfolk Press, 1968, 1975.

Bullock, Alan. *Hitler: A Study in Tyranny*. New York: Harper & Row, 1971.

Churchill, Winston. *Memoirs of the Second World War*. Boston: Houghton Mifflin Company, 1990.

Dawidowicz, Lucy S. *The War Against the Jews: 1933–1945*. New York: Bantam Books, 1975.

Delarue, Jacques. *The Gestapo: A History of Horror*. Translated by Mervyn Savill. New York: William Morrow & Company, 1964.

Delmer, Sefton. *Black Boomerang*. New York: Viking Press, 1962.

Evans, Richard J. *The Coming of the Third Reich*. New York: The Penguin Press, 2004.

Evans, Richard J. *The Third Reich in Power*. New York: The Penguin Press, 2006.

Fest, Joachim C. *Hitler*. Translated by Richard and Clara Winston. New York: Harcourt Brace & Company, 1974.

Friedrich, Otto. *Before the Deluge: A Portrait of Berlin in the 1920s*. New York: Harper & Row, 1972.

Gilbert, G. M. *Nuremberg Diary*. New York: Signet Books, 1947.

Gill, Anton. *A Dance Between Flames: Berlin Between the Wars*. New York: Carroll & Graf Publishers, 1994.

Goeschel, Christian. *The Criminal Underworld in Weimar and Nazi Berlin*. History Workshop Journal, April 2013, 75: 1, 58–80.

Göring, Emmy. *My Life With Goering*. London: David Bruce & Watson Ltd., 1972.

Hanfstaengl, Ernst. *Hitler: The Missing Years*. New York: Arcade Publishing, 1957, 1994.

Hartmann, Arthur and Klaus von Lampe. *The German Underworld and the Ringvereine from the 1890s through the 1950s*. Global Crime, 2008, 9:1–2, 108–135.

Hitler, Adolf. *Mein Kampf*. Mumbai: Jaico Publishing House, 2008.

Isaacson, Walter. *Einstein: His Life and Universe*. New York: Simon & Schuster, 2007.

Jenkins, Roy. *Churchill: A Biography*. New York: Farrar, Straus and Giroux, 2001.

Kershaw, Ian. *Hitler, 1889–1936: Hubris*. New York: W. W. Norton & Company, 1998.

Kershaw, Ian. *Hitler, 1936–1945: Nemesis*. New York: W. W. Norton & Company, 2000.

Kessler, Count Harry. *Berlin in Lights: The Diaries of Count Harry Kessler (1918–1937)*. Translated and edited by Charles Kessler, with an introduction by Ian Buruma. New York: Grove Press, 1961, 1999.

Koehn, Ilse. *Mischling, Second Degree: My Childhood in Nazi Germany*. New York: Puffin Books, 1977.

Lambert, Angela. *The Lost Life of Eva Braun*. New York: St Martin's Press, 2006.

Large, David Clay. *Berlin*. New York: Basic Books, 2000.

Larson, Erik. *In the Garden of Beasts: Love, Terror, and an American Family in Hitler's Berlin*. New York: Crown Publishers, 2011.

Lehrer, Steven. *The Reich Chancellery and Führerbunker Complex: An Illustrated History of the Seat of the Nazi Regime*. Jefferson, NC: McFarland & Company, Inc., 2006.

Longerich, Peter. *Heinrich Himmler*. Translated by Jeremy Noakes and Lesley Sharpe. Oxford: Oxford University Press, 2012.

Manchester, William. *The Last Lion: Winston Spencer Churchill, Alone, 1932–40*. Boston: Little, Brown and Company, 1988.

Marcuse, Harold. *Legacies of Dachau: The Uses and Abuses of a Concentration Camp, 1933–2001*. Cambridge: Cambridge University Press, 2001.

Mosley, Leonard. *The Reich Marshal: A Biography of Hermann Goering*. New York: Doubleday & Company, 1974.

Nagorski, Andrew. *Hitlerland: American Eyewitnesses to the Nazi Rise to Power*. New York: Simon & Schuster, 2012.

Padfield, Peter. *Himmler*. New York: Henry Holt and Company, 1990.

Read, Anthony. *The Devil's Disciples: Hitler's Inner Circle*. New York: W. W. Norton & Company, 2003, 2005.

Reed, Douglas. *The Burning of the Reichstag*. New York: Covici-Friede, 1934.

Reuth, Ralf Georg. *Goebbels*. Translated by Krishna Winston. New York: Harcourt, Brace & Company, 1993.

Rosenbaum, Ron. *Explaining Hitler*. New York: Harper Perennial, 1998.

Shirer, William L. *Berlin Diary: The Journal of a Foreign Correspondent, 1934–1941*. New York: Alfred A. Knopf, 1941.

Shirer, William L. *The Rise and Fall of the Third Reich: A History of Nazi Germany*. New York: Ballantine Books, 1960.

Speer, Albert. *Inside the Third Reich*. Translated by Richard and Clara Winston. New York: Galahad Books, 1970.

Strasser, Otto. *Hitler and I*. Boston: Houghton Mifflin Company, 1940.

Tobias, Fritz. *The Reichstag Fire*. Translated by Martin Secker and Warburg Limited, with an introduction by A. J. P. Taylor. New York: Putnam, 1963, 1964.

Toland, John. *Adolf Hitler*. New York: Doubleday & Company Inc., 1976.

Acknowledgements

FIRST AND FOREMOST, THANKS TO MY WONDERFUL editor, Flora Rees. Flora, working with you has been a delight. From your first email, I knew I was very lucky to be paired with you. Thank you for everything.

I am grateful to everyone at Headline, including Darcy Nicholson for her attention to detail and Bekki Guyatt for creating a cover that gives me chills every time I look at it. I owe a special thanks to Katie Bradburn in publicity for arranging the UK blog tour for *Prisoner of Night and Fog* and for taking such great care of me while I was speaking at the Edinburgh International Book Festival. Katie, I still agree with you that books, blankets, and hot chocolate are the perfect combination! Thanks also to Gillian MacKay for looking after me at the festival and keeping me supplied with yummy ginger tea.

I owe a big thanks to my UK agent, Caroline Walsh of David Higham Associates, and my US agent, Tracey Adams of Adams Literary, two fabulous women who are passionate about books. Caroline, I'll cherish getting to know you over lunch at the British Museum. And thanks to Renu Shah for hosting my UK cover reveal on her blog, The Page Turner.

Many thanks to my mother, Lynn Brostrom Blankman, who has been my first reader since I was old enough to hold a pencil. To Sara B. Larson and Sara Raasch, for critiquing early drafts. To Chin-Lin Ching, MD, and Scott Alexander Mooney, MD, for their advice on Daniel's compartment syndrome. I am especially grateful to Dr Ching for speaking to me at length about the exact nature of Daniel's physical limitations. Thanks to Esther Benoit, PhD, LPC, for advising me on abnormal psychology and family dysfunction. To Victoria Belfer Zabarko, for talking candidly to me about your own experiences with anti-Semitism during your child-hood. Daniel owes many of his opinions to you. To Pat Riter, interlibrary loan manager for the York County Virginia Public Library System, who tirelessly tracked down every single source I requested.

Thanks to my husband and best friend, Mike Cizenski, for his support. Mike, you listened to me go on and on about Nazis and *Ringvereine* without complaint, cooked delicious dinners when I was on deadline, and offered me endless encouragement. I couldn't have written this book without you. Thanks to my daughter, Kirsten, who makes me want to be brave. And to my dad, former reporter Peter Blankman, for raising me and my brother Paul on stories about the *Minneapolis Star* newsroom. I'll never forget your telling us about your assignment covering Ku Klux Klan meetings in the Northeast. Your passion for journalism helped inspire me to create Daniel.

And many thanks to the librarians, booksellers, teachers, bloggers, and readers.